THE SIX

ANNI TAYLOR

THE SIX

ISBN-13: 978-1548871369

ISBN-10: 1548871362

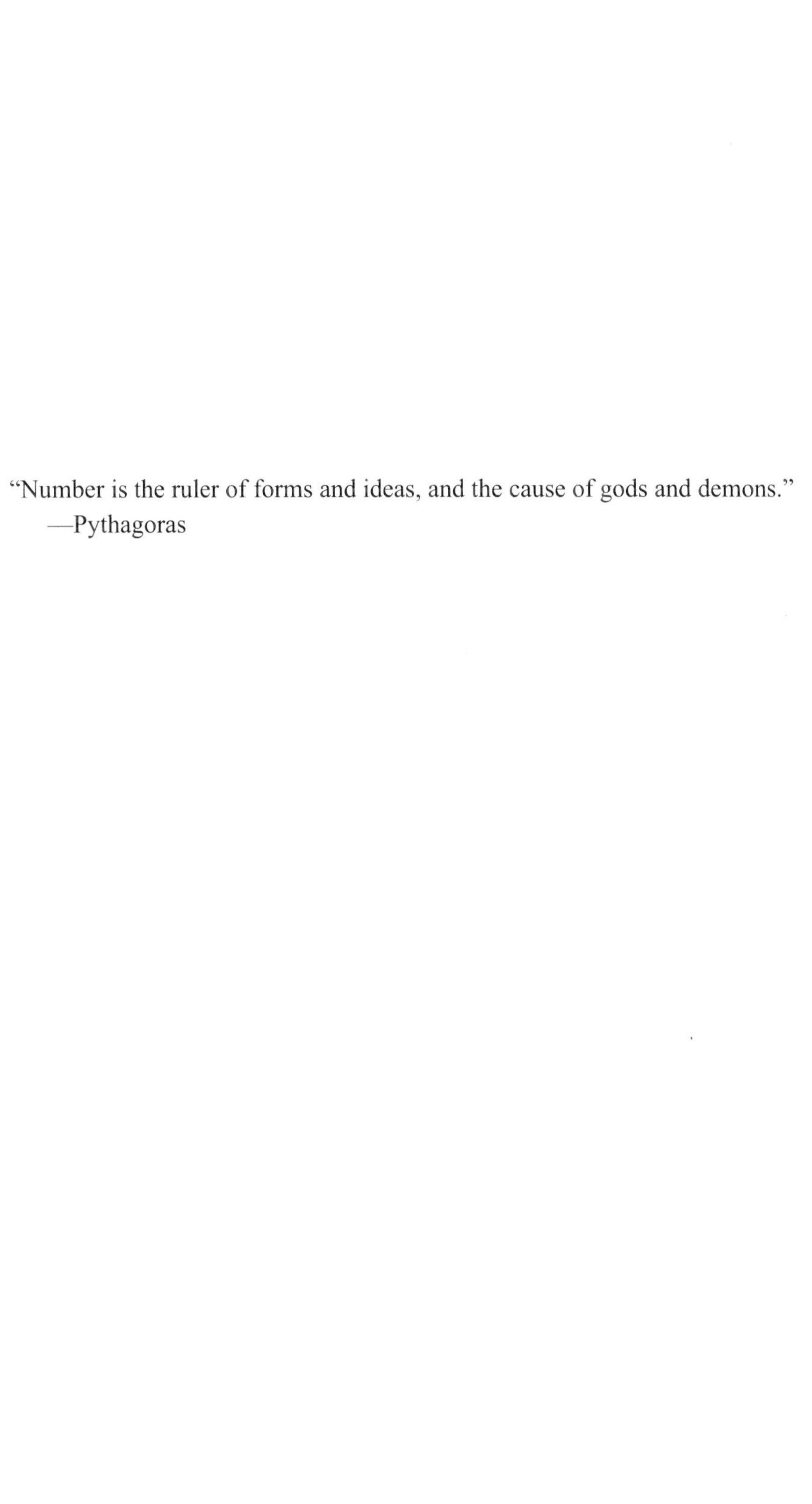

"Number is the ruler of forms and ideas, and the cause of gods and demons."
—Pythagoras

PROLOGUE

THE AIR SMELLED ALL WRONG.

I tried to drag myself from sleep, but my eyes refused to open. My head felt leaden and my limbs were strangely restricted.

Dank, coppery odours surrounded me. And the faint scents of seawater and cold sweat.

I wasn't at home. Because at home, the rooms reeked of cooking and crayons. The old rental house that I shared with Gray and our two small daughters always smelled of those things.

This place was nothing like that.

Where am I? What is—?

Strong lights began flashing in front of my face.

I jolted fully awake, my gaze darting downwards. Something was keeping me from stretching out fully.

Chains. I'm chained to the floor.

I'm sitting on cold stonework, my head against a hard wall.

There are others—either side of me—sitting in chains, like me. One of them starts singing in a strained, haunted voice, her words shattering into a series of unintelligible whispers and stutters.

The memory of the last few days crashed into my mind.

Black terror ran in pinpricking waves along my back and arms. *No. God. No* . . . this was no dream or nightmare. This was real.

I remembered why I'd been asleep. A few minutes ago—maybe more—I'd sworn out loud at one of my captors. He'd smacked me hard across the head. I must have passed out.

I wish I'd stayed unconscious. And never woken.

I'd travelled to this place voluntarily. Six days ago, I'd joined a program that was meant to heal me, make me better—along with twenty-seven others. It had taken two days, two flights and a boat trip to get to this monastery on a tiny Greek island.

I'd thought I was safe here. I thought I could trust everyone.

But I couldn't trust everyone. A trap had been set. People had been waiting behind the walls of the monastery, watching our every move.

A sudden round of choking gasps and cries echoed through the cavernous room.

I jerked my head up to see what was making my fellow captives cry out.

The lights were all on now—illuminating what had been kept in darkness before.

Horror spiked ice-cold down my spine at the sight in front of me. A scream tore from my throat, raw and sharp and broken.

Never in my darkest nightmares could I have imagined . . . *this*. A scene so terrifying I could barely comprehend it.

I need escape, escape, escape . . .

My thoughts sped backwards. All the way back to when I was a child. A desperate, flashing show reel of images, sounds, memories playing in my mind.

I heard the words my father used to sing to me—when I'd had a bad dream and couldn't sleep. Bob Marley's *Redemption Song*. Dad would grab his guitar and sing that.

I concentrated hard on Dad's familiar, gravelly voice.

But I couldn't keep hold of it.

The memories were already fading to black.

1. EVIE

ONE WEEK AGO

"MRS EVIE HARLOW? YOU MADE CONTACT with the casino yesterday in terms of a gambling problem?" came the voice on the phone.

Panic-stricken, I glanced across at Gray and our daughters, Willow and Lilly. They were laughing, rolling around on the floor of our living room and pretending to be sea lions. Two-year-old Lilly had invented that game.

Normally, I'd join the game. There was nothing better than being with Gray and the girls like this. Just being together and having goofy fun would make my heart swell to bursting.

Looking up, Gray grinned widely at me, making my heart glitch, his hair falling across his striking face. The next instant, my love for him dissolved into terror. I couldn't let him know what I'd done. Gray had no idea that I'd become hooked on gambling. Let alone did he know that I'd fallen so deeply into debt that I'd made a desperate plea to the casino for help.

I returned a quick smile and then rushed away to the sunroom. "Yes. Yes, I'm Evie," I said into the phone.

"My name is Brother Vito." His accent sounded Mediterranean. "I run a program that is quite unique. For people suffering from addiction."

"I'm not"—I hushed my voice—"an *addict*."

There was no hesitation before he responded. "The first step towards healing is accepting that you have an illness, an addiction. From that point you can begin to move ahead."

I exhaled slowly. "I can't join a program. I have children to look after."

"The treatment runs for just one week. Six days, actually. It consists of a set of challenges. One challenge each day. As an incentive towards your path of healing, we offer ten thousand dollars per completed challenge. In addition, we pay off all your debt."

Suddenly, I stopped being able to hear Gray and the girls in the next room. Everything was silent, in a vacuum. Brother Vito's words replayed in my mind as I mentally added those figures up.

All my debts paid off? A challenge each day over six days and ten thousand dollars each challenge? *That was sixty thousand.*

My throat felt like cotton wool were stuffed inside it and my tongue felt swollen and useless. I forced myself to speak. "That's incredibly generous. I can't have heard that right."

"It is a *very* generous program. We're a group of benevolent businesspeople who help a select group of addiction sufferers each year."

Just one week? Could I do it? Yes, of course I could do it. I couldn't turn this down.

"Tell me, Evie," he said, "what are you thinking?"

Scarcely breathing, I started planning how I could manage it without letting Gray know. Maybe Marla could take the girls. My friend Marla used to be a nurse who worked in a children's ward. She'd take excellent care of my girls. And she didn't get along with Gray, which was a bonus because it meant she'd try hard to keep him from knowing anything.

"I'm thinking ten different things at once," I answered breathily. "Is it local? In Sydney?"

Brother Vito gave a low chuckle. "I'm afraid it's a long way from Australia. The program is being run at a monastery in Greece, on a small island."

"*Greece?* That's out of the question for me. I can't—"

"Everything can be arranged."

"But I don't even understand how the casino would have a program like this, all the way across the world."

"We're not connected with the casino. This is a very select program."

"Are you a priest, Brother Vito?"

"No. Not a priest. You can think of me as a mentor. There are four mentors. We mentors refer to ourselves as brothers and sisters, but we're not religious. There are real monks at the monastery, naturally. They are the ones who designed the program. The mentors merely fund the program and oversee it."

"I—"

"Evie, I understand your reluctance. I'll leave you my number and let you think on it. The unfortunate thing is that you don't have long to decide. There is just one place left on the program. Only twenty-eight people can join it at any one time. They come to us from all different countries—America, England, China . . . I'm afraid you have just a day to decide."

"*One day?*"

"Yes. And one last but very important thing—the program must be kept in strict confidence. That means only you can know about it. There are many, many people out there who are desperate, but we cannot help them all. Do you understand?"

"Yes. Of course." I slipped the phone back into my pocket.

As I stood in the doorway watching Gray and the girls playing, a feeling of shame and dread washed through me. The debt that I was in was going to sink us.

I had to fix this.

2. EVIE

THE LAST FEW DAYS HAD BEEN A WHIRLWIND—trying to organise for Willow and Lilly to stay at Marla's and ensuring Gray didn't suspect what was happening. I felt terrible not telling him. But I didn't have time to think. I just had to act.

My head was filled with jetlagged fog after the long flight from Sydney airport. My stomach still felt the rock of the boat that had taken me across the Aegean Sea from the Greek mainland.

I stared through the night at the outline of a sprawling monastery. Far below, the ocean was an orchestra of giant drums and cymbals. Brother Vito was just ahead of me, showing me the way along the dark path.

In that moment, I could have believed it was all a dream. But a light rain began pattering on my bare shoulders, telling me the scene before my eyes and the crashing sounds in my ears were real.

I'm actually here. In Greece. On the island.

I need to pinch myself.

Who are you to get a chance like this, Evie? Make sure you don't blow it. Grab it with both hands and get yourself better.

Say it: you're an addict.

I'm an addict.

Brother Vito smiled at me like an indulgent parent as he showed me up the worn stone steps to the entry. "What are you whispering about?"

I hadn't realised I was talking out loud. "Nothing. Just . . . this is all so hard to process." "The monastery tends to have that effect on people. Try to see it as home for the next week, Evie. This will be your time to change everything you need to change." Brother Vito was far more handsome than I'd imagined him to be, his blonde hair silvering around his olive-skinned, angular face.

I nodded, swallowing.

I lugged my suitcase inside, lifting my face to the soaring ceiling. An enormous metal bird hung from a chain in the foyer, wings outstretched.

Brother Vito followed my gaze. "The bird was made in the forge."

I blinked, too exhausted to check my reactions. "There's a forge here?"

"Oh, yes, the monastery was built in the twelfth century. All of the original features are very much in use. It's very late—let's continue."

I followed him through dark halls that whistled around corners, coppery scents lifting from the stonework like ghosts.

"Let me take your luggage. You won't be needing it," he told me. "For the next week, you are to leave your former self completely behind. Everything will be provided."

"But I'll need my—"

"I assure you that you won't." His voice, with its thick Greek accent, was soothing but firm.

A moment of panic bubbled to the surface. This monastery was strange enough without my personal things being taken from me. I calmed myself, reluctantly handing over my suitcase, reminding myself that whatever they asked us to do must form part of the treatment. It was true that I needed to tear away all my denials and pretence about myself.

He stowed the bag away in a small room. "Come on, I'll show you where you'll be sleeping."

I stepped beside him into the pulsing darkness—the flicker of the wall lamps making shadows jump—avoiding the scolding eyes of the holy, centuries-old statues that lined the corridor.

A robed, hooded figure passed in the gloom far in front of us—the odd way that he looked back over his shoulder at me sending a nauseating ripple down my spine.

"The monks here are a silent order," advised Brother Vito. "They designed the program, but they take no part in it. You'll barely see them, apart from when they're preparing the meals."

Good, it's strange enough here without having to deal with shadowy monks as well.

I followed him to an enormous hexagonal room, in which the scene before me seemed otherworldly. Fourteen women slept in the beds, their hair fanned out on the pillows. Metronomes ticked and echoed on wooden shelves high above each bed. An arched window framed the indigo darkness.

"The men are in the room next door," he said in hushed tones, handing me two items of folded clothing. "The rooms will be locked. You'll be quite safe. Oh, and Evie"—he pulled out a small bottle from his pocket—"here's a couple of sleeping pills to help you through your first night."

He waited while I changed my clothes in the ancient bathroom and returned to settle into bed. With a nod, he clicked the door shut.

Darkness swept the room.

Jetlag moved through me in heavy, syrupy waves. Curling up, I tried to make myself sleep, but I couldn't seem to find the right spot in the bed. The ticking of the damned metronomes began to sound like a ceaseless march.

I ran my fingertips over the charms of the bracelet my husband had given me just days ago. I was supposed to have handed over everything to Brother Vito, but I'd hidden this. It was just a cheap novelty bracelet, but it was a gift only Gray and I would understand—the charms were tiny replicas of items within an online game that we played together.

I missed Gray already.

It was winter in Australia, and he and I went to sleep wrapped up together every night. He'd always fall asleep before I did, snoring gently into my temple. Or sometimes, we'd try to sneak in quick sex. On cue, our youngest daughter—two-year-old Lilly—would wake. She'd head into her big sister's room to cause a toddler brand of havoc. Willow would either protest loudly or giggle. The girls would end up in our bed, and we'd all eventually succumb to exhausted sleep like battle-weary soldiers.

I was so far away from Gray and the girls now. But this was a once-in-a-lifetime chance for me to make everything that was bad good again, and I couldn't throw this away.

A condition of the contract of this program was that I keep it confidential. There was no one I wanted to tell anyway. Because if I did, I'd also have to reveal secrets about myself: I'd have to admit that I'm a gambling addict and that I've racked up a debt so huge, I'll never be able to repay it.

There's yet another thing I've been keeping from my husband: two months ago, I tried working as an escort. I didn't get very far with it. But still, somehow, I got to that point.

How did I let all this happen? Why wasn't I smarter?

As sleep continued to elude me, the self-accusations skewered my mind. It'd started with Lilly.

From the time Lilly was a baby, she'd been sick—the trifecta of chest infections, ear infections and high temperatures. The doctors said her frequent illnesses were unlucky but normal. I was convinced it was our house. It was an old rental and the only house Gray and I could afford. Between the rising damp and the leaks and the dark rooms, it always smelled *wet* in winter. Cooking, crayons and mould—the constant smells of our home.

We needed money to move house, and we didn't have any money. So I'd decided I needed a job.

I'd made a list of all the things I was good at:

1. Cooking

2. Warcraft

3. Talking

4. Poker

5. Self-hate

There didn't seem to be many job openings for Warcraft gamers or self-haters, so that left the other three things on my list. I tried gaining a job as a kitchen hand at some local restaurants, but I couldn't get hours that would slot in when the girls were at daycare or when Gray was at home at night. And Lilly was sick too often for me to hold down a normal job anyway. So that cut out cooking.

I was down to two things on my list now.

~~*1. Cooking*~~

~~*2. Warcraft*~~

3. Talking

4. Poker

~~*5. Self-hate*~~

No one would pay me to talk. So, I'd turned to the thing I swore I would never do again after my brother, Ben, died. *Poker.* It was Ben who taught me to play.

I used to be good at poker. Ben's friends used to complain whenever I played with them because I'd win. I started entering local poker competitions, sharpening up my rusty skills.

When I began winning competitions, I began dreaming big. What if I could win enough for a deposit on a house? Gray and I could have our own home. And he'd be proud of me. Telling Gray that I'd scored a job at a city restaurant, I headed to the big poker tournaments.

But then I stepped from the casino poker rooms to the roulette table.

That was my downfall.

I quickly fell in over my head, into a pit of debt.

But now I'd been given another chance.

Just one week, and I'd be home again. If everything went to plan, Gray would never know where I really went or why.

3. I, INSIDE THE WALLS

THE LAST ONE OF THEM HAS arrived now in the monastery. Her face so pale and anxious.

In six days she'll be dead. Just like all the rest of them.

I would steal around now, if I had my way, and cut their throats one by one while they sleep. But I am constantly watched. The others will not allow me to steal their quarry from them.

Inside these walls, I wait.

The deaths are inevitable, one way or the other. Everything in the vast, cold universe is calculated. The numbers explain the existence of every last insignificant insect or the rings around Saturn that could be pieces of broken moons. Energy and time. Space and matter. Love and hate. Everything we feel is just calculations compressed and shaped into soft entities we call emotions.

Pythagoras knew. There are gods and demons in the numbers.

4. GRAY

THE LAST THING I THOUGHT I'D be doing today was telling Evie I'd lost my job. My stinking, worthless job.

Turning off the highway, I drove into the narrow, graffitied set of laneways that were a shortcut to my street. The laneways always reminded me of clogged arteries, choking everyone who passed through. I'd thought it'd rain, but the dark clouds dried out and stuck fast to the winter sky like old spitballs.

I'd stayed overnight in the city after attending my cousin's bucks party, and the Saturday traffic was just as busy as any weekday. Cousin Dayle was a law student with a city sneer in his upper lip and a Svengali-like devotion to his own bad jokes. But after getting unceremoniously dumped from my job on Friday afternoon, I'd headed straight from work to get blind drunk with him and the collection of jackasses he called his mates.

I'd slept in a hotel room until midday today, my eyes gritty and a twisting feeling in my gut.

I tried calling Evie again. I hadn't been able to get her on the phone yesterday or today. *Could she be angry with me?* It'd been Evie who'd insisted that I go last night with Dayle. She'd pointed out that I didn't have much family left in this world. Which was true. Both of my parents died young—drug overdoses—and I had no siblings.

But I'd been in two minds about going, right up to Friday afternoon.

I needed music—something fast, heavy and destructive. Rifling through my music discs, I took out a CD and pushed it into the player.

The angry, thrashing riff of Pantera's *Walk* pounded from the speakers.

I turned it up louder.

Louder.

But the music opened a valve that was only going to snap shut the second I had to walk in the door and tell Evie I'd lost my job. I knew her. My usually *talk-underwater* wife would go quiet, and I'd have to watch her struggle to hide that she was spinning out. *The rent, the bills, the groceries*—all of these things teetered on the edge of disaster every single week.

I needed something to make telling her easier.

Stopping sharply, I reversed and drove back around the corner, then swung the car around and parked outside Joe's. Inhaling a gasp of chilled air, I ran into his house for a $20 bag of pot.

Pot was something Evie and I did once every couple of months. Put the kids to bed, watch a movie, have a smoke. Kick back.

I'd kicked cigarettes five months and two days ago. Pot and alcohol were my last refuges. I convinced myself that those two things were a world away from the hard drugs that'd ended my parents' lives.

Later tonight, I'd pull out the weed, and once I was sure Evie was calm and sleepy, I'd drop the news.

When I walked into Joe's living room, he and his wife were sitting watching a reality TV rerun, their faces as worn and disintegrating as the fake leather of their armchairs. You could tell that whatever they'd been hitting in their lives—drugs, alcohol and cigarettes—they'd hit them hard. Both in their early seventies, they sold dope to *supplement their pensions*.

They tried to get me to stay and have a smoke with them. Sometimes I did. Today I didn't. Every time I'd sit down with them, they'd recycle the same old stories, in deep, smoke-burned voices.

Heading back to my car, I drove back around the corner to my street, threading through the beaten-up vans and wheel-less cars and a mob of kids on scooters and skateboards.

I pulled up short as two girls no older than eight stepped out in front of me, each pushing a stroller that carried a baby sibling.

Although the babies were rugged up with blankets, the girls weren't wearing anything more than tank tops and shorts. I watched them cross the street, the small, pixie-faced blonde girl stopping in the middle of the road to pat her squalling brother.

Driving three doors farther along to my house, I parked the car and rehearsed my act. Be casual. Don't spill the news to Evie until later tonight.

I walked into a strangely quiet house.

Our house was never quiet.

Normally, Lilly and Willow would be whooping through the house, pretending to be magic unicorns or killer ninjas.

No whooping this afternoon. No unicorns or ninjas.

No sound of music or the TV.

Nothing.

5. EVIE

SUDDEN FLICKERS OF MOVEMENT IN THE opposite wall stole my attention.

God, were those *eyes* peering in from a tiny hole in the stonework?

Yes, *eyes*, moonlight from a high window making the whites of them luminous.

Someone's watching me.

I jerked to a sitting position, rushes of cold prickles embedding themselves into my arms and spine.

The eyes glistened in the peephole.

Who was peering at me and the others? What was on the other side of that wall?

I willed someone else to wake.

The girl in the bed closest to mine murmured in her sleep, long, pale hair strung across her face. I choked back an impulse to run across and shake her awake.

I twisted around the other way.

A red-haired girl from the bed on my left side was silently observing me through the dim light. "Having a panic attack? I have those. Just . . . breathe. And cheer up, you're somewhere *good* for a change."

"Don't you see them?" A tremor ran through my voice. "The eyes, watching us."

Her face creased into a frown. "Ah, you're one of the druggies. Good, I'm not alone. The mentors said they'd put us all through rehab before we came here. But you still haven't come down off your high horse. Sorry, little joke of mine. *High* horse." She raised her eyebrows comically.

Not answering, I swivelled back to face the walls. There was nothing but a dark space where the eyes had been.

I let air fill my lungs.

"You really need to chill, or you'll never get through this," the girl said, softening her tone. Her accent was what I called *jolly-hockey-sticks*. Upbeat and very English.

"I'm sorry—" I flinched as the wailing, stereophonic calls of a flock of birds started up, my thoughts scattering. The bird calls were so loud and exotic they were almost alien, coming from somewhere out in the hills.

"Wow, you *are* a jumpy one," she said. "Hey, I'm feeling a bit jumpy, too. This place is weirding me out. And those birds are noisy."

I rubbed my arms. "I don't know what's making me so nervous."

"Don't sweat it. Why don't you try to get some sleep? It's a damned shame to waste time being awake when you could be snoozing." Yawning, she pulled the covers up close to her chin.

"Thanks. I think I'll do that." Wriggling back down under the blanket, I rolled to face away from her, feeling embarrassed.

Why didn't I just shut my big mouth? I must have sounded like a child.

The birds quietened, and I could hear the steady tick of the metronomes again.

I shivered as I scanned the walls, making doubly sure the eyes were gone.

No, not *gone*. They'd never existed in the first place.

I was jet lagged. Exhausted. Maybe even feeling the effects of Brother Vito's sleeping tablets. Enough to make me go a bit loopy.

My elation of mere minutes ago had vanished.

What's wrong with me? Things finally start going right and then I have to go and start inventing things to worry about.

The girl was right. I needed to chill, or I wouldn't make it through the challenges.

It'd been a huge rush to get here. A frenzied, whirling dervish of plans and decisions. I'd even pressed Gray to go to his cousin's bucks party. Gray didn't think a lot of Dayle, but I'd needed some time to organise things and make my flight.

The hardest thing was that I wouldn't be able to talk with Gray or my daughters for a whole week. That was a strict requirement of coming here. No outside contact.

I hated doing it this way.

But I hadn't had time to think about the right or the wrong. I just knew that I had to do *something*, else drag my family into a bottomless pit.

I'd never tell anyone about the things I'd done. Not Gray. Not my friends. Especially not my mother.

No one would understand.

6. GRAY

I CHECKED UPSTAIRS. SOMETIMES, EVIE AND the kids would be tucked up in our bed on a cold afternoon, watching a kids' movie on TV.

But they weren't there, either.

Even the cat, in its usual spot on the armchair, barely bothered to open one eye to give me its customary glare.

The house was cold. Evie normally had the oil heaters running. Both of our girls caught lots of colds in the winter—especially Lilly—and heating the house was the one luxury Evie insisted on.

I swapped back to thinking that Evie must be mad at me again. She rarely took the girls out on a cold night, and we hadn't gone this long without talking since we'd met. There had to be a reason she wasn't answering the phone.

She'd been strange lately. So up and down—for months. Some days dancing and singing with the kids. Other days almost refusing to talk. When I'd asked her why, she'd said it wasn't me, it was just everything. Well, damned if I could fix *everything*. Throw a couple of things my way and I might be able to patch them up. But I didn't even know where to start with *everything*.

I'd started thinking that maybe she was disappointed with her life. That she wanted more than I could give her. Once or twice, I'd caught that same look of disappointment in my eldest daughter's eyes when I'd explained we couldn't buy the crazy-expensive toy she wanted. And it'd killed me. Willow was only four, but she was just like a mini-Evie in many ways.

My thoughts burned to ash as I stepped through to the kitchen and saw the handwritten note on the fridge. It wasn't a grocery list or a dashed-off message or something Willow had scrawled. This was a short letter, signed by Evie.

Before I snatched it from the fridge, I already knew that things were worse than Evie being a bit mad at me.

Gray,

I'm sorry, I can't be here right now. I have to go away for a while, maybe a week or so. Sort myself out. We're fighting too much. That's not good for the kids or us. Please just give me the time that I need. Don't try to find us.

I'll come back soon.

xx Evie

Her words hit me square in the centre of my chest.

I'm sorry, I can't be here right now.

She left me?

I have to go away for a while, maybe a week or so . . .

How the hell did she think it was okay to take our kids and just go? No way was I going to be okay with not seeing Lilly and Willow for a week. Or even a day. She could decide to leave, but she didn't get to decide that she could take the girls away from me.

Why didn't I know things were getting this bad?

We fought sometimes—sure—but we rarely got to the point of yelling. We always made up. We were always a team.

I didn't know her, after all.

I squeezed the letter into a small ball.

This wasn't happening.

I'd find her and talk to her, and this would get fixed.

Taking out my phone, I tried calling her number for the twentieth time, but this time the recorded voice said the number was disconnected.

As I went to toss the letter into the trash, a noise at the front door had me doing a one-eighty.

Had Evie come back already? Had she changed her mind?

Of course. She wouldn't leave like this. This was just a bad day all around. We'd get past it.

Blowing out a stream of chilled air, I jogged along the hallway.

7. CONSTANCE

KNOCKING ON DOORS ALWAYS REMINDED ME of knocking on someone's skull and then hollering in their ear, *Let me in.*

People didn't want you at their front doorstep unless they'd invited you. Homes were a sanctum, a refuge away from the world. It was a wonder everyone didn't put *Never Disturb* signs on their doors.

But whoever lived here, I needed to disturb their peace.

I knocked again.

A slow panic squeezed through my veins at the thought of why I was standing on this doorstep. I'd found a note in my missing daughter's jacket that had this address on it.

I hadn't heard from Kara in three weeks. I hadn't even been able to wish her a happy birthday. She was just seventeen. I shouldn't have allowed her to go on this trip. *What had I been thinking?* It was my fault. Of course it was my fault. My bright and beautiful daughter, who'd finished high school early and was already in her second year of college, had been too young to leave our home in Mississippi and complete her second year of college here in Australia. But Kara was always so headstrong. Once her mind was made up, that was it.

I was about to knock again when a young man opened the door—his hair shaggy but his face clean shaven. His eyes held a measure of anxious anticipation—which vanished almost instantly as he stared at me. Had he been expecting someone else?

"I'm looking for my daughter." I fished in my handbag and produced a laminated photo of her. "Kara Lundquist."

His confusion seemed genuine as he glanced at her picture. "What makes you think she's here?"

"I just—" I stopped and started again. "I found an address on a piece of paper in a jacket of hers. *Your address*. And a name—Evie."

"Evie's not here," he told me flatly. "And I don't know your daughter."

"Then can I talk to Evie? Please?"

His fist tightened on a piece of paper he had crumpled in his fist. "Good luck with that. She just left me. Wrote a goodbye letter."

"I'm so sorry. Do you know where she—?"

"No. I have no damned idea where she went."

He just wanted me gone. He wasn't able to summon up any sympathy for a stranger and her missing daughter.

But I'd come a long way to find this house. It'd cost me well over a hundred dollars in cab fare from Sydney to this suburb in the middle of nowheresville. Not that the money had mattered, but it was the wasted time. I had no idea where I was—I'd simply shown the address to the driver and asked him to take me there.

The suburb reminded me of the town in Mississippi where I'd grown up. I lived in Lafayette County now, in a huge home on acreage. But I didn't always. I stifled a shudder as I glanced down the street. Old, leaning houses and rusting cars on front lawns with the grass growing right through them. I could almost taste the poverty in the air. And this man standing before me right now was a reminder of that life, too. Cheap shoes, cheap polyester shirt. He was young now and handsome, still with pads of baby fat covering his cheekbones and his eyes still clear. In a few years, the desperation of his life would wear him down. In bitter anger, he might start drinking too much, too often. And he'd turn into the man I'd lived with in my early twenties.

I took out a marker and scrawled down my phone number on the back of Kara's photo. I had twenty copies in my bag. "Please, would you call me if you do speak to your wife? I don't mean to be pushy. I'm just desperate to find Kara. I've come all the way from our hometown in the US."

Shrugging, he took the photograph. "Yeah, sure."

Behind him on the wall, a framed photograph of a smiling, fresh-faced family took pride of place—the man looking slightly awkward in a white shirt and tie beside a pretty, dark-haired woman and two little girls in red dresses. I guessed it was a Christmas photo.

"Can I ask your name?" I said in a last-ditch attempt to gather clues.

"Yeah, it's Gray. Gray Harlow."

Thanking him, I returned to the waiting cab. I'd hoped for more than this. If only I'd found the address in Kara's jacket pocket yesterday and had travelled out here then. It might have been his wife who opened the door, and she might have had the answers I was looking for.

My fingers were jittery as I closed the cab door and leaned back on the seat.

I needed to get myself to a doctor and grab a prescription for some Promaxa. The drug was for my anxiety and depression. My psych had refused to prescribe me any more of it. I'd been on it too long, she'd said, I was mentally stronger than I gave myself credit for.

What did she know? My three-hundred-an-hour psych didn't have a teenage daughter living in a foreign country. She didn't live with a husband whose love she'd never been able to *feel*. She didn't bear the weight of the crushing feeling of a wasted life.

Blinking back the sting of tears, I instructed the driver to head back to the city.

8. EVIE

I WOKE NOW, FEELING THE DRAGGING WEIGHT between sleep and consciousness. I hadn't felt this whacked since Lilly was a baby. I always woke just before Gray did, near six in the morning.

I hadn't slept in for years, not even on weekends. Willow and Lilly were always up so early.

I'd been dreaming of my brother Ben and me when we were kids—at the beach house that my parents rented every year. The beach house was a place apart, like it existed outside of everything. A place I could always go and find Ben. I hadn't wanted to leave the dream.

I stretched, warm under the covers. Even on my most stressful days as an adult, I'd wake in that lulled way of childhood, seconds before the worry came thundering back in. Those seconds saved me, I think. There was a sweetness in those seconds in between sleep and waking. A taste and a memory. Like my childhood summers of standing on sun-warmed sand with Ben, staring vacant-eyed at the distant salty haze, carelessly letting my ice cream soften and drip away to nothing. Ben and I would elbow each other to be the first to go when Dad whistled for us to come and help him clean his boat. In those days, I called the mornings to me and sent the sunsets away, never trying to keep hold of anything. Because there would be more summers with Ben and more melting ice cream cones.

I didn't know then that Ben's years were fast counting down and he soon wouldn't be here anymore.

Numbers, always counting. Numbers you can't see until afterwards. You had to make the most of every day, because the people you expected to wake up to tomorrow might not be there.

I wanted to take Willow and Lilly away somewhere like the beach house, but there had never been enough money for that.

Blowing out a sharp breath, I checked the clock on the stone monastery wall. It was near ten in the morning.

My thoughts switched back to Gray. He'd have found my note by now.

What was he thinking? Was he ever going to be able to forgive me for this?

The other women were gone, and the hexagonal room was still, except for the metronomes. I watched them ticking back and forth for a minute, wondering what the purpose of them was—each one on an otherwise empty shelf above each bed.

Remembering the *eyes in the wall* suddenly, I anxiously glanced around the room.

Nothing.

Still, I couldn't help but watch the walls as I rose and padded across the floor. I wore a hooded outfit of loose, cream pants and shirt that I'd been given by Brother Vito last night. All of the program participants were to wear this gear for the whole week.

Poking my head around the open doorway, I realised I had no idea where to go.

Had the challenges started yet? I'd be left behind. I dashed into the bathroom first—at least I knew where that was. I peered into the dim mirror as I washed my hands and face. I looked strange in my monastery gear, my eyes so large and uncertain.

Running my fingers through my hair, I headed back into the silent air of the corridor. The monastery seemed as if it were in twilight, though it was morning outside.

I made a wrong turn into a small, dead-end recess. On the floor beneath a forbidding, winged statue, some child had once painted a small court for a hopscotch game. Immediately, I pictured Willow and Lilly and made a mental note to teach them the game.

I jerked my head up sharply at the sound of scuffling on the other side of the wall. Maybe I'd found the others already? I just had to find the door for the room on the other side.

Running out of the recess, I almost bumped straight into someone—Brother Vito.

"There you are." He smiled, one eyebrow quirked. "What were you doing?"

"Getting lost."

"Ah, let me help with that," he said with a short laugh. "Come."

He led me along the hall to a library stuffed with ancient-looking books. He indicated a framed piece of torn, yellowish parchment illustrated with thin, hexagonal lines. "These are the original plans of the monastery, from the twelfth century. Shame it's not all there, but you'll get the idea."

"Wow, so old." Constructing the missing half in my mind, I surmised that twenty-four rooms encircled six rooms—all hexagonal and all exactly the same size—with a large gap in between the outer and inner rings. Yet another twenty-four rooms ringed the outside. "Why the odd-shaped rooms?"

He nodded, frowning as though the answer was complicated. "The monastery was built with the purpose of taking in the mentally ill and giving them work and lodgings. It was thought that the hexagonal shape of the rooms would give rest to the afflicted. Squares were thought to be too sharp and threatening. Circles roll too fast. Hexagons were the best compromise, apparently. When you step inside the monastery, you're meant to be stepping inside an ordered mind."

I gazed back at the dimly lit hall outside the library, thinking no one would willingly want to be inside the mind of this monastery. But then I considered the mentally ill who once lived here. "Did it work? Were the people helped?"

"Well, that's lost to history, I'm afraid. But it is a nice thought." He touched the map with a forefinger. "I'll give you a quick run through. Here at the top right, we have the old hospice—which we now call the dormitories—and the infirmary. And this is the library—where you are now, along with the scriptorium and the treasury. Next to the hospice, you'll find the balneary, which is where the bathrooms are located. At the top is the refectory, which is what the dining hall is called. The kitchen also is located here. At the bottom left of the map, which has been torn away, are the old monks' dormitory, which is where the mentors and long-term residents stay. The chapel is located in that quarter as well. Guests are not permitted to venture down that way." He paused, looking back at me.

"What if we want to go and pray?" I quipped.

His face broke into an easy grin. "You don't need a chapel in order to pray. We have wonderful gardens here if you find yourself needing a moment to commune with a higher power." It occurred to me again that Brother Vito was a handsome man. I knew my mother would think so, and he looked about her age.

"That sounds very new-age hippie," I remarked, wondering if he believed in God or not.

He shrugged, still smiling. "We accommodate everyone. If you want to believe in woodland fairies, we'll accommodate you, too." Turning back to the plan, he made a sweeping circle with his hand. "And outside the main building, we have the stables, the brewery, various barns and fields and the forge. The inner six rooms are where the challenges will be held. One room for each challenge."

I pointed to the very centre of the monastery, or at least what would be the centre if the plan was intact. The circle of six hexagonal rooms would have to leave a space in the middle. "And what is here?"

"There's nothing there. Just a dark space. Now, if you continue along the hall and head right, you'll find the cloister. It's a long, covered walkway that faces the garden. I'm sure you'd rather be out there than in here. Go and have breakfast. Are you hungry?"

"Yes, a little."

"Well, go grab what you can before it's all gone."

Following Brother Vito's instructions, I headed off. I found the cloister and wandered out gratefully into the thick, green foliage. Sunlight rushed down from a deep cyan sky, its warmth astonishing after the cool of the interior, gold streaks of sun glinting biblically along the top of the high stone wall. *Everything felt religious here, even the air.* I wasn't religious. but it gave me hope I could somehow be reborn during this week.

Past the top of a perimeter wall, I glimpsed the bare, reddish hills I'd only seen in darkness last night. And then I spotted them—the birds that had been making the startling, alien-sounding noise earlier when I was in bed. They were peacocks. Nothing more exotic than that. Their bodies were a startling, shimmering blue against the red soil of the hill. I'd never seen or heard a wild flock of them before.

I stepped along a path where sun-warmed scents of lavender eddied around me, spills of pink and red bougainvillea bright against the old stonework. Fruit weighed heavily on small mature trees—pears, figs and mandarins. Deep-green trees that I thought might be pistachios stood like a mini-forest. A waterway wound around the long curve of the nearby cloister, filled with orange-hued koi.

"So, what's your sin?" a voice came from behind me—high and female, the accent English.

I spun around. The girl was short and soft-looking, all her edges smudged and padded. Red bobbed hair framed large blue eyes and pillowy lips.

"My sin?"

"Yeah" she said, walking close. "Smack, cocaine, ice, prescription?"

"Oh . . . no. I don't take drugs."

"You were tripping on something this morning."

"That was *you* I spoke to? Sorry, it was so dark in that room." Of course it was her. The voice was the same. I'd just been so strung out by the thought of someone watching me, I'd forgotten her voice.

"It *was* dark," she agreed. "Plus, I've got my face on now. My boyfriend used to say I was unrecognisable without makeup. He died three months ago. Overdose."

"God, I'm sorry."

"Me too. He had a cute butt." A distinct note of sadness cut through her blithe tone. "So, why are you here? You don't win a spot on the program without earning it. You've been a bad, bad girl at something."

"I'm a gambler." It felt almost freeing to say it.

"Congratulations. Pleased to meet you." She extended a hand. "My name's Poppy. I think my parents must have seen into my smack-addicted future when they called me that. Y'know, smack being made from poppy-pod sap and all." She pulled a funny, wrinkled-nose face, as if she'd just told a joke and I was meant to laugh at the punch line.

Shaking her hand, I grinned. "I'm Evie. Named after a song that my dad liked. He was a Stevie Wright fan. So, you got here yesterday?"

"Yep. Like everyone else. Pretty crazy. I mean, *look* at this place."

"I know. Of all places I expected, this wasn't it." My grin turned nervous and tugged at the corners of my mouth. "How did you find out about the program, if you don't mind me asking?"

"Sure. My psych recommended it." Poppy pulled a comical face. "She said if I go ahead with the program, I have to go into it like my life depended on it. It's all so serious, isn't it?"

I laughed. "Yeah. I guess they think it makes the program seem very important and special. Makes sense. The mentors are putting a lot of money into this. I guess they want it to succeed. Brother Vito was the one who contacted me."

Her eyes squeezed shut. "Brother Vito? You lucky thing. There's something about him that's so . . . sexy. I know he's a *lot* older and all, but oh, he could just charm the pants off me. Literally."

"He *is* good looking and kind of charming." I knew what she meant, but he was old enough for the thought of that to completely squick me out. "So, where are the others?"

"In the garden. Just around the bend. I'm not a breakfast person at all, so I was going for a walk." She touched my arm. "I'll take you to them."

I walked alongside her, the scent of freshly baked bread reaching me before the outdoor settings of tables and chairs came into view. People were sitting there, baskets of round bread, cheese and fruit on the tabletops. A couple dozen heads turned my way. Half of them smiled encouragingly. The other half stared blankly.

"Everyone, meet our newest recruit and fellow desperado—Evie," Poppy announced.

I waved a quick hello.

Poppy took me to a table where two men were sitting together. "I prefer men," she whispered to me. "No drama llamas."

A small-framed blonde guy with a goatee reached to shake my hand. He looked maybe twenty-six or -seven. "Hi, I'm Richard. Underneath this manly beard, I'm stashing a fat baby chin and a bitter longing for Las Vegas. Don't ask me to shave it."

His words pulled a surprised laugh from me. I seated myself at the table, telling him, "I promise I won't."

"Good," he replied in his curt, American accent. "Because women tend to tell me to do that. They can guess I'm hiding things. Women are evil like that. Eyes like ferrets. All of them." He cast a meaningful sideways glance at Poppy.

Poppy giggled, sitting beside him. "Okay, I admit it. I told him to ditch the beard. I thought he'd look cuter without it."

"He'd look shite without that rug on his mug." The guy next to me turned to shake my hand. "I'm Cormack. As soon as I'm done here, I intend grabbing my prize money, packing up my Scottish skirts and heading off to the Amazon jungle. Going to trek from Columbia to Brazil. Get away from this world for a while. I'll only stop and lift my skirt should a comely wench cross my path, if she be willin'." He spoke in a deep Scottish brogue, his intense blue eyes vivid behind a scraggy array of long black hair and wild beard. He was perched on the edge of his seat, like he was ready for anything.

"Good to meet you, Cormack," I replied. "May you achieve your goals. All while playing the bagpipe."

"That would be grand." Cormack gave me a nod of approval, his face softening and changing in that instant. I smiled back, realising then that he wasn't as old as he'd at first seemed. His facial hair and intensity had thrown me. He was probably no older than twenty. A kid.

"Eat," Richard instructed, pushing a plate my way.

Suddenly famished, I grabbed two thick pieces of bread from the basket, dropped them onto the plate and buttered them. Then layered on some cheese, olives and tomatoes.

"It's homemade—the bread," Richard remarked, pulling a face I couldn't read. "And the wine. Everything here is home grown and homemade. I feel like I'm at some sort of hippie commune."

"It's not a hippie commune, dummie." Poppy sucked a cherry tomato into her mouth and then lisped as she spoke around it. "Monks grew all that food. Hippies aren't religious. I wonder what the treatment is going to be? I mean, they talked about challenges. Evie, did Brother Vito tell you anything?"

"Not much," I answered. "Just that there were six challenges, all held in the inner six rooms."

A glum look entered her eyes as she chewed and swallowed the tomato. "It's not fair they're not preparing us. It's making me stress, and stress isn't good for me. I get rashes in places you don't want to know about."

Richard shot her a look of feigned disgust.

"How hard can these challenges be? I'm going to smash them. They'll probably just be truth or dare," said Cormack, shrugging. "Some shit about laying your inner self bare."

"Better not be," said Richard. "Or I'll lay some inner-self truths on them that'll straighten their pubes."

"The challenges are probably all meditation," mused Poppy, idly using her long, painted-black nails to peel the skin from an olive. "I hate meditation. Makes me remember all the shitty things I've done."

I bit off a piece of bread. "Maybe they're not really challenges. Maybe it's just stuff like when they blindfold you and you trust strangers enough to fall and let them catch you."

Poppy nodded. "I went to a rehab group once, and that's what we did."

"Let's lay bets," Richard quipped.

"You'll be banished to toil in the monk fields for that blasphemy. Laying bets is gambling." Poppy shot him a fleeting saccharine smile.

Our table fell into a silence. I guessed the other three, like me, were desperate to be able to complete the challenges and get the money. But so far, we were completely in the dark.

"You mentioned Las Vegas before?" I asked Richard, trying to redirect the conversation. "Do I guess that you're a gambler? Like me?"

"Oh yeah," Richard said. "I'm a high-roller cowboy, baby." He shrugged. "I have to admit, it's pretty bad when the dealers all know you by name. But I just can't get that kind of high anywhere else. The nights where I win big I end up buying the whole damned place drinks. It's a party when Richard's in town."

A twinge of jealousy pinched me between the shoulder blades. "Okay, well, you're nothing like me. I didn't ever win that kind of big. And I wasn't gambling for the high either. It was for the money."

I wasn't sure if that was totally true. My wins had made me walk on air. They were addictive.

Richard raised condescending eyebrows at me. "People who go all in to make money never make it. They're too desperate. They either play too safe or take stupid risks. You gotta be a hustler. I get off on the hustle. This is what I do. All day long. I find business opportunities for the rich. I fly between my base in Vegas to London and Dubai."

A girl wearing a hooded top a couple of tables across leaned back and glanced at Richard. When she noticed me looking her way, she quickly turned her head.

Cormack rapped the edge of the table, suddenly agitated, his eyes set on Richard. "Then what in the bastarding fuck are you even doing here, man?

You'd have the money to just keep on bloody gambling. It's not a problem if you can afford it, right?"

"It's a sickness." Richard sobered. "I don't want to be sick anymore."

I could see from Cormack's darkened expression that he wasn't buying that. "Yeah, but you can afford to pay for treatment. You're a fat cat who's taking someone else's place in being here."

"Leave him alone," Poppy protested. "Richard needs as much help as any of us."

Richard raised his chin, looking past Poppy. "Speaking of help, the cavalry has arrived. Thank fug."

I twisted around in my chair. Brother Vito and three other mentors were stepping up to us together—two men and two women, all dressed in loose, white clothing. Brother Vito seemed so different from the man I'd met in his expensive sportswear days ago.

The four mentors together had a presence that made everyone's conversation instantly fall away.

"Welcome, welcome," started one of the men, his accent English upper crust and very educated. He seemed to be in his fifties, but I couldn't tell for sure. His hair was silver streaked, but his face was almost unlined, as if he spent each day in a peaceful serenity, not bothered by anger or worry. He held out his arms to us. "*Kaliméra! Kalos mas írthes*! You may call me Brother Sage. The monastery has been a second home for us for many years. We come here every year to run the program. We trust it will become like a home while you're here, too. Did you all enjoy your breakfast?"

Murmurs of assent echoed among the group. It was immediately obvious that he was the senior mentor from the assured way he spoke and the way the other three mentors looked to him.

"Good." A smile tumbled onto Brother Sage's lips, generous and broad. "We want you well fed for the tasks ahead. The rules of the monastery are simple. We are your mentors. You are our students. We expect that you'll follow direction and do your best. Beside me are Sisters Rose and Dawn, and Brother Vito. Now, I need you to know that we are mentors, not your agony aunts. We are not here to listen to all your ills. We are here to help you heal yourselves."

"What if some of us need agony aunts?" said Poppy to me in a stage whisper. She raised her hand above her head and called out, "What are the challenges?"

Brother Sage nodded at Poppy. “Well, I can’t tell you exactly what the challenges are, because that would destroy the element of surprise. But I will tell you that you must use teamwork to meet those challenges and win them. We’ll be dividing you into four teams. With each challenge, the four bottom-performing people will unfortunately be eliminated and will be escorted by boat back to Athens. Until we are left with eight people after the final challenge. We’ll then decide on the final six, with the two runners-up being given a bonus. The final six, as you are all aware, will not only be the recipients of the full sixty thousand dollars but will have their debts completely paid.”

Sister Rose clapped her hands together, then rested her chin on her fingertips, beaming at us like children on the first day of school. “You’ll see the first of the challenges tonight. You’ll enjoy it if you allow yourself to.” Her voice was American, her face as cheery and apple-pie round as a Sunday school teacher’s.

Sister Dawn nodded at Sister Rose. “That’s right. Put your heart into the challenges, and you’ll find yourself zipping through them.” She had the dark-skinned features of an Indian ancestry, her accent a blend of English and Indian, her eyes brown and comforting. “Brother Vito is about to give you all the wristbands you’ll need for the challenges. The display on the wristbands will flash with a number when your challenge is due to begin. The number will tell you which team you’re in.”

Brother Vito stepped forward with the box and began clipping chunky plastic wristbands onto our arms.

“How are you doing so far, Evie?” Brother Vito asked me quietly, fitting a wristband to my arm.

A gulp of air stretched my lungs. “It’s an adventure.”

“Good, good,” he said. “That’s exactly what it is. That’s how I want you to see it. Right to the end. I trust that you can get there.”

Internally, I felt like a Girl Scout being decorated with a coveted badge. I caught Poppy side-eyeing me with a slightly envious glance.

“At midnight,” Sister Dawn continued to the group, “you’ll hear the starting bells. They are church bells, and they are *loud.* I assure you that they will wake you. Together with the other members of your team, you will assemble here in the garden. From there you’ll be escorted to your challenge room. The teams are staggered so that each team gets their allotted time for the challenge." She turned to write on a large chalkboard: *Challenge One tonight.*

"At midnight? Why in the middle of the night?" spluttered a thin, bent-shouldered man from another table. "Seems a bit unnecessary. I'm a deep sleeper, and I don't like being woken."

"Shut it, Harrington," called Cormack from our table. "Maybe you want to think to yourself how you got here in the first place. You know that like all of us here, you told yourself you can quit your vice a thousand times over. But you never could do it, could you? Maybe if you beat this, you'll believe you can do it."

"That's the hope." Sister Dawn nodded. "You answered that perfectly, Cormack."

A plump, flabby jowled-man who reminded me of an English bulldog stretched his feet out into the sun. "My name is Eugene Bublik. I am an alcoholic. The amenities here are basic but sufficient. What I would like to know is the menu. I cannot do these challenges if I am not well fed. I don't like to be hungry." His accent was deep and heavy. I couldn't place it, exactly, but it was Eastern European.

Harrington turned to face him, giving him a disparaging look. "This isn't an Alcoholics Anonymous meeting, bud."

"Or a five-star hotel," called Cormack.

Everyone laughed.

"The meals will be more than sufficient, Eugene," said Sister Dawn. "I hope that answers your question."

A woman a couple of tables down from us stood. She was tall and severe looking, her dyed-black hair scraped back from her thin face, showing dish-water-blonde roots. Amateur tattoos ran down one side of her neck. "What if the team we're in can't complete a challenge due to the actions of one person? Does the whole team get punished?"

"There is no punishment here, Ruth," Sister Dawn assured her. "We take video recordings of the challenges and make determinations on the efforts of each individual."

"I really need this," stated Ruth. "I'm sorry for anyone who gets put in my team, but if you don't put in a hundred percent, you might see me bust out my mean side." She glanced around at everyone for effect.

Brother Vito gave a good-natured laugh, clipping a wristband onto

Poppy's arm. "Ruth, you won't need to get mean. I'm sure they'll all be pulling their weight."

"Ruth? More like Ruth*less*," muttered Richard under his breath. "She looks violent. I don't want to get in her team."

"Me either. She's missing a tooth, too—she probably fights people in alleyways. *Toothless Ruthless*." Poppy pulled her mouth down severely at Richard then lifted her eyes to Brother Vito, shooting him a smile that almost looked shy.

Brother Vito straightened, then dug his hands into the loose pockets of his clothing. "Look, everyone, don't worry so much. We're strict, but we're fair. Stay calm during the challenges and do your best. That's all you need to do. Any other questions?"

A pretty, brown-skinned girl raised her hand. "What's with all the ticking contraptions in the dormitory? Greta and Roxy and I can't sleep properly."

"You mean the metronomes, Yolanda?" replied Brother Vito. "They're there to help reframe your minds. Allow them to lull you. You'll get used to them." He smiled. "Now, why don't you all relax and get to know each other?"

With that, the mentors left the garden and returned to the monastery interior.

Richard's jaw pulled tight beneath his beard. "I don't know about any of you, but I'm not going to play this *calm*. I'm here to win. Right to the end."

Poppy high-fived him. "You and me, baby-chin. All the way."

He snatched his hand away from the hi-five. "Sorry, popsicle. I'm a lone cowboy. I walk this life alone."

"Awww, you can't mean that." She giggled. "Look, we already have cute names for each other. Baby-chin and popsicle."

Richard's lips formed a thin smile, his eyes remaining intent.

Poppy fiddled with her wristband. "They wouldn't even give us the smallest clue about the challenges. This is *bad*. God, I'm freaking. Seriously freaking."

Her anxiety rushed directly into my veins, replacing my blood with fear. "They wouldn't set us super-hard challenges, right? We're *supposed* to get through this. Just the people who slack off would be eliminated . . . right? But I hate it that we can't all get through to the end."

"Yeah, wouldn't it work better if they made it so that all of us got to the end?" agreed Cormack. "It'd look like a more successful program."

"That's not how business works," Richard scoffed. "And if they're smart, they'll be running this like a well-oiled business. They'll be weeding out the weak and only rewarding the winners. Because the winners'd be the ones most likely to kick their addiction, and the mentors know that. That would make the mentors look good. They get a higher success rate than they otherwise would. They're not gonna want to hand over sixty thousand to people who're gonna blow it all on drugs and end up killing themselves. How's that going to look?"

Ruth angled her head around and eyed our table, her expression haughty and suspicious. She seemed to have already gathered some kind of alliance at her table—Harrington and two others. With hunched shoulders, they spoke in conspiratorial whispers.

Ignoring her, Richard pulled himself to his feet and stepped across to the chalkboard. Richard rubbed out what Sister Dawn had written with the palm of his hand and started writing with a piece of chalk:

Challenge 1: 28 people = 4 groups of 7
Minus 4 losers
Challenge 2: 24 people = 4 groups of 6
Minus 4 losers
Challenge 3: 20 people = 4 groups of 5
Minus 4 losers
Challenge 4: 16 people = 4 groups of 4
Minus 4 losers
Challenge 5: 12 people = 4 groups of 3
Minus 4 losers
Challenge 6: 8 people = 4 groups of 2
Minus 2 losers
= The final six

"This is it, people," Richard boomed. "You heard what Brother Sage said. Here's the math. All you have to do is not get into the bottom four each night. What I want to know is what's involved in these challenges. If anyone knows anything, bring it to me. I'll pay part of my winnings for any snippets that are worth my while."

Richard had everyone's attention. I could sense the tension ticking in the air. We all wanted the end prize.

"Don't tell him anything," Ruth warned. "You'll never see him again after this. You won't see *any* of us for dust after this. And I know his type."

"And what's that?" Richard asked her, his mouth dropping open in mock indignation.

"You're a shyster," Ruth told him.

"And you're not?" Richard retorted.

"You don't know the first thing about me, and you're going to leave here not knowing any more than that." Ruth eyed him directly, raising her eyebrows snarkily, as if challenging him to a debate he couldn't win.

A blonde girl with her hood low over her face rose to her feet. I thought she was going to jump into the fray between Ruth and Richard, but instead she headed off into the garden, hands clutching her crossed arms. I realised she was the same girl who'd been in the bed nearest to mine. I decided to go after her and check if she was okay. Maybe she'd had an even rougher morning than me.

Yolanda and two women walked down to a sunny spot in the garden, stripped off down to their underwear and commenced sunbathing. The other two women were blondes, with botoxed, puffy-lipped faces. All three shot me bored looks when I asked if they'd seen which way the girl went.

I looked through the tangle of trees until I found the secluded spot where the blonde girl sat, dipping her bare toes into the stream. She glanced up suddenly, startled to see me standing there.

I knew her.

Her face was bare of the heavy makeup that had been packed on it last time I'd seen her, and she looked so much younger now—like the fresh-faced teen that she was, small constellations of pink moles on her cheeks.

She was the girl who'd introduced me to escort work.

Kara Lundquist.

9. I, INSIDE THE WALLS

IN THE DARKNESS LIES THE TRUTH. And in truth lies the darkness.

Happy stories are the things we tell to make ourselves feel better. But they are never truc.

10. GRAY

I HEADED OUT TO THE KITCHEN for a beer, but there wasn't any. I'd drunk it all during the week.

Instead, I mixed some cordial and water and parked myself on a stool.

I'd lost my job and family all on the same day. A hollow pit sat low in my stomach.

Evie hadn't given any clue that she was *that* unhappy with me that she was getting to the point of leaving. There'd been no *Gray, we need to talk.* I hadn't had a dread feeling looping at the back of my mind. I'd thought it was everything else that was wrong for Evie, not me.

Erase that thought. *It was me.*

I put my drink down too forcefully on the kitchen bench, making a small crack appear in the glass.

I tried calling Evie several more times, then gave up.

Mentally, I went through a list of places she could have gone. Not her mother's. She wouldn't go there. She and Verity had a strained relationship. Verity was one of those people who enjoyed cutting people down at the knees—even her own daughter. Evie could have gone to a motel, but she'd burn through a lot of money. And it wasn't like her to waste money like that—she was always so careful with the budgeting. So, that left Evie's friends. But how many of them would or could take in Evie and the kids for that long?

I drummed my fingers on the cracked glass, realizing I was past the dread of telling Evie I'd lost my job. I just wanted her here, no matter how she took the news.

My mind reeled back to yesterday, when weedy-faced Lyle told me I was no *longer needed.* He could barely hide his satisfaction when delivering his news. He was one of those types whose ego rested on his office desk, along with his name plate and stupid potted plant.

I'd taught myself coding—a scrawny kid sitting in his bedroom behind his computer, while his parents were in their bedroom asleep after injecting their daily heroin.

In later years, I'd been astonished to learn that even self-taught coders were in demand. There were gaps in my knowledge base though. I needed to go and study coding. But with a family to look after, I couldn't take time off. I needed to keep working. But I'd never once regretted having Evie and the girls in my life. They gave me a family—something I'd never really had.

I'd only been twenty when Willow was born. Evie had been twenty-two. Twenty-two had seemed so much older to me back then. She'd seemed like a woman who knew everything. Now that I was twenty-four, I knew that twenty-two was still a kid.

Were Willow and Lilly asking for me right now? They were used to me coming home each weeknight around six— each of them fighting to get closest to me. And they were used to me being there all weekend. I rarely went out with mates. I was happy at home. A dumb kind of happy, as it turned out.

The kitchen went dark around me as night fell.

I remained sitting there, like a lone drunk after the bar had closed, nursing a cracked glass of raspberry cordial.

Finally getting up, I headed out to the sunroom, opened the windows and let the cold air rush in.

And smoked the entire bag of weed by myself.

11. CONSTANCE

"MRS LUNDQUIST, THERE'S A GOOD POSSIBILITY she found herself a boyfriend, and that's why you haven't heard from her." The detective flicked his gaze my way before returning to my carefully laminated photographs of Kara.

"It's possible, but Kara's always been so conscientious about her studies," I insisted. "And she didn't mention any boyfriend to me."

The police station smelled vaguely of paint and sawdust. I guessed it had recently been renovated. Papers and folders were lying about in high, messy piles. Even the detective—Trent Gilroy—looked slightly messy, with his hair grown thick past his ears and the uneven frown line in his forehead. It all made me uneasy. I wanted the police station and the police to look sleek and efficient, like a well-oiled machine that could process the information I'd given about Kara and then locate her with laser-sharp precision. Detective Gilroy didn't look *well oiled*. He even looked slightly bored.

Gilroy drew his mouth into a noncommittal line. "We'll do our best to find her. But I will tell you that we don't have a clear idea that this is a missing-person case. Your daughter is almost eighteen, and she might think she's old enough to do what she wants, without telling anyone. We have lots of frantic parents of kids that age contacting us. The kid almost always turns up, confused that people were worried about them." He attempted a smile. "I know, they'd make it easier on everyone if they'd just stay in contact."

I didn't return the smile. "Please, that's exactly what's not making sense. It's just not like Kara not to stay in contact. We've always been so close."

He studied my face for a moment then drew a deep, audible breath. "So, you checked with the university?"

"Yes. She hasn't turned up to any classes for weeks."

"What about her friends? Other kids from her classes?"

"Yes, I've talked to them, too. No one's heard from her. Her roommate, Paige, dropped out of university two months ago. I had no idea."

"Your daughter didn't tell you about her roommate dropping out?"

"No," I said quietly.

"So, does that sound like she was trying to hide something from you?"

"I think maybe she didn't tell me because if I'd known she was living alone, I'd have tried to pressure her to come home."

"Was there any specific reason she wouldn't have wanted to come back home? She did choose to go a long way from home in the first place."

"She's just . . . headstrong." My voice sounded both stiff and weak at the same time.

He raised his eyebrows—just slightly—enough for me to know he was thinking things he wasn't saying. "Well, leave it with me, Mrs Lundquist, and I'll give you a call around this time tomorrow and let you know where we're at."

I was giving him the wrong answers. So far, I'd basically told him she was hiding things from me and that she was headstrong. I'd painted a picture of a girl who was likely to go off on her own.

By the sound of it, he'd been through this a thousand times with parents before, with the young person popping up again. *Please, please, let that happen for me, too. I want to be laughing about this tomorrow—about my mad-mom dash across the world to find my daughter.*

Gathering up my photographs, I rose from the chair and let Detective Gilroy show me out of his office.

Outside, the clouds had cleared to expose a wintry sun.

My phone rang. It was James, wanting an update on Kara. He'd wanted to come with me to Australia, but he was under an enormous workload at his job. My husband held a high-level position at the corporation he worked for, and he was always weighed under. It'd been him who'd told me to go directly to the police. I told him about Detective Gilroy and what he'd said. It was a quick conversation. James was about to head into a meeting.

I slipped the phone back into my handbag.

Putting on my sunglasses, I headed along the city street, finding myself in a large open area. I remembered seeing it from my hotel window—the Darling Harbour Precinct. Crowds, eateries, children's playgrounds, building work and noise.

A sign near the entrance to the Chinese Gardens offered tranquillity. Paying the small fee to enter the gardens, I went in and settled myself in a quiet corner of their café, looking out onto a pond of koi that was framed with willow trees.

I stirred milk into my coffee vigorously. Detective Gilroy didn't know Kara. He didn't know how special she was and what a terrible thing it was that she'd vanished. And he didn't understand that Kara and I were tight. We talked all the time. We were friends as well as mother and daughter. *Weren't we?*

I hadn't admitted to him that Kara wasn't exactly like most young girls. She was an aloof daydreamer who only really engaged in conversation when she was interested in the topic. Those were the times she'd light up and talk on and on. She had a fairly narrow range of interests—astronomy among them. A paediatrician had once assessed her as being both highly gifted and on the fringes of the autism spectrum. Her mastery of science and English had her finishing high school two years early and then heading into college at age sixteen. She'd lost contact with her old friends and had found it hard to make new ones. Not that it seemed to bother her that much. Most of the time, Kara seemed to drift along in her own world.

I'd been shocked when she'd first told me of her desire to finish her college education in Australia. *Australia of all places!* She had a friend she'd met at college—Paige—whose family was moving back to their hometown in Australia, and somehow Kara had decided that she would go too.

James had been firmly set against her going. As I had been. But I'd wavered under Kara's determination.

We'd flown with her to Sydney and helped set her up in student accommodation at the University of Sydney—a vast, sprawling Victorian structure in the centre of the city.

It'd felt like I'd chopped off my right arm when I'd flown back to Mississippi with James and left my little girl behind. In the six months that followed, I'd found nervous joy in all the photos Kara posted on Instagram and Facebook. But without Kara there at home, suddenly the gulf between

James and me was laid bare. Guiltily, I was forced to admit to myself that James was a wonderful man who provided me with a wonderful home and lifestyle, but there was no connection between us.

Kara, on the other hand, had seemed happier after she left home. She'd travelled to all kinds of places with Paige and new friends. She'd even found a casual job in an upmarket women's footwear store.

News of the footwear job had made me smile. It'd seemed an odd place to work for a girl who found the greatest pleasure in going barefoot. Kara went barefoot whenever she could.

She loved the feel of earth under her bare feet, the touch of rain and sun and snow on her skin.

Of all the five senses, Kara's strongest was sensory. I used to think that anyone would know just by looking at Kara that she was a girl who loved texture. Because she herself was so *textured.* Her skin was smooth and sun browned, with raised, pink moles on her outer cheeks. She had waves of kinky blonde hair that were gorgeously frizzy around her hairline, in colours ranging from white to a buttery dark blonde. Her eyes always seemed sleepy, as though she were experiencing more than she could see. She had a body made for running and climbing—long limbed and streamlined. From the time she was small, I couldn't keep her inside. She needed to be outside, rolling on the grass, playing with leaves, building forts in the sandpit, staring up at the stars at night . . .

Where was my barefoot, sleepy-eyed girl now?

12. EVIE

SUDDENLY, WITH KARA RIGHT THERE in front of me, I didn't feel as far away from my former life as I had just minutes ago. And that wasn't what I wanted. I needed to put my past behind me and put on a brand-new skin.

"Hi, wow, I never expected you'd be here." I settled down beside her, an orange koi wriggling past the sudden intrusion of my feet in the stream.

Her blue eyes were cold as she turned to me. "I don't want to talk. This is a competition, right? I don't need friends."

I flinched under the scorch of her words. Not only did she look different, but she sounded totally different. Her formerly sweet, Southern accent had given way to a harsher, almost metallic voice.

"Suit yourself." Picking myself up again, I stepped away.

Maybe none of us were going to become friends here. Everyone had their eyes on the money. How was this whole program even going to change us? Brother Vito had told me to trust in the process. But I was already having a hard time doing that.

I wound through the olive trees until I found a shady spot.

Sitting, I pushed my back against the smooth bark of a tree, already wishing Kara wasn't here. She was part of the *before*, and I just wanted to think about the *after*.

I wondered how she'd ended up on this program. I'd met Kara in the restroom of a casino. She'd been there with a wealthy man in his sixties—a sugar daddy. I'd just suffered a crushing loss after losing my last five thousand on the roulette wheel.

I'd walked away from the roulette table in stiff-legged defeat and into the ladies' restroom. In front of the bathroom mirror, I'd stood staring at myself—numb, *shocked to my bones* and unable to accept the results of the stupid decisions I'd made. My carefully styled hair had been stuck to my sweating brow, my slinky, expensive city dress twisted at the seams.

Gray thought all these trips of mine into the city at night and all the money I'd been bringing home were due to a job in an upmarket restaurant. But here I was, forced to face myself and the lies I'd told.

The sudden squeal of the bathroom door opening had caused me to shrink back from the mirror and turn away. I didn't want to have to acknowledge anyone.

A girl had burst in, running for a toilet and vomiting, clutching her kinky blonde hair back from her face.

"Are you okay?" My response was automatic. In truth, I didn't care. She was a stranger who'd probably just had too much to drink. At least that kind of problem was easily solved. She'd feel better now that she'd vomited.

She grabbed some toilet paper without looking back at me and hastily dabbed her mouth. "Yeah."

Rising awkwardly on stiletto heels, she blundered to the sink and noisily drank down some water and then spat it out. She wiped her mouth again, this time with the back of her arm. "Sorry. Not used to cocktails." Turning to the mirror, she ran her hands through her hair, fluffing it out and studying me with heavily lidded eyes. "What's your name? Mine's Kara." She offered a moist hand for a handshake.

"Evie."

"You look bad, honey. You should come back out there and have a drink with me. You'll get a bit happier, guaranteed." Her accent was American—sweet and slightly Southern.

"I don't feel like a drink, and I think you've had your limit." I sounded uptight.

"Oh yeah? Bet I could drink lots more now. And you'd feel better if you did. I saw you at the roulette table. You lost pretty badly."

I bristled. "Happens to everyone." I made a show of looking through things in my handbag, as though I'd misplaced something, and that was the reason I'd been standing here in the bathroom looking lost. Surely she'd get the hint.

"If losing makes you sad, maybe you'd be better off not playing," she persisted.

She sounded young. It was something a kid would say. I eyed her properly, letting my mind reverse engineer her heavy makeup back to a bare face. I was right—she was extremely young. A teenager.

I snatched some paper towelling from a reel and dabbed the sweat from my brow. "I'm not sad. Just angry with myself."

She shrugged a lazy shoulder. "There's a way out, y'know."

"Rob a bank?" My laugh sounded worse than hollow in my ears.

"No, you don't have to rob a bank. You're pretty. And smart. I mean, I've seen you here before, playing poker. You have to be smart to even play those tournaments."

"So, what's this magical way out?"

"You can make money just by talking with lonely people. Go on dates. Stuff like that."

"Escort services, right?" I said dryly. "That's what you're talking about? Well, I'm married."

"That doesn't matter. You don't have to sleep with them. And it's not being an escort, exactly. We're called *companions*. We set our own rules."

"That's what you're doing? That man you were with tonight—you're his *companion*?"

She lifted her pointed chin. "Yes."

"Yeah, it's not for me. Thanks anyway."

"Just trying to help. It's just a way of helping yourself when you have, y'know, an addiction."

"I don't have an—"

"If something's bad for you, but you keep doing it, isn't that a problem?"

"It just wasn't my night," I said stiffly.

Her pale eyes clouded, and she folded her arms in tight against her body. "I saw your face when you lost. And I can see you've been crying now. You're in a bad place, honey. I'm an addict, too. Just a different kind. I've been addicted to cocaine for the past four months."

"God. Cocaine?"

"I'm okay because I'm getting help. I'm staying with the man I came here with—Wilson. He gives me money, anything I need."

"Don't you have anyone else who can help you out? Friends? Family?"

She shook her head. "I don't have anyone here. I came out here from America to study. My second year of college. I had an Aussie friend I was sharing a dorm room with. But she's the one who got into drugs first. I don't know where she is now. I couldn't pay for the dorm room on my own. And besides, all the money was going toward drugs. I slept in homeless shelters for a few weeks. Before Wilson found me."

I softened my tone. "Can't you go home?"

"No. I don't want Mom seeing me like this."

"How old are you, if you don't mind me asking?"

She hesitated before saying, "Seventeen."

"You're seventeen? You shouldn't even be here."

She shrugged. "Wilson likes the roulette. So I come here with him. Better than hanging out in his apartment all alone."

She was still a child. A child that could be in danger, and she was all alone. I couldn't imagine Willow and Lilly ever being alone and at risk at this tender age, but if they were, I'd want someone to help them. "You don't know anything about this man. You could be getting yourself into all kinds of trouble. Might be the hardest thing you ever have to do, but you should just call your mother. Tell her everything."

"You don't know what that would do to her. I can't do it. Anyway, I know enough about Wilson. He's really sweet. He gives me all the dough I need."

"Look"—I pulled a pen and notebook from my handbag and scribbled down my phone number and address—"if you get into trouble, give me a call. Or if you need somewhere to stay in a hurry . . ."

"Thanks. But I'm okay. Like I said. These guys, money is nothing to them. I know another girl who got all her credit card debt paid off. Twenty thousand. They're nice guys."

Twenty thousand. Paid off. Those words seemed like some kind of fairy tale told in fairyland.

Taking my pen, she tore off a strip at the bottom of my note and jotted down the address of the *companions* website that she'd told me about. "You should think about doing what I do. It's easy. They just want your company, like I said." She handed it to me.

"Hey . . . thanks for trying to help. Really." I gave her arm a light squeeze. "See you. And . . . be careful."

In my mind, I was already walking towards the restroom door, beginning to make my way out of the casino and through the cold night to the train station. Thoughts of having to admit to Gray what I'd done seeped in like a caustic substance. But my body hadn't moved. I was still standing there in the exact same position.

Twenty thousand dollars. That was how much Kara had said the guy had given a girl. *Twenty thousand.*

God, why was that thought sticking in my head? I'd never do what Kara was doing. Not in a million years.

She looked at me slightly askance, and I guessed that she knew what I was thinking. A deep crease appeared on her forehead then, and she shook her head. "No, forget it. You're not cut out for this. Forget I ever spoke to you." There was a clatter of high heels as she ran from the rest room.

It was midnight when I returned home to my house in the outer Sydney suburbs.

Something was wrong. All the lights were on. It was way too late for all the lights to be on. I rushed inside, forgetting for a moment the terrible thing that I had to tell Gray.

Muffled noises and voices came from behind the closed bathroom door. Thick steam wet my face as I opened the door. All three of them were in there—Gray, Willow and Lilly—all in damp pyjamas. Gray had the shower running hot. He was sitting on the side of the bath, Lilly lying across his lap while he patted her firmly on the back. Willow was kneeling beside him on the bathroom mat, brushing back her sister's hair. Lilly was coughing—in that deep, croupy cough that she got too often.

The three of them stared at me through the mist.

Gray had work tomorrow. It should be me here with Lilly, or at least caring for her alongside Gray. I had nothing to show for my six hours away from home. I wasn't marching in there with a home deposit in my fist and the promise of a better life. All I'd done was to make things a thousand times harder for all of us.

Gray only said one thing to me as I took Lilly from him: *You didn't answer your phone.*

"Things were hectic at work," I muttered, holding Lilly close, feeling her clammy arms and legs against me, her damp clothing and hair. I turned my head away from Gray, kissing Lilly's cheek.

Uncried tears burned in my eyes. I didn't deserve to cry. Tears were for the suffering. Not for the one who was about to make her own family suffer.

I told Gray to go back to bed.

Willow watched her father leave the bathroom and then silently turned back to me, her dark eyes round and questioning. What was she thinking? Did I look guilty? Even at age four, she would come out with the most astute observations. I couldn't even imagine what she'd be like as a teenager.

"Go pick out a book to read, sweetie," I said. "I'll read it to you and your sister. We'll get you two into dry pyjamas, and then we'll all get some sleep."

That night, I got the girls off to sleep, but I didn't sleep at all.

The entire house seemed to smell of steam and mould. Lilly was sick yet again. My dream of a new house that didn't let in the rain and mould stretched further and further away.

Sometime between three and four a.m., I moved my last possible thing on my list of job descriptions to the top.

~~1. Cooking~~

~~2. Warcraft~~

3. Talking

~~4. Poker~~

~~5. Self-loathing~~

I was a good listener, and I found small talk easy.

Kara had told me that sugar babying didn't have to involve sex. It could just be dinner and conversation. At the back of my mind, I knew that it was a slippery slide, but I was beyond the point where I could think rationally.

I'd dug through my handbag for the website address Kara had given me and looked it up.

Somehow, the terror of chatting to men for money had started to dull in comparison to telling Gray or my mother about my gambling.

13. I, INSIDE THE WALLS

IT ALWAYS STARTS LIKE THIS, happy in the garden.

They come here in temptation.

They don't know that they will fall, one by one, into a hell of their worst imagining.

14. GRAY

I WOKE WITH MORNING SUN SLANTING across my face and a mouth drier than cardboard.

Evie wasn't beside me in the bed.

That wasn't unusual for a Sunday. I'd sleep in on Sundays, and she'd get up with the kids, except when she worked late at the city restaurant on Saturday night. But today was different, and with a sinking feeling I remembered why. Evie had left me. Was this something I was going to have to get used to—waking up without her?

The house was quiet and empty. In the kitchen, the notepad where I'd written down a list of Evie's friends was still lying on the bench top. Late last night, in a marijuana haze, I'd called every one of those names. None of them knew anything. Every one of them expressed their heartfelt shock that Evie had left me, but their concern of course was all for her. They immediately closed ranks. They were her friends—I got it—but this breakup was fresh and painful, and they'd always been friendly with me before. Not now. I was on the outside.

Finally, at midnight, I'd called Evie's mother, demanding to know if Evie was there. I'd gotten an earful from Verity and given an earful back. She said she hadn't spoken to Evie since the last time she hadn't spoken to Evie. When I'd told her that made no sense, she told me I was a drunken idiot. Which I'd also argued with. I hadn't been drunk.

I stared at the list of names on the notepad.

One name stood out.

Marla.

When I'd spoken to Marla last night, she'd been too nice. Marla was rarely nice to me. She'd married one of my good mates four years ago, and ever since the marriage went bust (six months into it) she'd hated both him and me.

Was Marla just being extra nice because finally she'd gotten what she wanted—Evie and me breaking up—or because of something else?

No, Marla, you don't have me fooled. You know something.

Running out to my car, I jumped in and drove to her street. I parked across the road from Marla's house, next to the 7/11. Close enough that I could see who was coming in and out. Marla couldn't easily spot me here, and if she did, I could just say I was buying a snack. She couldn't claim that I was stalking her, even though I was. I knew better than to just knock on the front door. She didn't open up for anyone except friends and family. I was neither. She'd insisted her landlord install a peephole in the front door. Somehow, that summed up Marla. She viewed life through a pin-narrow lens. I couldn't figure how she and Evie were even friends.

Heading into the 7/11, I bought myself a milkshake. I took it back to the car and settled in, switching the radio on.

The nine o'clock morning news started.

C'mon, Marla. You normally take Princess Pout to ballet lessons at this time, the daughter that looks and acts like a mini you. I know this is when you take her, because Willow was doing the lessons, too, before we stopped being able to afford them.

The door opened.

Damn. Just Marla and Princess Pout. She didn't have Willow and Lilly.

I'd been wrong about Evie and the girls being at Marla's.

I turned the key in my car's ignition and drove the car down to the exit of the 7/11.

Checking along down the street for oncoming cars, I caught sight of the shutters in one of Marla's windows flipping open. Two little faces poked out.

The faces of my daughters.

They *were* here. Which meant Evie was here with them.

I swung the car around into the street and parked. I waited for Marla to leave and then sprinted across the busy road.

I knocked harder than I meant to on Marla's front door, the frustration inside me boiling up.

What was I even going to say to Evie? The hell if I knew.

No one answered.

I took back my concern about knocking hard, and I hammered at the door. A second later, I stopped and sat myself down on the front step, my head in my hands.

People are allowed to leave people, Gray. You can't make Evie come home. You just have to ride this out.

"Dad!" came a soft, high voice to the side of me. Willow's voice.

She was peeking between the shutters, tapping on the glass.

"Honey, get your mother. Tell her to open the door."

A frown crossed her small face, and she shook her head. "She's not here."

"You and Lilly are in there alone?"

Lilly wriggled in beneath her sister's chin, jostling for position. Lilly shook her head too, copying her sister's gestures in that silent way she often did. She just stared at me, round eyed, as though she hadn't seen me for years.

I jerked my head around at the sound of a car engine.

Marla's car appeared in the driveway again.

Someone must have called her and told her to come straight back. If not Evie, then who?

Princess Pout jumped from the car first, her expression set in its all-too-familiar sulk. Marla stepped out behind her. "Gray, what are you doing here?"

"My kids are here. That's what I'm doing here. Where's Evie?"

"Look, I don't know. I'm just minding your girls."

"How could you not know?"

The front door cracked open. A woman with short, faded brunette hair and harsh eyes looked out. Marla's mother. She looked straight past me to Marla. "I told you not to get involved."

"Mum, let me handle this," Marla said.

"Handle what, exactly?" I demanded.

Three generations of women—Marla, her mother and Princess Pout—stared at me with the same slitted eyes.

Willow and Lilly burst from the house, running to me and hugging my legs and side.

"We're going now, girls," I told them.

"Maribelle," Marla said to her daughter, "I need to talk with Gray. Take Willow and Lilly with you."

Princess Pout tightened her lips. "But we were going to get my new ballet shoes."

"We will, maybe a bit later," Marla crooned.

"The girls are coming with me," I insisted.

"I can't stop you from doing that, Gray." She looked me directly in the eye for maybe the first time ever in her life. "But can we have a short talk first?"

I exhaled a breath through my teeth, stopping myself from grabbing Willow and Lilly and leaving right then. "Okay, we'll talk." I nodded at the girls to go back inside.

Marla folded her arms defensively. "Look, I don't know what's going on. But Evie asked me if I'd babysit the girls for a few days. For a week, actually. Seems that she just needed some time on her own."

"On her own?" I exploded. "Evie went away without Willow and Lilly?"

"Yes. And you're just going to have to respect that."

I lowered my voice. "The hell I do."

"No point getting like that with me, Gray. Evie's my friend. She needed help. What else was I supposed to do?"

"What exactly did she say to you?"

"She said you two weren't getting on. She . . . she was worried for herself and the girls."

"She said that?"

"Yes."

"Well, fuck. What did she mean by that?"

"I don't know. She didn't say."

"There was nothing wrong between Evie and me. Nothing."

Marla just looked at me silently, a faint accusatory look in her eyes.

"I need to talk with my wife. Call her now, wherever she is."

"I can't."

"Yes, you can. Just call her. Tell her I made you do it."

"No . . . she didn't leave me a number. She said she would call me."

"Oh, come on. Let's be adults here. As if Evie wouldn't leave a number. What if something happened with the girls?"

Her voice closed down, small and tight, like she was admitting to something she didn't want to tell me. "I . . . had the impression that Evie was maybe going to check herself in somewhere."

"What? You don't mean like a psych ward or something?"

"I'm not sure. She just said her mind was a jumble and she really needed some time to get herself together. She said I couldn't contact her where she was going."

To her credit, Marla looked worried.

Where did I go from here? The police? Yeah, I could imagine how that would go. They'd be on Evie's side. Abused wife flees home. No choice but to leave the girls at a friend's house for their safety. The cops would be looking at me with sceptical eyes, wondering what I'd done to Evie. *Hey, here's a guy who just got dumped by his employer. And his wife and kids ran away from him. He's not exactly stable, is he?*

I could try calling all the local mental health clinics, but they probably wouldn't tell me if she was there or not, especially not if she'd told them she needed to get away from me.

How did all of this even happen? What the hell spurred Evie to take these drastic steps? Was this the end stage of her strange moods over the last three months or so?

Marla was my only connection to Evie now. I had to try to stay on her good side. "Okay. I can see you're stuck in the middle of this. That's not fair on you. It's a lot for you to have to look after the girls. I've got time off work, so I'll take them." I wasn't about to let her know I'd lost my job.

She sucked her lips in hard. "I promised Evie I'd keep them here."

"They're my daughters."

"But Evie said—"

"Whatever Evie said, she's not herself. If she's checked herself in at a clinic or something, then her head's not where it should be. She's probably saying stuff that isn't quite right."

"I don't mean to get personal, but it sounded like there's been problems at home."

That sounded like the old Marla. *Of course you meant to get personal.* "We've had money troubles for a long time now. It gets to both of us. But it seemed like, with her new job, that we were starting to turn a corner."

I caught a flicker of quickly controlled glee on her face.. Trouble for Evie and me spelled trouble for our marriage. And that could only make Marla happy. Correcting herself, she drew her mouth down so far it nearly hit the end of her chin. "Well, if you two were fighting a lot, maybe it was having a bigger effect on Evie than you knew."

"I didn't say we were fighting a lot."

"Maybe she kept it all to herself then."

"Kept what to herself?" I wanted to wipe that self-satisfied look from Marla's face—a look she could no longer hold back.

Another possibility bled darkly into my mind. What if Evie hadn't gone to a clinic? What if she'd gone off alone to do something terrible to herself?

Would Evie do that? When someone committed suicide, their family often said it caught them unawares. Panic shot into my throat. "Look, Marla, I'm taking my daughters. Now."

"Why don't you just leave them one more night? Give you a chance to cool down."

"I don't need to cool down."

"I think you do. Just leave."

"What are you going to do if I don't? Call the police? I can save you the trouble, because I'm going there myself."

"Get real. You are not."

"My wife's missing, as far as I'm concerned. Something's very wrong here, and I'm going to find out what."

Realisation dawned on Marla's face as she studied mine. She touched her fingers to her mouth in alarm. "She just said she needed time alone," she said, repeating what she'd told me earlier, the resolve in her voice fading.

"Can you bring the girls out, please?" I kept my gaze level.

She folded her arms in tighter. "How are you going to work and take care of them?"

"I finished up the job this afternoon." *There you go, Marla. Another piece of information for you to gloat about.*

"You lost your job?" Her eyes opened a touch too wide to be authentic.

"Whatever. Give me my kids, and I'll go."

Marla looked like she didn't know whether to smile or frown, muscles wavering at the sides of her mouth. She had nothing left to argue. Hunching her shoulders, she marched inside. Willow and Lilly stepped from the house again, looking a little uncertain this time. I hoped they hadn't heard any of what I'd been talking about with Marla. As I took their hands and walked down the path, Marla and her mother watched. No doubt they'd be busily speculating on what had gone wrong at the Harlow house, trying to figure out what Evie had run away from—all the things that must be wrong with me.

I strapped the girls into their car seats and drove away. My first instinct was to head straight to the police station. But I needed time to think. What was really going on here?

Just how long had Evie planned this? A day? A week? I needed some more details before I made a statement to the police. And I needed to get my head around the reasons why my wife had left me.

Nothing was making sense.

THE FIRST CHALLENGE

15. EVIE

NO ONE WANTED TO RETURN TO the gloom of the monastery after breakfast. We stayed outside in the garden, hanging near the stream, eating warm fruit straight from the trees and feeling decadent.

Everyone took the chance to introduce themselves. I tried to remember them all, but I'd never been good with names. I knew I'd remember Poppy, Richard and Cormack. And probably Ruth. After ten minutes, I could recall only a few others. Louelle, an older American woman who liked country music. Mei, a petite Chinese girl with a severe gambling habit. Eugene, a chubby businessman from the Ukraine. Thomas, a teenager from Ireland who told the corniest jokes. Yolanda, Greta and Roxy—the three women who'd been sunbathing earlier.

When night fell in the garden, it felt like a thick crush of velvet, unlike any night I'd known before. Beautiful and dream-like and strangely suffocating all at once, lulling me with the heady scent of fruit ripening on the vines and trees.

In the refectory, we sat and ate a dinner of hot, fresh bread and soup.

Internally, I felt parts of myself relaxing, parts that had been wound up for so long they'd rusted tight. The daily grind of dressing and feeding young children, of trying to stretch the budget to buy enough groceries for the week, all the laundry and cleaning and worry. All the endless squabbles between the girls.

It felt as if drops of unseen oil were unspooling all the overwound parts of me.

Here, I was being fed, looked after, no one to worry about but myself. I was with people who were trying to help me, not judge me. That was the biggest thing. The not judging. Back when I'd found out I was pregnant with Willow, I'd been a smoker. The people who'd primly told me that a pregnant woman smoking was disgusting didn't help me at all. Cue my mother. Even Marla told me that women who smoke during pregnancy should be charged as criminals. It was Gray who helped me quit. He quit with me, and he was with me every step of the way. Gray didn't tell me when he lapsed and started smoking again. Not wanting to tempt me, he kept it well away from the house. He tried to quit two more times after that before giving up for good a few months back.

I grew nervous again as the bells signalled it was time to head to the dormitories.

Poppy squeezed my arm as we walked along the hall. "This is it. The first night of the challenges."

"I feel sick," I said in reply.

"Me too. But we just have to see it as getting one step closer to the prize, right?"

Kara knocked past me and was first to enter the women's bathroom. I glimpsed her staring straight ahead into the mirror as she brushed her teeth, her eyes fierce in the dim light.

Had something happened to her between when I saw her at the casino and now? I hoped she'd relax enough to talk to me.

She was already in bed and turned away from me when I filed into the dorm behind Poppy.

Poppy hugged me. "Good night. Sleep well, and good luck!"

Ruth rolled her eyes to the ceiling. "It's not luck if you know what you're doing."

The lights snapped off.

When the church bells rang through the room's loudspeakers at midnight, I startled from sleep, thinking I was at home and it was the fire alarm.

Lilly. Willow. Gray. In that order—smallest to biggest—thoughts of them flashed through my mind.

In a breathless panic, my eyes sprang open.

This was no fire alarm. It was *bells*.

Dimly lit lamps had automatically sprung on in the room.

I pulled out my arm from where it was folded underneath my side, a wave of pins and needles coursing through it. On the wristband, the digital display was flashing a green number one. I gasped a quick breath. I was in the first group to go out tonight.

From the other side of the room, Poppy held her bracelet up high. "One!"

Everyone pulled themselves to a seated position, checking their bracelets, looking halfway between sleepy and confused in the orange-hued glow of the overhead lamps.

Ruth held up her flashing bracelet, eyeing Poppy and me. "How in the name of all that's holy did I get in with you two?" She jumped from her bed. "Move it, people! The rest of the group must be from the men's dorm."

Poppy and I rushed to the door after Ruth.

Ruth rattled the lock, which was one of those panic exit devices—a horizontal bar that extended the width of the door. She swore when it didn't open. "How are we supposed to—?"

Then a loud click announced that the door had unlocked itself.

They locked us in at night? I didn't know that.

With cheers and claps echoing behind us, we ran out into the hall. The door shut automatically behind us.

Simultaneously, Richard and three other men raced out from the dorm next door.

I hadn't spoken to the men apart from Richard, all of whom appeared to be in their thirties or forties.

Ruth marched up to Richard. "*You?* My night just keeps on getting better. You'd better not be involved in any shady dealings that'll get us disqualified."

"Got it," Richard replied. "If I know anything, I'll be sure not to share it with you."

One of the men held his hand out to me in a handshake, his facial features disproportionally small, like a child whose head had suddenly ballooned. "I'm Duncan. I don't believe we've met." He indicated towards a big, clumsy-looking man with glasses. "This is Saul." He then pointed at the third man, a short guy with deeply olive skin. "And this is Andre. So, we've got our team."

I shook their hands in a series of quick grabs. "We have to go!" My voice was edged with an impatience that didn't sound like me.

Poppy nodded fervently.

We ran in the direction of the cloister.

The hallway speared into darkness. I wished the monks would use more light, but I guessed they lived too frugally for that.

The monastery at midnight was a different entity to the monastery at any other time of day. I couldn't have described it to myself in words. It was more a sensation, of being caught somewhere that no one should be. An in-between place. I guessed it was the age of the monastery bearing down on me—hundreds of years of history, the knowledge that people called *the afflicted* had once roamed the halls.

It seemed to me that I could hear the same kind of rustling, scuffling noises behind the walls that I'd heard in the morning. Like *things* were running along with us. Only, the sounds were even more muffled beneath the echoes of our feet pounding the stone floor.

No one else seemed to hear any of it. They were focused on the destination. I told myself that lots of old places had rats, and this place was *old.*

Still, I stopped and turned, looking back.

A ripple of clothing—monk's robes—vanished into the alcove I'd blundered into in the morning. I took a few steps back, peering into the alcove. "Who's there?"

There was no one in the alcove. Just the winged statue, staring back at me. There hadn't been any monk. What I'd seen had just been some trick of the darkness and my own fear.

"C'mon, slowpoke," Poppy breathed, running back and pulling me along.

I was holding everyone up. I had to forget everything and just concentrate on the challenge.

The four mentors were waiting for us in the garden, like statues in their white robes.

Brother Sage smiled warmly. "Ah, the first of our groups to begin the challenges. Are you ready?"

"I was born ready," Ruth told him.

"Good," he said. "The challenge room awaits you."

Brother Vito nodded at us. "Come this way."

We followed them to an arched doorway and through to a curved corridor. The inner six rooms were here.

Brother Sage unlocked the door of challenge room one.

"Remember," Brother Vito said close to me in hushed, reassuring tones, "just do the best you can do."

Inhaling deeply, I gave him a quick smile.

The door slid open automatically on being unlocked. As the last of us stepped through, the door swiftly closed again.

The room was exactly the same size and shape as every other room I'd seen in the monastery so far: hexagonal and enormous. This room was completely bare except for a wooden hexagonal prism about the height of my chest in the middle.

"Okay, so . . . where's the challenge? Bring it." Richard puffed out his shoulders.

"I think *this* is the challenge." I stepped up to the prism. The aged box was constructed of a dark wood, with six rectangular sides and a top and base that were hexagonal. On top it had six inlaid triangular-shaped panels of a lighter shade, the triangles all pointing inwards to a single point in the centre. "Maybe it's some kind of puzzle box. I bet the challenge is to open it. Though . . . I can't see any lid."

Poppy wrinkled her nose. "I hate puzzle boxes. I had one for a money box as a kid. I ended up smashing it open."

"Says a lot about you," said Ruth. Marching to the box, she placed her hands on its surface like a religious healer. "It's old and it's a beauty. They told us the rooms are challenges of the mind. We just have to figure this out."

"We've got twelve minutes," said Duncan, the guy with the overstuffed head and tiny features.

"Say what?" Ruth angled her face around, her brow deeply creasing as if annoyed by the interruption.

Duncan pointed at the only object in the room besides the box—an aged clock on the back of the door, with twelve illuminated markings around its perimeter. "The hand has moved halfway to the next point since we came in here. I'd say we've only been in here less than half a minute. That means we've got twelve minutes."

My breaths grew shallow. "Twelve minutes? We've got to *hurry*."

In a panic, the six of us examined the box, looking for any clue as to how it opened, hands moving everywhere over the box, prodding and pressing in frustration.

Richard thumped the box. "I'll kick you open in a minute!"

We all went silent for a moment.

"Wait." I listened carefully. "Do you hear it?"

"What?" Richard snapped in exasperation. "Angels singing?"

Poppy glanced at me then pressed the side of her face onto the box so hard that her cheek squashed flat like a child's against a window pane. "It's ticking."

"Ticking?" The short man, Andre, wiped a bead of sweat from his forehead. "Like a bomb?"

"How would I know?" Poppy squinted up at him with her free eye.

Pulling her away roughly, Ruth put her ear to the box and listened. "It's a metronome. Richard's thumping must have set it off."

Stepping around to another section of the box, I knocked on it and listened.

A slow ticking started.

I knocked again.

The ticking sped up. Another knock and the ticking sped up yet again, the sound echoing hollowly. I moved around the box to my right, bumping into Ruth. I began knocking again, this time knocking a fourth time. The ticking went back to slow on the fourth knock.

I stood. "What if below the six triangles are six hollow compartments, each with some kind of metronome device? They seem to go faster for three knocks then go back to slow again."

I glanced up at the clock. Eight minutes to go.

Poppy elbowed Ruth as she hurried to knock and listen to each section of the box. "Yep. Six metronomes. The pitch is different with each one."

"Wonderful." Duncan rubbed his eye as if he were still having trouble waking up from his sleep. "Six of those things, all running at different speeds and different pitches. We need to figure this out, people."

"Yeah," said Richard, raising a wry eyebrow. "That's really gonna help us."

"Well, they can't be mechanical," said Saul, breaking his silence. "They must be electronic, because they've got the ability to change. They're responsive." He shrugged. "I'm a mechanic."

"Seven minutes, people," called Duncan.

Ruth straightened, eyeing Duncan. "We can all see that."

"I'm just trying to hurry it along," Duncan offered.

"Hurry *what* along, exactly?" said Richard. "We don't know what we're doing. Until we do, shut the fuck up."

"It's not helpful to give me that kind of attitude," Duncan admonished. "I'm a team leader at work, and I know how to motivate staff. I've got twenty people under me."

"Well, I've got some unkind news for you," said Richard. "You're a—"

"Stop yapping!" Ruth frowned as she listened. "Some of these have the same pitch. Wait"—she moved around the box, still listening—"they're in pairs. Every two of them have the same pitch. It's just the speeds that are all over the place."

"Because of our knocking," I said quickly. "We've been knocking haphazardly."

"Yes." She nodded firmly, looking around at all of us. "Because of that."

"Then why don't we try getting the speeds to match with the pairs?" suggested Poppy, her voice breathy and tense.

"You got it, cupcake." Ruth wasted no time positioning everyone. She was doing exactly as she said she would—she wasn't going to allow anyone to get in the way of getting through a challenge, even if she had to physically move them herself.

Duncan stood back. We didn't need seven people to do this, and he evidently believed his role was to guide us through the challenge.

"Okay, people." Ruth inhaled sharply. "We need to get these speeds exactly the same. Three people need to listen and learn from the person on the opposite side from them."

"Now we're getting somewhere." Duncan raised his eyebrows in innocent surprise against Ruth's glare.

Richard, Poppy and I put our ears against the sides we'd allocated ourselves and determined the speed—slow, medium or fast. Then, one by one, we coordinated our speed with the person opposite.

"Nothing's happening." Duncan shook his head. "Now what do we do? We need to *think*, people. Try something else, quick!"

Ignoring him, Ruth stood back. "Just wait and see if anything happens. If anyone touches the box, I'll bite their fingers off."

Something whirred inside the box. Six triangular sections pushed upwards from the box. Each section contained a wooden metronome, ticking away at different speeds.

I raised my head to the clock. Six and a half minutes left to go.

A green light blinked just under the clock.

We'd done it. And way under time.

The tick of the metronomes echoed around the room now. Then, all of a sudden, the six of them went dead. There was just the sound of all of us panting and sighing in relief.

"Hey, what the—?" Richard reached in and picked up one of the metronomes. There were red, yellow and blue wires extending from the metronome to a small box that was marked *explosive*. He looked at the next. It was the same. "So, what would have happened if we didn't figure this out, huh? Was the whole shebang going to go kaboom?"

"I doubt they'd want to ruin this lovely box," said Ruth, inspecting the wires. "It's just a gag."

The door opened, and the four mentors entered.

"You did it! I knew you would." Sister Rose clapped her hands together.

"I'm pleased to tell you my team managed to complete the test in five and a half minutes," Duncan said, beaming.

"Indeed. Well done," Brother Sage told us. "We'll escort you to the library so that the other teams can complete this challenge, too. We have some wine waiting for you. It'll help you get back to sleep after your excitement."

We headed in the direction of the library, whooping through the hallways.

Ahead in the dark haze, a figure stood half hidden beside a statue.

"There's someone there!" I pointed. "I thought I saw him in the hall earlier."

"What in the blazes?" Ruth muttered angrily. "No one else is supposed to be out of their dormitory but us. Someone's spying on us."

"I think it's one of the monks." Saul squinted from behind his glasses.

"Well, why is he hiding?" Ruth marched forward. "What are you doing there?"

The person—a man—fled. He wore a long black gown with a symbol that I couldn't see clearly on the back.

"They're a silent order," said Richard with a yawn. "They don't talk.

And more to the point, who can blame him for trying to avoid talking to *you*?"

Richard shrugged as Ruth whirled around and shot him a scathing look. It was true that they were a silent order, which would explain the monk's reticence to interact with us. I wondered if they saw many strangers at all from year to year. Still, I wished they'd speak. I was finding it creepy as hell seeing them in random dark corners around the monastery.

When we reached the library, Richard was the first to drop into one of the plush chairs. He grabbed one of two bottles of wine from a small table in front of him and swallowed a mouthful.

"Strange the mentors allow alcoholics access to wine," commented Duncan, eyeing Richard.

Richard raised the bottle to Duncan. "Cheers. And I'm not an alcoholic."

"Well . . . *I* am." Duncan perched on the edge of a chair. "I'm pinning my hopes on this treatment changing my wife's mind about leaving me."

"Maybe they expect you to learn moderation." Poppy shrugged. "Because you can't get away from alcohol, no matter where you go. And there's only two bottles here. Well, only one bottle now that Richard claimed one all for himself."

"Still, it leaves me struggling more than the rest of you." Duncan sank back in the chair, looking miserable.

"This is supposed to be a celebration." Poppy poured herself a drink and raised her glass, clinking it against Richard's bottle. "But no one looks happy."

"I'm happy we got through it," I said quietly. "But it's the thought of five more challenges ahead that are like that one. Okay, so we had six or so minutes to spare, but six minutes can pass in the blink of an eye. We got lucky."

I expected Duncan to pipe up with something about teamwork, but he didn't.

Richard downed half the bottle. "Haven't any of you realised?"

"Realised what?" Ruth demanded, refusing the glass of wine Poppy offered to her.

Leaning back, Richard crinkled his brow. "It doesn't make any sense there's twenty eight people in the program. Twenty-eight isn't divisible by six. But everything here is divisible by six. Look around you. Hexagons everywhere. Six challenges. Six winners. And the monastery itself. Six inner rooms surrounded by twenty-four rooms which are surrounded by yet another twenty-four rooms. Six, six, six. Everything *six*." He sounded drunk already, even though he wasn't. "And we didn't need seven people to complete that challenge. We only needed, well, you know where I'm going with this . . ."

"Six," finished Poppy. "We only needed six people."

"So . . . ?" Ruth raised her eyebrows high at him for effect.

"So, what if," said Richard, "there's really only twenty-four of us? And the other four are here to check up on us and see how we're doing in the challenges? If I'm right, there's one person in this room right now who's not one of us."

Poppy giggled. "Wow. Paranoid much?"

But her voice rang hollow. Everyone had gone still, quiet.

It was a crazy thought. Wasn't it? Why would the mentors need to watch us this closely? They already had cameras in the challenge rooms.

"Okay then," said Ruth, "if Richard's right and there is someone here who's a mole, you'd better come clean, else you're going to have to deal with me." Ruth eyed Poppy. "Is it you, cupcake? I don't trust grown women who giggle. The sound grates on my nerves so much it gives me stomach ulcers."

"Well, I don't trust women who throw their weight around, like you," Poppy retorted.

"Oh, would ya listen to that?" said Richard. "Women are their own worst enemies. Always scratching at each other."

It seemed to me that Richard was doing more scratching than anyone, but I didn't say it out loud. I poured myself a glass of wine. I didn't want to think about the possibility that one of us wasn't *us*—just someone who was there watching and keeping score.

Out in the corridor, the bells chimed again.

It was time for the next team to enter the challenge room.

16. CONSTANCE

JAMES CALLED ME FOR AN UPDATE on Kara, asking if I was okay and if there was anything he could do. With a sigh in his voice, he told me that Ruby and Vonda had been to our house looking for me, wanting to know if I still intended acting as secretary of the volunteer Lafayette County parks and historical committee. I'd forgotten to inform them that I'd be out of the country for an indefinite period. James said that he'd let them know that Kara was missing, but they'd been a bit pushy.

It wasn't like anything the committee did was urgent. It had a say in the upgrading of the shared open spaces around the county, ensuring that heritage items were being cared for and that the parks and walkways were modernised and kept beautiful.

I listened to James, incredulous that Ruby and Vonda still wanted to know if I intended taking the minutes of their meetings after James told them what was happening with Kara. Ruby and Vonda were supposed to be my friends. The committee obviously meant more to them.

Well, bless their big lard-bucket asses.

Finishing the call with James, I stretched out on the hotel bed, too angry for the moment to even think about Kara.

What was I even doing on that committee?

This isn't who I am.

Did it really take travelling to a strange country on my own to realise that?

It had been a long time since I'd felt like myself. A long time since I'd felt . . . dangerous. Doing dangerous things. Making dangerous things happen.

I'd become *comfortable.*

I'd spent more than the last decade not doing a damned thing except committees and luncheons and dinners. Kara had been my one light.

The first year of college had been my year of glorious chaos. Driving too fast, slamming down Yellowhammers before a game, and skinny dipping in the murky waters of the Mississippi, Alabama. Alabama was where I'd chosen to go to college. I was the first person in my family to go to college. I'd wanted to get as far away as possible from the poverty-stricken place in which I'd grown up. I'd thought I was so grown up. So smart and cool and in charge of my future. But I was anything but those things.

Alabama was where I met Otto. In his second year of a medical degree, he'd been there at a club filled with college students, louder and prouder than anyone. He prioritised partying over studying, which I thought was incredibly edgy. He was teetering on a high wire, and I was too stupid to know it. Three weeks after our first date, he was kicked from his course.

He picked himself up, grabbed my hand, and kept running.

My world became a frenzy of living. Too much, all the time.

Otto was broken but beautiful. When he said, *I love you*, I believed him.

He was a trust fund baby. We lived in one of his parents' investment houses and painted the walls every colour of the rainbow. Just because.

Mere months later, we slid into heroin addiction. We were like children playing the game *What's the Time Mr Wolf?* blindfolded and at the edge of a cliff. I didn't understand then that heroin was the wolf and I couldn't recognise what had happened to us. Because we weren't like those images of addicts scoring hits in back alleys.

Otto and I got fat. No one thinks of heroin addicts being fat, but we were. As fat as only addicts with money can be. Between shooting up and smoking pot and eating takeout, we imagined ourselves as heroes of some never-ending action movie. But in reality, we spent most of our time slumped on the couch.

Other people moved into the house. When you have money and heroin, you have lots of friends.

Crazy things happened without warning or reason. A fire would start somewhere, and we'd all have an in-depth discussion about who was responsible for it before anyone took action. People I'd never seen before would suddenly appear in one of the bathrooms or bedrooms, casually brushing their teeth or casually having sex. I got pregnant, and it just seemed one more thing that jumped out at us from the field where crazy things lived. It all went on and on until the night a couple wearing superhero costumes jumped from our balcony onto a pavilion below, tearing a great big hole in it. One of the superheroes died.

The police came that night. Otto's parents flew in from Barbados, seeming more dismayed at the state of the house than the splattered superhero. All of our great friends fled, washing their hands of any association with us.

Otto had his trust fund stopped, and we were turfed out of the house.

We rented a little bedsit apartment for a while. Things got nasty between Otto and me. I can't remember why we turned on each other, but suddenly we were spewing toxic venom onto each other with impunity.

Still, we couldn't let each other go.

Me getting pregnant and then finding blood in my underwear prompted us to clean ourselves up and get healthy and kick the drugs. We rented a better place. An endless cycle of trying and failing over years. I did kick the drugs. Otto didn't.

In the aftermath, my psych would claim that Otto and I were addicted to each other, and she was right. We'd each injected ourselves into the other's bloodstream.

It had only ended when Otto decided that the pain inside himself could only be ended by killing himself. He said that every action needs a reaction of equal force to stop it. I didn't know the source of his pain—he'd never told me about his childhood, and I never did get a chance to hear it. He drove away one night in a black mood and died in a crash.

My psych's analysis of my love affair with Otto was filled with doom and gloom. She was wrong. It might have been doomed, but it wasn't all bad. My own analysis was like a sieve that continually sifted the relationship from year to year until what was left was a fine, velvety powder.

I still had Otto's ashes. His parents hadn't wanted them. I imagined the urn now, tucked away in the attic where James had never seen it, filled with Otto's velvety, intoxicating powder.

God, what was I thinking? Velvety powder? I was going nuts, going crazy, here alone desperately searching for my daughter.

But I couldn't stop thinking about Otto.

I blamed Ruby and Vonda.

These days, I had everything a person could want.

Yet everything felt hollow.

17. GRAY

WILLOW AND LILLY CHARGED INTO OUR house as soon as I opened the front door. They ran from room to room, as though they'd been gone for years and not just overnight at Marla's.

They tore about before making their final selection of toys—Willow with her iPad, Lilly with her collection of toy dinosaurs and dolls. I knew they'd been expecting to see their mother. Even the cat was prowling around expectantly. Things were different and upside-down. Evie was always here. I was the one who disappeared each day and headed off to work.

I stood in the kitchen, holding the bench top at arm's length, letting my head drop and inhaling slowly.

What was actually going on here?

In the past few months, Evie had been through peaks and valleys. Over-the-top happy and then just as quickly so down I'd suggest she see a doctor. Sometimes, I'd sensed she was secretive, which had hurt because she'd always been so open with me. Evie used to tell me everything, in so much detail my head would spin. But ever since she got the restaurant job in the city, she'd held back.

How much had she even told me about her job? She was vague about names of the people she worked with, vague about what she did all those hours.

A thought crept in—the kind you can't send packing. Was it another guy?

Hell.

Couldn't be. She wouldn't.

And her note said she'd be coming back. A woman wouldn't run away and have an affair for a week and then return to her husband. Would she?

Willow loudly complained from the other room. Lilly was being annoying. Lilly jumped in to put in her counter-complaint: Willow wouldn't play with her.

"Be nice to each other, will you?" I hollered.

That only unleashed a torrent of grievances on both sides, Lilly barely able to explain her issues with her sister before dissolving into shrieking sobs.

I stepped into the living room. "Play quietly and we'll get some ice cream later." Evie wouldn't be impressed. She kept telling me not to bribe the kids. But right now, I didn't have time for that delicate balance of patience and compromise that Evie used.

Lilly turned off her cascade of tears. "Promise?"

"Double promise." I gave her my serious-Daddy nod and then turned and headed for the stairs.

First things first. I was going to call the restaurant and see if anyone there knew where Evie might have gone. I didn't like calling her place of work, and there was no way of doing it without sounding a little bit suspect. Looking up the name of the restaurant that Evie had given me, I tapped the number onto my phone.

They sounded busy as soon as they answered. Lots of background noise. Music.

"Would I be able to speak with Evie?" I asked.

"Who?" The woman's voice was pleasant but hurried.

"Evie Harlow. She works a few nights there each week."

"I'm the manager. There's no Evie Harlow who works here."

Was she using a different name? "She's been there for a couple of months," I insisted. "Twenty-six years old. Brown hair. Brown eyes."

"I'm sorry. No one by that description works here. Most of our staff are guys. And there are two older ladies. Sorry, you've got the wrong restaurant." She didn't wait for my reply before she hung up. She'd been polite but firm in what she'd said.

I sat on my bed, stunned. I had the right restaurant. I thought back to the handful of times I'd called her while she was working. She'd always returned my call, never answering straight away. There'd been the sound of people talking in the background, sometimes music. I'd thought that was the sound of a busy restaurant. Obviously, it wasn't.

I was going to do the thing that I'd always sworn couples should never do to each other—check up on their internet browsing history. Evie and I had an unspoken understanding that we would never do that. I was sure it was more for my benefit than hers. She spent most of her online time on Facebook, sharing recipes and photos of the kids. Or chatting on parenting forums. Evie didn't need to know which porn sites I visited occasionally. She didn't need to know that I had a fixation with a certain actress.

But I was going to look at her online history. She had already broken the rules by running off and leaving our kids with Marla.

Like a thief in the night, I picked up my wife's laptop computer from her bedside table and sat back on the bed with it. The laptop was usually there. At night, when we were in bed together, we often spent an hour or two on our laptops, more often than not chatting about what we were looking at.

Had I been an idiot to think she was happy doing that kind of stuff with me? Did she want more than I could give her? Something*—or someone—*different? Was I going to find a heap of dating site links on here?

I started with her browsing history.

It was wiped clean.

Okay, I had more tricks in my toolbox. I tried typing in each letter of the alphabet—separately, to see which searches she'd made before. Lots of recipe stuff. That was typical Evie. She loved cooking.

A search came up for browsers other than google.

I hit enter and looked through the results.

She'd clicked on a result for a browser I'd never heard of.

So, my wife had a secret browser.

I opened up the new browser. She hadn't deleted her history here. I guessed she hadn't thought she'd need to, because I'd never find it.

Hell. Hell. Hell.

Links to a ton of gambling sites.

Online poker. American slot machines. Other kinds of gambling sites.

Evie had been gambling? The links ran back for months and months.

I scrolled back to the more recent links.

My blood suddenly ran cold in my veins.

There was a link for some kind of escort service website.

I clicked on it.

She was logged into it.

I clicked on the link that led to her account and then her profile.

Fuck.

There she was. On an escort website. *My wife.*

In a long red dress I'd never seen before. Red lipstick. Hair done in a way it never was—Evie usually just wore it back in a ponytail.

She'd given herself a name: *Velvette.*

My wife was a prostitute.

The proof was right there on the page.

A few heartbeats later, my mind connected the gambling websites and the escort site. The escort site had come after the gambling sites—had Evie been desperate for money?

It made sense. Terrible sense.

I clicked around the website. There were men on the site, too—older men. Sugar daddy types. Offering money, gifts and trips away.

Had Evie gone off with one of these men, for money?

I didn't even know which was worse: Evie cheating on me or Evie selling herself for money.

If she had gone off with a guy, what if he was an axe murderer?

I hadn't realised I was muttering to myself before I looked up and saw Willow standing at the door. Pressing my lips together hard, I quickly closed the laptop.

I could tell from her expression that she knew something was up.

Mummy was gone. Daddy was acting weird.

Maybe I should have left the girls with Marla. Too late now. "What's up, honey?"

"It's lunchtime. Can we have cheesy mac?"

"Doesn't Mummy usually make you sandwiches?"

She shook her head. "No, she makes us cheesy mac."

"I'm pretty sure that's not true."

"Lilly wants cheesy mac, too." Willow deflected her lie rather than admit to it. How had she learned to do that so young?

"Okay, macaroni it is. Just today."

"And you said ice-cream."

"Okay, yeah, and ice-cream."

"And apple pie for the ice-cream."

"Choose one."

A dead silence followed. Willow raced off downstairs. I knew that she and Lilly would have their heads together, holding a quick and frantic board meeting.

Willow's head appeared around the edge of the doorway a minute later, her expression serious. "We want ice-cream."

"Okay. Done deal. Go and get your shoes on, and help your sister with hers."

Willow sped away again.

So, what was I supposed to do now? My wife was most probably with some guy right now, doing who knew what. Should I just be waiting here like a chump for her to come home to me and the kids?

What if I signed up to the site—as a damned sugar daddy? Put up a fake photo and pretended to be a big shot, someone who dropped thousands at casinos every week. Even if Evie was busy with whoever the hell she was with right now, she'd have to answer someone like that.

Maybe later, after I'd made the kids lunch and got them ice cream, I'd think that idea was nuts.

I headed downstairs, my head feeling like it'd been chewed and spat out.

18. EVIE

THERE WAS AN AIR OF EXCITEMENT at breakfast. A few of us had been eliminated but all the teams had solved the challenge. We'd lost Andre. I'd secretly hoped it would be Duncan or Ruth.

Shade from the surrounding trees of the garden made a dappled, swaying pattern over us, putting us half in deep darkness and half in shimmering summer sun.

Richard plunged a knife into a peach and lifted it to his chin, eating it straight from the blade. "We're like gladiators, feasting after destroying the beast."

Poppy dabbed at his chin with a cloth napkin, like a mother fussing over a rowdy toddler.

Maybe the mentors knew what they were doing after all. That feeling of accomplishing the seemingly impossible was something you rarely got from everyday life. I had to replace the highs of gambling with better things, real things.

Kara sat at another table by herself, quietly sipping tea, hood over her head as usual and shutting everyone out. I was glad she'd made it through, despite the fact that neither of us wanted the other to be here.

Cormack piled his plate high with a doughnut shaped, sesame seed–coated bread that one of the Greek people told us were called *koulouria.*

Sighing, Cormack took a large bite of bread. "Damn if we didn't go too close to the wire last night."

"Not us," Richard boasted. "We had time to spare."

"And you made pains to tell everyone that in the dorm last night." Cormack munched his *koulouri*. "You big-headed bastard." He gave Richard a quick grin to show he wasn't serious. It seemed he'd forgiven Richard for being a rich *fat cat*.

"It was bonkers," Poppy breathed. "I feel like we just lucked our way through it."

"Yeah." Cormack shook his head. "They'd better give us an easier time of it tonight."

Brother Vito entered the garden, causing everyone to turn their heads. "I trust you all got some rest last night after your challenge. But if you were too excited to sleep, please find a shady spot and have a well-earned nap. Four people won't be continuing on, and they were returned to the mainland last night. But we wish them all the best in the future." He paused. "Please, give yourself a round of cheers for a job well done. *Yamas!"*

"*Yama*s!*"* everyone echoed, raising their glasses of juice and tea.

"I'll leave you all to your breakfasting," Brother Vito told us. "Eat well, and gain lots of energy for round two."

He strode away, back towards the interior.

Grabbing a *koulouri*, I followed him out. We hadn't seen the mentors at all between midnight and breakfast, and I wanted to tell him about the noises I'd been hearing.

"Brother Vito!"

He stopped and turned, surprised. "You should be in there celebrating, Evie. Your team finished in the shortest time."

I blinked, feeling stupidly happy at that small announcement. "We did?"

"Yes. By three minutes. Well done. You can be proud."

"Can I tell the rest of my team?"

"Of course. There are no secrets here. But in keeping with the history of the monastery, we do not boast about our accomplishments. We do not want to make others feel bad. We acknowledge our good fortune, and we apply ourselves to do even better next time."

I smiled. "That makes sense."

"You wanted something, Evie?"

"It's just that I've been hearing noises."

"Noises?"

"Behind the walls. Maybe even inside the walls. I think there might be a rat problem here."

"Thank you for letting me know. Perhaps rats moved in during the winter while much of the monastery has been locked up. I'll have the monks check it out."

"Good. It's kind of unnerving."

"I'm sorry you're feeling unsettled, but don't be surprised if the monks don't find anything. I'll tell you something. Sometimes I hear noises, too. And sometimes I even think I see people when I roam these corridors. Not much light gets in. And there is so much history here. I think my head is stuffed with so much of the past of this place that I can sometimes experience it as if it were happening now."

"I feel it, too. The monastery certainly has an atmosphere all its own."

"Yes, it can be overpowering at times. Would you like a glass of wine, perhaps, to settle you?"

I nodded. "I'd like that."

"Come this way." He led me inside and along the halls to the library. We stepped through the library and into what I remembered from the map as being the scriptorium. Hundreds of years ago, holy books must have been painstakingly written by hand here.

Brother Vito poured me a red wine.

I picked up a book from atop one of the tall piles of books on the desk, the name *Spinoza* on the cover.

"Spinoza is well worth the read," he said, pouring himself a glass of wine, "should you find yourself with some spare time and should you like to sit and think."

"He's a philosopher?"

"Yes. Seventeenth century. Spinoza said that we dream with our eyes open. We trick ourselves into believing we have free will, but free will is an illusion."

"It's not an illusion," I said firmly, surprising myself.

"No? You don't believe so?"

"We make choices all the time that change our lives. Like me coming here."

"But what forces were in place that brought you here? You might think one thing, but the universe has other plans for you."

I smiled wryly. "You mean, in religious terms?"

"I'm not a monk, Evie."

"I know. Well, for a while there, I used to believe that mumbo jumbo about the universe changing to help you achieve your goals. Like, if you had a plan, that was all you needed."

"And what stopped you from believing that?"

"Something that happened when I was seventeen. When the car that my brother and I were travelling in got wrapped around a tree. Two people died, including my brother. Now I think the universe is chaotic. No sense of rhyme or reason."

"I'm sorry to hear about your brother. I'd prefer to keep some faith and to think that somehow, things are all in balance. The people here believe it's all based on numbers. Everything, from our human wants to the grandest galaxy. I'll quote Spinoza—he said, *I shall consider human actions and desires in exactly the same manner, as though I were concerned with lines, planes and solids*."

A deep pain embedded itself in the middle of my forehead as I remembered the accident that took Ben's life. "I have a recurring nightmare about the car crash. Ben and I and the others are travelling on the road. It's a straight, long road. Lines of trees on either side. I can see the perspective of those lines ahead, like a long, thin triangle. It's like Ben is trapped forever inside the triangle. Sometimes, when I'm driving and a straight road appears in front of me, I get these flashbacks, and I have to pull over until the shaking stops."

Brother Vito held out his arms to me. I moved into them, and he held me.

"Your mind remembers what your eye did not," he said gently. "On that day, you wouldn't have even noticed the lines and the geometry of the scene. Your attention would have been on the people in the car or the small details of the scenery outside or your own thoughts. But in retrospect, you see it like Spinoza."

I nodded against his shoulder, suddenly back in the raw, helpless moment when I was watching Ben dying. "It's like Ben's life was closing down to a point, just ahead of us. But I couldn't see it then. We'd all been drinking, but that wasn't why it happened. The driver had a stroke and most probably lost his eyesight."

"Perhaps it was just going to happen, no matter what . . ." he said gently.

I shivered, not knowing whether that thought itself was soothing or not.

A female voice at the door made me twist around. "I'm sorry. I didn't—"

"Poppy?" I said, stepping away from Brother Vito. He dropped his arms.

She glanced with discomfort at Brother Vito and me. "I came looking for you, Evie. I got worried—you dashed away quickly, and I thought something might be wrong."

"No, I'm fine," I told her, flashing a quick smile.

"We were just discussing philosophy," said Brother Vito. "But I have some preparations to make for this evening's challenge, and so I'm afraid we'll have to leave it there."

Poppy peered at the book that Brother Vito snapped shut.

"Thank you," I told Brother Vito and walked out into the hall, out of his line of sight. The whole scene felt too intense to put into words—philosophy, geometry and Ben. I hoped Poppy wouldn't quiz me.

But she grabbed my arm. "Tell me everything. I mean, how lucky are you getting to talk philosophy with Brother Vito? I love philosophy. Not Spinoza—he's a sexist old windbag. But maybe Vito can come across me curled up in his library, reading one of the Stoics or something. And then he and I can have, y'know, the same kind of *in-depth* discussion you just had."

"It wasn't like that. We'd been talking about a . . . painful memory."

"I have lots of those. Maybe Brother Vito can give me some comfort, too." She winked.

"If you don't mind, I'd like . . . I just really need to be alone for a little while."

Poppy looked hurt for a moment but then either swallowed the hurt or had a change of mind. "Of course. I was just having a little joke with you. Go and curl up somewhere and have a good old rest."

"Thanks. I mean it." I met eyes with her to show her that I did.

Turning away then, I left Poppy behind as I wandered along the hall and into the garden.

Kara was sitting in a secluded corner, her arms locked around her knees in a large, round papasan chair, picking at her sleeve. She looked small with her limbs all wrapped up tightly like that, like a child. Today, I understood her wanting to distance herself from everyone else. Being here at the monastery was giving us all too much free time to think.

I stepped through the mandarin trees, the scent of the ripe fruit sweetening the air.

Sister Rose stepped through the garden, picking and gathering a bunch of flowers. She shot me a smile that was as apple-pie pleasant as her face.

A short distance away, Richard, Cormack and Saul were playing a card game, with pebbles for poker chips. For a moment, I ached to go and join them. Poker would take my mind away. *No, poker would take me some place I didn't want to be.*

I found Ruth and her cronies huddled together, talking in quick, sharp voices. Strategising. Harrington looked around at me with a squinty face.

All of a sudden, someone was shouting. One of the girls who'd been sunbathing yesterday—Yolanda—rushed through the garden. "Greta's gone! I knew she would. She's gone!"

Sister Rose ran up to Yolanda, flowers in her arms. "Are you sure? She might be having some quiet time inside somewhere."

Yolanda grabbed Sister Rose's arm. "No, listen to me. This morning she kept saying she couldn't last out the week here. She said she felt like she was dying without her drugs. Without ice. I went looking for her and found a ladder pushed against a tree. I think she climbed the tree and got over the wall."

Sister Rose looked stricken at the news. "Oh dear. She might have broken a leg jumping down from that wall. And if she tries to get back to the mainland by rowboat, things could go very badly for her. It's a very long way, and not all of the boats are seaworthy."

Thrusting the bunch of flowers at a woman nearby, Sister Rose took out a small walkie talkie from her pocket. She called for urgent assistance from the other mentors.

Whirling around then, Sister Rose frantically gestured to everyone. "We need to find her quickly. Would anyone like to help?"

A cranking noise shuddered in the air. The gates were opened by two monks. Everyone who'd been in the garden raced out to the bare, hilly countryside.

"There she is!" boomed Ruth. "Out there in the water."

Greta was a speck in a tiny boat, rowing out to sea.

"Thank you, Ruth," said Sister Rose. "It's all right, everyone, she's been found. She'll be safe. We'll go after her and bring her back safely."

Brother Sage sprinted out through the gates, stopping beside Sister Rose. She filled him in quickly.

Yolanda ran up to Sister Rose and Brother Sage, her dark skin streaked with tears. "She said she wasn't strong enough for this. She was right. I'm scared she'll try to get away again."

Nodding, Brother Sage sighed deeply. "Thank you for that information, Yolanda. We won't make her stay. She can return to Germany. It is a shame though." He turned to the rest of us. "To make up for the loss of Greta, one less person will be eliminated after tonight's challenge."

We sat on the hills and watched as the monks took out a large motorboat and caught up with Greta. Leaving the rowboat anchored, they helped Greta on board.

The motorboat sped towards the horizon.

19. I, INSIDE THE WALLS

THE KILLING STARTED YOUNG. BEFORE I knew there were others like me. Before I ever knew of the monastery.

I killed a man when I was seven.

Don't say you don't remember, Santiago, because I know you do. We were alone in the house.

This was how it happened:

Hello? Hello?

Is anyone here?

Bump, bump, bump downstairs. There's always bumpy monsters down there at night. This time, it must be a big one.

Santiago's eyes are huge in the darkness.

He's little as he walks across the bare floor and pokes his head out of our bedroom door.

Don't go down there, Santiago.

No! I told you no.

"The only way out is to kill things before they kill you," he tells me.

I shake my head as though I can pull him back to safety just by doing that. "The monster will hurt you."

He smiles. "Don't worry. I'm hiding knives under the bed. The knives make me happy. Do they make you happy?"

"No," I answer quickly. But I'm not sure of that.

The monster downstairs is opening things and shutting them again.

Santiago gives me a nod, and I know what that means. I know exactly what that means.

I help him crawl under the bed and search around for the hard metal of the knife blades. I've got dust on my knees and in my hair. I half choke and want to cough, but I stifle it, swallowing instead. My hair and face look white in the dark mirror as we step out into the hallway.

We tiptoe on the stairs.

The monster's crouching down in the living room. Looking in a cupboard. Making grunts and animal noises.

Santiago pulls me on, my hand in his tight grip.

The monster doesn't hear us.

Santiago makes the first stab, right in the monster's back. The monster jolts, cries out.

I make the second stab as he spins out. In his neck.

The monster looks angry, half crazed. He knocks me to the ground.

But Santiago hands me another knife, and I slash the monster's knee. *Slash, slash, slash.* The monster stumbles and falls, and it's too late for him now.

Santiago and I stab him and stab him until he stops moving.

We stab him until we feel better.

20. GRAY

WILLOW AND LILLY RAN SQUEALING AND giggling after I hauled them out of the bath, dropping their towels and doing their usual nudie run around the house. What was it about baths that got kids so excited? Actually, it was just the prospect of water that got them excited. When we went for a walk to the park, Lilly would cackle like a tiny, gleeful witch if she found the smallest puddle to stomp in.

Ordering them into Willow's room, I dressed them both in tracksuits. Evie usually took a lot of care when dressing them, and she'd spent a lot of money on outfits for them lately. Her restaurant job had meant she could buy things she couldn't normally. But bad luck—it was my rules now. And my rules were whatever was easiest.

Putting a *Toy Story* DVD on for the girls, I headed downstairs. The girls were snuggled together on Willow's bed.

I'd promised myself I wouldn't check the *companions* website again today. But that promise didn't hold.

Seating myself on the sofa, I grabbed the laptop and browsed to the *companions* site. I signed up. I had to pay a hundred and fifty bucks for the privilege. That hurt bad. I only had seven hundred in the bank. My week's wage. But I was driven. I had to talk to my wife.

I found a photo of an older guy online who looked rich, and I used it for my profile. My gut turned upside down as I wrote a quick blurb about myself.

A green symbol next to her username told me Evie had come online.

Pressing my back into the sofa, I told myself to keep it under control. Play the part, just like she was.

I clicked on the chat symbol for her profile.

Be cool. Smooth.

Me: *Hey, Velvette. I like your smile. Why don't we meet and you let me see that smile in person?*

Holding my breath, I waited.

Her: *Thank you! I'm afraid I'm pretty busy right now.*

Choice names spun through my head—all the names that men spat at women. *Whore. Slut. Two-bit skank.* I wanted to call her every one of them.

Play it cool, Gray.

Me: *Too busy for me? You're exactly what I like. I'm very generous with women I like. I can offer you trips, expensive gifts, money. Tell me more about yourself.*

Her: *I do a bit of Latin dancing. Morning jogs along the beach. I like a good red with good company.*

Evie didn't do any of that stuff. She had two left feet. She didn't even like red wine that much. She was playing a role.

Me: *What sex things do you do? Your profile didn't say much. Give me something.*

Her: *For a generous man, the sky's the limit.*

The blood rushed from my body.

Me: *Great to know. I have a shoe and foot fetish. I have a number of feathers that I like to tickle women's feet with. Interested?*

Her: *I'm wearing red stilettos and red nail polish right now. I would adore that.*

Breath gone.

Evie was too ticklish to even have her feet touched, let alone with a feather. She was really willing to do anything to please these guys. I had to shut out the other thoughts that spun through my mind. Thoughts of all the things she was doing.

Me: *How about tonight? Nine o'clock?*

How would I even swing that? I didn't know. I couldn't think.

Her: *Sorry, tonight is no good for me.*

Me: *Tomorrow night? Same time?*

Her: *You're the kind of man every girl wants. But I must apologise. I cannot see you. I am seeing a couple of gents at the moment and I don't have the time. Try me again soon.*

The green chat symbol went red.

My head thumped as I tried to put the pieces of the brief conversation together. She'd been running two different lives. For how long?

I regretted contacting her. I didn't need to know any of that stuff. I was just torturing myself.

The marriage was over.

THE SECOND CHALLENGE

21. EVIE

"HEY," POPPY WHISPERED TO ME AS the eight 'o'clock curfew sounded and we began walking towards the dormitory. "Are we good?"

"Of course," I told her.

"Cool, because I don't want you mad at me."

I shot her a smile. "I'm not mad at you. Hope we blitz our challenge tonight."

"We can do it. Bring it on." She didn't sound as confident as her words. Drawing in a breath through pursed lips, she tied her red locks up into a messy bun. "Hope Greta will be okay. She'll still get ten thousand for completing the first challenge. Maybe she'll use it to go into rehab in Germany?"

"Maybe she will." I didn't say what I was thinking privately. Some people weren't ready to be helped.

When I slipped under the covers in the dormitory, Kara was sitting rigidly on the edge of her bed, staring at me.

"Hope you go well tonight," I said awkwardly. I was out of earshot of anyone but Kara, but still, I was going to feel silly if she didn't answer me.

She fiddled with her wristband, remaining silent. Then she climbed into bed without another word and turned away from me.

Kara was so strange. Maybe she had a mental illness—and if she did, this wasn't the best place for her.

Settling down onto my pillow, I was surprised to find myself drifting to sleep. I thought everything would be running through my head, but I'd somehow found a sense of calm. I wasn't going to throw this opportunity away, and I wasn't going to let the actions of others make me doubt myself. Maybe talking with Brother Vito had helped.

When the bells sounded at midnight, I was ready.

I sprang from the bed.

Ruth's wristband began flashing first.

I stared at mine, waiting for the digital display to start up.

But two other women jumped from their beds, holding their bracelets high—Yolanda and the tiny Chinese girl named Mei.

The display on everyone else's wristbands remained blank.

The teams had changed. I hadn't guessed the mentors were going to change up the teams.

Poppy and I turned to each other in dismay.

"Oh well," Poppy shrugged. "At least we get to lose *ruthless toothless* for the night."

Ruth looked back over her shoulder at Poppy. "I heard that."

Pulling a face at me, Poppy refused to meet Ruth's glare.

The door opened, and Ruth and the other two women exited.

Inhaling slowly, I sat back on my bed. So, this was what it was like to have to wait.

My muscles remained clenched for the next fifteen minutes.

I'd almost begun to relax when my wristband flashed with the number two. I was in the second team.

A couple more people stood.

The first was an older woman who I knew nothing about except that her name was Louelle and that she was an American who liked country music.

The other person was Kara.

My heart fell a little. Kara was not going to be a team player. She tugged the hood of her top over her forehead. She didn't look in my direction at all.

The three of us rushed out into the hall.

Three men joined us from their dormitory—Cormack, Saul and Richard.

Mentally, I tried to calculate our odds as a team. We had six people this time rather than seven. Kara—a hostile teenager. Cormack—only just out of his teens, who, although he desperately tried to sound worldly, didn't have the experience of the older people. Saul—a man who seemed afraid to make a wrong step. Louelle, who I barely knew the first thing about. Richard, who had such a restless drive for the finish line he didn't seem to be able to concentrate on the task at hand. And myself, and I didn't place a lot of trust in *me*.

The odds didn't seem good.

We charged along the hallway together, at least giving the appearance of being a united front.

The same sound as the night before seemed to follow us, the rustling and the sound of feet.

Louelle and Saul turned to look at the left wall as they ran, frowning. They'd heard it too. But unlike me, the frowns quickly left their faces. They must have decided they had better things to worry about.

After the things I thought I'd heard and seen that first morning, I'd been jumping at shadows and listening hard for every creak. The monastery, with its age and its vaulted ceilings and hard stone spaces, was producing eerie, hollow noises all its own. And there might be rats too, but Brother Vito was getting the monks to take care of that.

I had to shut down any thoughts that might get in the way of a challenge. The challenges were about mental strength. And I had to be strong.

The mentors were standing together just as they had been the night before, their expressions calm.

"Without further ado," said Sister Rose, "your second challenge is about to begin. Be sure to look around you and think before you take action."

I wanted more from the mentors, some sort of clue. But nothing more was forthcoming. I could hear our group taking deeper breaths as we followed the mentors to the door of the second challenge room.

"We wish you well." Sister Rose opened the door and then stepped back to let us enter.

The room fell into complete darkness as she closed the door behind us.

"Smells like—" Cormack began.

"Seawater," Richard finished. "And I can hear a motor running."

Lights sprang on in a circular pattern.

A gasp rose in my throat.

"What in the weasel's piss is this?" Cormack's thickly Scottish voice echoed around the glass surfaces of the room.

Each of the six walls was made of floor-to-ceiling glass, schools of bright fish swimming in the water behind them.

A massive aquarium.

Baby sharks swam among the smaller fish.

Ancient-looking anchors and chains hung down into the tanks from the ceilings. Rocks and chests and scattered coins sat at the bottom.

All of the light came from bulbs within the aquarium itself. The only part of the walls that wasn't glass was the door through which we'd entered. Fish swam freely behind the glass above and at the sides of the door—except that the tanks were divided into six, with a glass partition between each tank.

The timer clock was fixed to the back of the door, as before.

Beneath my feet, the floor was covered in blue tiles. A hexagonal wooden prism occupied the middle of the room—almost exactly the same as the last one, except the inlaid sections of lighter wood had a different pattern. This time, the inlaid sections were six horizontal bands around the box, each about the height of my hand.

Everyone stood transfixed.

Panic spiralled through me. I didn't expect anything like this. What were we meant to do here? Was it just the box, or did the aquarium form part of the puzzle?

"Shouldn't we make some kind of start?" Kara walked up to a glass wall and tapped it. She pushed the hood back, the lights inside the aquarium catching the pretty curves of her face as her hair fell around her shoulders.

Cormack's *weasel's piss* scowl turned to open-mouthed wonder as he turned and looked across at Kara. She seemed instantly uncomfortable as she became aware of his eyes on her.

"Haven't noticed her before, huh, Cormack?" Richard winked. "Too busy looking at the sunbaking beauties, huh?"

Cormack corrected his expression. "What are you talking about, you mad thing? Anyway, forget it. We need to make a start, just like the girl said."

"I have a name. It's Kara." Kara raised her eyebrows to make her point.

"Kara." Cormack lifted his chin in a nod. "I'll remember that."

Richard made a derisive snort. "What you need to remember is that this is a competition."

"Everything in life is a competition," Cormack retorted. He stormed away to the wall opposite Kara, cupping his hands to peer inside the glass.

Richard made his way to another wall of the aquarium, whistling and sounding unhurried, but I already knew him well enough to know that it was an act.

Louelle stood by herself in the one spot, as though absorbing clues by osmosis. Saul merely looked lost.

I rushed to the hexagon box. The box had been the puzzle in the last challenge. Maybe the aquarium was just a distraction.

Putting my ear to the wooden surface, I listened.

No ticking.

No sound.

I went around the box, listening and knocking.

Nothing.

The box didn't sound hollow inside. It seemed solid.

Saul ventured across, watching but not offering help.

Moving back, I studied the surfaces of the box. There were tiny engravings in the middle of each horizontal band of wood. "Look, Saul." I touched a finger to a symbol on one of the six sides of the box. "You can only just see it. It's a—"

"Fish," finished Saul looking over my shoulder, holding his glasses out from the bridge of his nose to see the symbol better. "We need some better light in here. That aquarium is blinding me. Yeah, looks like a fish."

Trying to shield my eyes, I stepped around the box. "Okay, so six symbols of fish," I said quickly. "Scattered around these six bands. Is it some kind of code?"

"I'd say so," said Saul. "I run a puzzle toy business. It's a hobby—I don't make much money from it." His tone turned defensive as he added, "My wife and kids think it's weird."

"It's not weird. Any idea what this is?"

"My guess would be that the symbols have to match up."

I stared at him blankly. "Okay, Saul, but how?"

"Seems too easy, but you'd just"—he grasped hold of the first band —"and twist it."

Miraculously, the band of wood spun around, and he matched the top fish with a second fish. A smile cracked his face. Seeming to be on a mission now, he spun the third, fourth, fifth and sixth bands around.

Now we had a matching vertical line of fishes.

The hexagonal box was like a giant combination lock—like the metal, barrel-shaped lock that I used for my bicycle, in which I had to turn the sections of numbers around to match my number code.

A soft glow emitted from between each of the bands.

I gasped loudly, wanting to cheer, but holding back as I glanced across at the clock on the door.

The bulb below the clock remained stubbornly red. We hadn't solved the puzzle. This was just the first step.

Two minutes gone. Ten minutes left.

"That didn't do the trick," I said, panting now.

"Hold on," said Saul. "After you get the code right, you sometimes have to do something else." Tongue between his teeth, he examined the box all over. "Bingo!" He flipped up a lid on top of the box.

At the opening of the box, Richard and Cormack came running.

Inside was just a shallow shelf with six round depressions in it, each depicting an animal—an eagle, an owl, a dolphin, an octopus and others.

I checked the clock again.

Nine minutes left.

"What's this all about, then?" Cormack studied the images, his eyebrows puckering as they drew together.

"I know what they are." Richard pointed towards the aquarium, where Kara was still loitering, despite her urging us earlier about making a start. "There are coins at the bottom of every section. My father—the miserly old bastard—has coin collections coming out his razoo. These are old Greek coins. See this one of the bee? It's from the city of Ephesus. You can tell because it's got the symbols for epsilon and phi on either side of the bee. I spotted that exact coin in the tanks."

"Not just a pretty face, are ya?" Cormack blew out a tight breath. "But how's that gonna help us?"

Louelle gestured downward, in the direction of the door. "I think this might be the answer."

"You mean we just leave and forfeit the challenge?" Richard shook his head angrily.

"No," she answered. "Don't you understand? The floor is damp. All the way from the tanks to the door."

"What?" Richard demanded.

She looked at him askance. "Someone's been in the tank. We need to get in there, too, and fetch those coins."

"But there's no way in." I wanted to be Duncan and scream at everyone to *think*. It wouldn't help, but I couldn't figure this out.

"Unless we can sprout wings," said Saul. "But then, wings wouldn't be any use in the water. I—" He broke off as if embarrassed by what he'd said.

Something clicked in my mind. A pattern—on the back of the door. I turned back to study the door. On either side of the clock were two sets of vertical parallel lines, with horizontal lines in between.

Ladders.

They were made of the same metal as the door and had just seemed like decorative patterns before.

I shot Louelle a broad smile. "We've just found our way in."

Richard made the same realisation, and began racing to the door alongside me. We lifted the ladders down.

"Ladies and gentlemen, we've got ladders," announced Richard, as if he were announcing a sale in a department store. He didn't give Louelle any credit for her *damp floor* discovery.

I glanced back at the clock on the door.

Eight minutes left.

I watched the fish streaming past in the aquarium, trying to calculate how long it would take us to complete this task. "Okay, three of us to each ladder. Go!"

Cormack shrugged his shirt off. Louelle, Kara and I began stepping out of our clothing.

Saul backed away a step. "I'm not a good swimmer."

"Well, you have to get in there, Saul." Richard groaned under his breath. "Because I can't. Someone needs to be out here, directing the others to the coins. Do you lot have any idea how cloudy the view is going to be under there? You won't see shit."

"Trust you to make sure you don't get wet, mate," quipped Cormack.

That left only five of us. "Quick! We have to hurry," I breathed, turning to look at the tanks. The water looked damned cold. Would the baby sharks try to bite small chunks out of us? I had to trust they'd been well fed.

Louelle, Saul and I shared one ladder, and Cormack and Kara shared the other. Chill water rushed along my body as I jumped in.

Now, I had to get all the way to the bottom.

It was harder than I imagined to swim straight down. Despite kicking hard, I kept turning sideways. Determinedly grabbing onto the chains inside the tank, I ploughed downward. The small bodies of the fish slipped past my limbs.

On the outside, Richard raced from tank to tank, guiding people.

He was right. I couldn't see clearly through the water. I had to make several grabs at the coins before Richard finally gave me a nod. Relieved, I nodded back. My lungs were burning, and a sense of terror at being submerged this far down was beginning to gnaw at me.

Keeping the coin tight in my fist, I kicked to the surface.

Louelle was slow, still at the bottom of her tank. Cormack was the quickest, already onto the second tank. I stepped out onto the ladder as Richard moved it across for me.

Taking the coin from me when I was halfway down, Richard ran across to tap on the glass in front of Louelle and show her where to go. Her face looked pale and strained under the water. I watched her grab her coin and swim frantically to the surface, willing her to go quickly.

Cormack splashed to the surface, flicking his coin out triumphantly.

Richard caught the coin and rushed it back to the hexagonal box.

Saul made gasping breaths as he broke the surface and tossed his coin out to the floor. Richard ran back to take it.

I glanced across at Kara's tank. She was only halfway—why had it taken her that long? I realised then that she was struggling. Her challenge wristband had caught inside the link of a chain. She gave another couple of frantic tugs.

"Kara—she's caught!" I sprinted over to the ladder in front of her tank and dashed up it.

Cormack hoisted himself out onto the second ladder, shouting at Richard. "Why weren't you there to get her out?"

"I can't do everything at once," Richard protested. "I was checking the coins."

Cormack was behind me in a flash. We entered the tank one after the other.

Desperately, I tried to see clearly enough in the haze. I held the heavy chain while Cormack worked on wriggling the wristband free.

Somewhere in the murky water, a small orange light sprang to life. I saw a face illuminated by the glow. A woman held a candle, her face terrified. *Where?* Then I realised, the glow wasn't coming from inside the tank. It was coming from the outside. *The other side.* The tank that Kara was in must face the middle room of the monastery, the room that Brother Vito said had nothing in it. Then an arm reached out from the darkness behind the woman, extinguishing the light.

Was she one of us? It'd happened in a split second. Too quick.

Someone splashed into the pool above me.

Richard.

I thought he'd come to help, but he swam straight to the bottom of the tank and then straight up again.

I forgot about the woman with the candle.

Kara stopped struggling, her body going slack.

She was going to die.

Frantically, I pulled at Kara's wristband. A small stream of blood floated upward from Kara's wrist.

A shark swam near. Cormack kicked at it, and it retreated.

Richard climbed over the top of the tank wall and down the ladder. Hurrying across to the shelf on the hexagonal box, he placed the last coin.

Far beyond Richard, a light blinked from red to green—the light beneath the clock on the wall. We'd won the challenge.

But in here, in the tank, we were losing everything.

I felt my head grow hazy, like pins and needles. My lungs screamed for air. Cormack's movements were slowing. We were beginning to drown, just like Kara.

Hooking my fingers inside the bracelet, I tugged along with Cormack, my other hand still holding the chain.

Kara's arm came free.

Gathering her in his arms, Cormack swam upward.

The door of the challenge room swung open.

22. I, INSIDE THE WALLS

ONCE YOU SEE ME, THE REAL ME, it will be too late.

All the tiny things that worry you, they will all become like dust. Because you'll see, for the first time, the real monastery.

I will kill them all, every one of them, before the others get to them.

Santiago, stop worrying, stop fussing. Don't think.

None of this is our doing.

You can't change the universe.

23. GRAY

WHO WAS EVIE WITH AND WHAT was she doing?

I couldn't turn my mind off.

Taking a beer from the fridge, I went out and sprawled on a chair on the back verandah, from which I had a prime view of three neighbours' yards: a trampoline with half of the springs missing, a dented wading pool filled with dark water, and weedy vegetable patches. It was different in summer, here. Not any classier, but people actually used their yards then, and it all looked a bit more hopeful.

The sky darkened to a featureless shade of grey. It'd been raining for hours, and the day was about to smudge into night.

What happened next with Evie and me?

Divorce papers. That was what happened next. Nothing to divide up but a few sticks of furniture. I'd be seeing my daughters on the weekends.

No, scratch that. I'd go to court and try for full custody of the girls. Who knew what Evie was getting up to? But what did getting custody of the girls mean for me? Me not working for the next three years until both Willow and Lilly were at school? And never being able to build my career even after they started school?

After going through what I did with my parents, I always said I'd give my own kids a real family. My childhood had been brutal. Parents who were in and out of jail ever since I was small, both dying of a drug overdose one day when I was at school. I was the one to find them like that, slumped in their chairs.

Somewhere in the post-mortem of my marriage, maybe I'd figure out what went wrong. Right now, I was bloody clueless.

A series of small spasms travelled along my back and arms before I realised I was sobbing.

Lilly wandered out onto the verandah and curled up on the uneven wooden planks, wrapping her arms around my ankles. It was a thing she did when she was tired and wanted my attention but couldn't be bothered speaking. Lilly was economical with words.

I inhaled the chilled air, squeezing my eyes shut a couple of times to dry up the wet.

"Up you get, Lilly. Too cold down there."

Her cheek felt hot against my arm as I picked her up.

Too hot?

Angling myself back, I studied her face. There were high patches of red in her cheeks, watery eyes.

I carried her into the kitchen and set her down on the kitchen table.

It was Evie who always took care of taking the girls' temperatures when they were sick. I rifled through the medicine cupboard and found a thermometer.

Lilly grumbled softly as I pressed the button and held it inside her ear. It beeped at 40C/104F.

Okay, that was *hot*.

It was always Evie who made the decision about whether Lilly needed a doctor or not. Something about looking for other signs.

Lilly looked wilted.

Breathing faster than usual.

It was enough.

"Willow!" I turned and bellowed up the stairs. "Come down here, honey."

The silence on the way to the hospital was unnerving. Normally, I couldn't stop the girls from poking each other from their car seats or complaining that the other was making faces at her. But neither of them made a sound.

When we reached the emergency department, my heart sank as I saw that the chairs were three quarters full. A busy night. But the triage nurse took one look at Lilly and asked me to bring her straight in.

A different nurse took her temperature. "How long has her temp been at 40 degrees?"

"I'm not sure. The girls were watching a movie upstairs . . ."

"What about her breathing? How long has she—?"

Lilly collapsed on the hospital bed, a small, floppy doll suddenly without any bones.

The nurse yelled out something. Doctors and nurses came running. They rushed Lilly to another section of the emergency ward. Willow and I ran behind. I watched them lay her little body down on a bed to resuscitate her. She didn't wake again.

Willow grasped my hand so tightly that her small fingernails were digging into my flesh. "Did she die?"

"No," I told her firmly.

A nurse—or a doctor—I wasn't sure which, turned back to me. "Has she had an asthma attack before?"

I looked back at her, stunned. "She doesn't have asthma."

"It seems that she does."

"Is she okay?" She didn't look okay but I wanted them to *make* her okay.

"She's responding well. She's getting enough oxygen now."

When they'd stabilised her, they moved her to the children's ward.

Willow and I sat beside her bed, watching her sleep.

I was still in a state of terror.

Lilly had asthma? She'd been checked for asthma. Three or more times. She'd been checked for all kinds of things. The doctors had said she just had wheezy lungs. Something she'd grow out of.

An hour ticked past.

Willow slipped into sleep on the chair beside mine. I could remember what it was like to be four, thinking that the adults were in control. When you became an adult yourself, it became scarily apparent how not-in-control the adults actually were.

I needed Evie here now.

There was only one way of contacting her.

Switching my phone on, I navigated to the *companions* website and logged in.

Evie, I wrote, *this is Gray. Yes, it's me and I know what you've been doing. We're in the hospital. Lilly's really sick. She stopped breathing earlier. You need to get back here.*

Before I closed the page, I noticed a row of girls' photos slowly scrolling across the top of the screen. A carousel of girls to pick and choose from for wealthy sugar daddies. One picture in particular caught my attention—a young, blonde girl with day-dreamy sort of eyes.

Where did I know her from?

I clicked on the picture, and then I remembered. The woman who'd come to the door looking for her daughter—this was the daughter. The daughter's name had been Kara. She called herself *Lilac Lolita* on this website. Great name for an escort of what—seventeen? She was a kid. Was she trying to attract paedophiles with that name?

I shoved the phone back into my pocket.

Lilly slept on for hours, her fever dropping but not going away completely.

I caught snatches of sleep here and there, then I'd startle and check on Lilly and make sure Willow was still beside me. I wasn't used to keeping an eye on the girls like this. The only times I'd been alone with the girls was at home, and then only for a couple of hours here and there when Evie went to do some shopping or something.

Evie. Had she replied to my message?

I pulled out my phone and checked.

No reply.

Nothing.

I clicked on my *sent* messages folder, making doubly sure it had gone through.

Yes, I'd sent it.

Below my message was the conversation I'd had with her.

Nope, don't read all that again.

Don't do that to yourself.

In frustration, I clicked on Evie's profile again. Under her username —*Velvette*—was a record of the last time she'd logged in. One hour and six minutes ago. I'd sent the message about Lilly over three hours ago. She'd seen it. And ignored it.

I formed another message to her in my mind—a message filled with rage and accusations.

No softly-softly this time.

I checked again that the girls were sleeping and started typing.

The indicator beside her name went green.

She was online.

My brain flashed red as I wrote a short, sharp message and hit send.

There.

She was in no doubt now what I thought of her. I didn't hold back.

Cold satisfaction turned to confusion as the screen turned white.

Her profile had vanished.

Fumbling, I typed *Velvette* in the search bar.

The page returned to the home page of the website.

No username found.

I tried one more time, making sure I got the damned name right.

No username found.

She'd deleted her profile. She'd seen what I'd written about Lilly, and she'd deleted it.

Shivers rained down my back.

My wife had become a stranger.

24. CONSTANCE

FROM MY HOTEL ROOM WINDOW, I watched the endless journeys of ferries and yachts out on the dark Sydney Harbour. Just streaks of light on the faster boats, their crisscrossing through the night making me dizzy.

I wanted to feel a fresh breeze on my face, but there were no windows to open in this high-rise hotel. The recycled air had a clinical quality to it.

What was I going to do now?

Every path I'd taken so far in my search for Kara had led nowhere.

Had she been lying dead somewhere all this time? In an alley dumpster? Murdered?

I had to stop thinking those awful thoughts.

Stop thinking.

Dropping to the floor, I carried out my daily exercise routine.

Forty push-ups, forty sit-ups, variety of crunches and planks and squats. All up, it took just under an hour. At home, I also attended the gym twice a week and went for runs on a track along Sardis Lake. It was important to stay fit.

Clean body. Clean mind.

Push the negative thoughts out.

My skin warm and perspiring, I folded myself into my meditation position.

No, wasn't working.

Couldn't meditate.

Mind spinning.

Spinning.

Spinning.

Stretching over to the bedside table, I grabbed another four Promaxa tablets and swallowed them with a glass of water. I'd seen a doctor yesterday afternoon and told her I'd forgotten to bring my prescription to Australia. The doctor had only allowed me the 0.5 mg strength.

Doctors tended to make you feel like a desperado if you wanted more than they were willing to prescribe. *I wasn't addicted.* I'd just needed a little more to get me through these past few months. Surely I could decide if I was overdosing myself or not? Yes, I was feeling jittery and experienced a rapid heartbeat at times, but that wasn't the medication. It was my anxiety.

In truth, I didn't know which was which.

A mental picture of the note I'd found in Kara's jacket two days ago pressed into my mind.

Had Gray heard from his wife yet? Even if she'd left him permanently, surely some contact would need to be made. Child custody arrangements, personal effects and furniture. Lots of heated discussion and accusations and hurt.

I debated whether to call him again so soon. But I was desperate for answers. If Gray *had* heard from his wife, I knew I would be the last person he'd bother to call. It was up to me.

As I took out Gray's number from my handbag, I prepared myself to have the phone slammed down in my ear.

Steeling myself, I listened to his anxious hello.

"Hi . . . Gray. This is Constance Lundquist. I came by the other day looking for my daughter."

"Oh, right." Disappointment strained his voice.

"I was just wondering if—"

"My wife's not back. I haven't heard from her. I've got to go. I'm here in the hospital with my two-year-old, and she's about as sick as she can get."

"Oh God, I'm so sorry. Really. Sorry for bothering you."

I expected a rapid beep to follow as he hung up on me. But he didn't hang up.

"Look . . ." he said a moment later, stopping for a heavy breath. "I can tell you something about your daughter, but you're not going to want to hear it."

"What is it?" My voice sounded weak in my ears. *He did know something.*

"Lady, I'm just going to come out and tell you, then maybe you can quit wondering about where she's been and what she's been doing. Just like I've been able to quit wondering about my wife."

Taking in a rigid breath, I managed to say, "Perhaps you'd better explain."

"She's a prostitute."

"Excuse me?"

"I'm calling a spade a spade. I found both my wife and your daughter on a website where they do stuff with men for money."

I didn't know his wife or what kind of past she'd had. But Kara wouldn't do this. "You're mistaken. My daughter doesn't need money. I send her through more than enough."

"Well, maybe she wanted more than what you were sending. You can look up the website yourself. You have to register and pay if you want to try sending her a message."

A band of pressure tightened on my forehead as I emptied my handbag on the bed and grabbed a pen and notebook from the tangle of items. "Okay, yes, give it to me."

I wrote down a username and the name of a website, but I was shaking my head the whole time. "It must be another girl who looks like Kara."

"You can judge that for yourself. Anyway, I'll leave it with you."

The phone went dead.

Maybe I would have preferred he'd hung up before telling me any of this.

In all the scenarios I'd had in my head, this hadn't been one of them. I'd set up an automatic payment of $500 per week for food and accommodation —surely that was enough? And she'd had an extra job at the shoe store on weekends. What more did she need?

Of course he was mistaken. He'd barely even looked at Kara's photo when I'd shown it to him. I wasn't going to find Kara on this horrible website.

I took my tablet from the nearby desk and typed in the website name.

The homepage of the site wasn't what I expected. It was all very discreet. Just plain black, a logo and the word ENTER.

Giving myself a username based on an expensive car model, I signed up.

I began the search for *Lilac Lolita.*

So many girls. So many very young girls with variations on the name *Lolita.* I shivered as I thought of the customers who wanted their very own Lolita.

There she was.

My daughter.

Kara.

Unmistakable.

No, no, no.

She barely looked like herself. She wasn't the girl I'd said goodbye to at the airport. The face in the photo seemed so . . . deadened. The light gone from her eyes. How had she changed so much in such a short time?

It was incredible that Gray had recognised her from the photo I'd shown him—a picture of her sitting in the shady spot near our swimming pool, sweet in her white sundress. She looked nothing like that on this terrible website. In my mind, Kara was some kind of composite of baby, child and teenager. I wasn't ready for her to become a woman. I certainly wasn't ready for *this.*

Clicking on her photo, I brought up her profile page and quickly scanned the description she'd given. She said she wanted to be spoiled by a daddy figure. I was thankful the page gave no indication of thc intimate things she'd be willing to do.

She'd been a member for four months. She shouldn't be on here. The site said it did background checks. Obviously, they didn't, else they would have discovered her age.

It was too late to call the police station. I'd have to call tomorrow.

No, I couldn't wait.

I had to call.

Leaving the page up, I called the detective's number.

Someone else answered. A Detective Annabelle Yarris.

"Yes, hello, this is Mrs Lundquist. I recently reported that my daughter was missing—Kara. I have some new information."

"Is it urgent?"

"Well . . . it could be. I just found out my daughter signed up with an escort site. And she's missing. She's only seventeen."

"Okay, let me bring up her file. Kara Lundquist, correct?"

"Yes."

"Okay, I've got it. Can you tell me the name of the website you found her at?"

I gave her the details.

"I'll have Detective Gilroy look at this in the morning. Was there anything else?"

"No, not so far. But she could be in danger. Who knows who she's been seeing—?"

"We'll make sure we follow up in the morning."

Her voice was firm. Nothing was going to happen tonight.

A wall of exhaustion toppled over me as I ended the call.

I snapped my laptop shut. I didn't want to see that image of Kara anymore. Crawling up the bed, I collapsed on the pillow, my nerves fried.

Gray had found his wife on that site. What must *that* have felt like? His own wife. I realised now how Kara and Evie must have met each other. Through prostitution.

Kara, why?

My perfect little girl. What happened to you? Why did you do this?

What clues about Kara had slipped past me over the past few months? I'd thought she'd had everything she could possibly want or need. She'd come from a loving home. She was smart, beautiful and we lived in a lovely town close to the college she attended. James and I had taken her away on skiing vacations in New Zealand during the American summer. Island retreats in the Bahamas during the winter. She had everything money could buy. But love and money—the two elixirs of life—obviously hadn't delivered the magic they were supposed to. Whatever the formula was, I didn't know it.

Kara had been drifting away from me a long time before she disappeared. Sometimes, I couldn't form a picture of her in my mind. I wanted desperately to see her one way, but another, distant side to Kara would push into my mind.

I laid myself back on the bed, the mess from my handbag all around me—and fell into a half sleep, a strange, whirring haze that wouldn't allow me to shut my mind off.

25. EVIE

I POKED MY HEAD INTO THE sick room. Kara was sleeping in one of the beds, Cormack sitting on a chair next to her.

Last night, when the aquarium challenge was done and the mentors had entered the room, Brother Sage had been the one to resuscitate Kara. She'd stopped breathing, but she'd still had a pulse.

Cormack raised his bleary eyes. I guessed that like me, he hadn't slept well after returning to the dormitory. He had Kara's hand in his, lightly thumbing her fingers.

"How's she doing?" I asked quietly.

"She's not bad. Could have been worse."

I nodded, not wanting to think about how close Kara had come to drowning. "Why don't you go get breakfast? I'll stay with her for a while."

"Appreciate it." Drawing himself to his feet, he wandered out of the room.

Out in the hallway, I heard a group of people passing by. Then shouts and angry voices.

I stuck my head out the door in alarm.

Richard was standing with Poppy, Yolanda and a few others. Cormack was jabbing his finger angrily in Richard's direction. "You were prepared to let her die, you bastard."

Richard held his palms up. "Back off, son. I did what I had to do. If you—"

Before he could finish, Cormack took a couple of strides forward and punched Richard hard in the jaw. Richard staggered back, Poppy catching him.

"Leave him alone," Poppy cried.

"He almost killed her," Cormack accused.

"I didn't wrap her wristband around that chain." Cupping his jaw, Richard drew himself up to his full height. "I did the one thing that was going to finish the challenge and get the mentors into the room. I did the best thing I knew how to bring help. If you want to get mad at anyone, get mad at *them* for not rushing in sooner and stopping the challenge. They can all see what's going on in the room, right?"

Richard shrugged Poppy away and stormed off in the direction of the cloister. The others, except for Poppy, spoke in confused voices among themselves and moved off down the hall.

"You can try to talk yourself up, now, but I'm not buying it," Cormack called after Richard, but there was now a hint of uncertainty in his voice. He moved off towards the refectory, his shoulders tense and turned inward.

"I don't know what to think," I muttered to myself as I entered the sick room.

Poppy followed me in. "Richard was just trying to win, like we all are."

"A person's life is more important than winning a challenge."

She tilted her head as if reconsidering. "Guess you're right. But Cormack doesn't have to be so mean."

Both of us turned to Kara as she murmured in her sleep.

Get away. Get away from . . .

You don't know . . . you don't understand . . .

Poppy brushed her hair back from her forehead, the hair still damp from the night before. "Ssh, Kara, you're having a bad dream." She raised her eyes to me. "Poor thing."

"Wish I could help her," I said. "She's seemed really troubled the whole time she's been here."

Poppy eased herself back onto the seat Cormack had vacated. "We're all troubled, here. It's the house of trouble."

I jerked my head around at the sound of whispers—indistinct male voices. One thing they said was clear:

Kill them.

"Hear that?" I said urgently.

Poppy's fingers tightened on the armrests as she nodded.

Rushing to the door, I scanned each length of hallway.

No one was there. Everything still and silent. I headed back in and through the door that led to a storeroom—the sick room was a small annex of a larger space that held boxes, crates and medical supplies.

I looked back in at Poppy's wide, questioning eyes.

"I don't see anyone," I told her.

"Someone's playing a prank on us," she said. Raising her voice a notch, she added, "And it's not funny."

I stood listening for more, but there was only silence. I had a sudden, strange vision of Poppy, Kara and myself from far above the island—the three of us in this tiny room, hemmed in on all sides by hexagonal shapes, surrounded by high walls and the wide, restless ocean.

Threads of panic grew inside me. I felt unanchored, adrift in a strange, hostile world.

Go home now, I told myself. Two challenges means twenty thousand dollars. It's enough. *It's enough.*

No, it's not enough to pay off my debts. Certainly not enough to rent or buy a better house.

My thoughts must have been wild on my face, because Poppy was staring at me intently, shaking her head. "Don't weird out on me, Evie. Too many weird people here. Go get one of the mentors and tell them what we heard. I'll stay here with Kara."

26. GRAY

A SOFT, CROAKY GROAN CAME FROM deep within Lilly's chest. She was covered in sweat. Opening her eyes, she looked at me with a frightened gaze.

Grabbing the bedside alert button, I pressed it.

A doctor came rushing into the room to check Lilly.

"How long has she been like this?" She stooped over my daughter, listening to her breathing with a stethoscope, checking her pulse.

"Just now." I exhaled. "I'm not sure. Could have been a few minutes. I dozed off." That wasn't true. I'd been awake but distracted, sending my wife stupid messages. Guilty, I swept Lilly's dark hair back from her cheeks. "What's wrong with her?"

I wanted the doctor to give Lilly something to make her stop grimacing and sweating and crying out in pain. But instead, she called for backup. Whatever was wrong with Lilly, more doctors were needed to fix the problem.

For the second time today, Lilly was taken away from me. They mentioned spinal taps and other things that I didn't catch.

A day passed before the doctors were prepared to give me any answers.

They wanted to talk to me alone, without Willow being there. A nurse was arranged to sit with Willow.

I didn't like the look on the doctors' faces as I walked into the hospital office.

Grim. Serious. Expressions that set the mood before they spoke so that you'd be primed for their awful news.

And when the news came, it was awful.

The head doctor threaded her fingers together on her lap. "Mr Harlow, we've been conducting a series of tests, as you know, to try to better understand what's happening with Lilly. We have some results, and while we're not completely certain, things are pointing to a certain condition."

"What's she got?" My words tumbled out.

"At the moment, some things are pointing us towards a condition called cystic fibrosis."

"I've heard of that. It's people with bad lungs, right?"

"Yes, you could say that. It's a genetic disease. It affects the systems of the body that produce saliva, sweat and mucus. Even tears. People with CF develop excessive amounts of mucus, which leads to frequent infections—including lung and sinus infections."

My mind spun. "If Lilly's got this thing, why wasn't it picked up before? Evie—my wife—always had her down at the doctor's. She's had lots of tests."

"There is a newborn screening test for cystic fibrosis, but it does miss picking up on a small percentage of babies that do have the disease."

"What makes you think she's got it?"

"We conducted a sweat test, which showed abnormal levels of sodium and chloride. A positive sweat test is a key indicator. But we'll repeat the test tomorrow. Her chest X-ray showed a lot of mucus in her lungs. What you've told us about her history of illnesses also adds to the picture. Lilly's symptoms are similar to many childhood conditions, and, as I said, we'll need further testing to be certain."

"So, if she does have it, what happens now?"

She explained and I listened, but I couldn't grab onto any of it. All I wanted to know was, when will she get better? *What bag of medical tricks do you lot have up your sleeves?*

But they kept shaking their heads as they spoke, as though they'd lost their bag of tricks. Lots of words. Lots of head shaking.

Stopping, she eyed me squarely. "Do you understand what we're saying?"

I exhaled. “I can’t . . . I’ve been up all night. I’m trying, but you’re going to have to put it in a simpler way. Can you do something for her now, or will she outgrow it?”

“Gray,” she said. “If she has CF, she’ll always have it. But with good medical treatment and care, she has every chance of living a full life.”

“So, she’ll be okay? I mean, if we do everything we can to keep her from getting sick, she’ll be like any other kid?”

“We’ll cover all of that when we complete the tests.”

“I want to know now. If it *is* this disease, is she going to grow up and have kids and live until she’s a hundred?” Wanting to know the exact details of something was how my mind worked. I was a programmer. I needed to know if Lilly’s system was going to work as expected, or was this bug in her code—cystic fibrosis—going to infiltrate everything and bring the system down?

“I can’t tell you how Lilly’s life will go,” she told me. “Everyone is different.”

“Then tell me about the illness. Don’t leave anything out.”

She nodded. “I’ll keep it brief. The average lifespan of someone in Australia with CF currently sits at around age thirty-eight. Over half live past the age of eighteen, which is a much better outlook than it used to be. Women with CF can have children and do all the normal things, but there is a risk of passing on the disease to their children. Look, I don’t think we should go any further at this point. We just wanted you to know what we’ve been doing and what testing we’re undertaking on Lilly.”

Stunned, I just stared back at her, panic coiling in my stomach.

What if Lilly was in the half that didn’t live past eighteen? What if Willow lost her sister? How was Lilly going to plan her life while facing a life expectancy of less than forty?

Then came the next hammer. Medical costs. The government system would cover most of it, including hospital stays, but not all of the medication and specialists. And there was going to be a lot of those things.

How the hell was I going to get back to work and pay for all this and look after Lilly at the same time?

The doctors wanted to know about Lilly’s mother. Where was she and could I get her to come here to the hospital? they asked. As though I should be able to pull Evie out of a hat. They had no bag of tricks, but somehow I was supposed to have one.

Well, I couldn't pull Evie out of a hat. She was as gone as a person could get.

They then asked if I wanted to call anyone.

There was just one person I could call. Verity. Evie's mother. The last person I wanted to speak to.

I stepped from the doctor's office on unsteady legs.

Willow looked so small sitting on the plastic hospital chair. I'd gotten used to seeing her as my big girl, not the little four-year-old she was. I remembered bringing her to this hospital just after her baby sister was born. She was two then, and when I was cradling the tiny Lilly, Willow had suddenly looked like a giant in comparison.

The nurse who'd been sitting beside Willow gave me a quick, warm smile and headed away.

"When can we take Lilly home?" Willow stared up at me.

I exhaled a breath so tight I felt like I was breathing through a straw as I reached to hold Willow's hand.

Relax. Relax. Don't scare her. Lilly isn't going to die. Everything's okay. "Honey, she's going to be here for a bit longer. We want to make sure she's all better first."

"When's Mummy coming?"

"When she can."

"When is that?"

"I'm not sure."

"Where is she?"

"She went away . . . for work. To make some money. She'll be back soon."

"Doesn't she know Lilly's sick?" The tone in Willow's voice was imperious, sounding like a queen whose kingdom was falling apart.

"I haven't been able to talk to her yet. She doesn't know about Lilly."

At last, I got a small nod. Something I'd said had satisfied her. And Willow wasn't easily satisfied. She was like her mother, drilling down on a subject until she had enough answers. I pitied whatever teacher she'd get when she went to school next year.

Giving Willow's hand a final squeeze, I stepped out of earshot, took out my phone and looked up Verity's number. I'd only ever called her twice—on the days of the births of Willow and Lilly. Never before or since. She was going to know something was up the moment she saw my number flash on her phone's screen.

"Yes, hello?"

"Verity, it's Gray."

"*Gray?* Is something wrong?"

"Lilly's really sick. We're in the hospital. Westmead Children's Hospital."

"Oh dear. What's she got? Another virus? I told Evie—"

"It's not a virus. I . . . I need some help at the moment."

"So, Eveline got you to call me."

"No, she's not here."

"Well, where is she?"

"I'm not sure where she is. She . . . left me."

"Seriously? She left you? Well, it's all making sense then. She came by wanting money the other week."

"She did? I didn't know that."

"Yes. Why is Lilly with you? Didn't Eveline take her? What about Willow? Where is she?"

"She didn't take either of them. She left them with Marla."

"Marla? That twit? Oh, for goodness sake. Why didn't she just bring them here?"

"I don't know. You can ask me all kinds of questions about what your daughter's been doing lately, but I'm not going to be able to answer them. What I need to know is if you can give me a hand right now. I need to stay at the hospital with Lilly, but I can't keep Willow here any longer. She's already been here too long."

"Of course. I'll pack some things, and I'll come and stay until Eveline returns."

"You're coming to *my* house? I thought you'd—"

"Of course. It's too disruptive for Willow to bring her here. She's got all her things at her own home, and I can take her to preschool from there. Children need to be kept to a routine, even in times of crisis."

"Okay, sure. Thank you."

"Oh, and who's looking after your cat?"

I went silent. I'd forgotten *Socks*, the girls' cat. The cat had spent almost a day without being fed. "She's fine," I croaked. I'd ask Verity to heap her bowl up later.

Ending the conversation, I headed back over to Willow. "Honey, your nanna's coming to get you and take you home. I'll stay here with Lilly."

I could practically see my words cycling through her mind. "I'm not leaving here without Lilly. I'll sleep with her in her bed." She stuck out her small chin determinedly.

"Willow, hospitals are places for sick people. You can't stay here."

She held me in an intense gaze for a moment, a gaze that I was sure was saying that the adult world made no sense. And I couldn't give her any assurance that things would seem any different when she grew up.

Very little over the past three days had made any sense to me either.

Everything was caught up in some kind of crazy storm. I'd once heard about a place on earth where the electric storms practically never stop. Somewhere in Venezuela. Was it possible for my life to become like that from this point on?

27. CONSTANCE

A NOISE DRILLED INTO MY EAR.

I drifted awake.

My phone. *It was my phone.*

Please be Kara.

I twisted to a sitting-up position and snatched it from the bed. Outside the window, the world had grown dark. I'd slept for hours. I glanced at the clock beside the bed as I put the phone to my ear. Eight at night.

"Mrs Lundquist?"

I recognized Detective Gilroy's voice.

"Yes, it's me." *What did he know?*

"I've found out two pieces of information about Kara."

I held my breath, audibly, like a small child. "Okay?"

"It's nothing bad, so don't get too worried. The first thing is that she was picked up by police for suspected prostitution about a week and a half ago. At the Star Casino, Sydney. But there ended up being no real evidence, and no charges were laid. It seems she was seen there on a number of occasions by staff, and on each occasion, she was with an older man."

"Oh, dear God. At the casino?"

"Yeah, apparently. Anyway, I hope it makes you feel better that she's been seen about. The second thing is that I found out she's no longer in Sydney."

"She's not in Sydney? Where is she?"

"I'll explain. First thing this morning, I took a look at the website that you'd told Detective Yarris about. And it seemed to me that the girls on there are looking for sugar daddies. The girls are looking for gifts, dinners, trips away—"

"That's right. But what—?"

"Well, it was the *trips away* part of it that had me wondering. The trips can be within Australia, or anywhere in the world. The man gets company, the girl gets to see the world. That kind of thing. So, I did a check on any flights Kara might have taken in the past month. Seems that Kara boarded a flight for the UK about a week ago."

"*The UK?* She's not even here in this country? Who was she with? That man from the casino?"

"That I'm not sure about. She bought her own ticket—to London. So, there's a chance she flew to London by herself. Her flight might have nothing at all to do with the sugar daddy website. She might have other reasons."

"All this time," I breathed softly, "she was in London. She wasn't even here."

"Look, I'm not saying she's still in London. Just that she travelled there from Sydney. All I can tell you with any certainty is that she didn't return to Australia. Nor did she buy a return flight."

"Can you find out where she went after that?"

I heard the trace of a sigh. "I'm afraid not. I'll speak with London police, just to get her name in their system. So far, it doesn't look like a case of people trafficking or anything like that, but she is underage for the lifestyle she's been leading. I'll do what I can to have them follow it up, but there's probably not a lot they can do. And she's very close to turning eighteen. I'll call you again soon to give you a police contact name in London."

"Okay. Thank you. I appreciate your efforts." I ended the call, feeling like I was drowning with one hand still above the surface. There was hope, but I remained underwater.

In the detective's eyes, Kara was a young, independent woman. In my eyes, she was just a little girl. It didn't seem that long ago she was blowing out the candles at her tenth birthday party.

I called James. I needed to speak to him and hear his voice.

When he answered the phone, his voice was thick with sleep. I'd woken him in the early hours. He was tired, he said, from his business trip to New York. Briefly, I explained about Kara being seen at the casino and her flight to London, leaving out any mention of the men she'd been seeing.

James listened in silence, finally giving a confused, exasperated murmur. "What was she doing at the casino?"

"I don't know. Maybe she thinks she's all grown up now and wants to do adult things."

"Who was she with? I'm really disappointed in her."

"Me too. All I know is that the police know she was there on a few occasions. She was picked up for a . . . misdemeanour."

His tone turned quick and sharp. "A misdemeanour? Hell, what did Kara do?"

"Nothing, as it turns out. It turned out to be nothing. No charges. James . . . I know you're busy, but I need you. Can you meet me in London?"

"Sweetheart . . ."

"Just . . . please. Take some time off."

"I'm not sure that's such a good idea. You sound frazzled. That's not good for you."

"I *am* frazzled. At the end of my rope."

"Then come back home. What time is it there? Jump on a plane today. I'll get someone to find Kara—someone who knows what they're doing. We'll find her. Don't worry. Then we'll fly straight to wherever she is. And then she's coming back here to finish college. No ifs or buts. She's shown us she's not responsible enough to do this on her own."

James expected a lot from Kara. After all the money he'd spent on her education and all the time he'd spent patiently tutoring her in math and science, I understood why.

I relaxed a little. James had a plan. Soon, Kara would be back living with us in Lafayette.

"Okay," I breathed. "Okay, we'll do that."

"See you soon, Sweetheart. I'd better get some shut-eye. Big day tomorrow. Would you believe that Snowy tore up the sofa cushions again last night? I think he's really missing Kara."

Snowy, Kara's very white Japanese Spitz, had taken to chewing on things that he saw as belonging to Kara. Kara was the one to gather all the sofa cushions around her every time she sat to watch TV.

"Poor Snowy. I bet Kara's missing him, too."

"I'll bet she is." James begged off, yawning and making me promise to call him before I left Sydney in the morning.

I began packing my things into the suitcase. From the start, I should have done what James suggested—hire a private investigator. It'd been far too difficult trying to do this on my own.

Locking the suitcase, I perched on the edge of the bed, staring around the bland, lonely room. Should I try to fly out tonight? There was no point now in staying. Then another thought: should I get the ball rolling with a private investigator? James was busy—this was something I could do. I told myself it was too late to call anyone until I remembered that the time would be different in London.

Switching on my laptop, I checked international times. Eight p.m. in Sydney, Australia, was roughly three a.m. in America and nine a.m. in England.

I decided to look for someone now. Someone in London. I browsed through the results for private investigators. They were expensive—upwards of a hundred American dollars per hour—but money wasn't a problem. I just needed someone who'd do a thorough job.

I tried a couple of people first who said they had a high success rate. But I found myself listening to recorded messages on their answering machines. *No, I wasn't prepared to wait all day for a call back.* I wanted to talk to someone now. I came across the website of a lady named Rosemary Oort. The website wasn't as flashy as the others I'd looked at, but her words sounded comforting: *I research every case personally, approaching each one with enormous care and sensitivity. Sorry, but I do not take on cases of suspected infidelity.*

Maybe she was what I needed.

Picking up my phone again, I called her office.

28. GRAY

I JUMPED AWAKE IN MY CHAIR as the phone rang, snatching it from my pocket and answering it so as not to wake Lilly.

"Gray?" came the voice. "It's Verity. How's Lilly doing?"

I glanced across at Lilly's small form in the hospital bed. "Still sleeping. She's doing okay."

"Poor mite. Have the doctors said when she'll be coming home?"

"Yeah, maybe later today, maybe not. They're watching how she does on the antibiotics and steroids."

"Well, tell them from me they should keep her a bit longer. I'm still getting this house in order. It's a brothel."

I winced at the word *brothel*. "Verity, c'mon, it was a bit messy—"

"A bit? There's stuff everywhere! So much clutter. And there's the matter of mould around Willow's window. I was quite shocked. I'm dosing the entire room in mould killer."

"Evie's always taking care of the mould. Gets worse when it rains like this for days. She tried using the harsh stuff before, but Lilly broke out in a rash—"

"Nonsense. You have to kill it or it will come back."

"Okay, cool. I gotta go now. Doctor's just come in."

There was no doctor. But I was too exhausted to argue with Verity. I was raw. Everything inside me emptied out. There was no sleep in hospitals. Things beeped and rattled all night, and nurses and doctors came in and out.

A doctor suddenly appeared in the room, twisting reality and making me not have told a lie to Verity. I didn't know whether to feel cheated or virtuous.

"Mr Harlow," he said, "Lilly appears to be stable. And I'm sure both you and she would be more comfortable at home. You can take her home this afternoon, but if she develops any worrying symptoms, then bring her back in."

"How will I know? What kind of symptoms?"

He looked surprised. "If the fever returns or her breathing becomes rapid or strained, or if she just seems to be worse in some way." His forehead puckered into a deep V. "Have you managed to contact her mother?"

"No . . . not yet. But Evie's mother is staying with us at the moment."

"Oh, good. Before you go, I'll give you some information on how to clear the bronchial airways each day."

Three hours later, I gathered up my sleepy daughter and took her home. She didn't express surprise or ask questions, seeming to be in a distant, hazy zone of her own. I had the depressing thought that we all take this life journey alone, even children. They could get sick or die, and that cross was theirs to bear.

Even when Willow squealed and ran to give her a typically squeezy hug, Lilly barely responded. I set her up on the sofa with a blanket and her favourite soft toy.

Verity watched on with a wry expression, as if Lilly getting sick was somehow my fault.

I thought Verity would be rushing out the door as soon as I was back, muttering words about impositions and work commitments.

She didn't.

Instead, she showed all signs of lodging here for a long time. She'd nested in the sunroom, making a bed out of the futon, surrounding herself with various exercisers, salt lamps and devices. I later learned that a couple of those devices were an ionizer and sleep apnea machine. She seemed to need a great deal of contraptions to get by in this world.

Willow and Lilly's bedrooms smelled of strong bleach. Whatever germs and creeping mould had dared exist within those walls had been exterminated. I wasn't going to let the girls sleep in their bedrooms tonight. I'd drag their mattresses downstairs and make out like it was an adventure to sleep in the living room. I'd sleep on the sofa, to keep an eye on Lilly.

"Want a coffee, Gray?" Verity called from the kitchen.

"Sure. Thanks." Stepping into the kitchen, I parked myself on a stool.

While the kettle boiled, Verity straightened the mess of kids' drawings that were fixed to the fridge. Her nose wrinkled beneath the bridge of her glasses as she plucked one of Willow's drawings out and studied it. It was a drawing of her sister and herself, labelled with her tall, shaky lettering. "Lord knows why Eveline had to butcher Lilly's name and spell it with two Ls instead of one."

"She wanted it to match with Willow's name, I think." I'd never given the spelling of my daughter's name any thought. And why Verity thought it important to bring it up right now, I couldn't guess. "Hey, thanks for being here for them. It's been a bit of a slog the last few days."

She smiled. "They're lovely girls."

"Yes, they are." Closing my eyes for a moment, I rested my head on my hands. In the space of a few days, my life had turned upside down and emptied out its entrails.

My eyes opened to Verity studying me while she poured hot water into two cups. "I thought she'd leave you one day, Gray."

She'd caught me unawares. Being unawares with Verity was never a wise thing. She'd kick the chair out from under you when you weren't looking.

"She left the girls behind, too," I commented.

"She never was any good with responsibilities. That's why I thought she'd take off. Too flighty."

Did Verity know Evie better than I did? I'd fooled myself into thinking that I held that honour. I'd always thought she was completely wrong about her daughter.

"Well, maybe I'm just finding that out," I answered. "Anyway, she's made her choice. Now I need to concentrate on getting Lilly better."

But her eyes sharpened. She wasn't finished injecting her particular brand of *Verity* into the room. Not yet. "Perhaps Eveline couldn't cope with Lilly being sick all the time."

I stalled on my reply, not wanting to admit to Verity that Evie had been short-tempered lately with the girls. She'd seemed to have a constant short fuse. Their noise and squabbles annoyed her in a way they hadn't before.

"It's been tough for Evie," I finally conceded.

"Well, she's going to have to harden the fuck up when she gets herself back here." She pushed the coffee across to me.

I'd forgotten how much Verity liked to swear. She was someone who actually enjoyed swearing, rolling the words off her tongue like favourite delicacies. It was one of the few things I liked about her. When she'd had a few drinks, her harder side tended to soften, and she'd swear like a sailor. Unfortunately, she rarely drank.

"I'm pretty worn out, to be honest," I told her. "I don't really want to get into this."

Her expression adjusted. "Go have a rest. I'll get dinner sorted and watch the girls."

"Appreciate it." I headed upstairs and sank into my bed. I really did appreciate someone coming in here and making dinner and taking care of the girls. I just wished that person didn't have to be Verity.

I eyed Evie's things around the room. Her hoodies and jeans still hung over the chair where she'd left them. A family photo montage was lying half done on top of a tallboy.

I flipped back to thinking Verity was wrong about Evie. Whatever had gone off-track with Evie had happened recently. She wasn't restless and flighty. She'd always been the patient one, calmly breaking up the bitter death-matches between Willow and Lilly, instructing Lilly on using the potty for the hundredth time and somehow finding a core of strength when Lilly's night-time waking had her up all night. She'd been patient with me, too. When I'd had a shit day at the office with Lyle and his cronies, I'd sometimes download my frustration onto Evie, snapping at her. She'd tell me that she was going to walk away until I remembered that she was my wife.

Verity was trying to tip me off my feet. That was what she did best. She disoriented people, tied their psychological shoelaces and tripped them. It was what she'd done to Evie and her brother. It was why Evie'd had such a strange idea of herself when I'd met her. Evie had zero faith in her own ideas and decisions. She was always second-guessing herself. I'd ask her for her opinion on something, and she'd give me an answer, but then two seconds later, she'd pull back and tell me she wasn't sure. For a long time, I used to insist that she just make the damned decision. But I came to understand that when I made the decisions, she relaxed.

But I had to admit there was another side to Evie, one that didn't match up with the girl who wanted other people to be in control. When we played Warcraft together, she was ruthless, making calculated moves and annihilating our opponents. She was razor sharp and clever at those times.

No wonder I hadn't seen the day coming where she'd do what she'd just done. How far ahead had she planned this? And what was her end game? Did she plan on finding some rich guy and running off with him and never having to worry about money again? And what was the catalyst that made her decide that this was what she wanted and needed?

Anger started to burn in the pit of my stomach.

A loud knocking at the front door downstairs came thumping through the air.

Whoever it was, it wasn't Evie.

Verity answered the door, and I could hear two people, a man and a woman. From what I'd known of her, she normally gave door-to-door salespeople their marching orders, but she let them in.

Hauling myself up from the bed, I walked out to the stair landing.

Two police officers stood in my living room quietly talking with a shocked Verity.

The three of them looked upwards at me, stopping their conversation.

The female officer wore a concerned expression. "Mr Harlow, we need to talk with you."

"Sure." Willow and Lilly watched me from the sofa as I walked down the stairs, their eyes round and unblinking.

"Your grandmother and I are going to have a little talk with the police, okay?" I told the girls. "We'll just be out on the back verandah."

I showed the police through. Whatever they had to say, I already knew I didn't want the girls to hear it. I closed the door behind us as a further precaution.

"Okay, what's going on?" I said finally.

Verity jumped in first. "Gray, this is Sergeant Moss and Sergeant Gallinger." She indicated from the female cop to the male. "They've found Eveline's car."

"What?" My brain refused to compute that. Why had the police been looking for her car? Had Marla made a report that Evie was missing?

"Mr Harlow?" Sergeant Moss gave me a brief nod. "Your wife's car was found in bushland about an hour away from here."

"Bushland? Hell, don't tell me she crashed the car? She wasn't still in the car, right?" What weren't they telling me? Why were they hesitating and half glancing towards each other?

"It wasn't a crash," the sergeant told me. "She wasn't in the car. The car was deliberately driven into the forest then set on fire."

I blew out a slow breath of relief. "So, the car was stolen? You don't have any bad news about Evie?"

"No," confirmed Sergeant Gallinger. "But we'd like to get a few details straight. We estimate that the car was dumped and burned yesterday. But we've had no report that the vehicle was stolen. And Eveline's mother tells us that you're not sure where she is."

"Yeah, that's right. She . . . went away for a few days."

"And you've had no contact with her?"

"No."

"Mr Harlow, is that usual behaviour from your wife? Not to be in contact?"

"No, it's not the usual at all. Evie's never done this before. She organised to leave our daughters with a friend, and she left a note to say she was going away—for a week or so."

"Does the friend know where she is?"

"Nope, not according to her."

"Just in case we don't hear from Eveline, could I have the friend's details?"

"Sure. Her name's Marla Atkinson. Number 4 Brightfield Avenue. Just down the road near the 7/11."

"Okay, got it." Sergeant Gallinger cleared his throat, handing me a business card. "I understand. Well, we just wanted you to know about your wife's car. Do inform us right away if Eveline—Evie—contacts you."

I nodded, trying to process the fact that Evie's car was found burned in a forest.

29. EVIE

POPPY AND I DIDN'T HEAR ANY more of the whispers behind the walls. Brother Sage came to investigate the sick room. But like us, he found nothing. I knew exactly what he was thinking. We were just two girls who were feeling spooked.

"There *were* voices," Poppy insisted, obviously catching the paternalistic smile on Brother Sage's face.

"I'll sit with Kara, if you like," he offered, bending to check her breathing.

"No, that's okay," said Poppy. "I'm sure you've got more important things to do. We'll stay here." She turned to me for affirmation.

I nodded.

"Very well," he said. "But let us know the moment she wakes. We don't anticipate any lasting effects from her mishap, but we'd still like to make certain."

"She seemed to be having bad dreams before," I said.

"Did she?" Brother Sage tugged the blanket up over Kara's shoulders. "Hopefully they won't continue. It must have been an unsettling experience."

"Brother Sage?" Poppy widened her eyes.

"Yes?" he said.

"We're all feeling a bit raw after what happened to Kara," Poppy told him. "Could we have a little hint about what challenge three will be? Just to get a little better prepared mentally?"

I stifled a gasp. It was a bold thing to ask.

He chuckled under his breath. "I'm sure you don't want to gain an unfair advantage."

With that he exited the room.

Poppy gave me an innocent shrug. "Worth a shot."

"Hey," I whispered. "I thought I saw something when I was in the tank. Like, someone lighting a candle in the middle room of the monastery."

"The middle room?"

"Yeah. The one that has to be in the dead centre. There are six hexagonal challenge rooms—so they have to surround a centre hexagon, right?"

"I guess?"

"Didn't Brother Vito show you the map of this place?"

"No. Seems like he only does special things with you." A hint of jealousy hung in her voice.

"It was on the first morning. I was lost."

"Oh."

"Anyway, the walls of the tank are glass, right? And the tank I was in faced the centre room. I thought I saw a girl. But her hair was all over her face. And then . . . someone else quickly came and snuffed out the candle. She seemed scared."

She eyed me quizzically. "You weren't having raptures of the deep or something?"

"Only people who dive really deep in the ocean get that, don't they?"

She wrinkled her brow. "You're making me worry. You should have told Brother Sage. But you'd better be sure you saw something. I mean, we *did* just tell him we heard whispers in the walls."

I bit down on my lip, starting to question myself. I *had* been at the start of oxygen deprivation at the time. And the image of the girl had been murky through the water.

"How are you going?" she asked me in a concerned tone. "You seemed pretty bent out of shape yesterday."

"I'm fine. Talking to Brother Vito just brought up memories of Ben. He was my big brother. He died when he was nineteen. I was seventeen then." I eased myself into the chair beside Poppy's.

"Oh, rough." She frowned sympathetically.

"Yeah. It was really rough. Still is." I drew in a breath weighed with a sadness too deep to explain to Poppy. "Hey, how about you? How are you going? I should have checked. You know, especially after the way Greta left the island."

"You don't need to worry about me. The detox that the mentors sent me away on worked. But in some ways, that's bad. Because I can't shut things out the way I used to. I have to face everything."

"I remember you told me your boyfriend died of an overdose recently. That must be so hard."

She nodded, her eyes suddenly glistening. "Doug was a beautiful soul. A musician. He used to sing me songs he wrote. I was working at an art museum then. He'd pick me up from work at night, and we'd go to all the pub theatres around London. Sometimes, he acted in the plays the pubs put on. He was so talented."

"How sad. Such a waste of a life . . ."

"Yes. Such a waste. God, Evie, I'm a curse. When I was sixteen, I had a boyfriend a lot like Doug. His name was Evan, and he went to the same school as me. I thought we'd get married one day. We snuck out one night to go to a rave party. He took some pills someone sold him. And that was it. He died in hospital three days later."

I shook my head, unable to find words. Leaning over, I hugged her tight. A shudder ran through her body and I knew she was trying not to cry.

Her sleeve moved upward along her arm as she hugged me back. Horizontal scars crisscrossed her pale skin, some more faded than others.

Moving back, I touched her arm gently. "Poppy, what's this?"

She hung her head. "Oh. I've been cutting myself for years. Helps to let out a little of the pain. I know it's dumb of me, but I can't stop . . ."

I sat back on my chair, stunned. I wondered, then, about the stories of all of the challenge participants.

How did we all get to the point of signing onto a treatment program for addicts? Where were we all going from here?

30. I, INSIDE THE WALLS

HUMAN MINDS ARE LIKE DANDELIONS GROWING in dark rooms.

Thoughts lose their colour. Minds go to seed. And once they go to seed, there is no wind in the dark rooms to shake their deepest, darkest thoughts free. Only when they shake their withered thoughts free can they seed the new. That is what I have been taught.

All of them who came here, they don't understand. I don't know if I am sad for them that they don't understand or envious that they live in such ignorance.

31. CONSTANCE

ROSEMARY LEIGHTON SPOKE FAST, LIKE AN American from NYC, except her accent was definitely British. Clipped and precise. I'd only spoken to her briefly a couple of nights ago, but she'd agreed to take on the task of finding Kara. First, she'd requested that I pay a visit to the casino that Kara had been seen at. Rosemary wanted me to show Kara's photo around to the staff there in the hope of gleaning a little additional information.

I relayed to Rosemary what I'd learned after visiting the casino and then returning to my hotel room.

I'd found the casino a little intimidating. I didn't gamble, myself. Never had. I'd spent my life in a small town as a child and a college town after I met James. Not even during my wild years with Otto did I gamble.

Three of the casino staff had recognized my daughter from her photograph. The man she'd been seen with was Wilson Carlisle, an Australian man who'd been frequenting the casino for years. He was in his sixties, an orthodontist with a Sydney practice. I shivered to think of Kara being around this person.

One of the staff members—a gawky young man who served behind a bar—told me that he and Kara had taken cocaine together one night after work.

Cocaine.

One more shocking, terrifying piece of the puzzle.

The young man had been blasé about it. As if it were no big deal. I'd had to struggle to control myself, because I'd wanted to scream at him that it was a very big deal and that he'd had no right to head off somewhere with my daughter and use that vile stuff. But then he'd told me that the cocaine was Kara's. I'd walked away on legs that'd threatened to crumple underneath me.

"Constance," Rosemary said—*tapping at her keyboard*—"this Wilson Carlisle character has an interesting lifestyle. For a Sydney orthodontist. Yachting off the coast of France and Greece in the European summer. Contacts with some powerful people in the business and political arena. Actually, extremely powerful people." *Tap-tap-tap-tap*. "And . . . some activities I don't quite understand."

"What kind of activities?" I asked, concerned by her sudden change in tone.

"Let me do some research on it before I say too much. For now, I'll just tell you that he seems to be a member of some sort of historical society, and the society appears to have some unusual aspects that aren't adding up. I'm accessing a database used by law enforcement at the moment, often used to investigate people trafficking."

"Do you think he might have been trying to traffic my daughter?" I gasped, my throat suddenly feeling tight. "The detective I spoke to didn't think so."

"Well, at this point, I'd tend to agree. This case isn't showing any usual patterns. Perhaps his interest in her—as awful as this sounds—was just her young age. It would tie in with the theory that he was giving her money for the drugs she was taking. He possibly wanted to make her reliant on him."

"I can't even think about that. And I just can't figure out why she'd fly to the UK."

"She might have wanted an adventure. Young people are very mobile these days. They're jetsetters. Or—and this is another difficult thing to say—but she might have thought she'd find some wealthier sugar daddies abroad."

"Dear God."

"But we don't know that. We don't know anything at this point. But we *will* find out for certain. It will just take a little time."

"Of course. Is there anything else I can do at this end? I'll do anything. Go anywhere." There was a desperate, ragged edge to my words. I couldn't keep the terrible possibilities from my mind despite having claimed a moment ago I didn't want to do just that.

"I don't think so," said Rosemary. "Something might come up later, but I can't foresee anything at this point. If you'd feel better coming over to London, perhaps you'd better take the flight now."

I nodded as though she could see me.

James wouldn't be impressed that I was doing this. He was conservative, doing everything by the right paths. I'd thought I was conservative, too. But the things Kara had been involved with had sent me into a world of growing panic. When I'd told Rosemary I'd do anything she needed in order to find out more information, I meant it.

After finishing the conversation, I called the airport to book my flight.

32. GRAY

WILLOW SKIPPED FROM HER DAYCARE ROOM.

I'd left Lilly behind with Verity. I could tell that Willow was excited about something but trying to contain it. I watched her gaze sweeping the sea of mothers who'd come to collect their kids. Her expression fell when she saw me. I guessed she'd been hoping to see her mother. Each day, it was getting harder to explain to the girls why their mummy hadn't come back.

I bent down to hug her. "Have a good day?"

She nodded against my shoulder, her hair smelling of crayons and ripe bananas and the sandbox. "I drew a picture and got a gold star! And the teachers put it on the wall!" Grabbing my hand, she took me into the room and pointed at her painting.

"A gold star, eh?" I studied the picture, turning my head from side to side. "Nice mountain, honey."

"Dad, it's a whale."

"Just kidding," I teased, winking at her.

Marla moved near us, gathering up her daughter's cardigan and a gold shoe that looked way too fancy for day care. She startled as she noticed me. "Oh, Gray . . ."

"Hi."

"I—" Looking down at Willow, she motioned towards the wide door that led to the playground. "Willow, would you mind helping Maribelle find her other shoe? She left it outside somewhere."

"Can I, Dad?" asked Willow.

"Uh, sure. Go play," I answered then turned back to Marla. Had she heard something, and why did she look so nervous?

"How's Lilly?" she began. "I heard she was in hospital for a few days."

"Yeah. She was pretty sick." I wasn't ready yet to start telling people what Lilly was diagnosed with. It was too new. A specialist had just made a definite diagnosis of cystic fibrosis.

"I hope she's okay. If you need anything, I mean if you want me to mind Willow at any time, just call."

"Evie's mother's staying with us. We're okay, thanks."

"*Evie's mum?* God help you."

"Not much choice," I muttered.

She toyed with the glittery strap on her daughter's shoe. "The police came around to have a chat with me. About Evie."

"I know. I gave them your address."

"I was frantic when I heard about her car."

"Yeah, I have no idea what's going on."

"I'm scared for her."

I bit down on my lip as a picture of Evie in that red dress flashed through my head.

Marla waited for a woman and her son to step past us then said in an almost whisper, "Aren't you scared?"

"Of course I am." My words came out louder than I meant them to.

The woman half turned back to glance at us. It was obvious this was no everyday conversation.

"The police officer was asking a lot of questions," Marla continued. "About you and Evie . . . and your relationship."

"Guess they've got to be thorough."

"I didn't know what to say. I had to tell her what Evie told me."

"No problem. The note says it all anyway. She wanted a break."

"Well, she *did* say a little more than that to me. People are starting to ask me questions, too. About everything. People saw the police turn up at my house. I've had to tell them why. I had no choice."

"Wouldn't want you to hold back." I was done with this conversation. Marla didn't have any news about Evie. She was just fishing for some gossip. She wanted to be the person who knew things that other people were desperate to know. No wonder I'd heard Verity refer to her as *drama llama Marla* years ago.

Nodding a goodbye to her, I walked outside. Spotting Willow near a tree right down the end of the playground, I made a short, sharp whistle. A couple of mothers turned around to me with disgust on their faces. I often called Willow and Lilly like that when they ventured too far away. It wasn't the first time I'd earned a disgusted expression for it. It was usually the stuck up mothers who you'd hear calling their brats with quiet, controlled voices: *Adorabelle Rose . . . Baron Kingsley . . .* Suburban princess women who lived in the new housing estates with the perfect lawns. They always looked as if they'd rust right through if they opened their mouths any wider and yelled. At least I wasn't as bad as the parents who swore like sailors at their kids if they didn't come running straight away. Kids called Nathan and Ethan whose parents pronounced their names as *Nayfan* and *Eefan.*

Willow sprinted to me. Princess Pout followed reluctantly, her arms crossed tightly, probably annoyed that it hadn't been her choice to end the play session.

"Time to go," I told Willow.

She fell silent on the drive home, finally bursting into tears as we reached the driveway of our house.

I twisted my head around to her. "Did someone hurt you today? Do I need to bop someone in the nose?"

I got a small smile, but it fell away as soon as it appeared.

"It's Mummy, right?" I asked her. "Because she's not here?"

She turned to look out the window.

"I'm sorry. But I can't do anything about that."

"You said she was coming back soon."

"I know. But it's only been a few days."

"Maribelle told me that Mummy's never coming back."

"What? Well, that's not right. Don't listen to her."

"She said she heard her mummy tell it to someone else."

I opened my mouth to let fly an expletive but jammed it shut just in time. "It's not true. Come on, let's go inside. I made jelly earlier."

In the living room, Lilly was sitting propped up on the sofa with pillows and blankets. She had the colour back in her face that had been missing for days.

With reading glasses askew on her face, Verity was asleep on the rocking chair Evie used to use for breastfeeding the girls.

I looked from Lilly to her sister. "Who wants jelly? Hands up!"

Lilly's arm shot up. Willow begrudgingly lifted her fingers.

Verity roused and gave me a brief, tired smile.

I set the girls up at the table with bowls of jelly and custard. Lilly refused the first plate because the jelly wasn't cut into cubes. I'd made the heinous error of simply scooping it out with a spoon. After correctly cubing the jelly, I took the rejected plate of spooned-out jelly and sat down to eat it with the girls.

With my first mouthful of fluorescent, fake blueberry–flavoured jelly, came a knock at the front door.

Verity half rose from her chair, but I held up a hand as I crossed to the door. The knock had that sound that only cops use.

It was Sergeant Moss again but with someone new. A woman named Detective Lena Devoe, with sharp eyes and a sharp cut to her blonde hair, stood beside her.

"Mr Harlow?" said the detective. "We have some matters to discuss with you."

"Of course. My kids are inside, so I don't want to do this in front of them. Have you found out something about Evie?"

"It would be best if you'd come down to the station, and we'll talk about it there. Can you have someone mind your children?"

"My mother-in-law is staying with us."

"Okay, good. Let her know and then follow us down."

My heart galloped upward into my throat as I told Verity. I drove down to the cop station, trying to figure out what was going on. Had they found Evie and she'd told them I'd hit her or something? *No*—wrong. As bad as things had gotten, Evie wouldn't make up shit like that. Hell, had they *found* Evie—as in found her dead? Who knew what kind of men she'd been with?

I walked into Detective Devoe's office barely keeping it together, sweat dampening the back of my neck.

"Please have a seat," offered Devoe.

Sergeant Moss sat on a chair at the side of Devoe's desk, watching me thoughtfully.

The detective didn't hold back once I'd sat myself down. "Mr Harlow, I'm afraid we found more items at the site of the burned-out car."

I nodded as I swallowed, staring hard at the floor, trying to buffer myself for what was coming next.

"We found your wife's handbag," she continued. "With her wallet and driver's licence inside. We also found her shoes and a phone. They were all a short distance away from the car, burned and buried."

I didn't speak. I couldn't speak.

Breath gone.

All of Evie's personal things?

Burned? Buried?

Detective Devoe waited for a response, but when one didn't come, she handed me a couple of large photographs. "These were taken at the site."

I stared down at the pictures. One of disturbed ground, only a shoe heel showing. The next photo of a half-burned phone.

"What about Evie?" My voice broke hoarsely as I glanced up at the detective and sergeant.

"Are you worried we found Evie there, too?" said Devoe softly. Too softly.

"You didn't, *right*? You didn't find her?" I was begging. As though, if her body was lying there, they could rewind time and make it not true.

"Our unit is still searching the area," Sergeant Moss told me. "If she's there, we'll find her. We've also hauled the car away for forensic testing."

I stared from her to Devoe. They hadn't found her. "Someone could have stolen her car, with her things in it. Sometimes she used to leave her handbag in the car by accident. Too busy running around after the girls." I was telling the story I wanted to believe.

Devoe gave a nod. "Yes, that's entirely possible. Although people don't normally go about without their shoes."

A slow panic stirred inside me. But I refused to believe Evie could be dead. Despite everything, I still loved her. I couldn't just switch that off. Why did the police sound so damned negative, like Evie's death—*murder*—was a forgone conclusion?

Devoe leaned forward in her chair, eyes intent on me. "We're shifting this to a missing-person investigation, with a suspicion of foul play." She paused. "Sergeant Moss and I went to see a neighbour of yours the day before yesterday. Marla."

"Marla told me."

"She did?"

"Yeah. Just this afternoon. At the daycare centre when I was picking up my daughter."

"Okay. Well, she seemed very concerned about Evie. She said that you both discussed the possibility of Evie committing suicide. Is that right?"

I inhaled slowly, remembering having that terrible thought. "Yes."

"And that was on Sunday?"

"Yes."

"Is there a reason you didn't contact the police at that point?"

"No. I just . . . I ended up thinking she wouldn't do that. I mean, her note said she was coming back in a week."

"That's an unusual note, Mr Harlow. We normally find that when spouses leave the family home, they don't give a return date."

"Well, *she* did."

"Marla was also concerned that Evie had been upset of late. She said Evie told her that you'd both been arguing."

"There wasn't anything out of the ordinary."

"You're sure?"

"Yeah, I'm sure. Anyway, what has any of that got to do with Evie's car being stolen and Evie nowhere in sight?"

"We're just trying to determine the circumstances under which she left, to help us better understand. It might be important. It might not." She stood. "Well, we'll be in contact when we find out more."

Panic was a cold ball sitting low in my stomach. Evie could be in danger. I needed them to find her *now*. If they couldn't, I needed to. Standing, I half turned to go then looked back. "Wait. There's something else."

Detective Devoe's eyebrows shot up. "Yes?" She gestured me back to the chair.

I didn't take the seat she offered. "The reason I didn't contact the police is because I found out why Evie left me."

"Please, go on," she said quickly, dropping all pretence of that slow, measured tone she'd used earlier.

"The day that I figured out that Evie left the girls with Marla, I had the stupid thought that Evie might be cheating on me. And so I checked her computer. I found out that she'd been . . . working as an escort." Those words were still hard to say out loud.

"An escort?"

"Yeah. That."

"I'm guessing that shocked you?"

"It shocked me a lot. It's not the only thing. She'd been gambling, too."

"Does your wife normally—?"

"No. Never. She doesn't gamble. We don't have enough money for it." Leaning my head back, I stared up at the bland ceiling. I glanced back at Detective Devoe to find her eyeing me curiously.

"How did you find out about the escort work, exactly?"

"There's a website."

"Could I have the name?"

"Sure. I can even show you the last conversation I had with her."

A frown rippled her eyebrows. "You had a conversation with her? And this is *after* she left you?"

"Yes."

"Okay, then, I'd really like to see that conversation."

Using my phone, I browsed to the companions website, then logged in. Evie's profile wasn't there anymore, but my conversation with her was still there, in the message folder of my profile. And there was a tiny picture of Evie beside each of her messages.

Detective Devoe quickly read through the messages. "Do you mind if I take photos?" She said this while taking out a camera from a desk drawer.

"Go ahead."

She snapped pictures of each screen, then she clicked on Evie's username, which took her to an error page. "You know, Mr Harlow," she said, "These messages could be seen as you stalking your wife."

My breath stalled. "What?"

"I'm afraid that pretending to be someone else and then making pleas to your wife to come back does appear to be quite harassing. This message in particular—the one with all the swear words—does seem quite threatening."

"You're not serious?" I exhaled. "Look, I shouldn't have sent the first lot of messages. But our kid was sick and in the hospital, and I was crushed that Evie read the messages and didn't care."

"It sounds like you were pretty angry with her." Devoe's bland expression contradicted her careful, prying tone. Sergeant Moss was quietly observing her, as if learning how the business of being a detective was done.

"Yes, I was angry," I admitted.

"Did you talk with Evie again after that conversation you just showed me?"

"No."

"You're certain of that?"

"Look, why all the questions? Why is this all about me?"

"Please don't feel that we're focusing on you. Our focus is on finding Evie at this stage."

I didn't believe her. "I want to help search the grounds. Near Evie's car."

"I'm sorry. At this point, we're not allowing any members of the public at the site. There might be important things there that we've yet to find. And we have to finish the collection of fingerprint and DNA evidence."

"I'm her husband, not the public. I haven't even been told where the car was found."

"I'm sorry," said Detective Devoe. "But we *will* keep you up to date. Is there anything else you'd like to tell us?"

I shook my head. "No. I don't even know if what I just told you helped anything."

"It helped us build a picture." She stretched a thin smile across her face.

Stepping around her desk, she showed me to the door.

I returned to my car, half raging and half terrified. The detective had been like a dog with a bone once I'd shown her my messages to Evie. But far worse were those photographs of Evie's things.

Where was she?

At least if she contacted me and I knew she was okay, she could go off and live her new life for all I cared. I'd find a way of going on with the girls.

Or did something bad happen to her, after all?

A cold sweat pushed through the pores of my head. I couldn't go straight home and let Lilly and Willow see me like this. I wanted to find Evie myself, but I didn't have a clue where to start. I'd already called every one of her friends when I was looking for the girls.

Driving too fast through the strangled cords of laneways, I headed towards the highway. I just needed to drive. *Think.*

THE THIRD CHALLENGE

33. EVIE

I WOKE WITH A SHUDDER, INSTANTLY wide awake and ready, my heart already racing.

Twenty minutes to midnight.

Not long to go until the third challenge.

I watched Ruth and Kara and the others rousing from sleep in the minutes that followed. They were like me, waking close to midnight in anticipation. Kara had completely recovered from her near drowning. She was just like she had been before—aloof and unwilling to talk.

When the bells rang out, my muscles tensed. I was a racehorse, waiting at the gate.

Three women I barely knew were up first, shouting to each other, their voices high and excited but edged with fear. Everyone pretended bravado in the day hours, but at midnight, all of that was stripped away. The last challenge had changed us. It hadn't been hard mentally—it had just been hard physically. The massive tank and the shock of cold water and pushing your lungs to their limit. And what had happened to Kara stained the challenges with an element of danger.

Footfalls echoed as the first team sprinted from the room.

For the second time, I was forced to wait my turn.

I told myself it was fair to have to wait. But the truth was, I didn't want *fair*. All I wanted was to win.

Poppy left in the first team and Kara in the second.

My turn didn't come until the number three was flashing on my wristband.

I was just with Ruth this time.

When I rushed with her out into the hall, the men who met us were Duncan, Harrington and a young Chinese guy named Hop. There were five of us in the team. Internally, I groaned at getting Duncan and Harrington on my team. Duncan wasn't helpful at all. And Harrington only seemed to open his mouth to complain. I didn't know Hop at all.

The mentors greeted us warmly in the garden, Brother Sage showing us to the third challenge room. "We hope the wait wasn't too much to bear."

"It was brutal," Ruth told him. "There better not be any water this time, or else!"

"No water." Brother Sage gave a thin chuckle. "You'll find that it's completely dry in there."

We walked into another dark room. It had no smell or sound. No hum of a water filter, nothing mechanical. Just silence. All I could see was the red glow of the light bulb below the clock display. The door clicked shut behind us.

Then, one by one, each of the six walls was illuminated—each wall bare but for a single mirror. They were very old mirrors, gilt framed. But instead of clear glass, the surfaces were dark. The room held the usual hexagonal prism in its middle.

I inhaled a relieved breath. Nothing dangerous here.

What was the puzzle here? What did we have to do?

I rushed for the prism first, tapping and listening and trying to twist it.

Hop came to help me. But this box seemed to do nothing. It stood there silently, giving up none of its secrets.

I had to stop thinking of these things as boxes that could do a specific thing. They were there to act in sync with the rest of the room and with us, each one different. The box was uniform in colour, except for six lighter triangles on top, their points all facing outward. A six-pointed star with a hexagon in the middle. Five of the triangles had the letter I inscribed on them, while the sixth triangle had a zero.

"Well," began Duncan. "It looks like they've given us some mirrors to figure out this time. Six of them. We'd better get started."

Hop shot Duncan an odd sideways glance.

Ignoring Duncan, I glanced across at the mirrors. The glass was of a dark hue but not black. There was nothing remarkable about them.

Ruth muttered under her breath, breathing hard as she marched past me, staring into each mirror. "This is just too weird. And it's creeping me out. I don't like looking at myself. At home, I don't even bother. Why do I need to? It's not like I need to constantly check that I'm me."

"Best to leave your emotions out of this, Ruth," Duncan gently chided. "This is a puzzle. A question and an answer. It adheres to the laws of logic. Okay, everyone, getting back to business, can you spot any differences between the mirrors?"

Ruth turned around, scowling. "Go look yourself."

Duncan straightened, looking confused. "It's more efficient if I direct things."

"For shit's sake, go direct yourself to the nearest—" Ruth started.

"Watch your language," said Harrington, hunching the shoulders of his tall frame as though bad words physically hurt him. "No one needs to cuss to express themselves."

"Has everyone finished telling me off?" said Ruth. "Because you know, if anyone else wants to take a shot, go for it."

Hop looked confused by the whole exchange. "I think we need to talk about the box." He pointed to each of the six symbols. "We've got five of the letter *I* and one *zero*." He looked back over his shoulder. "If the mirrors match the positions of the symbols, then the zero is pointing at that mirror straight across from it."

"Finally, someone with a brain." Ruth didn't step across to the mirror though.

I rushed over and attempted to peer under and around the frame of the mirror that corresponded to the zero. "It's fixed to some kind of bracket."

Ruth was suddenly behind me, aggressively twisting the mirror. "It kind of swings. What's the point of being able to do this?"

I worried she was going to break something, and then we wouldn't finish this challenge.

"Hang on," Ruth said. "There's something on the back of this bad boy. A painting." Wrangling with the bracket, she pulled it up to arm's length and flipped the mirror completely around. The bracket folded back flush with the wall and out of the way.

The painting, like the mirrors, was old, on a religious theme, in rich golds, crimsons and royal blues. It was a depiction of a terraced mountain, all of bare rock. Ladders stretched upward everywhere on the mountain, with monks on the rungs—demons flying around the monks. Clouds ringed the mountaintop, a golden crown emitting light. Everyday people occupied the lower levels of the mountains, being prodded off the edges by the demons and falling into deep water. Drowned people littered the water below. On the middle levels of the mountain, virginal-looking women were holding onto large metronomes.

"The artist was obsessed with the idea of people either going to heaven or hell, wasn't he?" Ruth remarked dryly.

"The monks here seem obsessed with a few things." Hop scratched his temple. "Ladders . . . water . . . metronomes . . . hexagons . . ."

"Does anyone happen to know the artist?" I asked hopefully. Hell, I knew nothing about art. I'd spent most of art history class consumed by very improper thoughts of Cooper Cadwell, who had stringy, dyed black hair and drew morbid pictures of abattoirs.

The other four shook their heads.

I cursed under my breath. "Damn. Poppy used to work for an art museum. But she's not here."

"But what is it supposed to be telling us?" Harrington knitted his thin eyebrows together so tightly they formed a single line.

"Isn't it obvious?" said Ruth. "The gold crown in the heavens is God and the demons are the tormentors of humans."

"Well, yeah," Harrington replied defensively. "But where's the puzzle? The mentors are really making this one too complicated."

"The letter *I* could also be the Roman numeral for the number one," said Hop, running his fingers across the box's surface.

"A series of ones and then a zero?" Ruth's face creased into a deep frown. "Like a binary set of on/off switches?"

Hop nodded. "Maybe. If so, then the mirrors are the *on* switches and the painting is the *off* switch. Or, if we're going to get religious, then it could have religious meaning. I've studied the binary system at university. It was Gottfried Leibniz who refined the binary number system in the 1600s. The system reminded him of the Christian statement, *creatio ex nihilo*, which means creation out of nothing. Leibniz believed the binary numbers unified belief in God. Leibniz was very interested in the famous Chinese *I Ching*. I studied Leibniz along with the *I Ching*. The sixty-four hexagrams of the *I Ching* can all be represented by the binary system."

"A hexagram is six-sided, right?" I asked, trying to plough my memory of the geometry I'd learned at school.

"Yes," Hop told me, pointing at the pattern on top of the box—the six-pointed star that I'd noticed before. "The *I Ching* hexagrams also correspond to yin and yang. Yin being a broken line and yang being an unbroken line. Or, you can also say yin is a zero and yang is a one."

"The number *one* could also mean God," said Duncan. "My wife is a born-again Christian." His left eye twitched at the mention of his wife. "I've studied up on her books, trying to understand what she believes. In the Bible, God means unity. The number one."

Ruth dragged her fingers through her hair. "No, that doesn't make sense here. Because then you'd have five gods and one non-god—the zero."

Duncan raised his eyes to the clock. "*Ten minutes to go, people!* I think we might need to try to flip the other mirrors."

Duncan seemed pleased with himself, but Ruth gave every appearance of wanting to punch him. But for once, he'd gotten us back on track. The talk of yin and yang and binary numbers hadn't gotten us anywhere yet.

Racing around, we—other than Duncan—checked the other mirrors. The other mirrors were firmly fixed to the wall. All they would do is to allow you to angle them slightly to and fro.

I hated to agree with Harrington, but he was right. This challenge was infuriating. There were no clues to lead the way.

The others returned to the hexagonal box to continue debating God and numbers.

I stood gazing into the dark surface of the mirror. I realised then that I could see a vague illustration of the same painting we'd seen on the other side of the sixth mirror.

Why was it there?

As I angled the mirror to gain a better view, the lamp below the mirror cast a harsh light across my face, and I caught sight of my features. The illustration of the mountains and caves formed a face that merged with mine. The caves of the paintings made hollow places of my eyes, and the tumble of boulders into the water made my mouth look like it was hanging open in a silent scream.

Revulsion washed through me, and my stomach twisted.

But I couldn't look away.

I'd suddenly been confronted by the real and raw me. *The addict.*

All my pain, and the pain I'd caused others, was here. I wasn't the wife Gray needed. I wasn't the mother my girls needed. I hadn't been the child that my mother wanted. My whole life, my mother had told me about all the things I was lacking. I was never *enough.* I could see it all, here, now.

"This is it," I said, my voice hoarse. "*This is it.*"

I heard Ruth call from across the room. "What?" She walked up to me.

"They just want us to look into the mirrors," I told her as I watched her reflection. "If you angle the mirror, your face . . . changes."

"Well, I'm not doing it," she stated firmly. "That's not a challenge. That's a—"

"Who are we to question what the challenges are?" said Duncan. He surprised me by walking up to the mirror adjacent to mine and adjusting it. Within a second, Duncan's body began trembling. "Oh, I don't like this. I don't like it at all."

Hop stepped up to a mirror next, moving it until he saw what Duncan and I were seeing. "I look like my father. In one of his black moods. Telling me I need to do better. Study harder. Put in more hours."

"He sounds like a charmer," Ruth remarked.

"That's the last thing he was," said Hop, his voice different, almost raspy. "He hung himself in the kitchen of our home. Every time we sit down to dinner, my family has that reminder of him."

We all fell silent for a moment.

"That's awful," I whispered to Hop. Twisting around, I cast a pleading glance at Ruth and Harrington. "Let's get this over and done with."

"How do we even know this is what they want?" Ruth gave a rigid, unconvincing shrug. "Maybe the mirrors are just there to distract us."

"This is plain ridiculous," agreed Harrington.

I wanted Duncan to do his usual and remind them to be team players, but he'd plunged into silence, absorbed by whatever his mind was conjuring from the image in front of him.

"Maybe," I said. "But we have to try it. Get over there before I have to drag you there myself."

Inwardly, I was jelly. I never ordered people to do anything. Even with Willow and Lilly, I was too soft and patient.

Ruth swung her head around to view one of the cameras up high on the ceiling. "Is this really what you mentors want? *This?* It's insanity."

She walked up to a vacant spot in front of a mirror. Angling the mirror, she stared down into it, muttering darkly. "Okay. This is it? Really? The mentors will have to try harder. They can't get me with this. I already confronted my demons, years ago. And you know what? My demons can go to hell."

But she fell into a sudden silence.

I returned to my own spot in front of a mirror. The skull-like sight of myself wasn't any easier the second time.

Harrington begrudgingly took a place by the last mirror. "It's a trick. I've heard of an experiment where a psychologist had fifty people stare at their own image in a dark room until they imagined they saw their faces change into different things. All fifty of them got weirded out. Half of them saw some kind of monsters. Here, they're just speeding up the effect with this stupid illustration. Because we don't have very long."

I heard soft sobs. Hop and Duncan.

"If I saw him again in another life," said Hop, "I'd kill him with my own hands." I knew he was talking about his father.

Duncan made strange, discordant humming noises, like he was on the edge and trying to stop himself from completely breaking down. "Amelia never loved me. She doesn't love me. She married me because she didn't have a better option. Do you know what it feels like to look at your wife and see only loathing in her eyes?"

Ruth grabbed her mirror, shaking it. "I've seen you before. I've seen you . . ."

"Who have you seen, Ruth?" I asked.

"The demon inside me," she answered, her voice wavering in and out like a radio signal. "It won't let me go. It's been with me since I was sixteen."

"Let it go now," Hop urged her. "Leave it in the mirror."

"It's too clever." Ruth shook her head, and her shoulders trembled as she clung to the mirror's frame. "I had my first daughter when I was sixteen. That's the first time I saw it, laughing and clinging to my back when I was giving birth to her. I was high on drugs and in the worst pain of my life. When I was nineteen, I had my second daughter. I lost both of them. They took them away from me. For fifteen years, I've promised them I'd get them back and finally be a mother. But the demon always gets me. Heroin always wins."

I looked sideways at Ruth. "I have two daughters, too."

Her jaw muscles were tight as she returned a glance. "Hold them tight."

"This is me, who I am," said Harrington. "No more or less. Everything bad I've ever done, I see it staring back at me. There's me as a kid, locking our dog in a dark cupboard because I was being bullied at school. I can still hear him whimpering. Man, that's confronting . . ."

"I hear you," said Duncan. "I was bullied all the way through school. Why they chose me to pick on, I'll never know."

"We think we're gods," said Hop in a hushed voice. "That's what this challenge is telling us. Like the symbols of gods pointing to the mirrors. We think we're masters of our own destinies. But we're not. We don't even know ourselves. We're not in control."

"It's in the numbers," I breathed. The image before me seemed to suck inward, as if it were breathing, trying to draw me in. I began feeling disassociated from my own image, the gaping mouth turning into a mocking smile. When I turned away, the reflection of my face remained in the mirror, watching me.

Above me in the mirror, I saw a light change colour. I turned. The bulb below the clock had changed to green.

I could hear the breaths of relief around the room, but those breaths were ragged, conflict etched deep on everyone's faces.

This challenge had wiped me, confused me, picking me up and dumping me in a dark place. I was repulsed by myself, wanting to peel my own skin off and destroy the image I'd seen in the mirror.

There had been nothing to solve in this challenge. The challenge had been to see inside yourself.

I felt as if the ground beneath my feet were no longer solid.

34. CONSTANCE

MY PLANE TO LONDON TOUCHED DOWN in the early hours, just before dawn. Five in the morning. I dragged myself through the airport feeling lost and dazed—I was a terrible long-distance passenger. The long span of airport windows showed a bleak, rain-soaked day. Not the English summer I'd pictured.

I wished James was here. He'd deal with everything while I got myself together. He'd tell me what I needed to do. But I didn't have time to get myself together.

Here in the gloom and darkness of a strange country, sitting on the cold seat of a cab, I finally admitted to myself what I'd never been able to admit before. James was a father figure to me. That was what he'd always been. I had nothing else in the way between myself and that truth now. There was nothing here to hide behind—no charity dinners to attend with James, no shopping trips with Kara, no contractors to direct in maintaining our house and grounds, no useless knickknacks to buy.

Yes, James was a father figure. He directed me. That sounded odd, but it was comforting. My own father had never been a real father. There'd been no comfort in him. He'd been—still was—a bitter alcoholic prone to rages. James never raged.

Otto had been a bit like my father. Except that it was drugs instead of alcohol that made him so unstable, and I'd always felt that he loved me.

Otto, with his long hair and swagger and motorcycle, had been a complete separation from college life—one that I'd run towards. Everything with Otto had been a frenzy, even the simplest trip to a river for a swim. Because he'd insist on us swimming in that river naked at midnight. One night, we'd stolen a boat, jumped off overhanging tree branches into the black water and had sex on the river bank with willow leaves lapping our bodies. At the time, it'd seemed like we did things no one else did.

In a way, Otto had directed me, too. Everything had been so spontaneous, I hadn't noticed. But it had been Otto's wild imaginings I'd been swept up in, never my own.

Why did my thoughts keep returning to Otto?

I had a vision of myself in this cab, chasing Kara like some faded, aged shadow of her. As if I were actually here chasing my youth or some part of me I'd lost.

This trip was threatening to destroy the life I'd built.

The sun rose while the cab drove to my hotel. The weather grew impossibly bleaker, rain streaking across the windows.

The hotel room was better. Decorated in a style I called *cheerful chilled.* Lots of understated yellows and creams and muted greys. The room smelled of Italian coffee.

I showered and changed then tried to grab an hour's nap but failed. Whatever mechanism in my head needed to kick into gear in order to put me to sleep was malfunctioning. I washed down three Promaxa with a glass of water that tasted awful. Still, I couldn't relax. I tossed and turned on the hotel bed for the next five hours until it was time to meet Rosemary.

Rosemary wanted us to meet at a café. When the clock ticked around to ten in the morning, I combed my hair and stepped down to the foyer to call a cab.

The café was on Old Street, Central London. The cab driver pulled up outside a cosy-looking coffee shop. I wound my way through bicyclists and stroller-pushing women to the café and went to order myself a coffee.

I sat and waited. I hadn't seen Rosemary in person—not even a photograph. There were no pictures of her offered on her website.

A woman who'd just bought coffee and cake at the counter wandered through the shop looking for a seat. She sat next to me. "It's silly weather for July."

I nodded automatically. "I thought it would be sunny."

"I hope you're not too disappointed." She placed two bags of bread and fruit on the seat opposite, just like any of the women who'd been shopping around town this morning. "How are you, Constance?"

It was the first indication that it was Rosemary—the private investigator.

"Oh, it's you," I answered in surprise. "I'm fine. Just tired."

She wasn't what I expected. She was ordinary. She was the woman you passed in the grocery aisle who looked slightly frazzled and a bit worn around the edges. I'd expected a bit of glamour, someone who matched with the deep, quick voice. Even her name didn't seem a match. Instantly, I worried that she wasn't the real deal. This slightly frumpy woman couldn't find my daughter.

"Long flights are never much fun," she said. "Do you feel like eating? A slice of cake? The butterscotch tart looks quite good. I should have chosen that instead of the sponge. The cream tends to give me more trouble than what it's worth."

"No, thank you. I'm not much of a person for cake. Anything savoury, I'm first in line."

"Count yourself lucky. This sweet tooth of mine is a curse." She stirred her coffee. "I only just manage to keep from blowing up like a balloon." She glanced at a cyclist riding past. "At least I do that—cycling. I quite like riding about. It relaxes me. Ah, cycling and cake—the perfect balance. Do you ride?"

"Sometimes. Only with James—my husband. I'm more of a jogger."

"You do have a runner's body."

"Thank you," I said, though I wasn't sure if it was a compliment or just a statement. More than one friend had unkindly called me a *stick* due to my lack of curves.

"So, you've been to London before?" she asked.

"My fifth visit, I think. All the trips were for my husband's work—he has a lot of business here in the UK. I love London. There's so many interesting little pockets to lose yourself in."

"Yes, lots of pockets. That's a good description. My wish is that we find your daughter quick-smart and that the two of you are soon off exploring some of those pockets together."

I found myself panicking at the words *wish* and *we*. I wasn't interested in wishes. And this wasn't supposed to be a team effort between Rosemary and myself. She was the expert, and I was relying on her.

"I hope so." Swallowing a mouthful of coffee that burned my throat, I glanced away at the markets and busy foot traffic of the unfamiliar street.

Rosemary finished her cake. It'd looked so sugary it made me feel ill. A jetlagged, upset-stomach kind of ill.

"Are you all right? You look a little peaky," she said.

"No, I'm okay. Is there anything you'd like me to do today? I'm under your direction."

There. I'd made sure I'd established our relationship. We weren't a team. There was no *we*. I was contracting her to carry out a job. And I expected her to do it.

"I'm afraid you look like you're about to drop," she said. "When you've rested, we'll talk again and determine which direction we're going to take. For now, I'll tell you what I've learned." A wrinkle formed in her forehead. "Wilson Carlisle didn't accompany Kara here. He's still in Australia. I've done some more digging on the historical society that he's a member of. I'm not saying it has anything to do with Kara or where she is, but it *is* intriguing. So intriguing that I can't believe it's been under my nose for all these years that I've been working as an investigator. I've asked a couple of history professors that I know of for some information—they're a husband and wife who live in Athens. It appears the society has a connection with an ancient order. Well, either it's connected or the society *is* the order but doesn't want it known. I don't know which."

"What kind of ancient order?"

"I'm uncertain. The name I've sourced is Yeqon's Saviours."

"*Yeqon*? Sounds Arabic?" I said politely, wondering where she was going with this.

"It's from the Bible. As the Bible tells it, a number of angels were sent down from heaven to watch over humans. They were called watchers or Grigori. A ringleader named Yeqon led them into temptation, and they became fallen angels. This order appears to be using Yeqon's name. Which is a somewhat unusual choice."

My eyes darted about the café. This wasn't the usual cake-and-coffee conversation. No one could hear us, but still, it made me uncomfortable. This wasn't what we were supposed to be talking about. Was Rosemary slightly crazy? Or did she purposely invent wild stories for every client instead of actually working on the case, just to use up more hours and make more money?

"That's all interesting," I said. "But if it's unlikely to involve Kara, then do we need to pursue this?"

"I pursue every avenue in a case, Constance. Turn over every stone. It's why I've been successful. I used to take on infidelity cases. Cheating husbands and wives. There was only one case in which the person was mistaken about their spouse. In all the hundreds of other cases, I confirmed the person's fears and found out all the awful details. And the way I did it was to look into all the things that you mightn't think important. Things that other investigators had overlooked." She sighed. "At times, I think my client wanted affirmation that their wife or husband wasn't cheating. But then I had to tell them that their initial suspicions were right. I decided I no longer wanted to take on those cases."

"I couldn't even imagine giving someone that kind of news." I thought of James and how I'd never once suspected he was doing anything like that. "If it's okay, I'd rather just concentrate on where Kara might have gone. Sorry if I'm being blunt. This ancient order thing sounds very off-beat. I'm sorry if I sound anxious. I just—I *am* anxious."

"Of course you're anxious. Okay then. I've been running my usual skip-tracing process on Kara, but I will let you know that it's not the easiest thing to trace someone who's travelling through countries."

"Skip tracing?"

"That's just what investigators call the tracing of a missing person that's done over the internet and telephone. People very often leave a digital footprint that you can follow if you know where to look." Her forehead dented into a deep, triangular frown. "It does make it difficult if the person doesn't wish to be found. Kara doesn't appear to have used her social media accounts in many weeks. I've checked a number of escort websites, but I can't find Kara on any of them. Perhaps escort work is not among her reasons for coming here. Is there anything else at all that I can go on? What about Kara's university roommate—Paige?"

"The police tracked down Paige. Paige says she doesn't know anything about where Kara went. There's just one other person. A woman named Evie Harlow. It was Evie's husband who found Kara on that *companions* website. Evie knew Kara." I explained in detail about Gray and Evie.

"Would I be able to contact Gray myself?"

"I'm not sure. It was pretty awful last time I spoke with him. He was in the hospital with his very sick little girl."

"That's not good about his daughter. But the best chance we have of finding Kara is to move quickly. Would you mind trying him again? To see if he's heard from his wife yet?"

"It's probably the middle of the night over there—"

"It's about eight at night in Sydney right now," she cut in. "A perfect time to catch people. If it's not a good time, you can just apologise and hang up."

"Okay. I'll try." The coffee soured in my throat as I brought up Gray's number and called him. So far, my intrusions into his life had happened at the worst possible times for him.

This time, he answered in a tired, lost kind of tone. "Constance?"

"Yes, it's me. I'm so sorry to bother you, Gray. How's your little girl doing?"

"I've brought her home. The news wasn't good for her ongoing health, but we're coping."

"Oh no. I'm so sorry." Rosemary nodded at me, urging me to ask the question. "I hate to ask, but have you heard from Evie?"

"No." A flat, decisive *no*.

"Oh . . . okay. Well, I hope you do very soon."

"The cops found Evie's car."

"Her car?"

"Yeah. All burned out. And some of her things, too, buried in the ground."

My hand flew to my mouth. "*God*."

The calm expression in Rosemary's eyes switched. She made a revolving gesture, telling me to stay on the line and keep him talking. I understood. My instinct was to end the call and leave him in peace, but Rosemary wanted as much information as possible.

"Oh, Gray, that doesn't sound good," I managed to say.

"No, it's not good. I don't know what the hell is going on. The police won't let me go out there and look myself. They won't even tell me where. Some bushland area, apparently."

"And someone went to the trouble of burying Evie's things?"

"Yep. Her wallet and phone and shoes. All of them burned, too."

"That's terrible."

"You've got that right. How about Kara? Anything?"

"No. No trace. But I found out that she flew to England. The Darling Harbour police told me. I'm here now, in London, and I've hired a P.I."

Too late I noticed that Rosemary was shaking her head.

"Wish I had the money for one of those," he answered.

Gray was in such a bad place that I could sense the weight and strain in every word he spoke. But I needed to finish the call quickly now. I'd said the wrong thing and I didn't know how to fix it. I said goodbye and told him I'd call him if I heard from Kara.

I raised guilty eyes to Rosemary. "I'm sorry. I didn't think—"

"It's all right. I should have told you. It's just a habit of mine to keep everything as private as possible. Please don't tell anyone else about me."

"I won't. I haven't even told my husband. But that's because he'll fuss about me going ahead with anything. He worries about my . . . state of mind. I've been on antidepressants for a long time. Many years."

"We all have our crosses to bear. I'm glad you have someone who takes care of you."

For a moment—and only a moment—I glimpsed a piece of the person Rosemary must be. I guessed she lived alone and didn't have anyone taking care of her.

She sighed. "Sounds like things aren't going in a good direction for Gray's wife. I heard you say her things were found buried?"

"Yes." I recounted what Gray had said to Rosemary.

"Oh dear. Do the police have any idea who might have done that? Was it an expensive car? An insurance job perhaps?"

"No, I can't imagine it would be an insurance job. These people are dirt poor. From the look of Gray's car, it can't be worth more than ten thousand dollars, and I'd imagine Evie's isn't worth much more."

"Really? Hmmm, I wonder if the police checked if Evie left the country."

"I'm thinking she couldn't have if her wallet and phone were found? I'm assuming Evie would now be a missing person in the eyes of the police, so they'd check all that, wouldn't they? They did for Kara."

"Yes, yes, you're quite right. They would." Her eyes clouded. "Well, let's hope Gray didn't have something to do with his wife's disappearance."

"I didn't think of that. Oh God, I hope not."

"In my previous career, I was a detective. It was terrible how many times the culprit was the husband. Too many times."

"I first met Gray on the day his wife went away. He seemed genuinely distressed."

"Angry, too?"

"Yes, angry. He'd only just found the note she'd left him."

"I might do some investigating myself, seeing as Evie had some connection to Kara."

"I'm glad that Kara did leave Australia. After what happened with Evie's car. I mean, I just feel better that she's a long way from there."

"Understandable."

"So, you used to be a detective?"

"Yes, don't look so surprised."

"I just—"

"Because I'm not a big, burly man? I was with the police for fourteen years all up, eleven as a detective. I left a little over ten years ago, just after the accident. You see, my husband and daughter were in a boating accident."

"Oh no . . ."

"My husband drowned. My daughter, she was revived . . . but she never regained consciousness. I left the police force on compassionate leave. I never went back. My daughter hung on for years in a coma. Seven years. Then she died. She was twenty-one."

"I'm so sorry. That's tragic."

She nodded in reply. "I didn't know what to do with myself after she was gone."

"Is that when you became a P.I.?"

"Not long after, yes. I was offered a short stint as a private investigator by a former colleague—he also used to be a detective. It filled in the hours. Gave me some kind of purpose. I have a lot of contacts from my former profession. And I know what to say and who to talk to in order to find things out. I always did enjoy that aspect of police work. Putting all the pieces together and finding the answers. And so I decided to reinvent myself, giving myself a new name and going full-time into the P.I. business."

"Rosemary Oort isn't your real name? I thought your family might be Dutch or something."

She gave a brief, sad laugh. "No. I grow rosemary in the little memorial garden I made for my husband and daughter. And as for the last name, it's after the Oort cloud on the edge of our solar system."

"That's sweet, about the garden. And I didn't know there were clouds hanging out there in space."

"It's not so much a cloud. After the sun and planets were formed, there was leftover rubble. The rubble assembled itself into a spherical shape and remained there. That's what they call the cloud. I felt that way at the time—that my husband and daughter had gone on to form celestial bodies, and I was the rubble that was left behind."

"Yours is certainly a name I'll never forget."

"I don't normally tell clients any of what I just told you. But I look at you, and I can see hurt and sadness in your past, too. I thought you might understand."

I wanted to cry. But this wasn't the place to cry.

She was wrong about me though. Apart from losing track of Kara, my life had not been terrible. I'd lost Otto, but he'd been on a self-destructive track ever since I met him. No, my life was pretty wonderful. It *was*, right? Apart from my silly, middle-aged depression, I had a charmed life. A life I'd be returning to soon.

I felt a bit of a phony, because here was Rosemary, and she was the real deal.

My former reservations about her slipped away. She was exactly the person I needed in order to find Kara. Of all the things I'd gotten wrong so far, she was the one thing I'd gotten right.

35. EVIE

RUTH STORMED FROM THE THIRD CHALLENGE room. The challenge had been tough on everyone but especially on Ruth.

Out in the garden, the mentors stood abreast. The cool, damp air hung over us oppressively as we went to shake their hands.

I wanted the night done and the morning sun spilling in again.

"How did you all go?" asked Sister Dawn.

"You know how we went," said Ruth flatly.

"The mirrors are not an easy challenge for anyone except for those with the unmarked mind of a child." Brother Vito cast a look of sympathy at Ruth.

"You're damned lucky I didn't smash those mirrors." Ruth walked away and into the monastery.

"It was a cheap challenge." Harrington eyed the mentors with a haughty expression. "What is making people feel bad about themselves supposed to achieve?"

"I'm sorry you saw no value in it," said Brother Vito. "Well, you should all go wait in the library so that the next group can start."

Harrington swung his lanky frame around and headed after Ruth. Duncan and Hop went next, Duncan hunching as though he were being hunted.

I lingered. "Will there be any more challenges like that one?"

"No. You'll find that the challenges are all quite distinct," Brother Sage replied.

"I know that counselling services didn't form part of the program," I said, "but everyone's feeling a bit raw. Maybe everyone needs a bit of . . . debriefing or something."

"Thank you for letting us know, Evie," said Brother Sage. "We'll offer something in the morning. But for now—"

An echoing scream from inside the monastery broke through the conversation.

A man's scream.

Stunned looks passed among the four mentors.

"Stay in the garden!" Brother Sage instructed me before whirling around and running towards the cloister.

Within seconds, I was completely alone in the dark garden.

With the walls looming high all around and the sound of the scream still in my ears, the garden seemed like a dangerous trap.

I'm not staying here.

I rushed to the cloister, too.

As I entered the interior, a second scream travelled through the hall.

Ruth and Harrington and Duncan and Hop all seemed to come running from different directions.

"Wait." Hop panted a couple of sharp breaths. "Hear that? In the dining hall."

A bottle—or something—rolled along the floor on the other side of the wall.

Without another word, the five of us ran along the hall to the refectory door.

A gasp fled my lips. On the stone floor inside the doorway, a dark trail led to the kitchen, illuminated by the lamps in the hallway—*blood?* A waxy darkness shrouded the kitchen and the rest of the refectory.

"Who's there?" Ruth demanded.

A man burst from the kitchen, his eyes wild, his monk's robes rippling as he crashed past us.

My mind spun. Whose scream had we heard? This monk or another man?

Instinctively, I knew the answer.

Ruth ran into the kitchen first.

Tentatively, I stepped after her.

A narrow sliver of light exposed a man slumped over a chair, two knives wedged deep into his back. Foamy blood trickled from his mouth onto the floor.

Saul.

The man was Saul.

We inched closer, like children who'd just discovered a terrible yet incomprehensible thing.

Harrington pressed his fingers against the side of Saul's neck. "No pulse."

"I don't think it's possible to survive that." Hop gestured towards the knives, his voice stained with fear.

The sound of gunfire rang out, the first bullet pinging from the stonework but the second bringing forth only a dull sound.

I froze. Who—?

Then, Brother Sage yelled out, "*Vito!*"

The sound of feet running. Lots of feet.

My heart slammed against my ribs. What was happening out there? Who had the gun?

Everything turned quiet.

A woman's cry ended the silence—Poppy's. Suddenly there were lots of voices at once.

We headed out of the refectory and into the hall.

The mentors and challenge participants were gathered in a semi-circle around a fallen man—the monk that we'd seen. The monk was lying face down, blood oozing from a dark bullet hole in his temple, the back of his robes bearing a strange symbol—a ladder inside a hexagon.

Brother Sage had a gun in his fist.

"Saul's dead." Harrington indicated back towards the refectory. "Stabbed."

"Saul? *Oh, fuck . . .*" Poppy held a hand to her mouth, shaking her head in horror. Her team would have been in the library when Saul screamed. The last team would have just been released from the dormitories, ready for the challenge. Poppy and I exchanged terror-stricken glances.

"*No . . . Oh* no . . ." Brother Sage inhaled sharply, his eyes shocked as he gazed at the figure on the floor. "I hoped this man hadn't gone so far as to hurt anyone. He came at us with a knife. He had blood on his hands, and we knew he'd done something terrible. I had no choice but to shoot him."

Brother Vito and Sister Dawn rushed away into the refectory.

Richard pushed his way to the front of the group to get a better look at the dead monk. "Does anyone want to explain why Saul was even still here?"

Sister Rose shot a look of confusion at Brother Sage before turning to Richard. "I can't answer that. Saul was meant to have left the island hours ago."

"We need to find out why he didn't," replied Brother Sage grimly.

"More to the point," said Ruth. "Can you explain why one of your monks turned into a killer?"

"He doesn't belong to the monastery, Ruth. I've never seen him before." Dropping to her knees, Sister Rose examined the man's cloak. "What *is* this? This symbol?"

Brother Sage peered over her shoulder. "I don't know. But I have an idea. I've heard of a group that have an unhealthy obsession with monasteries, going so far as to dress as monks and trying to infiltrate the silent orders." Bending, he placed a supportive hand on Sister Rose's shoulder then took her hand and helped her rise from the floor. "They're quite mad," he added in his haughty English accent. "But I've never heard of them carrying out a murder."

Brother Vito and Sister Dawn walked back into the circle, their heads down.

"Yes, poor Saul is indeed dead. Five stab wounds to his back," Brother Vito confirmed quietly.

Ruth stared at the hexagonal symbol on the killer's clothing. "So, there could be more of these crazies here?"

"I'm not certain," said Sister Rose. "But I have the terrible thought that one or more of them might have posed as our monks to take Saul on board the boat. That could explain why he never left the island."

"What about the other ones of us that went with him?" cried Yolanda. "Does that mean they're still here? Maybe they got murdered, too."

"We need to find out if they returned to the mainland, post haste," Brother Sage told her. "There is another possibility. Saul might have thought that he could stay here and persuade us to keep him on in the challenge. He might have left the boat, unseen, and tried to steal back into the monastery, where he unfortunately came across the person who killed him."

Duncan folded his arms, tutting. "That does sound like the most likely theory."

"What's that supposed to mean?" Ruth fixed an intense glare at Duncan.

"It's just a question of morals," said Duncan. "Saul was a sex addict, after all."

It surprised me to hear what Saul's addiction was. I hadn't had a chance to get to know the quietly spoken puzzle box hobbyist.

Ruth's expression grew fierce. "And that makes you think you're better than him, Duncan? That you have better morals?"

"I think we'll end the speculation there," said Brother Sage. "We have other matters at hand. Until the monastery and grounds are thoroughly searched, I can't declare this island safe. I'm afraid you're all going to have to leave."

The group fell into a thick, shocked silence.

Sister Rose shuddered, rubbing her arms as if she were cold. "I can't believe any of this has happened. It's time to call in the police." She pushed her hand into her pocket. "My cell's back in the dorm. I'll use the library phone."

Richard walked straight up to her. "If you call them—the police—they'll have to interview us, won't they? I mean, we"—he gestured around at us —"are all witnesses. Two people are dead here. There's going to be an extensive investigation."

"Yes, of course." Sister Rose shook her head slightly as though she wasn't following.

Suddenly, I wanted to vomit. Not just because of Saul but, shamefully, for myself. I understood exactly what Richard meant. This whole thing was going to be splashed across the news. Everywhere around the world. And the reasons why we were here would be exposed.

Gray would find out everything about me. And my mother, my friends and everyone I knew. Immediately, I hated myself for thinking that way while the blood of two men was fresh on the stonework.

"Forgive the solipsism," said Richard, "but we were guaranteed privacy. My parents don't have the barest clue about my gambling habits, and I want to keep it that way."

"We're deeply sorry," said Brother Sage, looking across at him. "But this is nothing we could have anticipated. We'll do our best to keep it low key."

Richard just stared at Brother Sage before throwing back his head and bursting out laughing. "Low key? It's murder in a damned monastery. And a group of addicts undergoing a series of weird challenges as treatment. The media are going to go apeshit over this. I'm leaving. *Now*. Give me my money, and I'll get the hell out of here."

"If you wish," said Brother Sage. "You've completed half of your challenges, and we'll stay true to our word. You'll receive half of the payment."

"That seems fair." Duncan nodded around at the group. "Does everyone agree that seems fair?"

"I'm staying." Ruth's eyes were distant. "I want to stay to the end. I'm not letting this change things for me."

Richard cast Ruth a look that was almost menacing. "To hell with that." He turned back to Brother Sage. "This whole farce stops right here. We came here in good faith in the expectation that if we got to the end, we'd get our full amount of money. Well, you guys failed to keep us safe. One of us is dead. We're in danger of another one of us getting killed. Therefore, the right thing to do is to end the program now and give us the full amount."

Brother Sage pulled his thin lips in tight and small. "I'm afraid we're not going to be able to do that. It's not a reasonable thing to ask."

"Why not?" Cormack pressed. "Richard's right, as much as I hate to admit that. You know, the first morning that we were here, Richard told us that the reason everyone doesn't get through to the end is because you'd have to pay out too much money. Sending people off the island is just an artificial bit of gobshite. Well, circumstances have changed, and we should be compensated."

"Our budget is our budget, I'm afraid." Sister Rose's voice weakened under the glare of Richard and Cormack. "We're involved in lots of charity work. We don't have any additional funds allocated for this."

"Then maybe we should go by need," said Duncan. "Some of us require those funds more than others. If we all state our situation, maybe we'll get somewhere with this. I'll go first. My alcoholism cost me my job and my house. And then my wife told me she wants a divorce. My kids don't even want to know me anymore. I deserve a new start."

Cormack shot a questioning look at Richard. "You go next. C'mon, fat cat, 'fess up, then. You don't need the money."

"We're not going by *need*," Richard retorted. "That wasn't the deal we were offered. Who the hell here is going to start listening to Duncan? He's background noise at best."

Cormack grabbed Richard's shoulder. "You claimed you were here for the treatment. Not the money. Well, the treatment's done with. And you don't need any of the money. Do the right thing and leave it for the people who need it. Tell them. Tell everyone how much money Richy Rich is making."

Poppy moved in between Cormack and Richard, her eyes wet and reddened. "He doesn't have to tell anyone anything."

Richard's shoulders slackened under Cormack's grasp. "I'm not Richy Rich. The mentors know exactly what I am. When they—"

"You don't have to tell anyone your background, Richard," Sister Rose cautioned.

Richard's features twisted. "No, it's time I told the damned truth. When Sister Rose found me, I was living in the water channels under Las Vegas. Surviving on garbage scraps. In case you don't know, there's a system of rat-filled drains underneath Vegas that are taller than your head. A ton of people call them home."

Poppy's eyes filled with fresh tears. "You lived in a drain, baby chin?"

Nodding, Richard chewed on his lip. "Doesn't rain much in Vegas, so you're usually okay. But when it rains hard, you get flooded. All your stuff gets washed away. Sometimes people don't wake up in time or they're too drugged up to stand. They get washed away, too, and they drown. I saw quite a few dead bodies down there."

Cormack dropped his hand from Richard's shoulder but not without giving him a sceptical look. "So, what's with the high-roller stories?"

"Force of habit." Richard looked away. "I've been drip feeding my parents fake stories about myself for over two years."

"Maybe it's time to come clean with them?" suggested Poppy. "Maybe they'd give you some help?"

Richard snorted. "I might not be rich, but my parents are loaded. My father threatened to cut me out of my inheritance if I don't follow the script. My older brothers are both hot-shot lawyers, and it was expected that I'd become the same. Me pretending to be some kind of wealthy entrepreneur isn't making him happy, but at least it's been holding him off. But once this whole monastery thing hits TV screens across America, it's all over."

Ruth crossed her arms tightly. "Okay, enough of these true-life confessions. No one cares. Brother Sage, nobody except for us and you mentors know about the program. Why don't us challenge participants leave the island while the police are here and then return later? You could just say that Saul requested to come here on retreat or something. This way, we don't tarnish a dead man's name. He has a family who don't know about his addictions."

Sister Rose fumbled as she threaded her fingers together. "I do see your point, Ruth. We did guarantee you all your privacy. But I'm at a loss. We couldn't foresee this terrible set of events. But we can't make the situation worse by attempting to cover anything up. Also, you've forgotten that there are monks here. They certainly won't agree to lie to the police."

"I will sue the pants off every one of you if you go ahead with this," said Richard to the mentors. "Because if this goes public, I'll have nothing to lose."

I knew it was wrong—because we *were* here, and that made us part of what happened to Saul—but I couldn't make myself speak up. Maybe right and wrong wasn't so black and white. It was right that Saul's addiction didn't get splashed across every news outlet just because he had the bad luck of getting murdered. I knew exactly what the reporters would do with a story about sex addiction. And his wife and kids would bear the brunt of it. Saul's murderer had been caught and killed. Justice was already served.

Brother Sage's expression grew taut. "I'll meet you halfway. We will be informing the police of what happened here tonight. When the police arrive, we will tell them that you are here on retreat and that none of your names may be released to the media, nor may any photographs of you be released to the media. We will also inform the police that none of you witnessed any part of the discovery of the victim or the subsequent shooting of the murderer. We'll be asking the police to search the monastery and grounds to ensure that it is safe and that there are no more of these monastery invaders. Our program will continue, as planned. We have an entire day until the next challenge round."

Duncan clapped his hands together. "Sounds like a good plan. Is everyone happy with that?"

"Shut up, Duncan," said Ruth. "And yes, I'm happy. We just need to make sure everyone sticks to the same story." She shot a stern look at each of the challenge participants. "Anyone who doesn't stick to the story has to leave immediately and doesn't get their fat cheque. *Capisce*?" She turned to the mentors as if for affirmation.

Brother Sage gave a nod. "We're sticking our necks out for all of you. We'll expect you to play your part. The most important thing now is for everyone to remain safe. Everyone must return to the dormitories and remain securely locked inside."

"Wait," I said hesitantly. "I told Brother Vito about noises I've been hearing since the first morning. I thought it might be rats. But now I'm wondering if it was this man. We've seen someone at night in the halls. And that first morning, I even thought I saw eyes watching us . . . through the walls . . ."

People looked at me as if I was ever so slightly off my rocker.

"We'll make sure the police do a thorough search tomorrow," Brother Vito assured me, a placating tone in his voice. "The monks did a search for rat droppings but found nothing. It seems it was this person all along. He must have stayed out of sight when they were looking."

"Off to get some rest now," Sister Rose instructed us. "You'll be safe in your beds."

We were herded to the dormitories, Poppy reaching for my hand and gripping it tightly.

My throat felt dry and swollen, as if I'd been screaming ever since we'd found Saul. But I hadn't screamed at all.

Ruth and Harrington walked the hall together, a little in front.

"At least we're through the third challenge," Ruth was saying to Harrington. "Done and dusted. When I understood what the challenge wanted of us, I gave it the performance of my life."

Harrington snickered. "Yeah. Not hard to make people believe you're really feeling that shit."

Ruth swivelled her head around slightly, catching sight of me and then falling silent.

I felt burned. She and Harrington had just been *acting* in the challenge room? And now they were both crowing about it straight after we'd found Saul dead.

My skin prickled with cold beneath my monastery clothing.

Far away in the hills, a raucous chorus of peacocks started up.

36. GRAY

VERITY TOOK WILLOW AND LILLY OUT to a park for some fresh air. She was treating them to a special lunch at a restaurant after they left the park. She seemed to be relishing her time with them. For all the strange and annoying things about Verity, she actually did love Willow and Lilly. Shame she was so harsh with Evie, because that was bad for Evie and also meant she gave Verity a wide berth. The girls had largely missed out on bonding with their grandmother.

I grabbed my chance to go sit in my back shed and smoke a bag of Joe's weed, cigarettes and cold beer on the workbench beside me. I hadn't smoked a cigarette in months, but still, I'd picked up a packet.

I knew this was me running away from everything. I didn't want to do this every time things turned to shit, but I did. My friends who used pot didn't binge like I did. I'd been hiding the binges from Evie.

I'd been a heavy drug user before I met Evie. Not just pot but everything I could get my hands on. I'd hated myself at every step, following in my parents' footsteps. Evie had given me a different direction.

I leaned on my knees, head down, blowing smoke onto the dirt-crusted concrete floor.

It seemed like there was something I was supposed to be doing right now, something about Evie. But I didn't know what the hell it was. Maybe

I'd beg Verity for money and go searching for Evie. But where would I start? Where would I go?

Evie, where the hell are you?

A hundred possibilities flashed through my head.

37. CONSTANCE

I NEEDED SOME NEW CLOTHES. I'd packed warm gear for the Sydney winter, but I hadn't anticipated heading off to Europe. The London summer had produced a sticky, hot day. The grey rain of yesterday had been a ruse.

Leaving my apartment, I wandered down to the streets, looking to buy shorts and a couple of tank tops. I sweated horribly in the heat.

Young people moved in groups along Southwark Street, laughing, bumping each other, checking phones. High on life. The girls wearing tiny shorts and halter tops. The boys proudly shirtless. Backpackers, probably.

What was Kara doing right now?

If I could just *see her*, all this could end.

I found myself heading into a set of crowded food stalls. Scents of spicy Indian curries and Spanish paella. A sign proclaimed the area as Borough Markets. My first instinct was to about-face and flee.

But there was no point in doing that. Kara could be here.

I let myself thread into the crowd of people.

This was the London I'd loved on my previous trips. For minutes, I lost myself, buying earrings for Kara and myself, cute summery scarves and a couple of second-hand books to read back at the apartment.

Rosemary hadn't set me any tasks to do. I was free to keep wandering. I trusted that she was hard at work doing whatever it was that she did. I decided the best way of spending my time was to walk the streets in case Kara was out there somewhere today. It was the tiniest of chances, but at least it was something. Waiting in the apartment wasn't going to help anyone.

I peeled off a long-sleeved top and jeans in the changing room of a clothing store and stepped into a pair of khaki shorts and a black tank top. I didn't understand the sizes, so I'd just picked up what I thought would fit me. I knotted a multi-coloured summer scarf around my neck and put on the earrings. Looking at myself in the mirror, I felt mentally lighter.

I paid for the new gear then headed back out onto the street, tossing the old clothes in the trash. A trendy health-food stall advertised thirty-six different types of juices. Wheatgrass and kale and beetroot and exotic fruits I hadn't heard of. I ordered their Liver Zinger. I didn't ask what was in it. I didn't much care about the taste of things. It was the nutrient value that mattered.

I kept walking, through the markets and on to the music and song of several street buskers, muffled by the beeps and grinding brakes of the busy London traffic.

My phone buzzed inside my tote. Juggling the drink and the bag of things I'd bought for Kara, I fished out the phone. Rosemary's number was displayed on the screen. "Yes, Rosemary?"

"Hello, how are you?"

"I'm just out getting a few things. Not sure where I am now. I was on Southwark Street. All so incredibly busy!"

"Yes, you've arrived in peak tourist season." She paused for a moment. "Constance, I have a little bit of news."

I steeled myself. News could mean anything. It could be something extremely bad. "I'm listening."

"I'm not sure whether Kara's in the UK at all."

"What?" I stopped still, the light feeling I'd had earlier instantly vanishing. "Then . . . where?"

"I'm not certain. I've had a busy night and morning. It's Kara's close connection with Wilson Carlisle that's been concerning me the most. I don't know what his game is. And because I don't know, I'm pulling out all stops. The sooner we locate Kara the better. The fact that he had a young girl like Kara living with him tells me quite a bit about him. He might have been grooming her, gaining her trust. Let me explain further.

For the past few years, a great deal of my work has been in locating trafficked persons. Very young persons, I might add. From age twelve upwards. There are groups trafficking from the Balkans and former Soviet Union to London and Greece and other countries within northern Europe. And I—"

"You think Kara's been trafficked, don't you?"

"I honestly don't know. I'm not jumping to that conclusion."

"We need to go to the police. Get them in on this."

"Constance, please. I'm afraid there's nothing for the police to act upon yet. And it's not always a good idea to go in blindly. I'm afraid that I suspect a small number of people of high rank—police and politicians and others—of either turning a blind eye or having some involvement in certain shady activities. And sometimes, when you expose one of these bad apples, you lose all paths to your target. As a detective, I had that unfortunate experience. To put it simply, sometimes, exposing flaws means closing doors."

"Okay, I'm jumping the gun. But it's simply not like Kara to have anything to do with someone like Mr Carlisle. Something very wrong is going on."

"Look, there's a chance Kara could have just decided to go travelling. This whole thing might be nothing to do with Wilson or any other shady character. But, as I said, I've been monitoring trafficking pathways for years. And to that end, sometimes I'll take photographs of missing persons down to airports and docks. And so I did that with Kara's photograph."

I realised I hadn't let Rosemary finish what she was telling me before. "What did you find out?"

"I found out that Kara was seen boarding a private flight to Greece."

I hesitated, swallowing. "Are you sure it was my Kara? Not just another young blonde girl?"

"I showed them several photos, of different girls. I pretended to be looking for all of them. That's a method I often use. I know exactly what police would say. I just let them think I'm a plainclothes detective. Two of the staff members picked Kara out. And also, one heard her speak. He said she sounded like Blanche from *The Golden Girls*. That's the right accent."

For a moment, I let myself luxuriate in that thought. Kara had been *seen* and *heard*. Proof my baby girl was alive. I prayed she was okay. But the thought of her being trafficked was terrifying. "Where in Greece? Did they know?"

"Athens. But Constance, we can't be certain she's there. We don't know if she went somewhere else after that. This was days ago."

"It's the best we've got. We have to go there. *Right now*." I tossed my drink in the trash. "Should we go together or separately?"

"It could be a wild goose chase. I need you to remember that. Tracing people takes time, especially if they haven't put down roots anywhere. But yes, I'll be travelling there today. We can go together. It makes for a better cover to have two women travelling together. Dress touristy."

"I'm all ready to go. I bought clothes this morning."

"Wonderful. Then pack up your things and meet me at my hotel room. Room 2416." She gave me the name and street of the hotel. I committed them to memory. "Don't tell anyone where you're going."

"Yes, of course."

"There's something else."

"What is it?"

She hesitated. "The workers at the airport—one of them also identified Evie Harlow."

"*What?*"

"I know. It doesn't make sense. But he was certain."

"Why did you have Evie's—?"

"Remember you gave me her name yesterday? I looked her up online and then printed out photographs from her social media accounts. It was to cement her face in my mind in case I spotted her in any public photographs taken of Wilson Carlisle in Australia. To see if she has a connection with him, too. I didn't intentionally add her photograph to the pile I took with me down to the airport. I just needed a variety of girls. But one of the workers identified her."

"What if he just wanted the money you were offering?" I said dubiously.

"Of course that was the first thing to cross my mind. But he also correctly identified Kara, and he was also the one who correctly told me what her accent was like. He also said that Evie came the day after Kara. Which matches up with the timeframes."

"Is that enough? Did he hear Evie speak?"

"No. But he did describe a bracelet she was wearing. He remembered it because it was unusual. It was a silver chain with charms of tiny swords and war hammers."

"That *is* distinctive. I'll call Gray and ask him to confirm the bracelet."

"Constance, no, I'm sorry. You can't tell Gray. Or anyone. Not yet. Obviously, this is going to become a police matter at some point, at least in terms of Evie. Maybe in terms of both Evie and Kara. But I need a bit of time. Right now, there's no firm proof. I want something solid before we go to the police with this."

I felt like such a total beginner. Putting my foot in it and making mistakes. Rosemary was right.

"I'll see you soon," she told me and hung up.

I rushed back to my hotel and up to my room.

Where did Gray's wife fit into this? Had she faked her own murder and then gone off overseas? Had she and Kara met up somewhere in Greece? Nothing was making one iota of sense.

I'd been to Greece with James on his business trips. But really, all I could claim to know of it was a resort pool and some monuments. James had been off at his meetings while I'd basically stayed at the hotel. Greece was quite a few degrees more foreign to me than England. The difficulties rose in magnitude. There was also the nagging thought that Kara didn't want to be found.

I GAVE the cab driver the name of Rosemary's hotel.

The driver pulled up outside a modest hotel—at least, modest in comparison to the grand, vintage hotel opposite, even though it rose higher than the vintage hotel. I paid my fare, dumping some cash into the driver's hand and letting him figure it out. Pounds totally confused me. If he swindled me, I wouldn't know. There was a time that being swindled would have bothered me, but those days were long gone. I didn't need to count my dollars now.

I called Rosemary so that she could come down and meet me, but she didn't answer. Perhaps I was meant to go straight up. I tried the elevator, but it wouldn't budge. Apparently, I needed a keycard from the reception desk in order to operate it.

Deciding that I couldn't be bothered with that, I took the stairs. I was fit enough. At least, I thought I was. By the fifteenth floor, I was puffing and sweating profusely, my hands wet on the metal stair bannister. Now I had nine more floors to go. I dragged my feet up each stair, cursing myself that I wasn't doing more hill runs. I made a mental note to add hill runs to my schedule.

I stepped out onto the twenty-fourth floor. Snatching some tissues from my bag, I dabbed at my face. Rosemary had asked me to look like a tourist, and I did—just a sweaty, dishevelled one with her hair stuck to the back of her neck.

The halls were stuffy and narrow, the carpet worn, everything boxed in. I took a breath of air-conditioned air that didn't seem to have enough oxygen in it.

I located room 2416 in the rabbit warren of hallways. The door was slightly ajar. I knocked. And knocked again.

Perhaps she was in the shower and left the door open for me.

Would it be bad etiquette just to enter? Would she accuse me of being *American* if I did that?

Opening the door fully, I stepped inside.

God, please don't let me surprise Rosemary as she's walking naked out of the shower or something.

The room was empty, the decor as dated as the corridors.

"Hello? Hello?" Tentatively, I walked through and tapped on the half-open bedroom door. "Hello?"

I pushed the door open.

A scream rushed from my lungs.

Rosemary was here. On the bed. Blood all around her. Throat cut. Blood soaking into her white shirt and making thin trails into the waistband of her skirt. Her skirt was pushed up and her underwear gone.

I backed away, horror flashing in my mind. There was nothing I could do to help.

The taste of bile soured my mouth as I reached the elevator. I couldn't make it move. Fingers fumbling, I jabbed at the elevator emergency button.

"Hello" came a female voice. "Are you experiencing an issue?"

"Help . . ." I forced my suddenly rasping voice to work. "She's dead. *She's dead! Oh God . . .*"

38. EVIE

THE POLICE CAME AT DAWN.

They took the bodies of Saul and his murderer away. In the monastery scriptorium, a detective grilled each of us in turn about the events of the night before.

Poppy stepped out into the garden with red, weepy eyes from her police interview. "Poor Saul. I just can't believe this happened to him. Doesn't seem real."

Brother Vito appeared and told us that the police had requested we wait outside the monastery walls while they searched the monastery and grounds. We were led out through the gate and onto the hills, where the peacocks scattered in surprise at the intrusion.

Far below, a police boat chugged around the entire island, checking the perimeter.

I walked the hills with Poppy, Richard and Cormack, the sultry breeze lulling me into a sense that things would be okay despite what had happened last night. Even Richard and Cormack had completely mended their differences after Richard's revelations about living in the Las Vegas drains.

Beyond the bare hills, the island displayed vegetation and a small river.

"Found the vineyards." Cormack shielded his eyes from the sun. "Way over there."

We continued on to the vineyards.

Dark grapes weighed down the lines of carefully cultivated vines, the splatter of ripe grapes on the ground immediately reminding me of the blood I'd seen last night. I turned away.

"What a setup." Richard whistled. "They should open up some kind of tourist operation here. Who wouldn't want to come and stay at an authentic old monastery and taste the wine made under a Greek island sun?"

"Complete with monastery murders," quipped Poppy, still sniffling and dabbing at her damp eyes. "No thanks."

"That was a bit of bad luck," said Cormack. "But see it as an adventure. Something to tell the grandkiddies about. You know, like when you're very, very old and the most fun you've now got is to shock the family."

"Are you planning on having lots of grandkiddies, Cormack?" asked Poppy playfully. "Maybe with Kara?"

"Hell no," he answered. "Not me. No kids, no grandkiddies. When I'm old, I'll be buying a motorcycle and travelling the world. I'll write my story in chapters, on the walls of public bathrooms. And my story will be that outrageous that eager fans will follow from bathroom to bathroom, from country to country, until they reach the end of my story. And there they'll find me, dead at some road café. With a pen in my hand and a smile on my face." He smirked. "And the keys to my bike thrown where no bastard is ever going to find them. And the bike will remain there forever as a memorial. To my last stand on the earth."

I laughed, glad that Cormack was distracting me from my thoughts. "I'll read every word."

"What are you going to write about our time on this island?" said Poppy.

Cormack seemed to think for a moment. "I'll write that we were warriors."

Richard pulled a mock scowl. "Man, you go on with a lot of shit."

Cormack winked. "But it's good shit."

"I'll tell you what's good shit," said Richard. "And that's the monk's wine. And I bet they're holding out on their really good stuff. We've got to find a way to get into the good monk's wines before we leave this place."

Poppy gave one of her trademark giggles. "Yeah, let's get drunk as skunks on the monks' finest wine."

"Not now," said Cormack. "When this is over. I'm not putting up with any hungover bastards in the challenges. And we're down to sixteen people now. That's only four in each group."

"I hope I get you three in my group tonight. That's if the challenges are still going to run." I squinted at a series of teeth-like objects that topped a nearby hill to the left. "Is that a cemetery?"

"I love old cemeteries," cooed Poppy. "Let's go look."

We made our way up the craggy hill to the set of graves. The hill fell away at the summit to a sheer drop, the sea rushing in over rocks far below. The tombstones were cracked, with vines snaking through the cracks and covering the weather-worn inscriptions. I tried pulling away some vines, but none of the inscriptions that I found were legible. The stones had been out here too long.

"They certainly didn't bother looking after these graves," I remarked.

"You're right there," said Cormack. "Damned shame to let history go like that. Probably a wee bit too hard to tend the graves out here though. It's a bit wild and woolly. Probably fierce winds in winter, too."

Ruth stomped past us as if she owned the hills. Something about her always seemed kind of savage.

"I bet she'd push you off the edge if you looked at her the wrong way," said Richard darkly, echoing my private thoughts. "I still don't trust her. I stick by my theory. The mentors are using moles to keep a watch on us."

"Haven't you ever heard of a technobabble thing called cameras?" Cormack raised his eyebrows at him. "They're already watching us in the challenges."

"Yeah, okay," Richard replied. "But if there's one thing I'm good at, it's numbers. I wasn't lying about my gambling stories."

Cormack gave half a shrug. "If you're so good with numbers, why didn'ya figure out that gambling wasn't making you rich?"

Richard's expression grew strained and defensive. "I just had a run of bad luck. For a few years. It started when my boyfriend—*the bastard*—just up and walked out on me one night. I fell into a black hole with the black dog. Then I found out Jack had taken all the money I'd stashed away. I couldn't pick myself up after that."

I winced. "That would have added insult to injury."

"Yeah." Richard shook his head woefully. "Shows that you can't trust anyone. Everyone's just out to get you."

"Squeezy hug." Poppy wrapped her arms around him and smacked a kiss on his temple.

Sister Dawn appeared on the hill opposite, waving at us. "You can all come in now. The police have finished. We'll have a meeting in the garden in an hour."

"Where did she pop up from?" Cormack shoved his hands in his pockets. "Well, guess that's us then. We can get out of this blessed sun. Ruining my delicate Scottish complexion, it is."

"Play you a game of pool," said Richard. "And I'll flay the pants off you again. Figuratively."

Poppy yawned. "Didn't catch a wink last night. I bet none of us did. Going to go have a nap."

"I'm gonna stay and poke around the graves," I said, staring out to the ocean. I didn't want to go back to the monastery just yet, not if I could help it. Being out here in the open was a welcome reprieve.

"If you find out anything creepy, be sure to tell me." Poppy winked at me just as she turned and stepped away with Richard and Cormack.

I pottered around the graveyard until they disappeared from view and then walked towards the ocean. On a high outcrop stood the crumbling chapel I'd seen the first night I'd arrived here. As if drawn to it, I headed up the incline. The chapel, made of stone, had survived the centuries, but none of the interior furnishings remained—if there'd ever been any. The windows were just open spaces, with no indication there'd ever been glass panels fitted. It seemed like somewhere just to kneel and pray and be alone. Wooden steps led up to a small stone altar. A long, fraying rope hung from a brass bell that had developed a greenish patina. I wondered if anyone ever used it.

Closing my eyes, I breathed the salt-tinged air, trying to make myself believe I was standing on the beach with Ben. My parents would be making lunch in the holiday house, the constant boom of the ocean like a brain-washing chant calling Ben and me to it.

A sudden voice behind me made me flinch. "What do we have here? A little lost goat on the mountaintop?"

Snapping out of my daydream, I wheeled around.

Ruth stood in the chapel doorway. "Wasn't everyone told to go back?"

"I chose not to." I wasn't going to give her an explanation.

“Better take better care. You’ve seen what can happen to people who are alone and not where they’re supposed to be.”

Suddenly, I wished I hadn’t stayed out here. I hadn’t calculated being alone with Ruth on the edge of a mountain or trapped by her inside the chapel. She’d seemed different in the third challenge. But it had all been pretence.

Before I could answer, she shrugged and headed away, humming a tune.

39. GRAY

LILLY LET OUT A BLOODCURDLING SCREAM. I took two stairs at a time up to her room to find out that Willow had hidden her dinosaur in retribution for Lilly throwing her iPad.

I was too strung out to apply any parenting methods, instead ordering each of them to bed. I hadn't sent Willow to day care today because I didn't want Princess Pout telling Willow any more nasty stories. I didn't know if Marla knew the latest news about Evie, but I wasn't going to risk it.

But now, I had both of the girls home twenty-four-seven. With Verity telling me I was doing it wrong at every opportunity. A physical therapist had taught Verity and me how to do postural drainage and percussion on Lilly's back and chest—but naturally, Verity didn't trust me to do it right. Truthfully, I didn't trust myself. I didn't ever want to see Lilly that sick ever again.

Collapsing onto my bed, I tried to grab a quick sleep. Lilly had woken three times last night with night terrors, and I felt waves of exhaustion moving through me. Lilly had always had night terrors, only it was usually Evie who got up with her during the night.

The ring tone of my phone sounded, muffled under the pillow. Twisting around, I fetched it.

Constance.

She was calling again? What did she want? Updates?

Well, I wasn't interested in giving her updates.

I went to switch the phone off when a text message from her popped up. *Gray, we need to talk! It's urgent!*

She was exaggerating—surely.

I spoke a guarded *hello* into the phone.

"Gray. It's going to be difficult to talk where I am right now, but I need to tell you some things."

"Okay?"

"Look, I'm at a police station. In London. I can't talk for long. You know how I told you I hired a P.I.?"

"Yup."

"She's dead. Murdered."

"Hell . . . That's rough."

"It's awful. Really awful. I found the body. But I need to tell you what she found out. She found out that your wife came here, to England, and then went to Greece."

I sat up bolt straight. How did *your wife* and *England* and *Greece* fit together?

"Gray," she said, "did you hear me?"

"I don't get what you're saying."

"Rosemary showed Evie's picture to some airport staff in London. They identified Evie. She was here a few days ago."

"Evie doesn't even have a passport."

"I don't know how they got her out, but it seems that they did. On a private aircraft. She was seen here, Gray."

"They? Who is they?"

"I don't know. Rosemary had something to tell me about that. But now she can't. I'm all alone with this now."

"You said you're at a police station? Tell them all you know."

"That's the problem, Gray. Rosemary said there are people in the police force who we can't trust. She also said it's too soon and we need to find out more first, or the doors that are open now will be slammed shut. She was a detective and then a P.I. for years. I trust her judgment."

"Look, I don't know why your P.I. was showing Evie's photo around, but the people who said they saw her were mistaken. I think you must be upset because of what happened to your investigator and—"

"*No*. Of course I'm upset, but you have to listen to me. There's one thing more the crew member remembered. When he was guiding Evie onto the jet in London, he saw her bracelet. And he remembered it because it had tiny charms of war hammers and swords and things on it. He thought that was strange for a woman."

The muscles along my spine pulled tight. "I bought her that bracelet. Only a couple of days before she left me. She'd seemed really down, so I bought her something to try to make her laugh. I'd forgotten about it . . ."

"Gray, listen to me. This is real. This is happening."

Constance's sharp voice pulled me back. But was the bracelet enough proof? I didn't know Constance's P.I. and what she was all about. Something flashed through my mind. The bracelet hadn't been found at the site of the burned car.

I exhaled a tightly held breath. "I don't understand who would go to all the trouble of getting two women all the way from Australia to Greece. I know what Evie and Kara were involved with, but still, there must be thousands of women in Europe these people could have picked instead. And how did they get Evie and Kara to go along with it?"

"I don't know the answers," she said. "Maybe these people blackmailed them. Or threatened them. Look, please don't tell any of this to the police yet. I can't talk long, but I'll be in contact again soon. I've bought a new phone, and I need you to take down the number. Don't tell it to anyone. Buy a new phone yourself and don't call me on anything but that."

"Okay, I will." Constance sounded so different. I wrote the number down with a stub of one of Lilly's crayons, my head whirling with everything she had just told me.

"I'm frightened," she told me. "I'm certain Rosemary was killed because of what she was trying to find out. She was worried that Kara was being trafficked. It's possible that both Kara and Evie are in the hands of traffickers."

I let out an expletive. "Traffickers?"

"Yes. Or worse. In our first meeting, Rosemary mentioned a strange group named Yeqon's Saviours. It's possible they have a connection to this. She wasn't sure. The man my daughter's been with is apparently a member."

Browsing on my phone to an internet search engine, I began typing in the name. "Y-e-q-o-n?"

"Yes."

I had a quick search, but all I found was mumbo jumbo about fallen angels.

"Gray, I have to go. The police want to talk with me again."

The line went dead.

Wheels slowly revolved in my mind.

Evie had been gambling and dabbling in escort work and trying to make money. Someone could have offered her an incredible gig, some kind of work she could do in a week and come home again. Someone rich enough to get her out of the country without a passport. It all fit. Maybe it made a crazy kind of sense after all.

And if she'd been busy with a special gig, then it explained why she'd been too busy to meet up with random men from that *companions* website. That conversation still bothered me. There was nothing of Evie in that conversation. Like she'd suddenly turned into someone else.

A sudden thought pushed in. *What if it wasn't really Evie on the other end of that conversation?*

I recalled the crime scene that the police had shown me in the photographs. Evie's personal effects had been half buried, not buried in the way someone would bury things if they seriously didn't want those things to be found.

I held my head in my hands. *Evie, you sure left behind one hell of a mess.*

I jerked my head up again as Verity's voice pierced the air. She was standing in the door frame. "Detective Devoe and Sergeant Moss are at the door."

I nodded at her.

Running my hands through my hair, I checked that the girls were still in their beds and then headed downstairs.

The faces of the police were deadpan serious.

"Did you find out something else?" I asked.

"Yes," replied Lena Devoe. "We'd like you to come down to the station to give a statement. I tried to call, but your phone was busy."

"Yeah, I—" *No, don't tell them about the call from Constance.* "You want a statement from me? Why?"

"Please come down, and we'll discuss it there."

It wasn't hard to tell that they hadn't found Evie, but they'd obviously found out something that made things look bad for me. But I needed to ask the question anyway. "Have you found out where Evie is?"

"No, I'm afraid we haven't yet located her," said Devoe.

"Do I have to come down to the station?"

"No, you don't have to come," she said. "You're free to refuse at this point."

"You make it sound like I soon won't be free to refuse. What's going on?"

"We can't discuss that here." Devoe took a step back, as though she fully expected me to do as she'd just asked.

I glanced back at Verity, and she gave me an anxious nod.

I might as well find out what they knew.

Grabbing shoes and my wallet, I walked out the door to my car. And drove for the second time to the police station.

When I walked into Devoe's office, there was a pile of objects lying beneath a sheet of plastic on top of her desk.

"Sit down, please, Mr Harlow," the detective instructed.

I sat.

Devoe and Moss didn't sit. They arranged themselves near the items.

"Do I have your permission to record this session?" Devoe asked me.

"Record away," I told her.

She cast a steely look at me. "First, I need to tell you that you don't have to talk to us. You have the right to stay silent. And any statements you make might be used as evidence against you."

"Hell, I'm getting *that* speech. You're actually giving me *that* speech."

"It's just procedure, Mr Harlow."

I eyed her directly. "Fine. Go ahead."

"You're sure? You can get a lawyer before you talk to us, if you wish."

"Just . . . get started. You've hauled me down here, and now I just want this over with."

Thoughts ran haywire through my head. A dead investigator. Evie in London. Evie in Greece. The string of online messages that were nothing like Evie . . .

"Okay. I'm about to start recording." She pressed a button and then repeated her Right to Remain Silent speech. "Do you understand and want to proceed?"

"Yes."

"Okay, first thing I need to ask before going any further is a routine question. Are you under the influence of alcohol or drugs?"

"No. None of the above."

"Have you had either of those today?"

"No."

She snatched the sheet of plastic away from her desk. I didn't need anyone to explain the items to me. *They were bad.* A dirt-encrusted rope, a knife and thick tape.

Panic rippled through my stomach. Had someone hurt Evie after all? But then Evie's online messages slipped back into my mind.

Evie didn't send me those messages.

Whoever it was, it wasn't her. It was someone who knew nothing about my wife. I was being set up in every which way.

"Okay then," Detective Devoe continued. "We have three items on the desk. A length of rope, some tape and a knife. Do you recognise any or all of those things?"

I studied the items. "Yes, I do."

"Can you tell me who they belong to?"

"They're mine."

"Are you certain?"

"Yes. They're normally in our garage."

"You said they're normally in your garage?"

"Yes."

"Okay, now can you tell me where we found these things?"

"I'm going to take a wild guess that you found them at the place where Evie's car is."

"Did you put them there?"

"No, I didn't."

"Can you tell me how they got there?"

"No."

"No? Even though they're your things?"

"That's right."

"Mr Harlow, you don't seem surprised that these items of yours were found at the site. They were buried, just like Evie's personal things. Why weren't you surprised?"

Wherever Evie was now, she was still wearing the bracelet I gave her. She didn't throw it away in disgust. That meant everything.

"Mr Harlow?"

"I don't know why they were there."

"That's not what I was asking. I'm a little confused that you don't appear concerned that these particular items were found at the site. A rope? And a knife? Those are some very concerning things to find, wouldn't you agree?"

"Yes. I don't really want to think about it."

"What don't you want to think about?"

"*She's my wife.* I don't want to think about anything bad happening to her. I hope you can understand that."

"Did you know these three items were missing from your garage?"

"No, I haven't been out there. I've been busy looking after my daughters. The youngest was in hospital this week."

"I'm sorry about your daughter. Let me go over everything we have so far. It seems that your wife was afraid, which fits with her leaving you and with what Marla told us. We've seen you pretending to be someone else online in order to find out where she is. And now we've found your rope, knife and tape at a site where we suspect that Evie came to harm."

"That forms quite a picture." I didn't need her to spell it out any clearer.

"Mr Harlow, do you know what happened to Evie?" she said.

Sergeant Moss glanced from Devoe to me, raising her chin and pretending hard that she wasn't holding her breath.

"No. I don't. Can I leave now? You said I didn't have to be here."

She crumpled her shoulders, deflating a little like she'd been pricked by a needle. "Yes, you're free to go. We would like to get a bit further with this, though, and—"

I stood. "I've answered your questions and now I'm done."

"Okay then. Please do stay local. Let us know if you intend going away. We might have important findings to tell you about."

She was suddenly friendly again. A distant kind of friendly.

They thought I'd done something to Evie. I would have sounded even guiltier if I'd started raving on about the whole thing being a setup.

There was one thing I was sure of. They were moving close to an arrest. I didn't know whether talking to them had bought me some time or made it worse. It'd probably made it worse.

Far worse.

Hell, I could probably be arrested on the answers I'd given. I'd admitted to those things being mine. And apparently hadn't shown an appropriate amount of shock.

I walked out without another word and sat behind the wheel of my car, my heart banging away in my chest. The people who were involved with this, whoever they were, were dangerous. So dangerous Constance couldn't go to the police and tell them about what she knew. They'd killed her investigator without a second thought. Evie was in danger. And Detective Devoe was moving close to arresting me.

Things dropped into place.

Evie had been desperate to make some money. But she'd trusted the wrong people. Either she had no idea that Lilly had been sick, or someone was preventing her from contacting me or coming home. And Kara was somehow mixed up with the same people.

Nothing else made sense.

Now that I knew where Evie was, I had to go find her. But I only had a few hundred bucks in the bank now. Maybe less. Not even enough for a plane ticket.

It was an insane thought. People like me didn't go charging off around the world to search for a missing person. I wasn't like Constance with all her money and no responsibilities. And Lilly needed special care.

I wasn't even going to be able to look after my daughters if I got arrested. My girls would lose both parents.

Everything was closing in on me. I had to figure out my next move —*fast.*

40. CONSTANCE

I SAT STIFFLY IN THE CHAIR the detective offered.

"Mrs Lundquist," said the London detective, "we've been busy trying to put together a picture of Lydia's last hour. I—"

"Who?" I asked.

Detective Chief Inspector, Michael Hurst—a blonde, long-faced man in his mid-forties—seemed momentarily confused before nodding. "The victim's name is Lydia Garner. You knew her by her working name."

"Oh. Can we call her Rosemary?"

"Yes," he said gently. "We can call her that. Okay, we've been able to gain access to the security footage of floor twenty-four. The footage shows a maintenance person heading in and out of Rosemary's room about twenty minutes before you arrived."

"Could you identify him?" I breathed, sitting forward.

The DCI sighed. "I'm afraid he wore a cap down low over his face—and no, they couldn't identify him. We know that he's Caucasian, about six foot two and a large build. He entered a bathroom on the next floor down, washed off a knife and changed into everyday clothing. We can be pretty certain that this is our guy. We're running searches on sexual-assault offenders that are a match."

"You think it was a sexual assault?"

He looked at me strangely. "We won't have the lab report back for a while yet, but it seems apparent that something of a sexual nature occurred. Her underwear had been removed. Do you have reason to think it's something other than that?"

I opened my mouth to argue, but then I heard Rosemary's voice distinctly in my mind. *Don't tell the police more than you need to.*

"Of course," I said. "I just keep seeing all the blood and the terrible gash in her throat, and I—"

"Very understandable."

"I hope you can catch him quickly. Poor Rosemary. She didn't deserve this to happen to her. She was doing so much good. Finding missing people. We need more people like her in this world."

"Can you tell us more about that? You said you contracted her to search for your daughter?"

"Yes, Kara. She vanished while studying in Australia. Sydney police told me that she'd caught a plane for London."

"And Rosemary was attempting to locate her?"

"Yes."

"Hmmm, can you tell us anything that might help? Is there a possibility your daughter was mixed up in anything such as prostitution or drug running?"

"I don't think so. No."

"Well, there's a possibility that Rosemary was investigating something that triggered the murder. Or the man could have been a thief looking for cash or jewellery. The sexual assault—if it did occur—might have been just an afterthought. Of course, it's all speculation at this point."

He studied me thoughtfully. "We discovered two phones belonging to Rosemary. One of them was completely destroyed. We believe that Rosemary destroyed it herself, possibly at the time the intruder accessed her hotel room. Would you happen to know what she was using it for? It could help greatly in our investigation."

"I'm afraid I don't know anything about that."

"Well, do let us know if you remember anything during your conversations with Rosemary that was unusual in any way."

"I will."

"And Constance, there's a concern that this person might come after you, too."

"Do you think so?"

"There's a possibility. But what we can do is offer you a secure place to stay."

"I'll be all right. Maybe I'll even return to America," I lied.

"We might need to interview you further. You were the last person to have contact with Rosemary before she died. We really do need you to stick around." The DCI levelled his gaze. "Okay?"

"Yes, I'll do that. I'll pick a hotel that's a bit away from where I was staying before. I doubt anyone would be able to find me."

"Well, the offer of a police guard is there. Call us if you get worried. We'll do what we can to find your daughter." He smiled briefly, and I knew it was his turn to lie. He had a murder investigation on his hands. A teenager who was tripping around the world was not his concern.

"I'd appreciate that."

"We'll let you know when you can return home. Your husband's been on the phone with us, demanding you return to America," he said dryly.

"James was worried even before I travelled to the UK. He's probably getting a bit frantic now." James never actually got frantic. He had two modes: either calm or demanding. Mostly, he was calm. You knew things had gone haywire when James got rattled.

I left the police station, suitcase in hand. I'd been all ready to head off with Rosemary. Now, I didn't know where to go. I could ignore the detective and head off to Greece on my own. But I didn't have the barest clue where to go or what to do when I got there.

When I reached a park, I sat myself down. A series of shivers passed along my body in spite of the warm day. The police had suggested I see their recommended counsellor. *Seeing someone with their throat slashed was bound to be traumatising*, they'd told me. And it was, more than I could articulate. I kept seeing that image of Rosemary over and over. But I couldn't return home to James's arms. Not yet.

Rosemary Oort was not going to die in vain. She'd spoken about many things to do with the people that Kara might be involved with. And the strange historical group. I just needed to pick up the threads.

The old self-doubts came galloping in. *I couldn't do this by myself.* My whole life, I'd never really given myself permission to trust myself. I'd always let someone else take the reins.

Had it really taken me getting to the age of thirty-eight to realise that the people who took the reins were just more confident than I was? *Yes, it had taken me that long*. Other people weren't really any wiser than me. They just jumped on the horse and took the reins.

Kara was completely different to me. She made her own decisions, and she followed them through. She didn't second-guess herself. So like her father. That was why she'd been so bull-headed about coming out to study in Australia. Once she'd made her decision, I knew there was no turning her away from that path.

I wondered what Kara thought of me? *Weak?* Could she and I ever meet in the middle? Or would our relationship continue to wear thin? I knew parents who never saw their offspring once they'd grown. The thought of that was almost too much to bear.

Black and white ducks waddled across the grass to a murky pond, the first of them jubilantly flicking water about once they'd plunged into the pond. A group of backpackers cycled past, narrowly missing the ducks.

In that moment, I recalled my conversation with Rosemary in the café next to the bicycles. She'd been in contact with a couple who lived in Athens. A husband and wife who were both history professors. That couple should be my next port of call. Rosemary had been very interested in what they had to say—and I should be too, because if Rosemary had found something compelling about it, then it was worth investigating further. Even though I'd found talk of the ancient society all so strange.

There was nothing I could do for Rosemary now.

I had to steal away from London and fly to Athens.

41. EVIE

THE MENTORS GAVE THE CHALLENGE PARTICIPANTS a briefing session in the garden. They informed us that Saul's body was being taken home to his family.

The police had found out that Saul's murderer had come here on his own, arriving in a small boat—possibly before any of us had even arrived—and concealing himself. He was Italian, a man who'd belonged to one of the monastery-invading groups that Brother Sage had described, but they'd recently thrown him out due to odd behaviour.

The mentors told us that challenge four would be going ahead as planned tonight. At the end of the talk, any of us who felt they needed a counselling session were invited to attend the scriptorium and have a private chat with Brother Vito.

Poppy, puffy eyed from both her nap and crying, was among the group that wanted a counselling session.

I chose to find a quiet place in the garden where I still had glimpses of the sky. I needed to keep hold of the world outside the monastery, even though that desire seemed irrational when I'd only been here for five days.

The only view of the outside was of the sky and distant hills. There was no view to the ocean from the monastery grounds—the walls were too high for that.

I realised my mistake in thinking I'd found a private spot when I overheard Cormack talking in a lowered voice to Kara. It was the voice of a guy who obviously liked a girl a lot and was trying to impress her.

He asked if they could meet up sometime, after all this was over. Kara's reply was clear: *Sorry, I just can't. I'm not like other girls.*

Kara swiftly headed away.

Soft sobs came from the other side of the trees. I felt a wave of guilt at being here listening.

Someone else came. Shoes crunching on the pebbles.

"Are you all right, Cormack?" It was Brother Sage's voice. "I saw Kara running from here. She looked a little upset. And you do, too."

"Yeah, I'm okay." But Cormack didn't sound okay.

"Young love troubles?"

"We were talking and laughing and getting along. But then as soon as I mention seeing her outside of here, she gets all defensive."

"You'll have to accept that. Perhaps she's fighting a battle you don't know about. I'll have a chat with her sometime later today and see how she's doing."

"Sounds good. I know I shouldn't push. It's not like me to push. Girls are the one thing in life that have come pretty easily to me. Hope that doesn't sound big headed."

"Not at all." The conversation lapsed for a moment before Brother Sage spoke again. "Cormack, I've noticed you shaking a little the last couple of days. If you need any medication—"

"No. I'll be fine. I'll beat this down. You lot were kind enough to send me to rehab before I came here, and I'm almost clean."

"Good, good. Glad to hear it. Well, if you change your mind or you need to talk, you know where to find us."

Brother Sage walked away again.

After a minute, Cormack left, too. I hoped he wasn't trying to find Kara. I wished again that I knew what was troubling her. I wanted to help her, but I didn't know how. She wasn't letting anyone in. Maybe she'd relent and talk with Brother Sage.

Richard poked his head through at me from between two mandarin trees. "Hey, you. Thought I saw you head this way earlier."

"Hey." I smiled.

He looked behind him before he stepped through to stand before me, as if checking to see if anyone else was close by. "I got a bit worried before when I saw Ruth come back through the gates, knowing that you hadn't come back yet. I was starting to think maybe she did push you off a cliff." He winked. "Easy for the imagination to run wild in a place like this."

"I can handle Ruth."

"Are you sure? Those button eyes of hers give me the creeps . . ."

"I think she just goes out of her way to look fierce. Speaking of imagination, after seeing the first three challenges, I can't even begin to imagine what challenge four will be."

Richard sucked in a huge breath, blowing it out hard as he swung around on a branch and came to sit beside me. "I'd kill to find out what it is."

I winced. "Bad choice of words, considering . . . ?"

"Yeah. Sorry. I have a pretty black sense of humour at the best of times." His expression became serious. "I, uh, I've been hearing those noises you've been hearing, too."

"You have?"

"Yup. You said you saw eyes in the walls, too?"

It sounded so stupid when someone else said it. I plucked a leaf from the mandarin tree above and crushed it between my fingers. It smelled tart. "Just the first morning."

"Where?"

"The women's dorm. On the wall opposite the window."

"The men's dorm is on the other side of that." He paused to flash a grin. "Are you accusing us of being Peeping Toms?"

I laughed. "If the shoe fits."

"The shoe certainly doesn't fit *my* foot." He sobered. "But something else isn't fitting. This whole place. I calculated the area of the monastery—all the rooms and hallways. There's a lot of space that's unaccounted for. Just . . . empty space."

"It's the walls," I said, nodding. "They're either super thick or hollow. They have to be. I thought the same thing."

"You have to wonder if the police were told about that. And do the mentors know?"

"That's a good question. Should we talk to them about this?"

Richard lowered his voice, looking around again. "I don't think so. They seem to leave everything to the monks. Brother Sage just brushed you off when you mentioned it."

"True."

"Look." He dug down inside his shirt and pulled out a rolled-up piece of paper. "I've been busy. I stole some pencils and paper from the scriptorium early this morning. And I made the best damned map I could of the monastery."

He glanced over his shoulder before unrolling it.

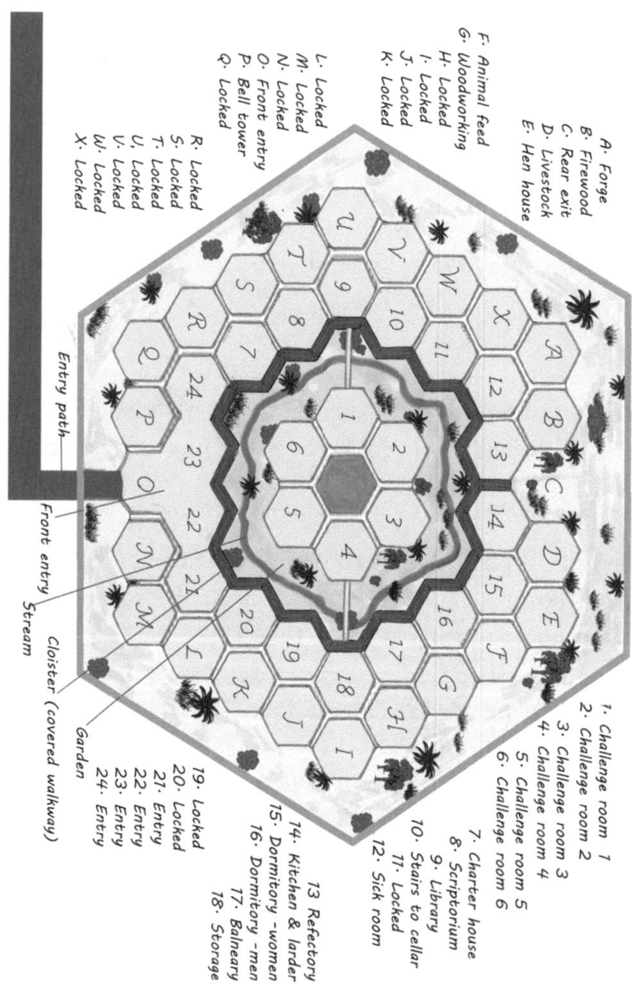

I studied his drawing. "This is good, Richard."

The map looked crazy when you saw it all at once. The inside ring of six rooms looked almost like an eye, with the centre room the pupil of the eye.

The garden itself was comprised of hexagonal spaces. A ring of twenty-four rooms surrounded the garden, and then there was an outside ring of another twenty-four rooms.

"We should go check out why there's all that empty space between the rooms." Richard quickly stowed the map away again.

"Ourselves? I don't know if that's a good idea."

"Look at it this way. The mentors haven't done a good job of keeping us safe so far, have they?"

"Nope." One of us was dead. Another of us had come close to drowning. "I remember something. The night of the first challenge, I thought I saw a monk right behind me. But when I stepped back to look into the alcove that he ran inside, he'd vanished. I thought I must have imagined seeing him."

His eyes grew intent, his voice closing down to a whisper. "Have you told anyone else that?"

"No."

"Bet a thousand bucks you weren't mistaken. Why don't we start there?"

Lowering my voice to match his, I nodded. "Guess it wouldn't hurt to have a look." I told Richard where to find the alcove.

Pulling myself to my feet, I dusted off my hands, letting the crumpled leaf fall to the ground.

"Wait," he said. "I'm also going to lay bets that Ruth is watching everything we do. Might look more suspicious if we go off somewhere together. How about I'll go first and you follow?"

"Okay. Done."

It felt all very cloak and dagger as I stood waiting in the garden and then made my way to the cloister. It also felt *wrong*. We should be going to the mentors with this. But I'd told them about the eyes and the noises, and nothing had been done. They hadn't discovered the man that would later kill Saul. *It wouldn't hurt for us to take precautions*, I told myself.

The cool air of the hallway enveloped me. No one was around. Good. I walked along to the alcove. Richard was there, next to the statue.

I frowned. "What are we going to say we're doing if someone comes along and sees us?"

Richard smirked, taking my face in his hands and smacking a kiss on my cheek. "That."

I inhaled a quick breath. "How's that going to work? I'm married and you're gay."

"People believe whatever they see. And do you have anything better?"

"No," I admitted.

Richard glanced upwards at the larger-than-life statue. "He's an ugly S.O.B., isn't he?"

"Very."

We examined the statue and the surrounding walls then stepped behind the statue. Beyond the statue was just a religious frieze framed by an arch. I tried pushing on the frieze and gasped as it moved back smoothly. The black space that opened up was just big enough to be able to slide inside.

Richard prodded my back. "You did it, girl."

Holding my breath tight, I stepped in.

Richard gave a low whistle as he moved in behind me. "We're in the belly of the beast." He pushed the door shut.

An immediate wave of claustrophobia washed through me. "It's damned dark in here."

"Stick with me, honey, and you'll be fine."

My mouth went dry as we walked along the passage. I wanted out of here already.

Up ahead, tiny pinpricks of light were the only salvation from the oppressive darkness and isolation. Where was the light coming from? Running up to the first of the specks of light, I pressed my eye to it. "Oh my God, Richard, look! Peepholes . . ." I peered out into the hallway that we'd just left.

"That's insanely weird," Richard muttered, taking a look for himself. "I wonder if Saul's killer made these holes? Probably not, right? An electric drill would make a hell of a racket."

I turned to peer into the dark tunnel ahead. "Maybe we should go back and get a lamp or something."

"We're here now," said Richard. "Might as well keep going. Hey, get behind me, kid. I'll keep you safe."

"Oh yeah? What are you going to do if a man comes at us with a knife?" I'd been joking, but the words sounded too real and possible in this strange, closed space.

"Karate chop. They won't know what hit them." Richard insisted on stepping around me and walking in front. We continued walking along the passage.

"Damn," said Richard, feeling his way around a structure in front of him. "There's a ladder here."

I moved beside Richard. The passageway ended in a wall. A simple wooden ladder led straight up.

The last thing I wanted to do was to climb up there. But if we were going to continue, this was the only way to go.

I ascended the ladder after Richard, breathing easier once I realised that it didn't lead up into some claustrophobia-inducing attic but instead just led back down and into the passageway. "I know what this is," I breathed, turning back to Richard. "This is the refectory door that we're climbing across. Otherwise the tunnel would have ended."

Richard nodded. "I think you're right."

We continued along, taking a sharp right turn, then up another ladder. The tunnel we headed into was high, and we couldn't walk upright any longer. We had to crawl.

"Whoa, we're going across the hall now," said Richard from behind me. He appeared to test it with his hands before moving forward. "Seems solid enough."

At the end of the overhead passage, a ladder led down, and the passage went left and right and straight ahead—up yet another ladder.

"This way." Richard stepped up to the ladder.

I stalled. "I don't understand this. This way should be heading out to the cloister and garden . . ."

"I'll be damned. I remember seeing a bulkhead that stretches right across the garden. So this is what that's for. A secret passage." He climbed the ladder quickly.

I followed hesitantly.

The peepholes stretched along the floor now, the light seeping through them growing brighter.

Crawling forward, I stopped to squint through one of the bright pinholes. I caught the briefest scent of fresh air. The sun lit up the tops of the fruit trees. The challenge participants were there, not guessing that Richard and I were overhead and staring down at them.

"We can't go any further," I whispered. "If we do, we'll be going across to the inner circle of rooms. Where the challenges are held."

The silence that followed told me that the direction we were headed in wasn't a problem for Richard.

"Richard," I said uneasily, "please tell me this wasn't the reason you wanted to do this in the first place?"

"Are you going to say that you don't want to know what's in the last three rooms?" came the reply.

"No." My *no* didn't sound as firm as I'd meant it.

"Look, it's not like we'd actually go into the rooms and solve the challenges," he added. "All we'd do is take a quick look."

"But if we got found out, the mentors would probably throw us out of the program. Without any money at all."

"That's the gamble, Evie. Gamble big, win big. You're a fellow gambler, and I know you understand that."

"Okay, now I'm sure you wanted to do this to get into the inner circle."

"Ding, ding, ding."

My heart hammered against my ribs. He'd tricked me.

But still, I didn't turn around and head back the way we'd come.

In the third challenge, my team had only just skidded onto the finish line at the last second. Seeing the new rooms might give me the slight advantage that would get my team over the line in the next challenges.

It's wrong, Evie. You know it is.

But something clouded over my sense of fairness. I had a family to think of. I needed the money.

I didn't speak as I followed Richard forward. At the other end of the bulkhead, we descended the ladder.

We were in the inner circle.

Almost immediately before us was a door, a lamp overhead dimly illuminating it.

"Don't touch it!" I cried. "It could be alarmed."

The door had a keypad and a strange square screen with a handprint marked on it.

Richard whistled between his teeth. "This thing scans your hand. Pretty high-level security for a pack of monks."

"So, what's on the other side of that door?"

He shook his head. "I'd pay good money to know that. If I had any, that is."

"We have to head back," I said quietly, not sure if I was glad or not that a door had stopped us.

Reluctantly, Richard tore himself away. We climbed the ladder and returned the way we'd come.

"Wait," I said. "Hear that?"

The sound of voices bounced through the passage.

Exhaling low, hard breaths, we rushed down the ladder in between the cloister and the hall.

"We're on the wrong side of the hall," I whispered.

"We're going to get ourselves lost," Richard hissed back. "Sorry. This is my stupid fault."

We moved along the passageway in the oily dark.

The voices faded.

A sudden glow spilled through a peephole.

Richard pressed his face close. "It's the scriptorium," he said so softly I barely heard him. "Vito's there."

I took my turn to peer into the peephole. Brother Vito was seated on the ornate, high-backed chair behind the desk. Candlelight illuminated his face as he wrote with an old-fashioned quill. The scene looked otherworldly, like I were peering back to the medieval era.

A woman moved into view—nude—her soft flesh like that in a medieval painting, red hair half spilling from a bun. It took a moment for me to realise that the woman was Poppy.

Brother Vito looked up at her, startled. "What are you doing?"

"I can't stand it anymore." Poppy tried to step around his desk. "I need something to make me feel better. Don't throw me out."

Brother Vito stood. "Get dressed."

Poppy whimpered. "But . . . you can recite philosophy to me while we do other things, and—"

"You need to remember that your place in the challenges is a privilege. Leave now, and I'll forget this happened." Brother Vito's voice was authoritative, with no shades of uncertainty.

Richard, hearing my stifled gasp, bumped me out of the way, clapping a hand over my mouth. He took another quick glance through the peephole.

Grabbing my arm, he pulled me away and along the passageway.

I waited until we were safely out of earshot to speak. "We can't tell anyone what we saw. For Poppy's sake, and for ours."

Richard's voice turned ugly. "For Poppy's sake? Surely you're not so innocent you don't know what she was trying to do? She was trying to gain an advantage. Sex for challenge points."

"She said—"

"I know what she said. I could hear it plain enough. As if she's going to tell Vito her real reason for trying to jump him naked. Poor guy. He looked mortified. Yeah, great counselling session that one was."

"She's probably just not herself. None of us are. And most of us would try to gain an advantage if we could. Look at what we just did."

"Let's just get back to the garden." Richard marched down the passage. I hurried after him, not wanting to be left in here alone.

We found our way back to the alcove with the statue and slipped out into the hall. We returned to the garden the same way we'd come in—one by one.

Everyone seemed too caught up in their own thoughts to even notice either of us had been gone. I guessed it had just been minutes, but it'd seemed so much longer.

I felt empty.

None of us here were *good.* None of us deserved this chance at the money.

42. I, INSIDE THE WALLS

I FOLLOWED THEM ALONG THE HIDDEN walkways.

They didn't see me. I know how to hide. I won't tell. I never tell anything I see.

I know you won't tell either, Santiago.

43. GRAY

I COULDN'T SLEEP NOW.

I pictured the items on Detective Devoe's desk. The rope and the tape and the knife. Devoe had told me that items at the site were being investigated for DNA and fingerprints. And blood.

I could lay bets on what was coming after that.

If the people who were trying to frame me had done their job properly, my DNA and my fingerprints would be found at the site. On things they shouldn't be on if I'd never been there. Maybe a trace of Evie's blood would be found on the knife.

My heart thudded. *Had these people hurt Evie?*

I had to believe she was alive for my own peace of mind, even if they did find her blood. You could get a smear of blood just by pricking a finger.

One thing was certain: there was a narrow window of time left, and that window was rapidly closing.

If I did the crazy thing and flew to Greece, I had the tiniest chance of finding Evie.

But if I did nothing, she might remain missing forever. And I'd be locked away for life in jail. Our girls would grow up not only without their mother but with the belief that I'd killed her.

My lungs compacted into tiny boxes until I could barely breathe.

I had to go.

I headed out to the stair landing. Willow and Lilly were already asleep, and so was Verity. Verity had moved from the sunroom to Lilly's bedroom, putting the girls into the one bedroom. She'd found the sunroom too cold and leaky, which it was.

Stepping up to Verity's door, I raised my fist to knock on it.

What was I going to say? Blurt out everything about the knife and the rope and the crazy story about Evie being seen flying to Greece?

Evie was her daughter. She deserved to know. She'd asked what the police had to tell me, and I'd told her that they'd found another couple of items but nothing significant. In truth, the items were significant enough to send me to jail.

But Verity was Verity. She'd think I was nuts, and she'd call the police.

I descended the stairs. And then began wearing a hole in the floor, walking from the kitchen to the living room and back again, trying to figure out who I could borrow money from. Almost no one I could think of would have a spare few thousand to lend me. Everyone was poor, like Evie and me.

I spied a set of elephant-shaped ceramic jars Verity had put on a high bookcase shelf in the sunroom. She hadn't finished shifting her things to the upstairs bedroom yet. Verity loved elephants—Evie had told me that. I could guess why. Because like elephants, Verity never forgot a single damned thing.

Wait, jars—didn't Evie once say that her mother kept money that she earned for cash jobs in a jar? Verity did extra bookkeeping work on the side that she never declared in her tax. She called it her *retirement fund.*

Walking into the sunroom, I picked up each jar in turn and opened the lid. Only the largest of them had anything in it. Stuffed with old phone and electricity bills. For an accountant, that didn't seem very efficient. I was about to put the jar back when I decided to fish the bills out instead. The bills were hiding wads of money underneath.

Swallowing hard, I pulled the money out of its tight hiding hole. Around five or six thousand.

If I took this, there was no going back.

This was stealing.

The doubts returned.

What if Constance's private investigator was wrong? What if it hadn't been Evie boarding a plane to Greece and she was lying dead in that forest, after all? Maybe this was what those people wanted—me running away and looking as guilty as sin.

I didn't know anything about what was really going on here. Except, if I was locked up in a jail cell, I'd never get the chance to find out.

I dashed off a message on a piece of notepaper:

Verity,

I'm sorry. I can't explain right now, but I'll be back in a few days. Please look after Willow and Lilly. Tell them Daddy loves them.

Gray

Briefly heading back upstairs, I grabbed my passport and a few clothes and things, stopping only to look in the room where Willow and Lilly slept together. They were cuddled together like koalas. I left the note on my bed.

I rolled the car down the driveway and down the road a short distance, hoping not to wake Verity. She slept pretty heavily. I worried that Verity wouldn't wake up for Lilly during the night if Lilly had a night terror or came down with yet another bug. But Willow was right next to her. Willow would surely go and bang on Verity's door until she woke.

MASSES OF PEOPLE milled through Sydney International Airport.

I kept a baseball cap on my head as I bought a ticket. I guessed I didn't need to do that—it wasn't as though the police were looking for me—but it felt better. I bought a seat on the flight that was going to get me to Europe the quickest. The flight chewed through an enormous chunk of Verity's money. Almost two thousand dollars.

I had less than half an hour before the gate would close. I made my way to the departure lounge and joined the queue. My hand was slick with sweat on the handle of my suitcase, heat making my skull prickle. I was going to bring attention to myself if I couldn't get control.

The line moved so slowly.

Shuffle and wait. Shuffle and wait.

I wanted to be in the plane and out of here. I looked behind, half expecting police to be rushing up to me. I had to stop that. Stay cool. I wasn't under arrest—*yet*.

Hell. Hell, hell, hell, hell. Security coming my way.

A man and woman.

"Sir, can you come this way, please?" the woman said to me.

"Sure." I forced a smile that was probably a big mistake. The smile was sure to look fake and nervous.

They took me aside and ran their handheld scanners over me.

"Can we check your baggage, sir?" asked the man.

"Yes. Go for it," I replied quickly.

He rummaged through my things, stopping briefly to ask me if I had anything to declare.

"No. Is there a problem?"

"Just routine," the woman told me. "A random check."

I relaxed. It wasn't me they were interested in but what I might be carrying with me. My fault for sweating wild panic back when I was standing on the line and making them suspicious.

Really smooth, Gray.

"Okay, you're good to go," said the man, giving me a wan smile.

It could have been worse. They could have taken me into a room and held me up with strip searches and questions. Even made me miss my flight. I'd heard of that happening.

I was the last one through the gate. Just minutes to spare now. Good. Because I wanted this plane in the air. Waiting was going to turn me into a sweat machine.

I found my seat and settled in.

The flight attendant gave the safety speech, and then the plane started down the runway.

I instructed myself to go to sleep if I could manage it. Because I wasn't going to stop running once I got to my destination.

44. CONSTANCE

I OWED IT TO ROSEMARY TO find the people who'd murdered her so cruelly. I'd dragged her into this. And she'd paid the price, in the worst way possible.

But I wasn't going to stay. The best way to find them was to find Kara.

I sensed that Rosemary would understand.

Rosemary's phrase replayed in my mind: *Exposing flaws means closing doors*. Remembering that had kept me from blurting everything out at the police station. I didn't know who I could and couldn't trust. I had to play it safe, else risk having every door that was currently open to me locked tight.

I couldn't *become* Rosemary, but I could use the things I'd learned from her in the brief time I'd known her. One of those things was only revealing the information that I absolutely had to. Leaving no stone unturned was another. And using a phone that couldn't be traced to me was yet another thing Rosemary had taught me—she'd shown me how to buy a phone to use for private conversations with her the day before she died.

Sitting cross-legged on the bed in my hotel room, I browsed the news online. I needed a distraction to keep my mind from spinning. It was a habit of mine to read the news every day. I always read every story at my favoured sites, collecting all the stories, all the terrible and quirky and strange things. People at their worst, at the end of their rope, on the edge. The stories made me somehow feel better and made me feel that my own life wasn't out of control.

I still had a news page open from Sydney. Back in Australia, I'd been anxiously checking Sydney news every day for stories about young girls who'd been found dumped and dead somewhere. There *had* been a girl, around Kara's age, but she hadn't been Kara. She'd been a pretty, dark-haired aspiring model. *Dead and dumped.* Like trash.

Today, the news was filled with murders. So many murders.

I felt ill suddenly. Leaving the tablet on my hotel bed, I grabbed a glass of juice. Like a drill sergeant or a priest hearing confession, I made myself pay the price for my obsession with the daily news—dropping to the floor and commencing ten push-ups. James had told me many times to quit reading the news so much. But I couldn't quit. I was addicted.

Inside my handbag, my phone jingled. I wasn't used to the new ringtone yet. No one had this number, not even the police. Except for Gray.

Fetching it out, I answered breathily. "Hello?"

"Constance. It's me, Gray."

"What's happening?"

"Just a sec. I can barely hear you. I need to go where it's less noisy."

The push-ups had made my heart squeeze, I'd gone at them so hard and fast. I held the phone to my ear and waited for Gray.

This was the first time he'd called *me* so far. Before, it'd been me calling and desperately wanting clues from him. Now, he obviously needed something from me. Perversely, a brief flicker of satisfaction passed through me. I wasn't the needy one now. Gray was knocking on *my* door.

A news story on my tablet caught my eye. *Suspect flees after knife and rope found at crime scene.*

Anger rattled inside me. Yet another person murdered, and the murderer trying to get away scot free. I clicked on the story. A strangled gasp rose and died in my throat.

A picture of Gray Harlow accompanied the text.

Police are seeking information about a person of interest in relation to a crime scene that has been established at an unidentified bushland setting in Sydney's western suburbs. The burned-out car of missing Sydney mother Evie Harlow was found days ago, with Mrs Harlow's handbag, phone and shoes found buried a short distance away.

Police also discovered a knife, tape and rope buried at the scene. These items have been positively identified as belonging to Evie's husband, Gray Harlow.

According to a close family friend, Marla Atkinson, Evie had recently left her husband due to problems in their relationship. Evie arranged for her two young daughters, aged two and four, to remain in safety with Marla. Mr Harlow allegedly took the girls by force the following day.

Presently, the girls are in the care of their grandmother.

Police are seeking urgent assistance in locating Mr Harlow.

If you have information, police are advising that you contact them.

Gray hadn't made any mention to me of a knife and a rope being found at the scene. And the news report said they were *his*.

My stomach tightened, and the dread feeling returned. Had I made an enormous mistake in trusting and confiding in Gray? If Gray had fled his home, where was he?

Wild thoughts rushed in unchecked.

What had he done?

Evie wasn't supposed to be dead. She was supposed to be a world away, in Greece, and very much alive.

But what if Rosemary was wrong? Perhaps she'd downloaded a photo of Evie that could look like any of a thousand young women. Evie was pretty in a way that a lot of young women were pretty—her hair and eyes and skin all of a perfect, fresh colour and smoothness but with no outstanding features. I'd have trouble picking her out in a crowd. As for the bracelet, for all I knew, lots of girls had them.

Rosemary's words about Gray fed back into my mind: *Let's hope Gray didn't have something to do with his wife's disappearance. It's terrible how many times the culprit turns out to be the husband. Too many times.*

I'd just assumed that the people Evie had gotten involved with were trying to cover their tracks when they'd dumped and burned her car. But I didn't know the first thing about Gray. He might be a bad person, too. I couldn't expose myself to something like that. I'd be better to cut off all contact.

"Whew!" Gray's voice came back on the line. "That's better. Huge crowd back there. Constance, we have to meet up."

His words shocked me, sending a wave of electricity across my bare arms. "Meet up? How is that possible?"

"I'm in London."

"*London?* You're here . . . ?" My voice trailed away.

He spoke fast, his voice filled with tension. "Yeah. Crazy, right? I just flew in. I'm calling from an airport phone."

"What are you doing here?"

"What do you mean? I'm here looking for Evie."

"Look, Gray, it might be better if we each tackle this on our own. You should go ahead and see what you can find out."

"I thought you'd be on your way to Greece." Disappointment and confusion edged his words.

"I was. But the police asked me to stay on here. And I feel like if I leave now, I'm going to be under suspicion, and then I'll be watched. And I don't want that. Better for you to head off to Greece."

"Okay. But then you're going to have to tell me what you know. I'm here because of you and what you told me."

Guilt burrowed through me. It was true that I'd called him and told him in no uncertain terms that his wife was in Greece. It made no sense at all that if he'd killed his wife, he'd come here in search of her.

Unless he was insane.

Yes, he could be insane. That might be the reason why his wife ran away from him. And he might have found Evie and killed her, and he'd been pretending all this time. And now he was coming after me.

I needed time to think, but anxiety was making my brain shut down.

"I wish I did know more," I told him. "But I'm afraid that Rosemary is dead, and everything she knew died with her." I hesitated before adding, "I have to go now. I wish you luck."

I pressed the *end* option on my phone and threw it into my bag, not giving him a chance to say more.

I should dispose of the phone. It served no purpose if I no longer wanted contact from Gray. Dear God, I was the one who brought him to Europe.

Puffing up the pillows, I crawled into bed. I wanted to escape from everything. Because everything I touched had gone wrong.

I slept for a short time but then woke into a terrifying silence. I switched on the TV just to create some noise, flicking from channel to channel. An English detective series was showing. I used to like watching these. Not anymore. It was all vile to me now, watching people murder others as entertainment.

Switching to a news show, I half sat up. I shouldn't have let myself nap

—I wouldn't sleep tonight. I'd lie awake for hours, haunted by the sight of Rosemary's bloodied and lifeless body.

They were showing the lighter end of the news. The squealing winner of a reality-show bake-off, an antique painting that had sold at auction for a crazy figure, a high-society charity dinner. I'd attended many such dinners together with James. They'd mostly been pretty boring, with a bit of celebrity spotting to break up the tedium.

In the background of an art show, a silver-haired man sported a much younger wife, the wife looking excited by all the attention of the press. But it wasn't his wife I was interested in. It was him. He was familiar—who was he?

The answer came to me. He was Wilson Carlisle, the man in the photographs Rosemary had shown me.

It was him. I was sure of it.

He was still in Australia when Rosemary last checked. But he was here now.

Instant revulsion crawled up my spine. He was the man that Kara had been staying with. Most likely, he either owned or rented an apartment near the Sydney casino that his wife didn't know about—the apartment Kara had lived in.

I needed to find out what Mr Carlisle was doing in London.

Somehow, I had to follow him.

If Rosemary was here, she'd know exactly how to do that. But she wasn't. It was all up to me.

THE FOURTH CHALLENGE

45. EVIE

JUST BEFORE SUNSET, THE MENTORS GATHERED us all on the edge of the cliff to hold a memorial for Saul. We tossed flowers from the garden down into a fissure where the ocean rushed in.

Poppy and I held each other while we cried for Saul, who'd had no idea that this island would be the place he'd draw his last breath.

I watched as Poppy cast an anxious look at Brother Vito as he passed by us. I guessed she was feeling pretty embarrassed at what she'd done and at Brother Vito's rejection of her. I'd already decided not to judge. Richard and I had done the wrong thing, too. Saul's death had left us all shaken and looking for easy answers.

I fell asleep that night in a black despair. None of us knew how or when we'd die.

Only the numbers knew.

I woke near midnight, the calls and screams of the peacocks shaking me from sleep.

I'd been inside a nightmare of my girls being at the monastery.

I'd turned a corner to see Lilly standing there, alone in a corridor, a cough hacking through her small chest, her eyes reddened and weepy. As I rushed to her, a voice called her away. Suddenly I caught sight of Willow standing at the other end of the corridor. "Come on, Lilly", Willow said. "You can't be with Mummy anymore." Lilly ran to her sister before I could reach her. I heard the two of them running, until they were on the other side of the wall from me. No matter which room I ran into, they were on the other side of the wall. The sound of their footsteps turned into scraping, rustling noises. I screamed their names. "Lilly! Willow!" When I spun around, I saw a man dressed in hooded monk's clothing, staring at me.

Sitting up, I folded my knees against my chest. I missed my girls. I desperately needed to see them, to hold them, to know they were okay. My fingers ached to touch their soft skin, their silky dark hair, their little hands. So much of what I did with the girls was touch: hugs, washing them in warm baths, changing their clothes, snuggling on the sofa with a well-loved book. And I missed Gray. In some ways, my need for Gray went even deeper. He wasn't *my other half*—he was my whole. When I met him, for the first time I saw myself whole, too. I could see myself reflected in his eyes, in his smile and the things he said to me when we were alone.

The fourth challenge was almost here. Just this one and then two more. And I'd be gone. *Or sooner if I didn't make it through a challenge.* I allowed myself to think about the house that Gray and I could buy and what colours we'd paint the rooms to make it ours.

I wondered what Saul had been dreaming of doing with his money. Whatever it was, those dreams died with him.

I waited in my bed for the bells. It seemed that hours passed. And the metronomes never stopped ticking. They were soldiers marching in some crazy, eternal war.

The challenges were nothing like I'd expected. These were no fuzzy, feel-good puzzles. They were strange and even dangerous. Who were the mentors, really? Why bring us all this way to a remote island where an order of silent monks designed the challenges? The monks weren't psychologists and didn't even have contact with the outside world.

I tried to doze and rest my mind and body, but I couldn't relax a single neuron or muscle. My fingers entwined in the bracelet Gray had bought me. The bracelet grounded me, calmed me.

But when the sound of the bells crashed through the room, I jerked upright, immediately tense.

The lamps in the room flickered on as they always did at midnight. The faces that stared at me and each other looked the same as I felt. No one had slept well, with the possible exception of Ruth, whose face held the same hard-set expression as always.

Raw anticipation needled my back.

My wristband flashed.

Number one.

My turn. First up.

I realised I hadn't even looked to see who else was in my group by the time I reached the door. Did that mean I was playing my own game now and had stopped caring about anyone else? I didn't know. Maybe Ruth had gotten inside my head. She was certainly playing her own game.

Yolanda's eyes met mine as I turned my head, pale brown against her dark skin. The bracelet on her wrist was flashing green. I barely knew her, having spoken with her only three or four times. She'd lost the friends she'd made on her first day here—the two blondes, Greta and Roxy.

Someone else appeared behind her. Ruth.

Harrington met us outside. My heart fell at getting Ruth and Harrington on my team again.

But this was my group of four for the fourth challenge and I had to make the best of it. Yolanda, Ruth and Harrington. Maybe they were cursing being put with me.

There were no whispers or rustling behind the walls this time as we rushed to the garden. The mentors stood silently beside the stream, encouraging us with serene, close-lipped smiles.

"You can do this," said Brother Vito. "But there can be no hesitation or mistakes with this challenge. You haven't got this far without either being extremely good or extremely lucky. If it is that you are good, keep faith in yourself and study the patterns carefully. If it is that you are merely lucky, may luck still be on your side."

That sounded kind of terrifying. I wasn't at all sure if I'd shown any skill in the challenges so far. Skill could continue. Luck couldn't.

The dark air smelled strangely metallic as we walked in, and the door closed behind us.

The lights flashed on all at once, blinding me for a moment.

My vision cleared, and huge objects came into focus.

Birds. Made of metal. Six of them. Similar to the metal bird in the monastery foyer.

The birds—each twice as large as a man—were suspended from the ceiling on thin rods that stretched down to about my chest height. With their wings straight out in flight, they formed a tight circle close to the centre of the room.

"Son of a—" said Ruth, scowling. "What *is* this?"

I peered between the birds. For the first time, there was no hexagonal box in the centre of the room. Instead, pieces of chunky wood in geometric shapes were scattered about the room.

"I'd lay bets those are the box," said Yolanda, pointing. "Looks like we're meant to put it together."

"Saul . . ." I said softly.

"Wasn't he the one who got killed?" Yolanda shot me a nervous, confused glance.

I nodded. "He was a puzzle box hobbyist. This one would have been right up his alley."

"Well, he's not here to help us," said Harrington in a pinched voice, as if Saul was being selfish. "Anyway, how hard can it be?"

"I don't know," said Ruth "I mean, how do the birds figure into it?"

"Fine." Harrington took a step back, crossing his arms. "Let's all stand here having a pleasant conversation, shall we?"

Yolanda's temple twitched, and she shot Harrington a scornful look. "You sound just like my mother. Passive aggressive. I had such a *pleasant* conversation with her in the mirror during the last challenge." Angered, she marched forward towards the nearest of the wooden pieces. Before she reached it, a sound vibrated through the air.

One of the birds shifted out on its metal pole. Then one by one, each of them did the same. The vibrating sound became a high-pitched whirring as the enormous birds began swinging to and fro.

Yelling out in fear, Yolanda fled, a bird beak narrowly missing her.

The birds began moving in sharp, erratic arcs.

We rushed back against the wall.

Heavy, whooshing sounds filled the air as the birds rose and fell in long swoops, crisscrossing each other's paths but never touching.

I raised my face, gazing up at the top ends of the pendulums that the birds were suspended on. The pendulums were suspended on metal balls and able to swing in any direction. The birds swung straight past where the hexagonal box should be.

Ruth did a slow clap. "Great work. How do we put that box together now?" She sighed then. "We're going to have to grab the pieces one by one and put it together back here."

"No," I replied. "The box goes where it always goes." I sounded certain. *Was I certain?* No, I wasn't. But it was my best guess. *There isn't time for second-guessing.*

"I'm with Evie," said Yolanda. "The box has to go dead centre. Something had to have been triggered when I walked over there before," said Yolanda.

"Maybe you should go *untrigger* it," said Harrington.

"Can't be that simple," Ruth mused.

"Here we go again," said Harrington. It was the first time I'd ever heard him criticise Ruth.

"No . . . *look* . . . the birds are moving in patterns," Ruth insisted. "Otherwise they'd be smashing into each other, right?"

Yolanda nodded. "But figuring out the pattern doesn't help us. We can get past the birds if we're super careful, but we can't put the box together."

"We have to stop the birds." I watched them swinging for a moment, mesmerised.

"They're working on some kind of motors," said Yolanda.

I continued to observe the paths and movements of the birds. "The birds get a bit wobbly when they pass over the puzzle pieces. Kind of like they're being held in place for a moment. Like . . . they're a giant version of those novelty paperweights that move about on magnets." I looked around at the other three. "If it's magnets, could there be magnets in the pieces of the box?"

Yolanda shot me a worried look. "I can't claim to be an expert on magnets, but I was a physics major before my life went off the rails. And if there's magnets in the puzzle pieces, we're in for a world of trouble. Because magnets that strong would be neodymium. They're crazy strong. Get in between two of those puzzle pieces, and you'll be crushed to death."

Ruth sucked her mouth in, making a popping sound. "Yeah, looks like magnets. Well, they didn't make this one easy."

I pressed the back of my head into the wall. "It's damned dangerous."

Harrington blew out a hard breath. "What choice do we have but to get out there and just do it? We've got to dodge those killer beaks and move those bad boys."

"The birds seem to be losing a bit of height in their arcs," said Yolanda.

"The motors started them off and the magnets are keeping them going. But air resistance will win out, and the birds will eventually stop."

"How long do we have?" demanded Harrington.

Yolanda shook her head. "I said I was no expert on this, and I don't know how it's set up. And we don't know how they're triggered. Once we go in, we could set the whole cycle off again."

"Should we try to work out the trigger?" I asked quickly.

"We could do that," said Yolanda. "But I don't know if it would help us. The birds could stay in motion for a long time just on this one trigger, with only a small loss of energy."

I spun around to check the clock, shocked to realise that I'd forgotten to look at it since I'd walked into the room.

Eight minutes left.

Ruth threw up her hands. "You lot are complicating things. I like things simple. If the puzzle pieces are magnets, why don't we just try flipping 'em? North and south poles and all that. If the magnets are repelling the magnets in the birds now, then maybe we can flip the magnets and make the birds stay tight."

"I want to hug you right now." Yolanda flashed a row of white teeth at Ruth.

"Touch me and die." Ruth glared at her.

"You women all have to hug me if I head in there first." Harrington creased the right side of his face in a wink.

"Like fun we will," Ruth called out after him as he strode to the first puzzle piece.

Ducking low, Harrington made a grab for the piece and turned it over. Yelping at the swift return of the bird, he sprinted back to the wall.

The bird didn't stop immediately, but its arc was interrupted. It moved chaotically for a few seconds before settling on top of the puzzle piece.

The four of us cheered out loud.

"Okay, people," said Ruth with the voice of a sergeant major. "Let's work out which pieces of the puzzle go on the bottom and which go on the top."

Staying hard against the walls, we moved quickly around the room, studying the pieces.

"Look!" I called. "See the pattern? The pieces with the pattern would go on top, right? Wouldn't see them on the bottom."

Ruth nodded. "You got it."

"And the pieces with the parallel lines could go around the sides, horizontally." Yolanda had both her hands out in front of her, moving them as though rotating an invisible piece of wood.

"Right, people," instructed Ruth. "I want these two pieces of wood first. We'll go in and stop all the birds. Then bring me the pieces I asked for. That way, we cut down on the number of birds in flight until the end. *Capisce*?"

Ruth had taken over and was already ordering us around. But that was her usual. And if it got this challenge done, that was okay with me.

Within a heart-stopping minute, we had every bird stopped and under control.

But not for long. Now, every puzzle piece had to come out, setting each bird off again.

Yolanda and I eyed each other from across the room and nodded. We grabbed the puzzle pieces Ruth had asked for.

Harrington waited by his piece.

Two birds were now in flight.

This piece of wood was heavy. Much heavier than I'd expected.

I lugged the solid chunk of wood across the room.

Wait. Stop.

A bird swooped past, sending a sharp breeze over my face and prickling every nerve in my body.

Run.

Yolanda made it to the middle of the room first, Ruth waiting there to take the puzzle piece.

Panting, I stepped carefully towards Ruth. Was this thing going to jump from my arms or what? I set it down on the floor and bent to push it the rest of the way. Frowning in concentration, Ruth took my piece and turned it to and fro before deciding how it fitted with her piece. She began sliding it towards the other. My puzzle piece slid to hers, crashing violently into place at the last moment with a loud clatter.

A grin spread over Ruth's face.

A bird was swinging our way.

"*Down!*" I screamed at her, then scrambled to lie flat as a bird headed straight for us.

Ruth threw herself to the ground. From the floor, Ruth pointed to two more pieces. "Those!"

Harrington was already standing by one of the pieces. I was closest to the other. Ducking a bird again, I ran to the other piece.

"Okay. Now!" Harrington yelled.

I moved my piece out.

Four birds were now in swing.

I weaved through the swinging birds.

Watch the birds.

Why did the monks even design this challenge?

Stop. You're losing focus. They don't give us anything too hard, remember? Another few minutes and this will be done. Another challenge over.

"No, I want Harrington's piece first." Ruth waved at me to stop.

Yolanda's scream echoed across the room. "Evie!"

I whirled around just as two birds were set to cross paths—straight through me. I went to drop to the ground. In the same moment, Ruth was beside me, knocking into me, sending my puzzle piece flying from my hands. The tip of a bird's wing sliced into my back.

I hit the floor backwards, my head slamming hard into the marble.

The room spun.

Silver flashes of enormous birds.

Yells and shouts.

Then darkness.

46. GRAY

I JUMPED IN A CAB AND instructed the driver to take me to a cheap hotel. I needed to get away from the airport, but I had no idea where to go. I couldn't even actually stay at a hotel—cheap or not—because they'd want ID. And I didn't want to identify myself.

I'd thought I'd be staying with Constance, but that plan had gone pear shaped. She'd been strange on the phone, like she couldn't get rid of me quick enough.

What her problem was, I couldn't guess. But I couldn't waste head space thinking about it. Maybe I'd go faster without her.

The Australian police were sure to know I'd flown to London by now. If they put out a warrant for my arrest, then travel was going to get hard. I couldn't stay anywhere under my own name. It was summer in Europe—I could sleep outdoors. Or find hostels for the homeless and nameless.

I bought a map at a newsagency and studied it, trying to figure how to get from London to Greece in the fastest time. With my thumb, I traced a route from London to Dover on the coast, then onto Calais, France.

I caught a series of trains to Dover. It wasn't as far as I'd thought it would be. England wasn't Australia—no huge distances to cover.

The weather stayed fine as I caught a P&O ferry from Dover to Calais. I'd had to use my passport for the ride. If the police were tracking me, I'd just made it too easy for them.

I stood out in the open, willing the boat to go faster.

An hour and a half later, the Calais docks were in sight.

"You've got the right idea," said a man who'd stepped next to me, an elderly English guy with a deeply furrowed brow. "Enjoying the sunshine while it lasts."

I went to answer, then stopped myself short. Better not to talk and cement my accent in anyone's mind. Giving him a polite nod, I looked out to the channel.

Undeterred, he repeated himself to a nearby woman, who was clutching the hands of her two small daughters. "Nice weather, what? Good to be outside in this weather, enjoying it while you can."

"We love the summer." She smiled. She and her girls had dark hair, reminding me of Evie and my own girls.

He gestured towards the Calais docks. "They've got that problem back again. I've heard that after the French bulldozed their whole camp, they've come back to squat. The Jungle, they called it."

Her smile faded. "The refugees don't have a lot of options of where to stay."

I walked to the railing and scanned the area around the docks. No police. The mention of refugee camps had given me a clue as to where I could sleep tonight. Breaking my silence, I asked the woman a few casual questions about the location of the camps. She told me about the Stalingrad district in the city.

As soon as the ferry docked, I found a bus headed to Paris then caught a cab into the areas where red, blue and green tents dotted the streetscapes. The tents had been pitched under railway bridges and near train stations. Some of the men were sleeping out in the open on sidewalks.

I had the driver stop at a camp beneath a high set of stairs. I spotted a group of French volunteers moving between the tents, giving out supplies.

Reminding myself not to talk, I stepped around the perimeter of the camp, watching. I was hungry and tired. But I had money for food, and I wasn't going to take the baguettes and drinks being handed out. I spied a large cardboard box filled with red plastic objects. Tents.

I grabbed one and quickly took it to the back of the camp and set it up.

Stealing from refugees—I couldn't get much lower. But I'd leave the tent here when I left. I was bone weary and could have slept straight away. I slipped my wallet and passport down my jeans and then tightened my belt. It wasn't the best solution, but at least no one was getting my stuff without a fight. My hope was that in the camp, I'd be safe from thieves rather than trying to go it alone.

Resting my head on my bag, I collapsed into an exhausted sleep.

When I woke, it was dark.

There were the ceaseless sounds of traffic and small crying children and people wandering between the tents, calling out to each other. It was hot tonight, the smell of urine coming off the pavement and into my tent. In winter, it would be intolerable. I imagined being here with Willow and Lilly. Lilly would be fussing and coughing all night long. Hell, with the illness that I now knew Lilly had, would she even survive a winter in a camp? Maybe she wouldn't.

First thing tomorrow, I had to find an internet café and start researching the historical society that Constance had told me about. If there was something I was good at, it was zeroing in on an elusive thing and figuring out systems. It was what I'd done for a job.

Whoever these people were, I was going to become the burrowing worm in their apple.

47. CONSTANCE

WILSON CARLISLE AND HIS WIFE STROLLED from their hotel, she holding a young child's hand. I hadn't realised they had a child. The blonde-headed toddler must have been with a nanny when the Carlisles were at the charity dinner.

I drew back beside a pylon, pretending to be absorbed in my phone. I wore ordinary gym clothes, my hair back in a ponytail and a baseball cap on my head. One look I did well was the upmarket gym look. Because those were the clothes I usually lived in. Hopefully, I looked like any woman staying at a hotel here and out for a brisk walk—and not like a stalker. Because tonight I was stalking the rich orthodontist, Wilson Carlisle.

Bibby Carlisle appeared to be prouder of the child than of the man on the other side of her, looking down at the boy more than a few times with a smile on her red-painted lips. She looked like a child herself next to her husband.

I knew from my research that Wilson had three older children—much older children. All in their thirties and forties. He and his first wife had divorced after five years, just long enough for her to spit out the three children. He'd had two more wives after that, the marriages all ending in divorce. His last divorce apparently happened due to a messy affair with a sixteen-year-old dental assistant. Somehow, he hadn't lost his licence to operate as an orthodontist. Following that train wreck was a fourth marriage to his current wife.

The stupid thought occurred to me that with him being an orthodontist, at least his former wives would have left the marriage with very good teeth. I almost giggled.

Looking up, I realised I'd lost the family around a corner. I quickened my steps.

Where had they gone?

They couldn't have gone very far with a toddler in tow.

I noticed an upmarket children's clothing and toy store. They must have taken the boy in there to buy him a treat.

Moving to the store window, I pretended to window shop. There were quite a few little Georges and Charlottes in there, all dressed like miniature adults of the 1950s. Wilson stood scratching his ear, watching Bibby place George on a giant rocking horse. He was probably wondering how he was going to ship that thing back to Sydney.

I couldn't hear, but it appeared that Wilson received a phone call, as he suddenly reached into his pocket for his phone and studied it.

I stumbled back as he turned and walked swiftly in my direction, passing through the door and out onto the street. He then stepped to a quiet spot, checking around him.

I needed to hear that conversation.

Pretending to snap photographs of a nearby theatre poster with my phone, I edged closer to Wilson. *I'm a woman who enjoys the theatre*, I said in my mind as I took the photos, as though passersby would somehow catch my silent message and be convinced.

Wilson was on the other side of a decorative partition. I could only just hear his lowered tones above the London traffic and noise. He was making lots of ums and ahs, listening to the other person.

"The husband's here," he then said clearly. "Cops know he flew into London. Why the fuck did he come all this way? If he wanted to run away, why didn't he take a slow boat to New Zealand or something? Someone needs to explain that to me. What the hell is going on?"

The husband? Could he mean Gray?

"Mistake to bury the knife," Wilson said. "Stupid fucking Australian cops took too long to find it. They don't deserve their fucking jobs."

My fingers almost froze on my phone as I pretended to snap yet another picture.

The knife.

This *was* about Gray.

"What about Constance?" he said. "She being a good girl and staying put here in London? I made sure Hurst told her she couldn't leave."

Blood drained from my face. He knew about me. And knew that I'd spoken with Detective Hurst. Therefore, he had to know about Rosemary. Questions whipped through my mind. *Had he ordered her killed?* What connection did he have to Detective Michael Hurst? Why would a detective take a directive from Wilson Carlisle?

The awful truth dawned on me. The detective was *one of them.*

I was just a thin partition away from Wilson. If he knew I was here, what would he do? I turned my head away, my chest tightening.

"Yeah. Get onto it pronto," continued Wilson in a sharp tone. "I can't do much from here. But I'll be there for the closing ceremony. You know I will. I never miss it."

What closing ceremony? Some charity event he was attending? I had to research that. If I got away from here alive.

Wilson sighed noisily. "Is Kara missing me? Tell her Daddy Wilson misses her. Little asshole broke my finger last time I saw her. Told me not to touch her again." He chuckled. "She told me to disappear into the black hole in the middle of the Milky Way."

My stomach folded in on itself.

Kara. *What had he done to her?* He knew exactly where she was. Kara had to be with the person he was speaking to, because he just asked them to tell her something. How on earth did I find out who was on the other end of that conversation?

I didn't gain anything useful from the rest of Carlisle's phone call.

I waited until he headed back into the store and then made steps in the opposite direction. I was too much of a mess right now to keep tailing him. A professional might be able to hold it together, but not me. Not now. My eyes brimmed with tears.

Kara, how did you get mixed up with Wilson Carlisle?

These were dangerous, bad people. Were they traffickers?

Who did I need to contact? Someone who was an expert in rescuing people caught up in sex trafficking? But I didn't know who I could trust. I couldn't trust the police.

And how was I going to find Gray now? I had no way of contacting him.

As I caught a cab back to my hotel, I realised I wasn't safe there anymore. Wilson would be sure to know where I was staying. Detective Hurst knew where I was; therefore Wilson knew.

I made a decision: I was going to travel to Greece and find an expert who rescued trafficked persons. I'd seen documentaries about such people—they'd just been volunteers on their own, hacking paths through the tangled, dangerous jungles of the traffickers. That was what I needed. Someone who worked outside of the system. Someone who couldn't be corrupted.

THE FIFTH CHALLENGE

48. EVIE

THE MONASTERY, IT WAS WARPING MY MIND. A feeling of being reeled in and at the brink of being consumed. My dreams had been invaded by three-dimensional shapes that folded out into endless hexagons. Forming and reforming. Everything in perfect order. Phi. Binary code. Birds of prey. Myself, running through the dark halls. Trapped and re-trapped in geometric prisons. Everything in a balance that cared about nothing, not even the numbers upon which it was all based.

I woke struggling to breathe. Staring around me, I realised I was in the recovery room where Kara had been. My hand reached automatically to a large, hard lump on the side of my head. It hurt. *How did I get that?* Confusion spun in my mind until I remembered. Ruth had pushed me into the path of a metal bird in challenge four. I didn't know anything that happened after that.

Poppy's fingers gently stroked my arm. "Evie, you're awake . . ."

I half sat. "What happened? Do you know?"

"Just give yourself some time to—"

"Tell me!"

She set her lips together grimly. "You guys lost your challenge. Sorry."

My heart fell. "Am I out of the program?"

"No. But Ruth and Harrington are."

I sucked in a breath of relief. "God. Really? Can't say I'll miss them."

"Me either." She suppressed a giggle. "Harrington apparently copped a bird beak right to his shoulder. He's too injured to continue."

"Okay, well, that's not good."

"He was a jerk. Anyway, it's breakfast time. Feel okay to walk out there with me?"

"I've been asleep all that time?"

"'Fraid so. You must have needed it."

"Let's get out of here." Rising, I let Poppy help me to my feet.

I spent the day of the fifth challenge out in the welcome sunshine and green of the garden, barely moving and barely speaking to anyone. People left me alone, apart from Brother Vito and Sister Dawn, who came to check on me a few times.

Yolanda stepped up to me just as the sun's last rays were burning themselves out. She sat on the low bough of a tree beside my chair. The shade of the tree turned her skin colour to the deepest of browns. "Hey."

"Hey."

"Is your head okay?"

"I'll survive, I guess." I managed a smile.

"Sucks we didn't make it to the finish line." "Looks like I got the order of the puzzle pieces wrong."

"What happened? I saw a bird coming your way and called out to you and then I was busy dodging birds myself. All of a sudden, you were on the floor and Harrington was bleeding."

"Ruth pushed me out of the way. Just because she wanted Harrington's puzzle piece first."

She gasped. "That's crazy. I've only been in one challenge with her before. But, oh yeah, she doesn't care what she has to do to win a challenge. She's such a strange person." She leaned her head back against the trunk. "Is this program helping any of us? I just feel on edge all the time."

"Me too. At least there's just today and tomorrow to get through."

"Can't wait. Scary though. I've built this whole fantasy thing up in my mind where I have a new shiny life. But I don't know if I can do it."

"What were you doing, before here?"

She half shrugged, twisting her long black hair around her fingers. "I don't even know. One minute I was in college and everything was good. The next minute my boyfriend of four years dumped me. I felt like the world's biggest loser, y'know? I came close to killing myself. Instead, I started going to every party and having every drug and sleeping with every guy. Just to kill the pain. I got kicked from my course. And that should have been enough to shock some sense into me. But by then it'd become normal just to wake up and have a pipe, y'know? Everyone I was hanging out with then was smoking ice. It didn't seem like this crazy thing that was going to steal your life away. It just made me feel . . . good. When I saw my old boyfriend in the street, I didn't even care anymore. Because I had something better."

"I get you," I told her. "That's addiction. You don't realise it's so destructive because it makes you feel better about yourself."

Nodding, she sighed. "You can guess the rest of my story. I had to make money somehow. I don't want to go back to any of that. I want to press a reset button."

"This—*the program*—is the reset button." Even as I said it, I only half believed it.

"Man, I hope so. Hey, what's your story? You're from Australia, right?"

"Yeah. I was an ordinary mum in the suburbs with a husband and two small daughters. Willow and Lilly. I got hooked into gambling. Just trying to make our lives better. But it didn't. I got into a terrifyingly huge amount of debt. Happened so quick. My next stop was trying to make some money as a kind of escort—a sugar baby. I'd go to dinner, chat with the guy, and hope he'd take me shopping afterwards to buy something expensive. Some did, some didn't. One man—a chartered accountant—bought me a handbag with a two thousand dollar price tag. I sold it on eBay the next day."

"Did you sleep with them—those guys?"

"It was heading there. But I didn't quite get to that point before Brother Vito contacted me. It's nothing I ever thought I'd do. But people have no idea of the things they'll actually do when they hit rock bottom. When their backs are against the wall."

"You get it." A small sob cracked Yolanda's voice. "That's exactly how it was for me. Some of the girls I worked with were fine with it, but they were the ones who knew exactly what they were walking into. It's the ones like us who are desperate who end up hating ourselves."

The last of the light slipped behind the tall walls of the monastery.

Everyone headed inside.

Like every night, we sat in the refectory and amused ourselves in the hours before dinner—reading, playing cards and chatting. There was no room set aside with comfortable armchairs or sofas—it seemed that the monks must work from dusk to dawn and had no need of such things.

Everyone seemed to be shouting—their voices bouncing off the stone, hexagonal walls. Challenge four had left us all charged with adrenalin and fear of what was coming next—fear we were trying hard to cover up.

I was glad for the quiet of the dormitory after our meal of pot roast.

Quiet, calm. A space to regenerate.

But in my bed, with the lights out and the metronomes ticking, I couldn't rest. I'd lost the last challenge. If the fifth challenge was even rougher and I lost it too, I'd be out of the program. My debts wouldn't be paid. I'd get thirty thousand—for my three completed challenges. That would only pay for half of my debt. I'd still be in way over my head.

My life so far seemed like a stack of failures, one on top of the other.

My mother had kept me well informed of my failings when I was growing up. There was something wrong with everything I did. I'd been blissfully ignorant that Ben was her favourite until the age of twelve, on the day I first got my period. It was the same day Ben sprained his ankle playing soccer. My mother told me to quit fussing and had presented me with a packet of sanitary pads. But she'd nursed Ben and his ankle all afternoon.

For a while, it was okay because Dad and Ben made up for what my mother lacked. But Dad died the year I turned thirteen, of a brain tumour. Ben died the year I turned seventeen.

Everything turned to ashes.

Until I met Gray.

And now I'd gone and burned it all to the ground again.

My mind replayed something Ben said the month before he died, when he was just nineteen—his voice serious but his eyes smiling: *Once you're born, you have the responsibility of making yourself some sort of a life, something that justifies the grand privilege of having won the race out of millions of sperm and thousands of eggs. You made it. Surely after winning against such odds, there should be a winner's life ahead?*

I had to start winning.

At midnight, when the bells woke me, Ben's words were still in my mind and silently on my lips. An anger seared my insides. Anger at the winner's life Ben hadn't had a chance to pursue. Anger at myself for losing at life. Anger at Ruth and the monks and the mentors who were making my time here so hard. Anger at the monastery for making me feel so defeated.

Good. I'd use the anger to get through this.

Over half the beds were now empty. There was just Poppy, Kara, Mei, Louelle, Yolanda and myself in the women's dorm now.

Poppy and I were in the second group to leave the room. I loved Poppy, but I couldn't help wishing I'd gotten put with Louelle or Yolanda instead. From what I'd seen, they were better at the challenges. But still, Poppy tried hard.

Out in the hallway, Duncan met us. I couldn't conceal my raging disappointment at getting lumbered with him in my team. "You'd better pull your weight, Dunc. If you try to stand there and direct like a traffic controller, I swear I'll punch you in your soft belly."

Poppy inhaled sharply in surprise.

I wanted to feel bad about what I'd just said and apologise, but I had no apology left in me.

Duncan's temples flushed. "Was that necessary? We haven't even gotten to the challenge room yet."

Not bothering to answer, I whirled around and sprinted towards the cloister.

Poppy caught up with me, panting. "You okay?"

"No. You?"

"No," she admitted.

We reverted to silence as we ran out into the garden.

Something had changed in the mentors' faces. Their expressions were serious, almost unyielding. As if they were guiding us on how we had to be to get through this.

"This challenge will test you in a different manner to the last," Brother Sage told us. "It's mental rather than physical."

Bracing myself, I replied, "You mean, you're not going to try to kill us this time around?"

"What happened was unfortunate." Sister Rose's words limped on her thin lips. "Sometimes people get over-enthusiastic in the challenges."

"It's not enough to keep saying things are *unfortunate*," I accused. "It's not enough. That challenge was dangerous."

Poppy curled her fingers around my arm. "Let's just get this challenge done, Evie. At least we know it's an easy one."

Brother Sage raised his eyebrows. "I didn't say it would be easy."

I shrugged Poppy's hand away. "What is any of this doing for us? It's starting to feel like we're performing puppets."

Duncan's eyes widened with surprise, looking from me to the mentors and sucking his mouth in—like a small child trying to look pious when another child was being naughty.

Brother Vito offered me his customary warm smile. "There has been a great deal of value gained by these challenges in all the previous years. You will see."

I held his gaze for a moment. "I hope so."

"We can't hold up the challenges," said Sister Dawn firmly, holding out the palm of her hand to guide us towards the entry to the inner rooms. "This discussion will have to continue tomorrow."

"Please," Poppy whispered as we walked along the hallway. "Don't ruin your chances. You're too close now."

"I couldn't hold back," I responded. But Poppy was right. I might have just blown it. The first time I'd stepped inside the monastery, I'd told myself to hold it together. But I was either doing a miserable job of that or the challenges really were too extreme, and this place really was too strange and too dangerous. I was fast losing perspective.

We stepped into an inky-dark fifth room. Every light off. I jammed my eyes shut. I didn't want to see the dark. I didn't want to yield to it. Things were going to happen on *my* terms.

Yet the sense of being swallowed whole was overwhelming.

We stopped just inside the doorway. I didn't trust that metallic creatures weren't about to swoop on us.

"Get it started," I said under my breath, my voice sounding fiercer in my ears than I felt.

Lights snapped on one by one around me. I let my eyes snap open.

The lights were dim. The room was bare, apart from a tall object in the middle that was draped with a black velvet fabric.

The object had to be one of the hexagonal boxes, but why was it covered?

"I'm not touching that," Poppy muttered somewhere close to me.

"Well, there's definitely something under there," said Duncan predictably.

I glanced across at him, wondering how he'd managed to get through challenge four. He would have had to run and dodge like everyone else instead of standing and trying to lead the action. A dark part of me wished I'd seen it.

We were hesitating, losing time.

Was that what the mentors expected? That because of the last challenge, we'd do anything not to set things in motion? What had Brother Vito told me? He'd said humans were creatures of habit—once stung, forever fearful.

Stepping up to the stand, I grabbed the edge of the velvet and flipped it over, exposing what lay underneath: six projectors sitting atop the hexagonal box. The projectors were modern, about the size and shape of a large digital clock, all facing outwards. Each of them was clearly labelled from one to six. The hexagonal box merely seemed to act as a stand for them, though I couldn't be certain of that.

I peered back over my shoulder at Poppy and Duncan to gauge reactions. Had I triggered something terrible that I wasn't yet seeing? But the two of them looked nothing more than curious, stepping across to the projectors.

"They're all attached to these rings," said Duncan curiously.

There were two metal rings running around the top of the hexagonal box —an inner and an outer, the inner ring a little higher than the outer.

"Should we turn them on?" Poppy widened her eyes at me, as if asking me if it were okay.

"What does everyone think?" Duncan nodded his head thoughtfully as he crossed his arms. "If we press the on button, what do you think is likely to happen?"

"We see some films?" said Poppy scornfully.

"Then we'll have to make a decision on whether to press the buttons or not. Because touching the buttons could set off a chain reaction we're not prepared for." Duncan sounded unaffected by Poppy's sneer, but he licked his lips anxiously.

Without looking in Duncan's direction, I pushed my thumb down on the button of the projector marked with the number *one*.

"Evie," came Duncan's reprimand, "I don't think we'd yet decided . . ." His voice faded.

My eyes tracked the silvery cone of light from the projector to the wall directly opposite.

The jittery film was old and washed of colour, like something that had once been shot on Super 8 and then copied to a modern medium.

In the film, a girl of about twenty slept in a bed. A metronome slowly swung to and fro above her on the wooden shelf. There was no sound. The film was shot here, in the women's dormitory of the monastery.

"Might as well see the rest." Poppy seemed emboldened as she took a couple of steps clockwise and turned the next one on. She glanced at Duncan, as if daring him to say something. He didn't.

The second film showed the girl passing underneath the bird-of-prey sculpture in the entry, glancing upwards at the bird as she ran. Did the bird mean something to her? Had she been through the fourth challenge and the bird reminded her of that?

In the third of the films, she continued on outside and through the gates of the monastery and then into the hills. Peacocks scattered as she raced up a steep incline. The girl kept looking behind her. The combination of the grainy quality of the film and the jitter made it hard to see her expression.

Was she scared?

Excited?

God, please don't let her be scared. After what happened to Saul and Harrington and Kara and even myself, I was already scared enough.

She stopped at the graves. Stepping forward tentatively, she looked behind her. Who or what was she checking for?

My skin prickled and grew cold as I viewed the fourth film. Hooded, menacing figures rose and stepped out from behind the graves. They wore long black garb. Their faces appeared painted white, having a luminosity in the night. They stood facing the girl. I could only see the girl from behind, but I could sense her terror by the stiff lines of her body through her thin nightdress. The wind blew her hair sideways as she backed away a step. The figures then filed out from the graves and towards the girl in two lines.

"What the hell is that all about?" Poppy gaped at the clip before moving on to start the next film and fumbling for the on button.

I spun on my heel to face the next film clip—the fifth one. This one showed the girl running again, this time along the jagged hilltop that led to the chapel. She dashed inside.

Breath caught in my lungs as I watched the sixth film. The figures were advancing on the chapel. The film stopped and started several times, the figures advancing on the chapel each time—my heart stopping and starting along with the film. I was terrified for the girl. The rope that hung from the chapel's bell swung in the wind, reminding me of a hangman's noose.

A sick feeling wound through my insides. I wanted to be out of this room and far away from these images. But I was stuck here, with the films looping over and over again.

"These are insane." Poppy's voice held a nervous giggle that she cut short. "I mean, I know the mentors said this one was a challenge of the mind, but this is just . . ."

Thoughts raced through me. *It's just another challenge. You can and will get through it. Think, think, think . . .*

"What if they're in the wrong order—the films?" I suggested. "Maybe it's all just a bad dream. Like, the film of the sleeping girl should be the last film?" Even as I said it, it sounded like wishful thinking.

"Let's try it," said Poppy in a breathy voice. "Anything to get this challenge *done*." Frowning, she tried to pick up a projector. "But they're fixed in place."

Duncan screwed up his small, snub-nosed features. "I think you'll find that the projectors can run around on those rings, like tracks."

Poppy glanced up at him. "You're good for something, aren't you Dunc? I bet you've got model trains at home."

"As it happens, I do," he replied. "I have a working model railway layout that almost entirely takes up a twelve-by-twelve–foot shed. It has mountains, towns and lakes and took me five years to complete."

I was worried that Duncan was about to launch into a story about his trains, but instead he applied himself to sliding the first projector around the inside circular track. As the film of the sleeping girl crossed with the fourth film—of the graves—something strange seemed to happen.

"Wait! Stop it there!" I breathed, pointing at the screen. The two projected films were merged on the wall. The girl in the bed now seemed to be sleeping on a grave, with gravestones surrounding her.

"Hell's bells." Poppy gaped at me.

"Let's try the others." I moved the second projector around on the outside track, trying to find two projected images that made a different scene.

"There!" yelled Poppy excitedly as the second film superimposed itself over the fifth film. Now, the girl ran along the corridor as before, but the two lines of hooded figures walked in lines on either side of her—looking like ghosts inside the walls of the corridor.

There was one last set of films to pair up.

Noticing my trembling fingers, Duncan took over, rotating the third projector around on the metal ring until it overlapped with the only film left—the sixth film. The two films put together showed the girl running into the chapel on the hill, but now the group of hooded figures were circling the chapel, ominously closing in.

All six films automatically stopped looping and locked into the scenes.

We'd gotten it right.

Our heads turned in unison to the clock.

The light remained red.

"There must be something else," Poppy whispered. She turned her face back around to the films. "Oh my God . . ."

I wheeled around.

Something was happening with the three sets of superimposed films.

The films had begun to *continue*. But each set of projected images now operated as one, as though the films had merged inside the projectors as well. Somehow, there were now just three films, looping in pairs on six projectors.

In set one, the girl woke on the stone grave on the hill, terror on her face. She jumped up.

In set two, she ran away towards the cliff. Hooded figures rose from behind the gravestones and filed out in two lines, following her.

In set three, she ran into the chapel. The figures surrounded the chapel. I held my breath as one of the figures turned and looked . . . *at us*. His face was completely in shadow inside the hood that he wore.

Poppy stumbled backwards. "Damned creepy shit," she muttered.

What were we meant to do? Hadn't we already done all we could?

No, there was something else. Think.

"Let's forget about the *scary-as-hell* fact that it looks like that guy is staring right at us," I said, "and work out what he'd be looking at in the actual scene."

"That would be the cliff edge." Duncan nodded. "The aspect where he is now, he'd be looking directly that way. I can picture that from the day when we were all out there on the hills. After poor Saul died." He gazed at the man in the hood as if transfixed.

The hooded man broke away from the group. And headed towards us. I felt a chill bite into my stomach.

Duncan threaded his hands together nervously. "I hardly think this is necessary. What's this all about? I don't like this man. No, I don't like him much at all."

For the first time that I'd seen in a challenge, Duncan took action. With quick movements, he rotated the first, second and third projectors back to their original positions.

Now, there was a film projecting on all six walls again.

The films all went blank.

Then every film snapped on again. All showing the same film—of the man on the cliff edge advancing towards us. He lifted a knife in his fist.

"Oh no," Duncan muttered. "That wasn't the idea."

The films began showing flashes of something else.

The girl in the chapel.

The hooded man advancing.

The girl lifting something in the chapel—the stairs?

The hooded man advancing.

A hidden passage appearing beneath the raised stairs.

The hooded man advancing.

The girl entering the passage and lighting a candle.

The hooded man advancing.

The girl running along a dark passage.

The hooded man advancing.

The candlelight showing a door ahead.

The hooded man advancing.

The girl opening the door.

The hooded man running, knife raised.

A flash of images so quick my mind couldn't register them.

A sudden nausea rose in my stomach. Duncan and Poppy made gasping, stuttering sounds, no longer watching but trying to turn away and cover their eyes.

Panting hard, I rushed to turn off the projectors. Anything to stop those images.

No, turning them off wouldn't win the challenge.

What hadn't we tried?

How could I undo what we'd done? How could I send the hooded man away?

I rotated the first, second and third projectors to align with the sixth, fifth and fourth projectors. The opposite to how we'd done it last time.

Again, the projected images on the wall went blank.

The man appeared again, tilting his head at me as if listening to a sound I couldn't hear. He then turned and walked back to the chapel.

Holding my breath, I glanced at the clock.

Green.

I didn't feel the usual jubilation.

Whoever that girl was, she hadn't *won*. The film didn't show her escaping.

I had the distinct sensation of winning the battle but not the war.

49. GRAY

MORNINGS AT THIS REFUGEE CAMP IN Paris were just as chaotic as the nights. Little kids crying and people calling to each other and a general sense of confusion. The fact that I didn't understand their language, nor that of the host country, only added to my own confusion. I'd fallen back to sleep sometime during the night.

In a sudden panic, I checked for my wallet and passport.

Still all there.

Pulling out fifty euros, I left it on the floor and zipped up the tent.

As I emerged, a bearded man eyed me in surprise, sizing me up, silently questioning me. *Who are you? Why are you here if you're not one of us?*

I shot him a tight smile and headed off down the street, feeling bad that I got to walk away.

Sun sparked from a greenish canal, tourists already sitting along it, a couple of them adventurous enough to be splashing about in the water. A sign stated: *Canal de l'Ourcq*.

Outdoor eateries were beginning to open up, the smell of coffee and hot food making my stomach feel as empty as a canyon.

I bought a full breakfast at a café and ate quickly. My heart tugged as I watched children dart and play around the chairs, sun glinting on their hair. If Evie and I had money, it could have been us here on an overseas trip and Willow and Lilly playing tag. Instead, lack of money had seen the two of us just trying to make it through from week to week. And now we were caught up in a world so dark and dangerous that we might not walk out of it alive.

I needed to talk to my girls. If I didn't do it now, there might not be another chance. I wanted to make sure they knew why I'd gone.

Locating a public phone, I called home.

Verity answered quickly.

"It's Gray. I'm sorry, but I had to go."

"Gray! You've got a nerve. What did you—?"

"I'm looking for your daughter."

"You're looking for Eveline? Where are you?"

"I'm a long way from there. Can I talk to Willow and Lilly, please?"

"They're in the yard, playing."

"Are they okay? How's Lilly?"

"I don't need to tell you you're in serious trouble, do I?"

"I know. I know that."

She went silent for a moment. Then, "You took my grocery money, Gray." She was fooling herself calling it her *grocery money*.

"I'll pay you back. Every cent."

"Look, it's all right. I don't need it." Her voice had changed, gone down a few notches in harshness. She sounded almost friendlier, if that was possible for Verity. "Gray, if you will, I'm a little confused with Lilly's treatment routine. Could you explain the steps to me again?"

"I'm sorry as hell about leaving all that with you. You'd be better off getting that info direct from the doc again—"

"Okay, but right now do you remember what to do with the postural drainage? Lilly's here patiently waiting for me to start. She's such a good girl."

I frowned. "You just said the girls were out playing."

I exhaled hard as I realised what she was doing. The police were there with her. *Right now*. They had the phone tapped, and they were indicating to Verity to keep the conversation going. And she knew I'd stay on the line if it was about Lilly's treatment.

"Tell them I love them," I breathed, and hung up.

I doubted the police had even needed me to stay on the phone to find out where I was. They could find out locations instantly these days, couldn't they? And a public phone was a fixed line—the location could be pinpointed. Maybe they wanted Verity to keep me talking in the hope I'd give away information about what I was planning to do. No wonder she'd called her *cash-in-hand income* her *grocery money* with the police there listening.

Okay, so the police now knew exactly where I was. I had to keep moving. And I had to look different, somehow.

I stalked the streets, searching for a pharmacy. Luckily, the French word was close to the English: *pharmacie*. I bought some brown hair dye then headed away to find a pub with a restroom.

Passing up the more popular pubs, I came across one that was looking a bit empty, apart from a few backpackers and elderly men. That was what I needed. I picked out a beer from the menu—a *Gavroche*. I swilled the fruity, malty beer in my mouth while waiting for the restroom to be vacated. I watched as an old guy stumbled out, slurring a song, and wandered back to the bar.

I made my way to the restroom and sat inside a stall. I doused my hair with the dye. It stank, but it was supposed to work within a few minutes. There wasn't much ventilation in the tiny space. With my eyes watering and a chemical taste in my throat, I washed the dye out in the restroom sink, first rinsing out the sour, beer-shot vomit of the drunk who'd just been in here.

My hands on the sink, I raised my head to study myself.

Dark-haired me looked a lot different to blonde-haired me. I looked older, more serious. Even a little bit criminal. Maybe the events of the past few days had made me look that way, or maybe my mind was playing tricks on me. I hadn't done anything wrong, but still, I was on the run from the police.

I straightened, forcing a friendlier expression.

Moving close to the mirror, I scrutinized my dye job. I had a few dark dye stains smeared around my hairline. I scrubbed the stains and my head the best I could with the soap and then rinsed it again.

Replacing the baseball cap, I walked out, stopping to ask a table of backpackers if they knew where any internet cafés were. They pointed me in the direction of a library. I jogged along the canal and towards the street they'd indicated.

I passed a newsstand with turnstile racks of postcards and greeting cards out in front. I bought a detailed map of Greece. I caught sight of a news item on the front page of a newspaper. The story was in French, but I recognised my face easily enough. Below the picture of me were images of Evie's blackened car and the rope and knife. The only word I understood was Interpol. And I could guess that this meant there was now a warrant out for my arrest. No doubt, police had found my fingerprints on things that proved that I'd been at the scene of Evie's burned-out car. The police already had my fingerprints from my misdemeanours as a teenager.

Taking my change, I quickly headed away, adjusting my cap to sit lower on my forehead.

Anyone reading that story would think I was dangerous, someone who'd murdered his own wife and was on the run in Europe. I recalled Constance's response to me in our last conversation. Had she seen a story like this and started to believe I killed Evie? The more I thought about it, the more I was convinced. Every time I'd seen a news story, I'd believed it without question. Now I knew that the other side of the story might not be so clear-cut.

After a few turns and backtracking, I found the library.

Sitting at a library computer, I typed in the word *Yeqon*.

That brought up a chaotic assortment about angels being sent to earth, Yeqon being one of them. But he wasn't a good angel.

This wasn't helping.

Next, I tried searching for the historical society. They had chapters in a list of different countries. No specific locations or contact details. A pretty secretive society that certainly wasn't welcoming to new members.

But Rosemary the investigator had been able to find out a bit more about them and so could I.

I needed to reverse engineer this. Set off a pinball and see how many targets it could hit. And then zero in on each of those targets. At my job, I'd often had to reverse engineer code. And sometimes I had to search for the needle in the haystack that was screwing up the code. When code went wrong, you had to go back and find out if the program was terminally screwed or if there was just a comma in the wrong place. A wrong comma could destroy everything.

I used the internet's Wayback Machine and other snapshots of web pages that were dead and buried. Were there any old pages of the historical society I could find here?

There wasn't much. I found an old Geocities website with no text but a few photographs, taken from a distance. The pictures immediately struck me as odd. They weren't snaps of a meeting. These were more like surveillance photos. Multiple pics snapped of a group of people walking and close-ups of faces—all blurry. Who'd put up this website? Maybe the person had tried and failed to capture the interest of the police, and in desperation they'd put the information out there online, like a beacon. But this was fourteen years ago. And there was no context to any of it.

I paid the library extra for access to a Photoshop module and started working on reversing the blur of the photographs. Motion blur could be fixed if all the information was still in the picture. You could get it back to a pretty sharp image. Verity had once been shocked when I'd fixed a couple of blurred photographs that had been the last ones taken of her son, Ben, making them clean and sharp. It'd been the only time I'd ever seen her cry.

I was in luck. Within minutes, I had the pictures fixed. Maybe the person who took the shots was nervous as hell they'd be discovered by the society, and they'd forgotten to keep the camera steady.

Now I had much clearer faces and images to work with.

I frowned, looking closer as I blew one of the group photos up large. Three of the people were wearing a type of robe. Freemasons, maybe?

I zeroed in on the person closest to the foreground. A woman. She wasn't facing the camera, but maybe that was good. Because there was a symbol on the back of the robe.

What was that?

I isolated the symbol and sharpened it with the Photoshop tools. It was basically a ladder stretching diagonally across a hexagon. Monks were climbing the ladder, winged angels and demons surrounding. The symbol looked ancient.

Next, I scrutinised the faces. I didn't recognise the Wilson Carlisle character that Constance had told me about. Maybe he looked radically different fourteen years ago.

I copied each face in turn and kept it in a separate folder. *I'm coming for each one of you*, I whispered under my breath. *I'm going to find out why you people were at that meeting.*

I returned to the picture of the symbol and tried an internet image search on it.

I sat back, stunned, as similar images came straight up.

The other images had a name. The Ladder of Divine Ascent. A religious symbol dating way back. Twelfth century. Monks ascending heaven on the thirty rungs of the ladder, each rung a different stage of the journey.

Okay, so these people were a religious group? That ruled out the Freemasons. So what I had so far was an ancient religious group hiding behind a historical-society shopfront. That sounded nuts. If these people were traffickers, they weren't like any traffickers I'd heard about. They were a cult.

Constance's investigator had been right. This group were religious nuts. Religious nuts with bad vices and criminal dealings.

This symbol was a little different to the ones on my screen, but I needed an expert to take a look and tell me what it all meant. *A priest?* The only church I'd ever heard about in Paris was the Notre Dame—the church everyone had heard of. But I couldn't afford to spend the time in the hope that a priest would agree to see me or that they'd know anything about the symbol, especially if it was as old as it seemed.

I had to get to Greece and figure it all out there. Besides, the Australian police knew I was in France, and I needed not to be here anymore.

Putting the photocopies away carefully in my bag, I exited the library.

How did I get to Greece now that Interpol were involved? I didn't have a clue.

50. CONSTANCE

I STEPPED FROM THE COOL AIRPORT AT ATHENS, only to be soaked through with sweat within minutes. Sweat trickled between my breasts, pooled in my navel and then seeped along the waistband of my shorts.

I stood under the broad sunlight, not wanting to know what the back half of my clothing looked like.

Summer in Greece was stupidly hotter than summer in England. I pictured Rosemary. Rosemary wouldn't have let any of this slow her down.

I'd looked up the names of people working against people trafficking, and now, somehow, I had to track them down.

The crowd pressed in on me from all sides—businesspeople and families excited to be starting their summer holiday. Walking up to a line of yellow taxis, I directed the driver to take me into the city. He asked me for a location, and I couldn't tell him. I hadn't planned that far ahead. All I knew was that I didn't want to head straight to my hotel. Wilson Carlisle knew who I was, and if he was trying to find Gray, then he might have people keeping an eye on me, too. The driver suggested the Acropolis Museum, and I nodded. Going the tourist route might throw them off-track and cause them to discount me as a danger to them. At the same time, I knew I couldn't win at this game. They had the advantage in every way. I just had to hope they had little interest in me.

A welcome cool enveloped me as I entered the museum. I wandered among the artworks, stopping to grab a cold drink and a bite to eat at one of their cafés.

I stepped through a display named the Archaic Gallery. All white, with soaring ceilings. Marble statues stood on rectangular stands among thick round columns. The statues were clothed and unclothed, dismembered and with missing parts, and had me sweating anew. These relics of an ancient world were all so *other* in contrast to the world I inhabited. Too vast and too strange.

I leaned against a stone column, letting a wave of nausea pass through me. I needed to take my anti-anxiety pills. This was all too much, and I needed to find a centre of calm. For Kara's sake.

Deep inside my bag, my phone tinkled. It wasn't the ringtone of my regular phone. It was the private phone. I'd forgotten to throw it away. I answered tentatively, wondering if the police or a stranger had somehow gotten hold of this number.

"Constance?" came the voice.

"Gray?" I breathed, then gathered myself, trying to sound like I wasn't astonished to hear from him. "What's been happening?"

"I've been doing a bit of hitchhiking, that's what."

"Listen, I'm sorry about how I was last time we spoke. I—"

"Don't sweat it."

"I feel bad. I shouldn't have just left you high and dry. I'm just . . . incredibly stressed. And I—"

"You thought I hurt my wife."

"No . . ."

"Where are you now?"

"Greece. I'm in Greece."

"Why did you decide to go to Greece? You said the police wanted you to stay in London." His voice, in that peculiar Australian way, sounded both serious and casual at the same time.

"I know. They still do. But I had to keep looking for Kara."

"So, where are you right now?"

"The Acropolis Museum, Athens."

"Alone?"

"Yes. Why—?"

"I'll see you there. In about twenty."

"You what?"

"Twenty minutes. Outside the entrance to the museum."

"You're in Athens?" I spoke that louder than I meant to.

"Yes. But Constance . . . if you call the police or if I see anyone or anything suspicious, you won't see me at all."

I couldn't blame him for being cautious, not after our last conversation. "Gray, trust me, it's just me here. There won't be anyone else."

"I hope so. I'll be there soon."

He hung up. The distrust in his voice was my fault, and it was up to me now to repair the damage and show him that I was on his side.

51. EVIE

RAIN POURED DOWN ON THE GARDEN.

I ached to take my breakfast and eat it outside, but I'd have been washed away in the downpour. A thick, melancholy light was trapped within the monastery halls and rooms—acid grey and unrelenting, tinting everything and everyone with its dull poison.

The projected images of the fifth challenge still stained my thoughts. It seemed to me that the images flashing too fast to register in the last section of film were even worse than what I'd seen.

Duncan had lost his place in the program afterwards, and he'd been sent home. I didn't judge him as harshly in retrospect. He'd done the best he could with what he understood of the world. Poppy had been unable to stop crying after the challenge. She'd hugged me and said she couldn't take any more. She wanted out. The mentors had allowed her to take the place of someone else who was supposed to be eliminated. We promised to keep in contact after the program was over. And then she left. Poppy had always been too sensitive for these challenges, especially so soon after the death of her boyfriend. It felt empty here without her.

Just one more challenge. Then I'd be leaving this place far behind.

I wasn't certain how I'd remember the monastery. There were so many hollow spaces and unseen parts. Two people had died. I still couldn't grasp it all and make it fit together. Perhaps that would be the final challenge—to understand my time here and the monastery itself.

As I took my plate of soup and bread from the kitchen into the refectory, I took a quick glance around at the small group of people sitting at the table and felt a keen sense of loss. This was what was supposed to happen, and I should have been overjoyed to be among the second-last group. But I wanted everyone here making it through to the end, especially Saul.

Another missing face was Kara's. She hadn't given me the chance to know her, but I hoped she'd head home now and go back to college.

The others at the table gave me a nod as I sat down. We were the last eight participants: Richard, Cormack, Mei, Louelle, Thomas, Yolanda, Hop and myself. Two would be eliminated. Then we'd have the final six.

We ate in silence for most of the meal. The soup was good, but after a minute or so, it seemed to me to be saturated with the same grey hue as the rest of the monastery, the taste turning bitter. I couldn't finish it.

"Well, here we are." Cormack pushed his empty plate away.

"The home run." Richard sipped a noisy spoonful of soup. "We all go home in brand new beautiful skins. We're butterflies." He slitted his eyes at Hop in a comical way. "All except for Hop, who told me on the first morning that he has no intention of changing his degenerate ways."

Hop grinned self-consciously, but then his smile slipped. "I've kind of figured out a few things about myself since then."

"During challenge four?" I asked gently.

"Yes, the mirror," Hop replied. "I saw my future, and I didn't like it. When I go back home, I'm going to be a new man."

"That challenge was bad for me," said Mei. "I saw the faces of the men who used to come into my room every day and night. I was nine when I was abducted and made to work as a prostitute. The mirror made me understand that as a child, I felt like I took the spirit of those men deep inside me and that I became just as ugly."

Louelle and I reached out to Mei, hugging either side of her.

Yolanda bowed her head, suddenly crying. "I don't want to go back to being who I was. But what if I'm just no good at being anyone else?"

Richard winked. "Chin up, buttercup. When I become a pilot for real, you can become my co-pilot. Imagine that, huh? Pilot Yolanda, stepping off a light plane in Saudi Arabia, tossing her beautiful hair around in the breeze.

And none of the rich sheiks can say a darn thing about it. Because she's about to fly their asses somewhere."

Sniffling and drying her eyes with the heel of her hand, Yolanda grinned.

Thomas stirred the dregs of his soup, looking for a moment like a child who didn't want to finish his dinner. He wasn't far off being a young child—I'd found out he was just sixteen. "Now that I've kicked the drugs," he said, "I'm going to study to become a chef. I wanted to do that before my mum died. I've given my dad hell over the last two years. But I'm going to do things right, now."

"Yay, Thomas." Yolanda clapped her hands together.

Louelle toyed with a spoon, spinning it back and forth. "Good on you, Tom. What I'm going to do is ride back to my town with my head held high, all guns blazing. There's been a heap of whispers and gossip about me over the past fifteen years or so. But my husband and kids have stuck by me, and I owe it to them to be a wife and mom they can be proud of. I lost my job a year ago—but I plan on getting that back now."

"Here! Here!" Cormack raised his glass of orange juice.

"What about you, Evie?" asked Louelle, dipping bread into her soup. "What are Evie's plans once she ditches this place?"

I breathed in deeply, feeling the air grow heavy in my lungs. "First thing I'm going to do is to go and stay at the beach for a few days with my husband and kids. Just that. Doesn't matter that it's winter back home. Then I'm going to tell him everything. If at the end of it, he hasn't served me with divorce papers, we'll buy a little house." None of it sounded real as it left my lips.

"Sounds like a perfect plan," mused Louelle. "I'm lucky my husband didn't divorce me. And that my kids still talk to me. I was a librarian. Fell off a stepladder putting a stack of books away and did damage to my hip bones. From that moment, I became addicted to painkillers. I'd feel so high and on top of the world, I'd even drive around town like I was on some kind of racetrack. Thank God, my kids are teenagers, and they'd grab the wheel from me. I started drinking, too, when the doctor started restricting the amount of painkillers I could have. I embarrassed my family constantly, and the days just slipped past me. That's not gonna happen anymore. It's all too precious. I didn't grow up in a happy family, but I'm going to make damned sure that my own family is a happy one." She nodded firmly. "Okay, who's next? Spill."

"Well, I'll be moving on out of that Las Vegas drain," said Richard in his American drawl. "Maybe I'll get out of Las Vegas altogether. Too much temptation. Don't know where I'll go. But I've got a few business ideas. Watch this space, people. Ah, look at Cormack mooning about Kara, like a puppy that got left behind. You have to let that one go, son."

Cormack lifted his chin. "Lots of lasses back where I'm from."

"Yes, but you've got your mind stuck on one particular lass," Richard pressed.

"Okay," Cormack admitted. "There's something about her I can't stop thinking about. I'm going to convince her to give me a shot if it's the last thing I do."

"Your bucket list is looking a bit sad, my friend," Richard joked.

"I'm nothing if not passionate. We Scots are a wild bunch. Whatever I go after, I'm all in," said Cormack. "Maybe we should all meet up again somewhere in six months and see how we're all doing. And we'll reminisce about the old days. At the monastery."

Louelle grimaced. "No thanks. If it's all the same, I don't want to remember this place. My grandmother used to say that buildings took on the minds of the people who lived in them. And this place gives me the shudders."

I took in my surroundings again—the murky tones, angled walls, metronomes and strangeness, and I could see what she meant.

Gazing down at the table, I ran my fingertips over the Warcraft bracelet —my link back to Gray.

Outside the arched windows, the rain was like a second skin over the monastery, maybe not drowning us but slowly and surely sealing us in.

Just one more day.

52. GRAY

I STUDIED THE SCENE OUTSIDE THE Acropolis Museum, using a pair of binoculars I'd bought. One minute, it seemed like crazy overkill to be taking precautions like this. But the next minute it hit home that I was a criminal who had won himself the attention of Interpol.

Early today, I'd paid a couple of truck drivers to take me from France to this country. If they recognised me from a news story, I hoped the money would keep them quiet.

Constance was standing alone, wearing white.

I focused on the people around her. Was anyone watching her? Was anyone alone and loitering?

She walked a short distance then stopped, looking nervous. I scanned the crowd, trying to spot anyone who was specifically turning to keep an eye on her. If anyone was watching her, they were doing a good job of hiding it. Unless they had better binoculars than me.

Putting the binoculars away, I cut through the crowd, ready to run if anyone besides Constance moved towards me.

I walked up on her blind side.

Constance startled when she caught sight of me. As soon as she recognised me, she grabbed me in a hug then shrank back quickly. "I'm sorry, that was probably wrong of me. I'm just so glad to see you."

"Good to see you, too."

Her face brightened in relief. "You look different. If I didn't see your face close up, I wouldn't have known it was you. Gosh. Here we are. Greece. Crazy, right?"

"Yeah, crazy. I passed the Acropolis on the taxi ride here. It just popped up out of nowhere."

"I hope you can come back here with your lovely little family one day. Under better circumstances."

"I didn't hurt my wife." The words slipped out unintentionally. The mention of my family released something deep inside. I guessed I needed to speak the words out loud. I loved Evie and the girls. But right now, almost no one knew that but me.

"I know you didn't hurt her," she said.

I turned away for a brief moment, trying to cancel everything out—all the noise inside my head and around me. "Constance, I want you to tell me everything your P.I. told you and anything else you know. So that we're both on the same page. And I'll tell you what I know."

She eyed me in surprise, but she nodded. "Let's go for a walk. And I'll explain what's been happening."

She went over everything in detail. About meeting Rosemary in a café and how she died and their phone conversations. She told me about the bracelet again.

Evie was here. Within reach. I just had to find her.

Constance's voice turned brittle. "I've been trying to do as Rosemary would do. And doing a terrible job at it. I need to get better at it, because my daughter needs me to be. I did manage to follow Wilson Carlisle for a night."

I whistled, not expecting that. "How did *that* go?"

"Nerve-wracking, that's how it went. He . . . mentioned Kara."

"Hell."

She sucked her top lip in, nodding and squeezing her eyes shut. "Yep. That was so hard to hear. They've definitely got her."

"And Evie? Did he talk about her?"

"No . . . but he did say they should have made sure the knife and things were found sooner by the police."

My knees suddenly sagged. I knew they'd done the setup, but to hear it was something else. "You heard him say that?"

"Clearly."

I shook my head, wondering if Evie and Kara even realised what kind of people they were with. It seemed that they'd gone willingly, although I couldn't be sure of that. It didn't always take a weapon to force someone to do something.

"Wait," I said. "Is that the exact moment you decided it wasn't me who buried that stuff?" I met her eyes.

Her shoulders hunched a little, and her gaze dropped. "I'm sorry. Yes. Please don't think bad things of me. This whole thing is just too much to grasp."

"I know. I get it."

"And now, we're in Greece. *Greece*." She threw up her hands in confusion. "Where do we start?"

"Wish I knew. Where are you staying?"

"The Electra Palace. It's where James and I have stayed before."

"Starting from now, Constance, you're going to stop being predictable. So, your suitcase is there in your room?"

"Yes. I had it taken there to my room straight from the airport."

"Great. Leave it there. Don't go back there at all."

"But all my things—"

"You can buy more things."

She sighed, her eyes anxious. "You're right. Someone somewhere knows that I booked that hotel and they're thinking they can keep an eye on me there."

I nodded, sucking in a breath. "Does anyone know you're here? Friends? Family?"

"No, no one yet. Not even James. I just decided to do this after hearing Wilson's conversation."

"Keep it that way. Don't tell anyone." I didn't sound like myself. But I didn't know how else to be right now. "Hey, I've got some things to show you. That group—Yeqon's Saviours—I found out a little about them."

Her eyes enlarged. "What did you find out?"

"I found some photographs and a weird symbol. Let's go someplace where no one's going to look over our shoulders."

We stepped across to a low wall that had a drop behind it and sat while I drew out the photocopies. "This is them. The *Saviours*. At some kind of meeting." I told her what I'd learned about them.

"They're not traffickers . . ." Her voice fell away in hushed confusion. "What are they? And what do they want with my daughter and your wife?"

"We need to find out what their game is. I'm hoping this gives us a clue." I showed her the close-up of the ladder symbol. "Maybe I need to see a priest to tell me what this symbol means."

"I'm not sure that a priest could help you." She sucked in her lips, studying the images. "They might be able to tell you what it's not, but not what it is. If you know what I mean."

"Yeah. I know. I had the same thought. What if the priest has studied religious history—maybe we can find someone like that?"

"That gives me an idea. Rosemary sourced her information about the Saviours from a pair of Greek history professors. They're apparently a married couple, here in Athens."

Stashing my photocopies back in my bag, I jumped from the wall. "Let's go."

53. CONSTANCE

I TOOK OUT MY TABLET TO look up the history professors.

Gray eyed me in alarm, taking the tablet from my hands. "No. From now on, no using your internet. The police or whoever else can track you through that if they want."

"But how are we to get anywhere from here?"

"We either do it old school or use an internet café."

"Old school? Okay, well, maybe they might be able to give us some information here. It's an ancient history museum, after all."

"Good idea."

I left Gray to wipe my browsing history from the tablet while I headed back into the museum. The strange mix of the cool modern interior and ancient artifacts closed around me again. I inquired at the information desk about a married pair of history professors here in Athens. The girl at the desk didn't know, but she asked a couple of others who did know of such a couple. An older lady wrote down two names on the back of a museum brochure. *Rico and Petrina Vasiliou.* They were professors of ancient Greek history, and they lived in an apartment block near the National & Kapodistrian University in Athens, not too far from the Acropolis Museum.

When I returned to Gray, he stopped me from calling them on my private phone, insisting that we should use a public phone. His eyebrows pinched together, his eyes wary in the shadow beneath his cap. "You don't know who alerted the Saviours about Rosemary, right? It could have been the professors."

"God . . ." I didn't trust myself to speak for a moment. It really could have been them. "But if they're connected to the Saviours, why would they have given Rosemary any information at all?"

He nodded. "Makes sense. I just can't figure out how all the moving parts fit together, you know? How did the killer find out about Rosemary?"

"It must have been something she was researching that tipped him off. We have to be careful, Gray. I didn't tell anyone about her. Not even my husband, because I knew he'd worry."

We located a pay phone, and I tried calling the number we'd been given.

Petrina Vasiliou answered. I told her we were from an international historical society, here researching Greek monasteries. She replied to say that it wasn't her area and tried to shuffle me off with a couple of numbers of other professors of history. In desperation, I almost mentioned Rosemary's name. First, I tried telling her about the symbol we'd come across, describing it in detail and saying that we were interested in sourcing its origin.

Her interest seemed immediately piqued, though she also sounded hesitant. She invited us to come over after her husband, Rico, arrived home from work.

Holding back a sigh of relief, I looked across at Gray and nodded.

THE SIXTH CHALLENGE

54. EVIE

I WOKE WITH SKIN LIKE A fish, cold and wet. I'd been sweating, dreaming that everyone here was somehow gone and I was the last person. The monastery had sealed itself, and there was no way out, as if the windows and doors were its eyes and mouths and it had shut them all tight. I was trapped inside an insane mind.

Breathing steadily, I reoriented myself.

I had to calm myself. Exist in the moment and close everything else out. Focus on the prize.

If learning the ability to focus under intense pressure was what the mentors had intended, then it was working. There had never been a time in my life when my surrounds had seemed so alien, my dreams so harsh, and days when I'd had to fight so hard not to pack it all in and run.

Yolanda, Louelle and Mei slept in their beds near me in the dormitory. Outside the high window, rain still surged through the inky night.

Evie, you're okay. No matter which way it goes, it's okay.

Still, panic shot into my chest and throat, making my breaths shallow.

Why did I feel so much like a prisoner going to the gallows? Maybe it was because each challenge just felt so enormous to me that I might as well be facing hurdles a hundred feet tall. If I was meant to be feeling like a winner by now, then the program had failed. Maybe in retrospect, when we were sailing away from here, I'd finally feel healed. Things always looked different in retrospect, as though you'd suddenly been given a new set of lenses to view them through.

I thought of Gray and the girls and knew that I already saw my life with them differently.

When the bells rang, the tiny screen on my wristband remained dark. The other women left the room one by one as their wristbands flashed, the rest of us chiming *good luck*. Until there was only me left in the room.

Almost a complete hour ticked past in the empty room.

Finally, my wristband flashed number four. I was in the last of the four teams.

Richard stood outside, his pucker of forehead muscles belying the wink in his eye. "Ah, so my final partner in crime is Evie. Makes sense it would be you."

"Let's smash this." My voice echoed hollowly down the hall.

We ran, for what would be the last time, out to the garden to meet the mentors.

"You've made it this far. You hardly need any words of encouragement," Brother Sage told us. "Just do what makes sense to you, as you have in every other challenge."

The mentors guided us to the sixth challenge room.

We stepped into almost total darkness, the blinking red bulb below the challenge clock the only point of light in the room.

The door closed behind us.

Nothing. No sounds, no smell, nothing being shown to us.

"Ah, guys . . . mentors . . . I don't think your lights are working," Richard joked.

"C'mon, c'mon, c'mon," I breathed. "Show us what you've got."

"Not funny." Richard walked a short distance, exhaling loudly.

I turned. A light had sprung to life, but only the light of a candle.

The man who held the candle began walking in a small circle around a hexagonal box in the centre of the room. He wore the loose garb of the monks, and his feet were bare.

Okay, there's the box. Same as always.

What else was in this room? My memory of the fourth challenge sharpened. I wanted to step across the room, but I hesitated.

Richard strode forward and made it to the middle of the room unscathed. Emboldened, I followed him.

The box seemed solid, with no markings or symbols. We carried out our usual tests on it—knocking, listening, trying to twist it or move it somehow.

The monk continued to walk in a circle, on the outside of us.

"Hey you." Richard stepped in front of him. "What are we supposed to do here?"

The monk stopped, but that was all. He gazed at Richard with vacant eyes. When Richard moved, the monk resumed his circular walk.

"We'd better search the room," Richard muttered. "Meet you back here."

I nodded, breath catching and holding like a fist in my stomach. What if there were more monks just standing there in the pitch darkness of this huge room? "We'll zigzag back and forward from here to the wall. If you find anything, call out and stay there. I'll find you."

"Yeah." Richard disappeared from view.

I began my search, to and fro, moving a little to the right each time. "Anything?" I called, not so much expecting that he had but just wanting to hear his voice.

The silence before Richard answered seemed an age. "Nope. Nothing here."

Richard and I met up again, panting.

I looked back over my shoulder at the clock. We'd wasted four precious minutes.

Shooting an anxious glance at Richard, I moved into the monk's path. "Give us a clue."

The monk reached inside his clothing and produced a scroll.

"Thank you," I said, trying to hide my shock.

"Bingo. He responds to commands." Richard took the scroll and picked at the twine that held it closed. "When we first came in, you said, show us what you've got. The guy showed you what he was holding—a candle."

"Okay . . . okay," I said, collecting my breath. If it was that simple, we had this challenge in the bag. "Get it open."

Richard rolled out the scroll on top of the hexagonal box. It contained an illustration of a cave, some people chained up and a fire.

Raising his eyes to me, Richard made a derisive snort. "Plato's Allegory of the Cave. I learned this in the first psychology class I took at college. It's kids' stuff."

I looked closer. In the cave, a line of chained prisoners stared at a wall.

Behind them, a fire burned. In between the fire and the prisoners, there was a puppeteer—making a shadow puppet on the wall for the prisoners.

"What does it mean?"

Richard screwed up his face. "Something about shadows. I don't remember. Hell, I was smashed at the time."

I whirled around to the monk. "Tell us what this means."

He didn't answer.

"Show us what this means," I demanded.

He remained staring at me blankly.

I looked back at the picture. The mask that the puppeteer was holding up reminded me of the awful faces in the mirror in challenge four. The prisoners' heads were restricted. They couldn't turn around and see what was behind them. "So, all the prisoners can see is the shadow, not the real thing?" I asked Richard urgently.

"Yeah." He nodded. "That's right. But the shadow pictures I saw back in college were of animals or something. Not that image."

I could practically hear my heart ticking as I looked at the clock again.

Four minutes left.

"Give us anything else you have to show us," Richard told the monk.

The monk stared straight ahead, unmoving.

"All right," Richard muttered. "So, there's nothing else. This is it. What are we supposed to do? Make our own shadow puppets?" He bent his head as if thinking hard. "Give me the candle, monk."

Again, the monk didn't move.

"Richard, you already asked him if he had anything else to give us. I don't think we're meant to have the candle."

Richard jabbed an angry finger at the monk's chest. "You. Make shadow puppets."

We waited.

Nothing.

Three minutes.

I could hear Richard breathing now. He pointed at each of the prisoners, of which there were five. "The five senses. Sight, hearing, smell, touch and taste. I remember that much. Plato was making a point that they couldn't rely on their senses to work out what was real and what wasn't."

I bent my head over the picture. I should have worked that out. Each of the prisoners was subtly touching a different part of their body with one of their hands—eyes, mouth, ears, nose or body.

The clues were all here, in this picture. Clues that were based on Plato but also clues that were made especially for this challenge.

Two minutes.

The challenges were simple. Designed to be completed within time. Don't go crazy. Go simple.

But what? What were we missing?

If we couldn't use our five senses, what was left?

Thought.

Mind.

Brother Vito's numbers and inevitability.

The monk had nothing left to show us. The answer lay somewhere else. Richard and I had found nothing on the walls or floor. Unless we'd missed something.

No, the answer wasn't anything we could find by touch.

If there was anything else out there in the room, then it was moving around. Evading us.

If it was evading us, then it was human.

One minute.

My palms sweated as my hands formed fists by my sides. "Whoever else is in this room, show yourself."

Richard jerked around to me, eyebrows raised.

No response.

But then a glow. A candle being lit. And a face—a mask—that matched the mask in the picture.

"*Holy—*" Richard exclaimed.

Then another candle from the other side of the room, and another and another and another.

Five monks, all wearing the masks.

Six monks altogether. But because we'd only seen one, we'd assumed there was only one.

I shivered internally at the thought of these masked people silently stepping around us in the darkness.

The clock stopped with seconds to go.

The bulb below turned green.

Richard and I stared at each other. *It was over.*

55. GRAY

RICO VASILIOU WAS WAITING FOR us on the landing of his apartment.

"*Yassou, yassou.*" He pulled a surprised Constance in for a hug and then gave me a back-slapping hug, his shirt smelling of tobacco and olives. "Come in, you both."

We'd given him and his wife fake names—Michael and Lara. I repeated our new names in my mind as I entered the apartment so that I didn't slip up.

The apartment was large and airy. Bright artworks covered the walls—all of a bay with white Greek houses dotting the hills. Everything in the apartment was decorated in clean whites and blues. The round-edge, ornate door frames were distinctly Greek.

Rico's wife came out to greet us. "Hello and welcome. I'm Petrina. Can I get you two a cold drink? The heat must be stifling out there." She was short —short hair too. Together with her large, expressive eyes, she had a kind of pixie look.

Rico and Petrina seemed genuine. But I remained wary.

"Oh, yes, please—anything cold would be lovely." Constance mopped her brow with a handkerchief.

I nodded. "Cold would be great."

That didn't seem to be enough information for Petrina. "Iced tea, Retsina, ouzito?"

A single, deep wrinkle appeared between Constance's eyebrows. "I don't drink anything alcoholic or caffeinated."

"Make mine alcoholic," I said quickly.

Petrina smiled warmly. "I'll get you ouzito, Michael. Retsina can be a little strong if you're not used to it. And water with lemon for you, Lara?"

She showed us out to a tiny balcony where the view swept far into the city.

Constance watched her step back inside then turned to me. "They seem okay?"

"Maybe." I whispered back. I stuck my head over the balcony railing and checked the street below. What would we do now if two carloads of Yeqon's Saviours thugs suddenly screeched up? We'd be trapped.

I wanted to zip this up quickly so we could get out of here.

The Vasilious returned together. Rico placed a platter of bite-sized things on the table—olives, sliced cucumbers, triangles of pita bread, three little cups of dip and some cheese-filled eggplant rolls. Petrina set down two glass jugs, one of water that had ice and sliced lemon floating in it and another of what I assumed was ouzito.

"I hope you like it how I make it," Petrina told me as she poured a glass. "It's got ouzo, sugar, soda water and lime. I didn't have any mint, but I prefer the lime anyway."

I sipped the drink. "Tastes good to me." I didn't tell her that I'd never had ouzo before, let alone ouzito. I liked it, so I wasn't lying.

Constance delicately touched a pita bread triangle to a cup of dip as though she were anointing it. I guessed nothing on the plate was her kind of food.

Petrina tucked stray strands of hair behind her ears, her eyes bright. "So, you two are students of Greek history?" She looked from one of us to the other, seeming to be asking more than she was saying. I guessed she was trying to figure out who we were and why we were travelling together.

But I wasn't going to volunteer any information. "Yes, that's right. We're interested in ancient symbols. Can I show you the one we've come across?"

Rico nodded, downing his ouzito. I caught a flicker of something in his eye. Apprehension?

Reaching for my satchel, I took out the photocopy and handed it to him.

He studied the picture, looking up at me twice before he spoke. "What is your interest in this symbol?"

"We just want to know what it is and where it came from, originally," I told him.

"It is based upon the Ladder of Divine Ascent," he said. "See the thirty rungs of the ladder? It signifies the thirty steps to reach the highest level of religious perfection. Each step is an instruction. Created at the request of the Abbot of Raithu in 600 AD, his monastery being on the edge of the Red Sea."

"So, it's an old religious symbol?" I asked him. "Is it possible to trace where this particular one came from?"

"It is old," he replied, "but it's not religious. Not this symbol. If it's religious artifacts you're after, I would advise you not to pursue this one." He passed it to his wife. She looked at it briefly, her eyes clouding.

"Our study would be incomplete," Constance protested. She glanced at me in a half-anxious way that I was sure our hosts noticed.

"Yes." I forced a smile. "We've come a long way to find out more about this."

"You're seeking someone," said Petrina flatly. "Aren't you? Someone who is missing."

I leaned back in the chair, confused at Petrina's question and trying not to look defensive. "That's not why we're here."

But she eyed me levelly. "Are you sure, Michael? Who are you two, and why *are* you here? At first, I thought you were perhaps a couple, despite the difference in accent and age. But I can tell by your body language that you are not."

"I didn't think we'd be given the third degree," I muttered. "We're just—"

Constance's sudden change of expression burrowed underneath the exterior I was trying to project. She shook her head, closing her eyes and pressing her lips into a thin, guilty line. "We're looking for my daughter and Gray's wife."

I turned to watch Rico and Petrina's reactions. Constance had not only told them what we were doing here in Greece, but she'd just said my name. If the Greek newspapers were running stories about me, it wouldn't be hard for them to put two and two together.

Constance's eyes snapped open as she realised she'd given away too much, giving me a look of open-mouthed alarm.

Rico exhaled a low, weary grunt. "Two people? A daughter and a wife?" He exchanged looks with Petrina.

I kept both Petrina and Rico in my line of sight as I gulped the last of my drink. I didn't know the first thing about these people. How had Petrina figured out we were looking for someone? Again, I felt trapped, here on the ninth floor with only a narrow set of stairs for an exit. If someone with a gun —or a knife—was waiting on the stairs for us, Constance and I might not leave this building alive.

"You didn't want us to know, but we know," Petrina said to me in a gentle tone. "You wouldn't be so interested in this symbol otherwise. I also know you won't take our advice and leave this alone, because you're seeking loved ones."

"Can you help us?" said Constance, breathy and tense. "Please."

Rico's brow indented itself with deep, crisscrossing lines. "We can't promise anything. But to go any further, I must insist on you showing us some identification."

There were just two courses of action now: get up and leave or go for broke. Constance stared at me with round eyes, waiting for me to decide. I had far more to lose than her in revealing who I was.

I decided to show them my ID. Constance followed suit. They asked about our missing relatives, and we told them about Evie and Kara. I left out the part about the police seeking me for murder, but they'd easily be able to find that out for themselves now.

Rico stood. "Let's head into the living room. There is much to talk about."

Were the Vasiliou couple really going to tell us more, or were they just stalling for time now they knew for certain who we were? I couldn't put aside my increasing nervousness at being here.

"I need to know," I said, as Constance and I followed them but before we'd seated ourselves on the sofas, "how you knew we came here looking for missing persons?"

Rico sighed heavily. "Please, sit, and we'll tell you how we knew."

Constance and I stood rigidly in the living room, and I could tell that she was wondering, as I was, if the Vasilious were our way forward or if we'd just stepped willingly into a trap.

56. CONSTANCE

RICO AND PETRINA FACED GRAY AND me with serious expressions that were edged with something I could only call dulled fear. Yellow Athens sunlight streaked in from a window, catching a cloud of dust motes—the unseen occupiers of air suddenly made visible.

I felt the tension in Gray, as evident as if it were another presence in the room. I knew the balance of everything was hanging precariously. Whatever the Vasilious were about to tell us would either end everything or begin it.

Gray and I sat, ready to listen, ready for whatever came next.

"This is not a happy tale," Rico began. "It's about a family who once came to us seeking their loved one. The year was 1992. They were an English family with a young daughter and a teenage son. The son, Noah, had been in trouble for many years prior. Lost to the drug culture. He was offered a place in a special treatment program. They offered him money for taking part in the treatment, a chance to start again. He told this to his parents over the phone—and he apparently accepted this offer." Rico paused. "His parents never saw him again."

"What kind of treatment?" I asked, confused at how this story connected with the things Gray and I had discovered.

Petrina placed a hand on her husband's knee. "A treatment for his addiction. The treatment centre was meant to be somewhere here in Greece. Noah wasn't meant to say anything about this program—he'd signed a confidentiality clause—but he did. That was the last they heard from him. The boy's parents were beside themselves, of course, when week after week went by without a word. They came to Greece in search of him. They were not rich people—they sold everything they had and bought an old motorcycle to get around on. Tragically, they were killed in a road accident not long after we met them. They were on their motorcycle when they were run off the road on a steep mountain bend. The driver of the other vehicle never came forward."

"That's awful," I breathed. "But why did they come to you about Noah? You're history professors."

"Like you," Rico told us, "they'd found out some information about the symbol you showed us. We were their last resort after the police couldn't help them. It was the worst decision for them, I'm afraid."

Gray was concentrating steadily on their faces. He still seemed wary, as if weighing everything they said against some measure of his own.

Petrina gave a silent sigh, her shoulders rising and falling. "We made some discoveries, and then those discoveries led the couple to discover more. But they were murdered before they could tell us what they found out. It would have been better if we hadn't agreed to help them."

"They were murdered?" I gasped. "It wasn't an accident?"

"I don't believe it was an accident," Petrina answered. "Most people would stop or at least try to get help. The driver of the car did neither."

An uneasy feeling embedded itself in my lower spine. "That's terrible."

"Yes, it is terrible," said Petrina. "At the time of their death, their ten-year-old daughter was staying with us—Jennifer. She was devastated, naturally. There was barely any family that could take her, just a couple of elderly relatives that weren't certain they could cope with a child. Anyway, Jennifer wanted to remain with us. And so that's what happened. We raised her. We always wondered if she might head back to England when she turned eighteen, but she didn't. She stayed in Greece and took up her parents' cause."

"What do you mean, *her parents' cause*?" asked Gray. "You mean finding her brother?"

"Exactly." Petrina gave a nod. "We were terrified for her, as it was a dangerous thing for her to do. But she's thirty-five now. A lot of time has gone past."

Gray leaned forward, resting an arm on one knee. "Is she still looking?"

Petrina seemed uncomfortable with his question. "No. It's been twenty-five years. She did end up returning to England and making a life there."

Gray raised his chin in a slight nod, but his gaze remained intent. He was so different to the lost, angry young man I'd first met at his doorstep clutching his wife's note. He seemed so focused, like he was constantly running calculations in his head.

"What a difficult time Jennifer must have had with losing all of her family," I said to Petrina. "I'm glad she had you and Rico."

"We're glad we had *her*." Petrina's eyes turned wistful. "She was a lovely child. Loved to swim and paint pictures in equal measure. She could have gone far with either passion, but she didn't wish to."

Rico squeezed his wife's hand, which was still on his knee. "Now, you two will want to know what we know about the symbol you brought to us. What we know isn't much, I'm afraid."

"Yes, please tell us whatever you've got," I pressed and then prepared myself. I sensed Rico was holding back, and I wanted him to tell us everything.

"The symbol is very, very old," he told us. "It is like the Ladder of Divine Ascent, but it is turned upside-down. The monks on the ladder are looking back to the earth, not to heaven. The demons are not trying to prod them off from the ladder. These people are not seeking God."

"They're *Satanists*?" When I'd arrived in Greece, I'd been prepared to pursue the sex trafficking avenue. I'd gone from that to thinking the Saviours were a religious cult. But this could be worse. *Far worse.*

"We're unsure," Rico said. "Even if they are, not all Satanists share the same beliefs. People are often surprised to learn that some groups of Satanists believe in neither Satan nor God nor any spiritual being. And not all Satanists think that human sacrifices or harming people is a good idea. And I haven't known any large satanic organisation being so under the radar as this one. If you want new members, you need to be at least a little open. How such an order as this survived from the twelfth century, Petrina and I cannot fathom. It doesn't make sense."

"How do you know they have survived all that time?" Gray asked. "Couldn't the group of today have just made their own symbol?"

"We discovered drawings of it in books," replied Rico. "From different centuries. And different countries. This symbol—and the group belonging to it—has somehow been with us all that time, in the background. Like a shadow."

"I hired a private investigator," I told Rico and Petrina, almost whispering. "Her name was Rosemary. She found out a name. Yeqon's Saviours. That's all I know."

"Yeqon's Saviours, yes," Rico confirmed. "After the fallen angel. That's what they call themselves. So, you and your daughter were the reason Rosemary contacted me. She didn't tell me why." Deep lines etched themselves across his sun-browned forehead. "You said the investigator's name *was* Rosemary? You don't mean to say she has died?"

"Yes. Murdered in her hotel room," I told him.

Petrina gasped. "*No*."

A shudder ran along my spine. "I was the one who found her. They haven't found the person who did it yet."

Petrina and Rico locked gazes for a moment. I couldn't tell what they were silently communicating between themselves, but I could see the worry clearly etched on their faces.

"I'm so sorry," said Petrina at last.

"As am I. But we will continue." Rico rose from his seat and walked across to a bookcase that was well furnished with aged, thick books. He selected a book and brought it to the coffee table. The cover and paper seemed ancient and fragile.

He carefully turned the yellowed pages until he found a page that contained the exact same symbol that appeared on Gray's photocopied image. The text on the page opposite was in Greek.

"You see, here it is." He kept turning pages, stopping on a page that contained an illustration of people drowning in water, all wearing robes. And then another page, which showed dead, thin people strung up on a wall, multiple knives and implements piercing their bodies.

A tremor passed through my chest, making my heart jolt. "What is all this?"

"Nothing good." Rico sighed deeply. "Whoever they are, they seem to deal in death. I'd repeat what we said earlier, about staying well away, but it seems you already know this. Especially after what happened to your investigator, Rosemary."

I nodded sombrely, barely able to breathe.

He closed the book, returning it to rest on the table. "I'm sure you don't want to see more of these images. If you keep looking for your loved ones, you could both end up like Rosemary. Or like Jennifer's parents. That is your reality."

"I can't turn back," I told him. "She's my daughter. I can't."

I turned to Gray, expecting him to back me up, but his eyes were set firmly on a large piece of paper that had fallen from between the pages of the book to the floor. I'd thought it must be a loose page, but when Gray reached for it, I saw that there was a drawing on the other side.

"Could I have that, please?" said Rico sharply.

The drawing was of an island—houses on the hills in the background, fishing boats in the foreground. It was easy to tell that whoever had drawn this had painted the artwork on the walls.

"Jennifer drew this, didn't she?" Gray raised his eyebrows.

"Yes," said Rico as Gray handed him the painting. "Just one of her thousands of drawings."

Gray gestured towards the paintings on the walls. "The drawing's signed with a J. It's the same bay as in these paintings. Is that where Jennifer lives?"

Petrina's expression grew taut, her large eyes opening even wider. "You can't go and see Jennifer. She cannot be part of this."

"How do you know she doesn't want to be part of it?" said Gray. "Maybe she never stopped looking for Noah."

Rico stood. "We can't place Jennifer in danger. She's in enough danger just by being alive. In telling what we told you, we were hoping to show you what danger you're in, in the hope of saving your lives. The more you search, the closer you move towards your deaths. I'm sorry about the loved ones you've lost, but you must go home to your families. What you're doing is a fool's mission."

Gray rose to his feet, facing Rico. "There's something you're going to find out soon. The police are looking for me, under the suspicion that I killed my wife. Back in Australia. After she went missing, her car was found dumped and burned and her things buried. Alongside a knife, rope and tape from our garage. The Saviours want me in jail, and they almost succeeded. My wife and I have got two small daughters. Right now they've lost both of us." His jaw pulled tight. "How many families have the Saviours destroyed? How many more are they going to destroy?"

Rico and Petrina stared at Gray with shocked, chalky faces.

My legs weak, I stood next to Gray. "Please . . . Gray's right. If everyone keeps running scared, how will these people ever be exposed?" My voice broke. "How will it ever end?"

I knew as I spoke that I was asking too much. Rico and Petrina, for all intents, must love Jennifer as their own daughter. Now I understood the fearful expressions they'd held before. Their fear wasn't for themselves but for Jennifer.

I also understood the thing that I'd sensed they were holding back on, the thing that would give Gray and me a direction to head in.

It was Jennifer.

57. EVIE

THE LIGHT BULB BELOW THE CLOCK had flashed green and the clock had stopped.

My knees weakened.

We'd done it.

The end of the sixth challenge.

I didn't know yet if I was among the final six, but I was so close I could taste victory on the tip of my tongue. I pictured Gray and the girls. I could go back to them soon and make everything right. We'd buy a little house, and it would be all ours. Just one more set of challenges. All held in one night.

I wanted to scream in relief, but I was beyond that point.

Bring on the boat.

Take me home.

The door of the sixth challenge room slid across.

The four mentors bowed as we reached them, smiles flickering on their otherwise serious faces.

Sister Rose placed garlands of flowers around our necks, and we shook hands in turns with the mentors.

"You got to the end." Brother Vito clasped my hand in both of his. "Be proud, Evie."

It was yet another velvety night out here in the garden. Everything still.

No breeze at all ruffling the leaves. Everything in suspended animation. I could believe the stars and moon had stilled in the sky.

We waited breathlessly to hear whether we passed through into the final six or not.

"You two kept your cool and you figured things out," said Brother Sage to us. "You used teamwork and courage and trusted your intuition. You are in the final six." His smile spread wide.

Richard didn't hold back. He bellowed as if he'd just won a war. I joined in—our cheers and whoops sounding like a huge crowd of people were invading the garden instead of just us.

We turned then as four other people joined us. Cormack, Yolanda, Louelle and Hop. Thomas and Mei hadn't made it.

"Yes! You two got through!" Cormack gave a low whoop, giving a celebratory punch to our shoulders and then turned to the mentors. "How can we thank you lot for what you've done for us? May the road rise to meet you. May the wind be always at your back. That's an old Irish blessing. My grandmother's Irish, God bless her."

"Your gratitude is more than enough thanks," said Sister Dawn. "Now, you can take your time returning to the dormitories. I realise you're excited."

"The dorms?" said Richard, deflated. "No celebration?"

"I'm afraid you'll need your rest," Brother Sage told us. "The final set of challenges will take everything you've got. And then comes the celebration."

The other mentors gave us warm parting smiles and nods before they stepped away.

Richard collapsed onto a swinging chair that hung from a nearby tree. "They're certainly sticklers for routine."

"I'm too wired to go back to the dorm and sleep." Cormack walked behind Richard, launching himself onto the back of the chair, making it swing high into the air. He whooped again, this time in a loud voice. "I'll not get a wink anyway."

"Me either." I wriggled into the swing seat opposite Richard. "Not yet. We should just stay out here a while."

Louelle stood apart from us, her arms crossed and staring at the sky. I couldn't decide whether I thought she was odd or lucky. She seemed to always be in her own space, not bothered by what was happening around her.

Yolanda's eyes brimmed with excitement. "We've done it. The next six challenges are just for fun. They have to be. We've already won. We won, people, we won!"

Hop looked exhausted and dazed, leaning against a small tree, but he cracked a smile at Yolanda's enthusiastic speech.

Cormack began singing the "Leaving on a Jet Plane" song at full pelt.

"With that voice, everyone will be glad you left," Richard remarked.

"Shut your face," Cormack told him. "Or I'll serenade you with the whole thing. Or I would if I knew all the words. Maybe I'll just substitute different words, for your listening pleasure."

"Maybe I'll box your ears before you get a word out," said Richard. "Let the grownups have some relax time."

"Do your worst," Cormack said. "I'll be on my way to see Kara in a few days. Nothing's going to give me a frownie face."

Richard shrugged. "Still beating that dead horse? One thing I know is money, and I can tell you she comes from money. Girl like that is not going to take up with someone from the wrong side of the tracks. Sorry to be the one to give you the bad news."

"Piss off, Richard. You bitter little bastard." Cormack, still smiling broadly, jumped from the chair, almost sending Richard careening sideways into a tree.

Richard emerged from his seat. "Yeah, well, life made me that way. Stick around long enough, and it'll make you that way too." He paused, tilting his head. "Hang it. This is supposed to be a celebration. Wine and women and song and all of that. Well, maybe just the wine for me. Hold the women and song."

Cormack whistled, nodding and slapping his thigh, seeming to instantly forget that he was angry with Richard. "Yeah, where's the wine this time? We're just supposed to go to sleep like good little children? Well, I don't want to be *good*."

Richard gave a devious wink. "Me neither. What about we sneak down to the cellar for a bottle of good, home-brewed monk wine?"

"What a sterling idea. I wouldn't be a good Scotsman if I didn't have a drink to celebrate a win," said Cormack in a slightly hesitant tone, as if trying to convince himself that Richard's idea was a good one.

Richard let out a victory howl. "Let me drink enough, and I'll be Scottish, too, before the night's out."

Hop spoke for the first time since we'd left the sixth challenge room, threading his finger nervously through his short black hair. "What got us here in the first place was not making good decisions. I'm not doing anything that might jeopardise things now."

I pressed my lips together hard. "Yeah, we're too close to walking out of here."

Richard and I had already been lucky not to be found in the walkways between the walls. No one even knew we'd done that.

"What are they going to do?" Richard drawled. "We can say we were just trying to do as they asked, but we were too excited to sleep. Like kids on Christmas Eve. So we needed something to help us sleep. That's where booze comes in."

Louelle turned to Richard. "The gate to the cellar's got an old rusted chain and lock on it. I checked."

"You alcoholic, you," said Richard, tutting playfully. "Then how on earth do the monks get down there? Must be another way."

I caught Richard's eye in alarm, silently warning him not to tell about the secret passages. If the others found out, they might accuse us of looking into the challenge rooms and gaining an advantage. The mentors might strip Richard and me of our win. It was better left unsaid.

The side of Richard's face twisted into a grin when he saw my discomfort. "Or . . . we just find something to cut the chain."

"I've seen bolt cutters in one of the garden sheds," said Cormack, raising his eyebrows like a comedian telling a joke.

"Bolt cutters, hey?" Richard thumbed his goatee. "What are we waiting for?"

"I don't think you should do this." Louelle stepped in front of Richard. "I won't be drinking. I'm not going back to my family with alcohol on my breath. Never again."

"Well, the demon alcohol is not my vice, Lou. And I demand a celebration. I'm not going to see any of you after this." He softened his tone. "We won't empty their cellar. Just a few bottles."

He, Cormack and Yolanda hi-fived each other and stepped off in the direction of the sheds.

Louelle and I exchanged tense glances. It wasn't just what they were planning to do that had me worried but the fact they wanted to do it at all. Had any of us even learned anything in our week here? Were any of us really changed? What if I went back home and started doing the same thing all over again?

Louelle tipped her head to the side, looking up at the sky again. "Something feels . . . off."

"Off?" Hop asked.

"You don't feel it?" A frown drew her eyebrows together. "When I was a kid, Mama used to drag me and my brothers to church every Sunday. We all hated it. But it felt like people were trying, you know? Trying to be good, even if they weren't. It felt warm and kind of safe. But this place, it doesn't have that feeling."

I wrapped my arms around myself, wishing Louelle hadn't spoken. I wanted to be encased in a winners' bubble and on a high. But the victory already felt hollow in some way I couldn't put a name to. I glanced upward sharply at the bulkhead that stretched across the garden. Was anyone watching us from there right now?

"It's fine," I said sharply. "It's just that the challenges have shaken us. Maybe we should stick with the others." I started walking, wanting to shake my sudden unease. "Let's go. Hop, are you with us?"

"Guess I am." He managed half a grin, but the apprehensive expression in his eyes contradicted it.

We met the other three as they returned with the bolt cutters and headed into the monastery together.

"Changed your mind, eh?" said Cormack.

"No, just keeping an eye on you lot," I quipped.

"Hey," Richard said in a stage whisper. "The mentors will have gone to bed, way down the other end of the monastery. They won't hear us. We'll just head down the stairs, grab a couple of bottles of red, race back up again."

Like a bunch of petty thieves, everyone's shoulders seemed to hunch a little as we made our way along the hallway.

The monastery interior was as silent as a tomb, as alien to me as on the night I arrived.

Pressure bore in on me from all sides, the hexagons bearing against each other. Was Brother Sage right? Was everything scripted, predicted by numbers? I could almost sense all the working parts of the monastery. The metronomes ticking away in synch. The garden stream running in an endless circle. The centre of the monastery and the tiny burning flame. The smallest, most inconsequential thing loomed large in your mind here, everything examined in isolation, under a microscope, from six different angles.

Love could be destroyed by numbers.

Minutes: the time it took for the blood clot to trigger the minor stroke that would momentarily take a driver's vision away and cause him to crash the car.

Seconds: the amount of time it took for Ben to go from alive and laughing to dead.

One second: the time in which it could take Gray to say to me, *I don't love you anymore.*

58. GRAY

WE ARRIVED ON SIKINOS IN THE middle of a rainstorm. The island where we hoped to find Jennifer. White, block-shaped houses were set into bare hills. The air was steaming hot.

The Vasilious hadn't told us Jennifer's address, but they'd seemed resigned to the fact that things had been set in motion and that we needed to talk with her. But they hadn't wanted to be complicit in just handing her over to us.

We'd found out her full name easily enough—Jennifer Bloom. A simple internet search for her paintings was enough to tell us her name and that she lived on the Greek island of Sikinos. Constance and I had studied Google maps of the island, locating the exact bay that Jennifer painted so much. It'd taken eight long hours by boat to get here.

Now, we just needed to find her.

The shops were shuttered against the storm, with only one café open. Constance and I made a beeline for it and stood dripping under the awning.

I peered inside the window. The café carried paintings on the walls—paintings that matched Jennifer Bloom's. A man in his sixties or seventies sat outside on a stool, smoking a cigar.

"Hello?" I called, crossing to him. "We're looking for Jennifer Bloom."

He shook his head. "I don't know." His accent was thick.

"She painted the pictures inside your café. We were told she lives here."

"I don't know," he said again in a casual voice.

"Is there anyone about who would know?"

He shrugged. "I don't know."

I made a guess that the locals had been asked not to give away her home address to any strangers on the island. Or maybe he didn't like giving away information for free. I was considering trying to give him a tip when Constance stepped up behind me.

"This is getting us nowhere," she whispered.

I turned, walking a short distance back with her to get out of earshot of the man. "So what do we do? Go door knocking?"

"Why don't we just go find her ourselves?" She marched off straight into the squall.

I grinned in spite of myself, following her. She could have taken one of the paths that led to the houses along the level land near the shoreline, but she didn't. She immediately began climbing the rocky hill that led straight up.

Rivulets of water ran from my forehead down my face and into my collar. "What made you decide she lives up here?"

"She's an artist," said Constance, raising her voice against the hard patter of rain. "She'd want the best view, not convenience."

There were forty-odd houses on this side of the hill, their bright-white exteriors defeating the gloom. Curtains moved aside as we reached the top. Two determined sightseers on this small island was probably not a common sight. We were bringing attention to ourselves, but we didn't have much choice.

"Every house here looks exactly the same," I said. Worse, we'd only seen it from the inside looking out.

You'd better have a business sign out in front of your house, Jennifer Bloom.

I prowled ahead, looking closely at every house that could be the one, mentally trying to flip it and figure what the landscape aspect would be like from the inside.

But it was Constance who stood looking at a house that looked similar to the others, turning back to me and nodding. "This is it."

I stopped, puzzled. "How do you know?"

"In one of the paintings, the windowsill is painted deep blue. And there was a little collection of animal statues on the sill."

I stared at her for a moment, trying to remember. I'd noticed the bay and the boats and the architecture, but not any set of windowsill statues. "Okay, lead the way."

The walkway to the house was up a heap of slippery stone steps. There was no guarantee that she'd be home or, if she was, that she'd answer the door. We could spend hours waiting it out.

Constance knocked, a gentle tap that I could barely even hear. Reaching over her shoulder, I rapped hard.

The door opened.

I sucked in a breath of wet air, relieved.

A slight woman about Constance's age stared out at us, her blue eyes intense, light-brown hair back in a ponytail. "Come in. You'll get washed into the bay if you stay out there any longer."

"We're—" Constance started.

"I know who you are," she said. "I'm Jennifer. I'm the person you're looking for, right? Well, you found me."

She stood back and let us into the wood-panelled hallway. "Let me take your coats. And I'll put a towel down for your shoes and socks."

A couple of minutes later, we were standing barefoot in her small living room. The interior was simple and fresh looking, with knickknacks crowded in everywhere.

I caught a distant view of the ocean through the window—the same view as in the painting. "Rico and Petrina told you about us?" I asked, curiously.

She crossed her arms tightly. "They told me to leave the island. I know they felt really bad they'd given information about me away."

"They didn't give it away," I told her. "We figured it out."

A tense look entered her eyes, and I could guess that she was running scenarios through her head, trying to establish whether or not she should send us packing. It was true that we posed a danger to her.

Instinctively, Constance padded across the room in her bare feet to pick up a tiny ceramic cat from the windowsill. "I love these."

"They belonged to my parents," said Jennifer, "and my grandmother and great-grandmother before that. Not much of an heirloom, I guess, but they're very special to me."

Constance replaced the cat more carefully than she'd picked it up. "I'd love to have something like this handed down to me. So much family history. So many precious memories."

Jennifer raised her eyebrows. "Can I get you two a hot drink? Coffee or tea?"

Constance and I both asked for coffee, and Jennifer left for the kitchen. "Come through," she called.

We followed Jennifer's path to a surprisingly large kitchen. Half the wall space was of stone and the rest of blue-painted plasterboard. Everything old but well cared for. A wide archway led to a studio filled with paintings. There were three easels with paintings in progress. Almost all of the work was of ocean scenes.

I took a sip of the home-brewed coffee. It tasted especially good after being out tramping about in the storm. I nodded my head towards the studio. "Are they all of this island, Jennifer?"

"Yes, mostly. I sell them on a few different islands around here. The tourists don't know the paintings are of Sikinos. They don't care either, I suppose. It's the mood they're after."

Chewing my lip, I decided to start the conversation that I'd come here for. "Rico and Petrina must have told you we're after some information."

Jennifer didn't bat an eye. "Then you have a problem. I have nothing to talk about. I live in the here and now. See my paintings? Every day I paint what I see—how the bay looks in the different seasons and time of day. There is nothing else."

I felt my jaw and throat muscles tightening. "I'm not sure I believe you. You stayed in Greece all this time for a reason."

"Look around you," she said, "and you'll know why I'm here. Well, look on a day when it's not storming. It's beautiful. And I was raised in Greece from an early age. It's my home."

Cold disappointment rose inside my stomach. "Is that why you saw us today? So that you could tell us that and get rid of us?"

"I don't have anything of interest to tell you. I'm sorry, I just thought you should know that. You could waste a long time in Greece waiting to talk to me. I made it easy for you."

"We appreciate it," Constance said before I could reply. "We can't afford to waste any time. My daughter is just a teenager. I need to find her."

Jennifer turned to look outside the kitchen window. "I'm sorry about your daughter."

Constance exchanged quick, wary glances with me. I guessed she was telling me to keep my mouth zipped. I was pressing too hard.

"We have a few people we can try next," Constance told Jennifer. "There's a trafficking expert who's agreed to meet with me."

Jennifer's hands closed firmly around her coffee cup. "Trafficking? Is that what you think happened to her?"

Constance gave an uncertain nod. "Everything else is leading to a dead end. All of these things about an ancient order are all very interesting, but I can't imagine it could have survived all this time. There's probably just some thin connection." Twisting around, she peered into the art studio. "What you said about the seasons—I can see it so clearly in your work. You've captured the light beautifully. So calming. I wish I could take half a dozen home with me. But my husband is an art collector, and he only hangs the pictures that he thinks will be a good investment." She flinched, as if startling herself. "Oh, I didn't mean that yours wouldn't be. I just meant that—"

Jennifer smiled for the first time since she'd invited us in. "You meant that he only buys the paintings of well-known artists. Not a no-name woman in a tiny Greek village who only paints in order to earn a living. It's okay. I'm not offended. That's exactly what I am, and I don't aspire to be any more than that."

"You have far more talent than what you're admitting to." To embolden her point, Constance took her coffee and strode into the studio. She stepped about, examining the pictures. "Your brushstrokes are lovely. I've learned a lot about painting techniques through my husband." Bending, she looked through one of the three racks of pictures, each rack holding at least twenty. Jennifer must output a serious amount of work.

Constance stopped still when she reached the last of the paintings on the rack. I craned my head and caught sight of paintings of an olive-skinned, wiry man in a boat and diving underwater, and others of a pasty-skinned young man staring directly out from the canvas.

Looking back at Jennifer, Constance frowned. "These are incredible. Who are they?"

"The man is just someone I know. A friend. And the other pictures are of my brother," Jennifer said, her expression growing rigid again.

I remembered her brother as being the one who'd disappeared. Noah. I wanted to jump in and start asking questions, but I held back. Constance was managing to do what I couldn't—get a dialogue going with Jennifer.

"Your friend is beautiful. And your brother's eyes . . ." Constance shook her head. "So soulful and expressive."

"He was troubled," Jennifer admitted. "I didn't understand that at the time, because he was so much older than me. But I understand it now."

"Yes, I can see the pain on his face." Constance turned back to the picture. "It almost hurts to look at him."

"My brother was a drug addict and a gambler. Noah would put a bet on anything. When he was working—which wasn't that often—he'd put all his money through the slot machines. My parents kept bailing him out, and then he'd tumble straight back into the pit . . ." Her voice trailed away. "Noah wanted a big life. He wanted to do everything and go everywhere. But he didn't seem to be able to get to the first rung. I'd wake sometimes in the small hours when he'd stumble home. And he'd be full of chat about his latest business idea or a girl who was the love of his life. He spoke to me like I was an adult. I didn't mind. But nothing lasted with Noah. Not even Noah himself . . ."

"He sounds like a lot of young men who lose their way. I had a boyfriend a lot like that, once," said Constance. "His name was Otto. But then, it's true that I also lost my way back then." Gliding the rack back into place, Constance returned to thc kitchen. "Those paintings of Noah are so different to your paintings of Greece. It's hard to believe the same person painted them."

"Now you know," said Jennifer in a flattened voice. "That's the person behind the sunshine and fluffy clouds. A blank canvas is a thing of terror. I tackle that terror anew each and every day, and I never know what I'll put down on that canvas."

"The sunshine and clouds mostly win?" Constance offered a smile.

"Yes," Jennifer agreed. "They mostly win the fight."

"You're a survivor." Constance sucked her lips in, her eyes sad. "I hope I can have your strength, because I'm going to need it. Can I show you a picture of Kara? She's my daughter." Without hesitating, Constance drew out one of her laminated photos from her handbag. "This is her."

At first, Jennifer put up a hand like she was going to refuse to look, but she relented and took the picture. "She's a pretty girl."

"She was last seen with a man named Carlisle," said Constance with a bitter tone in her voice.

A flicker of recognition seemed to pass through Jennifer's eyes, but she quickly adjusted her expression. I swallowed, still holding back.

Constance hadn't even asked Jennifer if she could begin this conversation. She'd burrowed in through another route, and it'd worked. So far. Constance, despite all her uptight nervousness, had some surprisingly steely stuff inside her. I made a guess that if she got past her anxiety, she'd be a dangerous person to have as an opponent.

"And Gray has pictures of his wife and family." Constance indicated towards me.

Grateful for the cue, I wasted no time in pulling out my wallet and flipping it open in front of Jennifer. "That's Evie. And Willow—she's four. And Lilly—she's the baby."

"Cute family," Jennifer said. "The little one is adorable."

"Not always. She's got us all under her thumb." I gave a rueful laugh. "She was really sick just before I left. The doctors finally found out what she's got. It's cystic fibrosis."

Jennifer frowned sympathetically. "That's harsh."

"Yeah. Evie doesn't even know." Out of nowhere, everything hit me fresh, like a punch to the stomach. I put my wallet away, turning and staring hard through the window, my vision blurring.

I decided to stay quiet again and allow Constance to handle the conversation with Jennifer. And I didn't trust myself to speak right now. It was like Evie was right there in front of my eyes.

"Rico and Petrina told me what brought you two to Greece," said Jennifer.

"We're determined to keep going until we find Kara and Evie," said Constance.

"I'm sure they told you about the dangers?"

"Yes. And I can tell they're very worried about you."

"They needn't worry about me. I've looked after myself for a long time."

"But they do. Like all parents. I know they aren't your biological parents, but I could tell that as far as they're concerned, you're their daughter."

"Yes. Rico and Petrina made a life choice not to have children. And then they got me." She laughed wryly.

"They couldn't have sounded prouder of you."

"They're Greek. They're proud of *everything*." But she couldn't hide the small smile on her lips.

Constance returned a warm smile. "We don't want to cause them any worry in us being here. I know you want answers about what happened to Noah, and we want answers, too."

"But I'm afraid I can't help you," Jennifer said. "People just . . . vanish sometimes. And they never come back. That's how it is."

Constance didn't waver. "I don't believe you've accepted that."

Jennifer's shoulders collapsed inward, and she cradled her coffee mug to her chest, her expression suddenly changed. "I expect to die doing what I'm doing. Is that what you want for yourselves? Gray, you've got two young daughters. And Constance, you have your husband. You should both go home to them while you still can."

"I can't," I said, breaking my spell of silence. "I can't do that without knowing I did everything in my power to bring the girls' mother back to them. And, anyway, if I go home, my girls will lose me anyway. I'll be arrested for my wife's murder. Didn't Rico and Petrina tell you about that?"

"Yes, they did. You were set up. I was forgetting. Setups are a classic move on the part of the Saviours."

"They've done that kind of stuff before?" I asked her, exhaling a tense breath. "Framing people?"

"Yes, but not usually. Framing people is messy. They generally choose to kill the ones who pose a risk to them. Rico and Petrina don't know about any of this except what happened to my parents and Noah. You mustn't tell them."

"Well, they know about us now." I rubbed my jaw, thinking hard. "Look, if you're still looking for Noah—and I think you are—you should team up with us. Maybe it's time you stopped going this alone. It won't help Noah if you wind up dead."

"I don't think my brother is still alive, Gray."

I tried to adjust to this new piece of information without showing my surprise. "You don't?"

"No. It's been far too long. But I need to know what happened to him, and I need the people responsible brought to justice. If I don't kill them myself, that is. I'm quite sure that the only reason they've left me alone is because I was a child when my brother disappeared. All trails had gone completely dead and cold by the time I was old enough to continue my parents' search. The Saviours don't realise that I never let go of Noah. They know I've made some investigations over the years, but they don't know how much I know or how tenacious I am."

"Sounds like you're their worst enemy," I said.

"I am. And to continue, I need to stay beneath their radar. I can't join with you. I'll become too visible. I'm close to finding out where and who, and I can't risk outsiders giving my game away."

Constance leaned forward on the kitchen bench, a determined look set fast in her eyes. "But what if we know things you don't? We didn't tell Rico and Petrina all that we've discovered."

I knew that Constance was mostly bluffing. We'd barely found out anything. We needed Jennifer far more than she needed us.

Jennifer hesitated for a moment, setting her cup down rigidly on the bench, her head bent.

I was quick to wipe the shock from my face when she nodded.

59. CONSTANCE

BUNDLING A TOWEL AROUND MYSELF, I stepped from the shower. I was a little plumper than I had been when I left my home in the States, my hips not quite so angular. I hadn't been watching what I ate at all. I'd have to correct that when I got back home.

If I ever got back home.

Jennifer had generously offered her house to Gray and me to stay in. She'd sent us off to have hot showers, and I was immensely grateful. I'd been hot and sticky beneath my damp clothing.

I padded down the hall, making a right-hand turn into the small area that led to my room. The door to Jennifer's room lay open, a steamy breeze drifting in through sheer, fluttering curtains. The storm had ended abruptly while I was in the shower. The sunshine and fluffy clouds of Jennifer's paintings had returned. I took a quick peek into her room from the door-frame. Her bedroom furnishings, like the rest of the house, were simple. Whitewashed wood, clean lines. One of her paintings hung on the wall over her bed. The blues, greens and yellows were exactly right. You could feel the warmth radiating from the canvas. Hear the rustle of the swaying branches and the slap of waves against the fishing boats.

I gasped as a figure appeared at Jennifer's window. A man. Naked. Climbing in backwards over the sill. His hair wet and body damp.

My scream sounded like a squawk as I stumbled back. "Jennifer! Someone's breaking into your house!"

Gray had already jumped into the shower seconds after I'd left the bathroom. He wouldn't hear.

Jennifer rushed into the hallway and peered in at the man standing in her room. He'd grabbed a sheet and had it wrapped around his middle.

"No, it's just . . . Sethi." She smiled.

"You know him? He often comes in here like—?" I broke off, suddenly embarrassed. He had to be a boyfriend or some such, surprising her. He'd been naked, after all.

Sethi grinned. "Bad decision." His accent was deep, melodious, Greek.

"I'm sorry." I shook my head, not knowing where to put myself. "Goodness, how silly was I?"

Jennifer's laugh tinkled in the air. "You weren't to know. Sethi and I are very good friends. He's been away for a couple of weeks on a fishing trawler. He's a fisherman."

"Apologies," I said to Sethi. "I must have given you a shock, screaming like that."

"I was more scared than you." He winked.

"Clothes are optional in my house," said Jennifer lightly. "That's why Sethi didn't think anything of coming in here *au naturel*. He likes to surprise me sometimes."

I frowned, remembering something. "The man in your paintings. It's Sethi, isn't it?"

She nodded. "Yes. We've been together for seven years. We don't live together. I like my space. It works better this way."

I eyed Sethi intently. "The paintings of you underwater just looked so . . . free."

"Ah," he said. "Those paintings are from the stories I told Jenny of my younger years. I grew up on Kalymnos Island. My brothers and cousins and I were all sponge divers. We learned to dive deep and hold our breath a long time. It is a proud tradition on Kalymnos—sponge diving."

The way Jennifer gazed at him as he spoke, I could tell she was besotted with him.

"I should leave you two alone . . . to catch up." I beat a hasty retreat to my room and closed the door.

The same sultry island breeze that had been filtering into Jennifer's room had found its way into mine, too.

I pictured the catch-up that Jennifer and Sethi must be having. And then tried to shake it from my mind. But still, my mind wandered back to the paintings. They'd been so sensual and lovingly drawn they made me ache.

James had never been anything like Sethi. He wasn't spontaneous or sensual. His eyes didn't light up in the way Sethi's did when he looked at Jennifer. He'd never surprised me the way in which Sethi apparently liked to surprise Jennifer.

Life with James had been very ordinary. Go for a run every Saturday morning, walk the dog, check in with each other about basic things to do with the running of the house. Of course, James was away a lot on business trips, but he'd always maintain the routine when he was there. He was fit and lean and expected me to be too. Perhaps that was a good thing. Without his standard to adhere to, I was sure I would have indulged my sweet tooth more. I'd probably be fat. I'd been fat when I was with Otto. Now, I looked good. I never had to worry that the clothes I bought wouldn't fit well. I had a lot of pride in my toned thighs and flat stomach and the feeling of a belt cinching in my small waist. When James would come up behind me and place his hands on my waist, I used to glow. He'd fit his hands to me like I was a finely tooled machine that was beautiful to touch and hold.

I didn't know what was wrong with me—James had given me so much. I couldn't expect to have everything. Passionate men weren't wealthy businessmen, it seemed. Did Jennifer and Sethi have the right idea in living apart? Did it make them desire each other more, fuelling a lust that often disappeared too soon in a relationship?

Next door, the bed creaked softly, the headboard knocking against the wall twice.

Dressing quickly, I headed out to the garden to have a cigarette. Smoking was my guilty secret. James would be disgusted if he knew. I only indulged a few times a year, strangely feeling like I was regaining a little of my former self when I did. The cigarettes were my dirty little touchstone.

I found a secluded spot inside an olive vine grown wild over a trellis. I smoked two cigarettes in quick succession, just for good measure.

Someone jumped in front of me.

Gray. He must have had a two-minute shower to be out here so fast.

"Caught ya red handed," he joked, his hair soaking wet and plastered to his head.

I felt fourteen again, when my father had found me smoking in the back shed. "I don't normally do this. I don't even know why I bought a pack. I haven't smoked for at least ten years."

He shot me a broad smile. "Quit explaining. I didn't mean to make you feel bad. Hey, where's Jennifer? I didn't see her in the house. She hasn't run out on us, has she?"

"She's . . . busy."

"Mind if I have one of your smokes?"

I held the pack out to him. "You, too?"

"Yeah."

"I felt like one as soon as I got to Athens. I've never seen so many people smoking. It was kind of freeing. I guess that sounds ridiculous."

"No, it doesn't." He paused to light the cigarette from my lighter.

I sighed. "I feel bad about being so persistent with Jennifer. I'm not like that normally."

Blowing out a stream of smoke, he threw back his head, nodding. "People like us, we don't do things like this. We don't run about interrogating people and tracking people down. I almost feel like I can't get a grip. Do you know what I'm saying? Like whatever Jennifer tells us is just going to send us further down the rabbit hole. And things are going to get crazier, but we're not going to get any closer."

In that moment, Gray sounded like the twenty-four-year old that he was. He'd held up a front since I'd met up with him here in Greece. But he wasn't much more than a kid, just seven years older than Kara.

"I know," I sympathised. "I'm on edge every second."

Gray found himself a seat on a log and launched into a set of stories about his two girls, as though trying to ground himself. It was easy to see that he loved them dearly.

Jennifer and Sethi walked out into the garden, carrying trays. They'd made sandwiches on sourdough bread, piled high with different cheeses and tomatoes.

"Hope you're hungry." Jennifer set her tray of drinks down on a nearby table made of the same stone as some of the walls of the house. Sethi placed his tray beside hers. "I brought the bread and tomatoes with me today. I didn't know Jenny would have visitors, so it is good timing."

"Count me in." Gray picked up a sandwich. "Hey, *ef-ha-ri-sto*. I hope that means thank you. I've been hearing people say it here."

Sethi raised his eyebrows, smiling. "Almost right. Say it with more gusto and I'll know you meant it. And, hey, you're welcome."

We ate while Sethi talked about the catch and life at sea on a fishing trawler. Jennifer was clearly entranced by him, watching him closely as he spoke.

The humidity out here was making me sweat. Already, I needed another shower. I realised that I was barely ever in humid environments at home. Everything was air conditioned: the house—all five thousand square feet of it, the shopping malls, my car. I jogged around the lake in winter and autumn and swam in our heated pool during the summer. I was never really uncomfortable. But here, it was a different world. I could imagine sleeping in the shade outside during the hottest part of the day and then staying up late at night chatting and socialising. I could step into a different mood, like stepping straight into one of Jennifer's paintings. It was a vision that stood outside of everything else—a life that only someone who wasn't me could lead.

Jennifer sipped on a glass of iced lime and soda. "I guess we should start."

"I'd like that," I said, my vision of lazy Greek days dissolving in an instant.

"I'm not so sure that you will like it when I'm through," she said in a quiet tone.

Gray took a wary, sideways glance at Sethi, and Jennifer caught it.

"Sethi knows all that I do," Jennifer told us quickly. "You can feel comfortable talking in front of him. He served in the Hellenic Army for six years—all Greek men have to serve about a year. He saw some of the worst things people can do to each other." She paused then, glancing briefly at him as if for confirmation that she could continue. "But the worst thing that he experienced happened back at home, when a thief broke into his house and murdered his wife, right in front of their child. Sethi was away in the army at the time. He was left with a burning hate of those who treat human life so cheaply."

"Damn. I'm sorry about your wife, mate," Gray told him.

I sighed in horror. "So awful. How did you manage with your child after your wife was gone?"

"I have a close family," he replied. "We all helped raise Anxo—my son. He's grown now."

Jennifer leaned back on her seat, holding onto Sethi's arm. "I have files and files of disconnected clues. Enough to create a media storm. But not enough to convict anyone or provide enough evidence to the police, and so I'm holding back. But I've learned terrible things. I'll tell you a little about everything, from the beginning." She paused, as if figuring out exactly where to start. "When I turned seventeen, I left the home that Rico and Petrina had given me, and I went to live on my own. In Athens. They wanted me to go on to university, but I had other plans. I took up odd jobs—enough to live on and pay rent. More often, I had night jobs—waitressing and things. By day, I slept and followed people. I followed them all over Europe."

"So dangerous for a young girl," I gasped.

"Yes, but no one else was looking for Noah by this time. The police had stopped many years ago. Rico and Petrina had spent a lot of money hiring private investigators, but it all came to nothing. I had to do what I could, for Noah." She licked her bottom lip, stopping to take another drink. "I could tell Rico and Petrina were growing suspicious. I thought maybe they suspected I was going the same way my brother had—into the seedier side of life. They thought maybe becoming addicted to drugs. When I was twenty-two, I decided I had to move further away, where they wouldn't see or hear of anything I was doing."

"That's how you ended up here?" asked Gray.

"Yes. *Somehow*. I can't even tell you why I chose this island."

"She knew she would meet me," Sethi quipped.

"Maybe I did." Jennifer flashed a smile at Sethi. "I felt safer here. I began painting for a living, and I've been doing that ever since." Her eyes became a little distant. "I found out about other people who'd gone missing. And I found out about the Yeqon's Saviours society. It was by luck I found out about them. One morning about five years ago, a London lawyer named Alastair Bastwright turned up at St James's Park, London, with cuts to his head, rampaging and yelling out strange things. He'd been in a car accident near the park and had sustained a number of injuries. He was raving about the thirty steps to enlightenment and boasting that he'd killed more people than people had had hot dinners. He said he was going to kill more and that no one could stop him."

I recoiled. "Oh, God."

Jennifer nodded. "Everyone just thought the head injury had caused him some sort of temporary madness. He was a respected lawyer, a married man with four children. He was placed in a London psychiatric ward. When I heard about it, it gave me an odd feeling that everyone was missing the real story. I went to London and convinced the hospital staff that I was a close relative of Alastair's and needed to see him. I spent only fifteen minutes alone with Alastair in his room—that's all the time they would allow me. They said the things he spoke of were too disturbing for a young woman to hear. But what I found out in that space of time . . ."

Sethi squeezed Jennifer's shoulder while she took a breather.

Swallowing and growing pale, she continued. "Alastair spoke in horrific detail about tortures and murders. Not just by him but by a large group of people. I won't tell you these things in detail, but it all made me sick to my core. I listened, and then I fed him names—names of people I knew had gone missing either in Greece or in a country close to Greece. I also gave him Noah's name. He didn't know Noah, but he knew three of the names. Two women and a man. Hailey, Andrew and Yanis. He described them, and his descriptions were correct. There was no doubt at all that he knew them. It isn't as though these people had been in the news. They'd just been among the thousands of people who quietly go missing every year. He described their tortures and how they begged for mercy. He described—"

Jennifer's body grew rigid, as if she were reliving the scene in the psychiatric ward. From behind her, Sethi gently stroked her arms. My instinct was to tell her she didn't have to go on—it was obviously too painful and still raw. But I couldn't do that. I needed her to tell her story. In the back of my mind, I was pushing thoughts of Kara away. I didn't want to associate her with the victims Jennifer was talking about. I couldn't bear it. I glanced at Gray, and I saw something approaching murderousness in his eyes. I knew he was thinking of his wife being at the hands of these people.

Jennifer shook her head. "He described how they took their last breaths and what their last words were. After that, he began speaking so fast that half of it was gibberish. Talking about predators behind walls that no one could see, watching their victims." She took a shuddering breath, gathering herself. "I went to the police with what he'd told me. Barely an hour later, someone crept into the ward where he was being held and killed him. In the media, it was reported as a suicide."

"How do you know it wasn't—a suicide?" I asked.

"They said he hung himself with his belt. He hadn't been wearing any belt. He'd been wearing hospital pyjamas. The police dismissed everything

I'd told them, saying that the knock to his head had merely triggered a psychotic episode. My best guess is that the accident didn't cause a psychosis but just released the inner workings of his mind. The head injury affected his ability to keep his mouth zipped about the things he'd been involved in and about Yeqon's Saviours."

"We know the name, Yeqon's Saviours," I said bitterly.

"A few people know of it," said Sethi. "But ranks seem to close around the name. As soon as mention is made of it, it is shut down. People die."

Jennifer bent her head in acknowledgment. "I have come close to finding out where these people gather so many times, but I am always blocked at some point along the line. I admit that I still can't quite grasp the whole thing. How is it possible such a thing as this has survived for so long? For centuries? How is it possible that more than a handful of people are involved? There has never been anything like this in the world."

I became aware of my surrounds again, realising I'd been holding my breath and caught deep inside Jennifer's story. I'd seen the ancient illustrations in Rico's book, but some part of me had desperately hoped that the modern-day version of this group just practiced rituals and that they weren't the same as they'd been in the distant past. "It just doesn't seem like it can be real . . ."

Jennifer inhaled deeply, letting her eyes drift open to the sky. "And I think that's why no one has believed me. It's impossible. Less than one percent of the world's population are serial killers. They're rare."

Gray rose suddenly and strode away to the side of the house, his shoulders hunched, stopping to stare out at the ocean.

"I fear the talk of serial killers has become too much for him," Sethi said to me.

I nodded softly. "It's too much for me, too. I need a break."

Pressing her lips in firmly, Jennifer reached to touch my arm. "Go. We'll talk more when you two are ready."

I stepped along the stone path to where Gray was standing. Silently, I offered him a cigarette. We remained there for the next several minutes, puffing away furiously, trying to find an equilibrium on the horizon. But the whole world had been tipped.

"I'll tear these people apart if they've touched a hair on Evie's head," Gray said finally.

I couldn't speak. I didn't want to put a coherent voice to my thoughts.

Gray stubbed the cigarette out on the ground then strode into the house. He returned a moment later with a folder and laid it on the table where Sethi and Jennifer were. "This symbol. The thirty steps. The same stuff that the Alastair guy was raving about. We need to find out the source of the symbol." He sounded desperate, showing them his photocopy of the monks descending the thirty rungs of the ladder.

Walking back to the table, I looked on.

"Rico and Petrina told me they showed you the historical books containing this symbol," Jennifer said to Gray. "For a while there, many years ago, I confessed to them what I was doing. Just after the incident with Alastair Bastwright. I was horrified and terrified, and I needed support. I drip-fed them tiny pieces of information, certainly not everything, because if they knew it all, I knew they'd throw everything at trying to stop me. For the next year, they researched the Saviours with me. But it became too dangerous. Good people that I talked to about this symbol began dying —murdered."

"Are Rico and Petrina still looking for clues about the Saviours with you?" I asked her.

"No," she replied with a definite tone. "After the spate of murders years ago, I pulled back. I couldn't risk more people dying. I didn't tell them about the murders, but Rico and Petrina could still see how dangerous it was getting. They made me promise I'd give up the search, and I promised them I would. I was lying, of course."

Gray eyed her with a heavy expression. "I can see why you had to stop involving other people. So, did you ever find out anything else about the symbol?"

Jennifer shook her head. "Not anything useful. I've been concentrating on finding out who's in the group and what they're doing. But that's proved damned difficult, too. They've wrapped themselves in many layers of secrecy."

A short spell of silence followed.

I sat myself down on one of the wrought-iron chairs. "Do you happen to know anything about Wilson Carlisle, Jennifer?"

"Yes, I've got a couple of folders of information on Mr Carlisle," Jennifer told me. "Nothing that could incriminate him. I've followed him many times on his trips to London. But I can't follow when he takes off on a boat, helicopter or plane. I always lose him."

"I followed him for a few hours." I stiffened as I recalled his words about Kara.

Jennifer shot me a look of alarm. "You followed him? That's a risky thing to do. Very risky. Wilson is certainly unusual, in that he's much more flamboyant than any of the others I've suspected of being part of this. I think he's a bit of a loose cannon. I wouldn't be surprised if he ends up dead."

"I hope he does," I said darkly.

"No." Jennifer waved her hand in a dismissive gesture. "That's not what we want. We need them alive so I can continue to investigate them. I only have strong suspicions about three. I was intending on heading to London to follow Wilson tomorrow."

"You're leaving?" Sethi raised his shoulders in a deep sigh.

Bowing her head, Jennifer turned to him. "I'm sorry," she mouthed.

"Always, I return home and off she goes," he said to Gray and me, giving a sad shrug. His eyes showed a quiet worry.

"I know a couple of names," said Gray, laying out the rest of the photocopies on the table. "I found these images online and I found out who at least two of them are."

Jennifer's forehead puckered as she read Gray's notes and viewed photocopies. "How did you manage to dig these up?"

"I know a few different ways of pulling out old information from the net," said Gray. "I think these were taken by someone spying on the group. They were fuzzy as hell. I cleaned them up and made them sharp."

Jennifer's eyes were suddenly rimmed with tears. "This screen shot of the text under this photo here—it says *For no no boo.*"

"Yeah." Gray studied her changed expression. "Does that mean something to you?"

She nodded. "That's what I used to call Noah when I was very small. I'd heard someone call him by his full name—Noah Bloom—and I began calling him *no no boo.*" She took a full breath. "My parents took these photos . . ."

I swallowed, saddened by the wistful gaze on Jennifer's face. Sethi pressed his face to Jennifer's shoulder in mute comfort.

She raised her eyes to Gray, wiping away the wetness from her cheeks. "You did a great job. My parents must have been trying to keep a record of what they'd found out. But these photos might just be what prompted the Saviours to kill them."

"Do you recognise any of the names and faces?" said Gray, his tone intent but gentle.

"Yes," she said. "Both of these people are dead. I thought they were victims of the Saviours. Now I know better. The Saviours are quick to kill their own if there's any chance of being exposed—these two must have posed a risk."

Gray sat heavily on a seat, his eyes clouding with disappointment.

Sethi kissed Jennifer's temple and then took a close look at the photocopies himself. Suddenly, he slammed a hand down on the table. "*Gamóto!*"

"What did he say?" I whispered to Jennifer.

"He said *fuck*, basically," she told me, turning to frown at her boyfriend. "Seth, what is it?"

"This landscape behind the people," Sethi said. "I know it. It's Greek."

Gray ran a finger across the hilly backdrop of the photocopy. "Where? Where is it?"

"I don't know the name of it," Sethi told us. "It's not a place you go by any accident. It's a tiny island. Nothing on it except for an old monastery and a silent order of monks. No one is allowed to enter. I went there just one time as a teenager, with my father. We were looking for my uncle and his fishing boat. We found my uncle later in another location. But the island, I cannot forget it."

Jennifer's voice was tight and raw when she spoke. "You're certain?"

Sethi nodded, his full lips firm. "I have never been so much certain. This rocky mountain peak that is shaped like a fist? Look, it has an old chapel on top. The chapel was crumbling when I saw it, and it doesn't look any different here. I'm sure I could find it again."

"And look at the date of the meeting," said Jennifer in a hushed tone. "It's this week—the week the Saviours always seem to gather. This has to be the place where they take their victims to."

"But there's a monastery there. Monks . . ." Sethi's tone was doubtful.

"It's no monastery," said Jennifer. "And these are not monks."

Sethi and Jennifer stared at each other for a moment.

"This is it, then." Her tone was quiet and understated. But the weight of what she'd meant was evident in her eyes.

A silent message passed between Gray and me. Whatever happened next, we were going to see this to the end.

60. EVIE

I HADN'T GIVEN THE CELLAR ANY consideration before nor had I ventured down this way. But then, I wasn't an alcoholic. That wasn't the cross I bore. I wondered how many of the alcoholics had noted the location of the wine cellar on the map and had wandered down here, hopeful they could grab a bottle without anyone noticing. No wonder the monks kept it securely locked.

I stood at the chained gate with Richard, Cormack, Louelle, Hop and Yolanda.

Cormack winked at us and then turned to apply the bolt cutters to the chain. He grunted with the effort.

The chain fell away.

The cutters in hand, he pushed the gate open. "Time to party."

"Better have some quality wine down there." Richard pinched Cormack's cheek and stepped past him. "Age before beauty."

Cormack snorted in reply.

We filed down the winding stairway after Richard.

The smell hit us about halfway.

I couldn't guess what it was, but if this was the smell of fermenting alcohol, I wouldn't touch a drop of it.

Richard stopped short, craning his head back at us and covering his lower face with his sleeve. "Jeez, what the hell? Smells rank."

"Oh man." Cormack spat on the stair. "You're not wrong. This can't be the damned wine cellar. Maybe it was once, but not anymore."

Odours of rot and sickly things reached me, and I had to stop myself from vomiting on Yolanda's back. "Let's get out of here."

Yolanda nodded. "This is foul."

"Just wait," said Richard. "I want to see what the good monks are keeping down here. Dead animals? Nothing shocks me. You don't live in a drain for two years without seeing it all. I'll go down there and take one for the team."

"Dammit," said Cormack. "I'm coming, too. If there's one decent bottle of red down there, you'll grab it and go drink it by yourself. After you, m'lady."

Keeping his arm across his face, Richard continued on, going faster now, as if he just wanted to get it over with, until he disappeared from view.

A sudden choking sound punctuated the air—Richard's voice.

"*That* bad, huh?" joked Cormack, running around the spiral staircase.

I looked back at Louelle and Hop as we followed behind the others.

The wide floor of the cellar came into view.

A scream rose inside my chest, but no sound came.

A scene that shocked every one of my senses.

A long, medieval-looking half wall spanned across the cavern directly ahead. People were slumped against the walls, chained. Dead or unconscious, I couldn't tell.

Blood in their hair. On their faces. On their clothing.

Blood on the walls.

The people—they were *us*.

Us.

The challengers.

Kara, Mei, Thomas. Even Ruth . . .

The stench of blood and decay so thick it was suffocating.

A table held an array of knives, swords and other implements I couldn't name.

Beyond the wall, an enormous door was open a sliver. I glimpsed people —bodies—hanging up high against a stone wall.

My chest wall stiffened against my gasping breaths.

With a roar, Cormack burst past Richard. "Kara! Kara!"

She was curled up in a corner of a cell, her face against the stonework, blood spattered on one side of her clothing.

"Fuck this." Richard knocked hard into Yolanda and me as he rushed back up the stairs and away.

I twisted my head around. Richard was gone. Louelle and Hop remained behind me, their eyes huge and unblinking.

Fear shot down my spine.

The chance to get out of here was *now*.

Richard had run. We could all run.

There were killers here in the monastery. *How many? How many were there? And who were they?*

Cormack cut the chains from Kara's wrists.

She woke groggily.

Yolanda stood numbly, making a keening sound in her throat.

Louelle ran alongside me, her hand suddenly clutching mine. "We get who we can and then we go tell the mentors." She paused for a second, her voice grown deeper. "Kill anyone who comes at us."

I stared at her—nodding, but barely.

I couldn't feel my legs beneath me as I ran with Louelle.

Cormack pulled the broken chains away from Kara's wrists and ankles. Next to Kara, Ruth was chained and doubled over. I tried to rouse her, but she was either deeply asleep or unconscious.

I crouched down in front of Kara. "Are they down here—the people who did this to you?"

Kara turned her face to me, her eyes glazed and distant. "They're everywhere."

My fingernails dug into my flesh. "What do you mean, they're everywhere?"

"You will see." She let her face rest across the bloodied wall again.

"What about the others?" I persisted. "Where are they?"

"Floating . . ." Her voice limped out in whispers, her face still against the wall.

I wasn't going to find out anything from Kara. My breath caught as I exchanged glances with Cormack. "What if the mentors are all dead?"

He swallowed, his cheeks drawing in and hollowing. "It's war, then."

Jumping up, I ran to the table and snatched up two large knives.

I had a better view from here inside the second room. Were the killers in there right now?

I caught sight of a pale, red-haired girl, strung up on the wall, in between two men that were hanging just like her.

Poppy.

She'd never left the island.

Blood rushed through my head and limbs.

With wooden legs I stepped to the door of the second room and peered through the gap in the door.

The room was hexagonal. Twelve people were strung up on the walls, two to each wall. Some of them missing one or more limbs. Dead, all of them. Including Poppy. Metronomes ticked away on twelve steps far below them, like a funeral march. The people must have been asked to walk onto the steps before they were hoisted up on the ropes.

My entire body grew cold.

The monastery hadn't suddenly been invaded by a band of murderers. The entire cellar was set up for murder.

God, the monks.

It was the monks.

My mind screamed at me to leave. *Escape.*

But I couldn't leave without checking, without being certain everyone here was dead.

I pushed the door all the way open and stepped inside.

Duncan half raised his slumped head to me, his eyes dulled. *He was still alive. Somehow.* Five knives were pierced through his body and into the wall behind.

"Duncan . . ." I could barely speak his name.

"This isn't a good place, I have to warn you," he rasped.

I fumbled with the hoist, already knowing it was useless. No one could save him. "We'll get you down."

"All told, it might be best if you kill me." His voice chillingly matter-of-fact.

"*No* . . ."

"I was the safety officer at my work. If you remove the knives, I'll bleed out."

"I'll get help. I'll get help, Duncan." But I'd vacated my words before I'd finished saying them.

He stared like he was no longer seeing me. "Tell my wife I did love her." His head slumped again, chin hitting his chest.

I whirled around, checking the others in turn. All had been tortured to the point of death. Except for Poppy. Maybe. *Maybe.* She had cuts all over her body, but none seemed deep enough to kill her. But I couldn't tell what else they might have done to her.

With a cry, I ran to her and used the hoist to lower her to the floor.

Please wake. Please wake.

Don't be dead.

I knelt down to her crumpled figure. "Poppy, please . . ."

Her eyelids fluttered below a dark bruise on her forehead.

There. She was alive.

Working quickly, I sawed at the ropes around her wrists. I went too fast, making a small, shallow cut on her skin.

"Oh, hell. I'm sorry. So sorry." Carefully, I pulled the ropes away from her rope-burned wrists.

Her eyes sprang open.

"I didn't mean to cut you. I—"

"Evie. *Evie, Evie, Evie . . .*" She kept whispering my name as if nothing made sense, not even the fact that I was here in front of her.

"She's in shock," came a voice behind me. I turned to see Richard.

He bent to scoop Poppy in his arms. He met my eyes as he rose, shifting Poppy's weight so that she settled against his chest. He looked as terrified as I felt.

I nodded, both shocked to see him and unsurprised.

Yolanda and Hop ran around the room, desperately checking all the others.

"They're all dead. All of them," breathed Yolanda.

Louelle stood at the doorway, sweat glistening on her face and chest. "We get out of here now. Or we don't."

A straggly, unsteady group of people stood behind her, their faces numbed with terror—the people that had been freed from the cells. Kara was among them, her shoulders caved inward and head down.

"Only seven?" I asked Louelle.

Louelle expelled a quick, sharp breath. "We can't wake the others. They're unconscious. We have to leave them."

Richard headed out with Poppy. I rushed behind him, shooting a glance back at Duncan. It was already too late for him.

"There's another way out!" Yolanda gestured frantically past the cells.

In the dim light, I saw what she was pointing at. A door with a small glass section.

We charged towards it.

Cormack got there first, pulling Kara along with him. Kara shook her head, holding onto Cormack's arm and stopping him from touching the door. "There's an alarm. Do you see it? And how would we get through those locks? There's no use. They'll be back here soon. There's no way out."

Richard found a flashlight on a shelf nearby and shone its light onto the locks. There were two solid bolts securing the door—too large to cut through. I could see nothing but darkness through the glass panel, nothing to tell me what was on the other side.

Most of the people we'd released had already turned away and fled, rushing for the stairs.

Louelle steadied a disoriented Thomas as he fell against the wall, his eyes dazed. "C'mon, kid, you can make it," she told him. "We can't go this way. We're going out up the stairs. Put your arm around my shoulder."

Hop stepped across to support Thomas's other arm.

How are we all going to get out?

Don't think now.

Just run.

61. CONSTANCE

SETHI AND JENNIFER BEGAN MAKING PLANS, leaving Gray and me to our own devices. I grew increasingly nervous.

Wasn't it time to bring in the police? We had a location now. And some names.

But Jennifer had insisted that going to the police with this would do nothing except to get us all killed. She was certain that there were members of the Saviours among high-level police, only she didn't know who. In desperation, I'd suggested contacting the media. She'd levelled her gaze at me and asked me what I thought would happen if we did that. With a growing terror inside, I'd understood. Before such a thing even went to air, the Saviours would destroy all evidence, including their victims. Victims that included Kara and Evie. And then the Saviours would simply start up again, somewhere else.

I watched as Jennifer and Sethi packed a bewildering assortment of gadgets, speaking to each other in quick, rushed voices about ammunition, guns, cameras, signal interference, infrared devices and counter-surveillance.

They tried to shut Gray and me out of the discussion, but Gray was having none of it. He was adamant that he was going along on the trip. I decided that I would go, too. For all I knew, this might be the last time I would see Kara.

Jennifer and Sethi battled our assertions, telling us it was too dangerous and that we weren't trained for this. But we won, in the end, partly I think because they knew that if we were with them, we couldn't panic and run to the police.

Sethi went to get his boat ready—Gray going to help him. Jennifer excused herself and returned to the house.

Jennifer had instructed Gray and I not to contact anyone—not family members and not even Rico and Petrina. I hadn't spoken to James since I was in Athens. No one was to be contacted until Jennifer and Sethi had been to the island and returned with evidence. All phones and tablets were to be kept switched off.

I was beginning to suspect that Jennifer had lived too long all alone. Except for Sethi, she had no one. She had no trust for anyone. But this was too big for Jennifer and Sethi to tackle by themselves.

Waves of rage, fear and frustration passed through me.

What if the four of us travelled to the Saviours' island but then never returned? The knowledge of where the island was would die with us.

The photocopies of the Yeqon's Saviours photographs were still lying on the table outside. I snapped a couple of quick pictures of the hill and the chapel with my phone and then headed away for a walk on the cliff edge. My heart nearly jumped through my chest as I sent the pictures through to Petrina, asking if she knew where it was. I didn't tell her where the image had come from. If she and Rico had noticed it when they'd viewed the photocopies before, they hadn't said anything.

I kept walking, my muscles forming knots. I could be jeopardising everything. But Jennifer didn't own the search for the Saviours, even if she had been looking for most of her life. Gray and I were searching, too.

Petrina's reply text came back quickly. *Please call me. I have information.*

I called her, reminding myself not to sound anxious.

"Where are you?" Petrina asked.

"We're still on Sikinos. With Jennifer and Sethi."

"Sethi's there?"

"Yes. He seems nice."

"He is. I'm glad Jennifer has someone like him. How is she?"

"She's fine. We've had a lot to talk about."

Petrina sighed. "I'll bet you have."

"We just had a chat. Nothing too major," I lied. I waited patiently for her to tell me what she knew about the chapel.

"Constance, where did you get that picture you sent me?"

"Oh, Gray and I have been looking at all kinds of things, trying to find clues. This is just something we couldn't find any information on."

"Well," she said, "as it turns out, it's extremely interesting. You must tell me later exactly where you found this. This discovery is going to cause quite a stir in Greek history circles. Rico and I went down to search at the library. We have special access to a rich catalogue of Greek literature that ordinary people do not. We found the chapel—it's of a particular style that we were able to find the origins of."

"Wonderful. Can you tell me where it is?"

"Well, that's a little more difficult. We couldn't pin down an exact location, but it is definitely situated on an island between Greece and Turkey. The chapel belongs to a twelfth-century monastery. What is interesting is the history of the monastery."

"Oh?" I didn't want to know the history. I wanted a location.

"Yes. It seems that the monastery was built by an order of monks, all based on the number six, which was thought to be one of God's divine numbers. Many facets of the building, including the shape of the rooms themselves, are based around the number six. The rooms are all hexagonal, apparently. Like the cells of a beehive. We read that the monastery was built with the purpose of taking in the people with mental illnesses from the surrounding islands. Of course, they didn't have the same understanding that we do now of mental illness. They believed they were afflictions that came from demonic power. The monks aimed to destroy the power of the demons and restore health to these poor creatures."

"Goodness, well, I guess we can assume that didn't work very well," I replied.

"I would guess not. It seems that the monks even went as far as to install secret passageways through which they could observe the patients and see if their methods were working. Apparently, there was even a passageway they ran from the chapel into the cellar, where the monks kept the worst of the patients. The history is murky after that point. We couldn't discover what happened."

"How bizarre." I held my breath for a moment. "Were there any maps of the monastery, showing where these passages are? Or any drawings of the exterior?"

"Unfortunately, no." Her tone changed. "I'll ask again what your interest is in this place? I'm finding it difficult to believe you found it by accident. It's quite obscure."

"It's nothing, really. Like I said, Gray and I are casting a wide net, and he happened to find this. I'd ask Gray exactly where he found it, but he's . . . gone out fishing with Sethi."

"Fishing?"

"Yes," I said weakly.

"I haven't been able to get in contact with Jennifer this morning. Could you tell her I'd like to talk with her?"

"Of course, Petrina."

I ended the call, thrusting the phone into my pocket, feeling like I was betraying everyone. Petrina's worst fear was that Gray and I were going to pose a risk to Jennifer. And it turned out that we were doing exactly that. Jennifer was about to head into extreme danger, and I hadn't even warned Petrina. I knew it wasn't fair of me to risk her daughter to save my own.

But I couldn't force myself to call her back.

I hoped they could all forgive me. I saw what I'd done as leaving a breadcrumb trail, just as Jennifer's parents had done when they'd uploaded the photos of the Saviours' meeting to the internet.

Gray sprinted up to me as I returned to the grounds of Jennifer's house. "We're going now." He was breathing hard, his expression taut and determined.

62. EVIE

THE PLAN WAS TO STAY TOGETHER. Stay quiet.

But some of the people we'd freed from the cells scattered once we reached the top of the spiral stairway. Before we could stop them.

Kara tried to run, but Cormack still had her hand tightly gripped.

Blood pulsed wildly in my temples, images rushing through my mind like a frenzied show reel.

Dead. Dismembered. Chains. Hooks. Knives. Blood.

So much blood.

We had no plan for what to do next. I didn't blame anyone for running. It seemed safer to stick together, but splitting up might be the only way any of us were going to survive.

Our group was now made up of Cormack, Kara, Louelle, Yolanda, Hop, Richard, Poppy, Thomas and me. Most of us were armed with knives, but that was no defence against a horde of murderers, especially if they had guns. And the three of us that had been rescued were still groggy.

"Richie, you can put me down," whispered Poppy. "I'm okay."

"You're in no state to walk," he said.

"Yes, I am," she insisted. "They'd barely . . . started on me yet. I'm slowing you down."

I glanced at her in horror, gory images in my head of what she'd witnessed.

Richard gingerly set Poppy down on her feet. "Who did all this? Who are they?"

Her eyes enlarged. "The same people as the one who killed Saul. There's more of them."

Yolanda stared down the dark hall. "I don't know about the rest of you, but I'm heading straight for the front door."

"If the front door's not locked, the gates will be," said Louelle. "And those gates are freaking high. But I'm with you."

"Me too." Hop nodded, breathing hard. "The best way forward is usually in a straight line."

"We'll find a way over the damned gate." Cormack started walking, pulling Kara along.

"Wait," said Poppy. "Shouldn't we warn the mentors?"

Cormack stopped and looked back over his shoulder. "We've got no guarantee they're not dead. I'm not wasting any time."

Richard and I locked gazes, each of us knowing what the other was thinking.

"There's another way." Richard gestured towards the wall. "Through there. The walls are hollow."

Cormack spun around fully. "How the hell do you know that?"

"It was accidental. No time to explain," Richard said. "But the passages would have to run all the way to the front."

"Let's do it!" I stared at Richard, trying to calculate the difference in time between just running for the door and heading around to the entry to the hidden passages. Every way we could choose to go was dangerous.

"Sounds like a good way to get trapped." Yolanda shook her head emphatically, her mouth trembling.

"Yeah, why the fuck would we squeeze ourselves into some tiny space?" agreed Cormack.

Kara tilted her head back, staring fearfully at the ceiling. "If you don't want to be seen, don't go where they can see you. They can follow your every move out in the hallways. You know there's cameras up there. If the killers have access to the cameras . . ."

"We have to take that risk," Poppy cried. "I'm with Yolanda and Cormack. I'd kill myself before being strung up on that wall again. You don't know what I was forced to watch in that room. I need to get *out* . . ."

I wanted to grab her hand and run with her, but images of Gray and my girls flashed through my mind and crowded all else out. Kara and Richard were right. The cameras would see our every move. It was better to try the hidden passages.

I whirled around to Richard and Kara. "I'm with you."

They both nodded.

"Fuck, I'm with you lot, then," said Cormack.

"You can't just leave us." Yolanda's eyes grew huge, her dark skin looking ashen.

"Please come," I offered, then shot Poppy a pleading look.

But Yolanda and Poppy shook their heads, backing away. Louelle, Hop, Yolanda and Thomas started away down the hall—Thomas now steady enough on his feet to run by himself. Poppy stood by herself, trembling.

"Hey, popsicle," cried Richard to Poppy. "I just carried your ass out of there. The least you could do now is be grateful and try to live. You get yourself here, now."

She'd only taken one step towards us before Richard had run back and grabbed her hand. I exhaled hard in relief.

We sprinted to the alcove with the hidden passage.

Richard wriggled in and opened the doorway.

Cormack gave a low whistle. "You've got some serious explaining to do, Richie boy."

Richard ignored him, herding us all in and closing the door again.

Immediately, I felt entombed.

In my mind, part of me was still running for the gate, in the open air. Along with Louelle, Yolanda and Thomas. But I hadn't taken that option.

Richard led us, pulling out the flashlight he'd found in the cellar. We tore through the passages, me pulling Poppy along and Cormack pulling Kara.

We reached a point where the passage branched off into two directions.

"I heard something." Kara's voice echoed dully through the air. "To the left. We'd better go right."

Our party of five stopped still, listening.

"What did you hear?" I whispered.

"I don't know. Voices maybe," Kara told me.

"But that path goes the wrong way. We need to go left." Richard took out a knife from his pocket, the blade gleaming silver in the glow of the flashlight. He snapped the light off. "Better not show ourselves until we have to.

I'll take anyone on. I've been in knife fights before—I've told you I was living in the drains. And I always win."

"Let's do it." Poppy's voice shook in the pitch darkness.

"But what if there's too many of them to take on?" Cormack said under his breath. "I think we need to head to the right."

"You'd go anywhere she leads you, wouldn't you, lover boy?" came Richard's voice.

"We're going," said Cormack firmly.

I heard he and Kara move off.

"Please come," Kara urged the rest of us in a low breath.

"Sorry," replied Richard, his tone brittle and tense. "I came in here to get out the quickest way I can. Poppy, Evie—you with me?"

I wanted *out*. Desperately. "I'm with you."

"No," I heard Kara whisper, but waves of claustrophobia and fear spiralled through me. If the killers hadn't already discovered that their victims had been freed, they soon would. There was no time left.

What had we done? Were Louelle and the others at the front gate now, escaping? Maybe we shouldn't have come in here at all, but we were here now, and we just had to keep going, no matter what.

Drawing out two knives and clenching them in both fists, I stepped away with Richard and Poppy into the maw of black. Kara and Cormack pleaded with us again. They were two headstrong kids in love, and nothing could convince them they were wrong.

I anxiously checked our location at the first peephole I could find. We were no longer walking alongside the wall. I looked through into a supply room. Shelves of folded clothing like the outfits we were wearing. And metronomes—all still.

Poppy's fingers pressed gingerly into my shoulders. "Evie? Why are you stopping?"

"I found a peephole," I told her, trying not to sound guilty at telling a lie. I already knew about the peepholes. "There's nothing to see."

The three of us kept winding our way through the passages, my heart thrashing against my ribcage as I anticipated someone jumping out at us at any moment. Richard kept the flashlight off.

"Are we going the right way?" said Poppy softly.

"I'm good at finding my way through dark tunnels," came Richard's reply. "But this place confounds me."

"We're lost, aren't we?" My hands had grown numb on the handles of the knives I held, my grip still tight. "Wait, did you hear that?"

Somewhere down the passage and around a corner, there was a scuffle of feet. Then silence.

Richard blew out a hard breath. "It's on."

Switching on his flashlight, he charged forward, a knife held high in his right hand.

I ran behind him.

The beam of the flashlight bounced around an empty passage.

Whirling around, he sprinted down another passage.

I turned to check behind.

Poppy was gone.

No.

"Richard!" I called, but he'd already run too far.

Had someone grabbed Poppy? Did they have a hand clamped over her mouth right now, and were they about to hurt her?

I ran back, retracing my steps.

The passage curved around. I understood now. The passages were winding around the hexagonal rooms. That was how we'd become lost.

I heard Poppy's cry. I stopped dead still for a moment, frozen. I wanted to turn and head away. Save myself. But I couldn't. I couldn't leave her like this.

I raced around the curve of the wall, catching sight of Richard and his flashlight beam coming from the opposite direction.

With Richard here, the two of us could save Poppy.

Richard cast his light to and fro, searching.

Poppy stood with her back flat against a wall, terrified.

Someone leapt from the darkness, knife in hand. They plunged the knife deep into Poppy's side. Poppy screamed.

The assailant glanced my way.

Kara.

Confused, I cried out for her to stop. She'd mistaken Poppy for a killer.

But Kara pulled out the knife and held its tip to Poppy's throat. "Come closer, and I'll slice her veins."

Richard stopped short. "What the hell are you doing?"

Kara looked back to me again. "Walk past me. We're going this way."

"Please, Kara," I begged. "Why are you doing this?"

Poppy moaned, clutching her side, dark blood staining her top. "Get this psycho away from me . . ."

"Do it," Kara ordered me, her Southern accent steely, digging the knife into Poppy's throat.

I obeyed, stepping around her and up to Richard.

Cormack came running up behind Richard, panting. "Thank God. I lost Kara and couldn't find—" His words gagged in his throat as he drew close enough to see. "What . . . ?"

"Your girlfriend just stabbed Poppy in cold blood," Richard told him.

"Cormack, I had to do this," Kara told him.

"*This* is why you ran away from me?" Cormack's face was white. "What the fuck is wrong with you? Who the hell are you?"

"Please don't ask any more questions. Just keep walking. The way I tell you to," Kara told him, her eyes hard.

"No." Cormack shook his head. "You give me that knife and go. I don't care what happens to you after that."

Poppy moved her head to one side as Kara moved the knife lightly over her neck. "One cut and she's dead. See this vein? If I slice it, the blood will spurt so far and fast she'll lose three pints before you can blink. Her heart will race in a desperate attempt to pump blood through her body. Another blink, and her blood pressure will drop and her small blood vessels will go into survival mode, trying to do the job of the heart. But it will be too late."

"Please," Poppy whispered to us, her eyes wide and terrified. "Help me."

I tried to rush to her, but Richard pinned me against the wall. "She'll try to kill you, too. She's one of *them*." He stared at Kara, dropping his hold on me. "You're one of them, aren't you? The killers."

"Please," I begged Kara. "Let me wrap up her injuries."

Kara shook her head. "I can't do that."

My knees went slack as I leaned against the wall. "*You* . . . you were trying to set me up. From that time I met you in the casino. That Wilson guy is behind this thing, isn't he?"

Kara refused to answer.

My breaths were ragged in my throat as I turned to Richard. "But if she is one of them and she knows her way through the walls, then the other killers do too. We're sitting ducks in here. We have to get out."

"You did a good job of pretending," Cormack accused her. "You had *me* fooled."

"I didn't fool you," Kara said to Cormack calmly. "I told you that I can't be with you. I told you I'm not what you see."

"I never thought you could be *this*." Cormack's lower lip trembled, and his teeth set hard together.

Kara's flat expression remained unchanged. "Well, I *am* this. I've always been this. We need to hurry now. We've wasted too much time already."

"We can't trust you now," Cormack told her. "Not after what you've done."

"The people you call *the killers* will be here soon," she said. "You have one chance. I'll take you down to the shore."

"She's going to kill us all." Poppy's voice grew ragged, breathy. "That's what you plan to do, isn't it?"

I could hear my own heartbeat in the moments that followed, the air disturbed but silent as Kara refused to answer.

"Kara, who are you?" Cormack demanded, his voice as hoarse as it was broken. "Who are the killers? You owe us at least that much."

"Yeqon's Saviours," she answered.

The sound of feet echoed in the passageway.

Kara turned her head sharply.

Panic churned through my stomach, blood roaring in my ears. We were stuck here.

Richard switched off his flashlight, plunging us into darkness.

There was a large group of people coming in this direction.

Please, please don't come this way. If we stay here and stay quiet, maybe they'll go another way.

A dull thud came as someone fell roughly to the floor.

The feet were running now. The people had heard us.

We'll be butchered right here.

Else taken down to the cellar and killed there.

We had to run. Poppy would be left behind, but we had no choice. None.

Footfalls came from the other direction.

Too late. We were trapped now.

Flashlights strobed the air, slicing across our faces and bodies.

In the snatches of light, I could see that there were over a dozen figures.

They were almost upon us. Silhouetted. Hooded. Terrifying.

I prepared to die, my mind blanking out.

"What's going on here?" Brother Sage's voice boomed down the long, narrow space.

Jerking my head around, I searched the figures until I found his face. It *was* him. I hadn't imagined his voice.

My body slackened in relief. The mentors hadn't been murdered. Neither had all of the monks been slaughtered.

We weren't alone here.

"Well, thank fuck it's you," cried Richard, his voice shakier than I'd yet heard it.

Kara had vanished.

I looked around for Poppy. She was slumped on the floor. Running to her, I dropped to my knees and lifted her top to just above her navel. "We need a bandage—now!"

Poppy shivered uncontrollably under my hands. She'd lost so much blood already. Kara's cold words about how long it would take Poppy to die sprang into my head.

"Here," Cormack told me under his breath. He tore off his shirt. I tried to wrap it around her.

Poppy struggled to sit, her voice raspy and strained with agony. "Kara was just here," she told Brother Sage. "Bitch stabbed me."

"Get Poppy to the infirmary," ordered Brother Sage. "Before we lose her." He half-turned then to speak with one of the other monks.

I frowned, shielding my eyes from the harsh glare of flashlights. I knew the monk that Brother Sage was speaking to. But from where?

My stomach hitched as the answer came to me.

Wilson Carlisle.

The man that had been at the Sydney casino with Kara.

He wasn't a monk.

Brother Sage turned around a fraction more.

I caught a split-second view of the back of his robes.

A symbol.

A ladder inside a hexagon.

The same symbol the person who'd killed Saul had worn.

Everything inside me crushed to a single point, a single thought.

We had not been rescued.

The monks were not monks. The mentors were not good.

What had Kara said they were? Yeqon's Saviours*?*

Gasping breaths rattled in my lungs.

Brother Sage finished his conversation with Wilson and fixed his gaze on me, a sudden knowing look curling his lips. "Get this lot down to the cellar. Brothers, three of you go and find Kara."

"What the hell?" demanded Richard. "Do you have any idea what's happening in the cellar? There are people—" He broke off suddenly, making a low moan as he came to the same realisation that I had.

Wilson grinned at me, shrugging.

"*Fuck.*" Cormack tried to run and barrel his way through the men behind us.

"You bastard!" Richard charged straight at Brother Sage with his knife held straight out.

But the Saviours grabbed both of them and held them tight.

Brother Vito strode forward from between the dark figures in front of us. Bending down, he gathered Poppy into his arms.

He shot me a resigned look. "I'm sorry, Evie."

Poppy rested her head against his chest. "About time, Vito."

I stared from her to Brother Vito.

"*Poppy . . .?*" My voice crushed to grains.

Poppy cast a dark look in my direction. "You ruined it. I get a kick out of being hung up in the cellar. All these cuts on my body? Brother Vito did them. We do this every year. As a special anniversary treat between lovers." Sighing, she eyed Richard. "Awww, cheer up, baby chin, I really do like you."

Brother Sage clapped his hands together. "Hurry, go find the rest of them. There should be about seven."

Poppy giggled. "They were trying to make a break for the exit."

"They made it out there," said Brother Sage. "They're being rounded up at the moment. Well, this year's event has certainly been different. We need to get things back on track."

I stared in numb horror at the hooded figures that I'd believed I could trust. "Why?" I whispered to Brother Sage.

He tilted his head as a dismissive look entered his eyes. "People like us have been among all of you for centuries. And so we'll always be."

63. GRAY

THE MOON WAS COVERED BY CLOUDS as our boat cut through the black water. I couldn't make out a mass of land ahead, but Sethi assured us it was there.

Echoing cries filled the air, long and plaintive, like the cries of small children. "What the hell is that?"

"Peacocks," Sethi told me. "It's deafening when you're close to them. It's good. The noise will help give us cover."

Jennifer was staring straight ahead, like she hadn't heard the birds at all. "There's the island."

Constance hadn't spoken on the entire trip, just sitting and looking out at the ocean.

We landed on a pebbly shore. Reeds or tall grasses—I couldn't tell which—rustled and swayed in the breeze.

Clouds shifted from the moon, exposing a long line of boats on the left side of us, anchors stuck deep in the sand. I spotted the chapel up high on the hill, the large cross on top jutting darkly against the moonlit sky. I couldn't see the monastery from here, but that was good.

If we can't see them, they can't see us, right?

I knew that was a logical fallacy, but I needed something to hold onto. Jennifer and Sethi had been using gadgets to interfere with any surveillance devices on the island long before we even arrived. I had to hope they knew what they were doing.

Sethi jumped out and into the water. "At least we don't have the worry of hiding the boat. Our boat shouldn't be noticed among all of these."

I followed Sethi into the water, helping him tug the boat into shore. Jennifer and Constance climbed out. I caught Constance's arm as she stumbled on driftwood.

She jerked her head up at me. "God, this place. It feels . . . *bad*."

I knew what she meant. Everything we'd heard about the Saviours had suddenly crystallized into something physical.

On a far hilltop, large, dark shapes moved.

I froze on the spot. If whoever was on the hill had watched us sail in, we were sitting ducks. Then I realised what they were. Peacocks. Their bodies were big enough—with their long, full tails—to resemble a man crawling. At least the peacocks might act as a kind of cover for us.

"You and Constance stay here," Sethi told us. "Behind this rock. Keep your heads down. Until Jennifer and I return."

"What are you going to be doing?" Constance asked anxiously.

"Looking for thermal imaging cameras," he said quietly. "They give off a kind of heat we'll be able to detect with our counter-imaging. If there are any, we'll disable them."

Constance and I kept behind the rock, tense and waiting. When Jennifer and Sethi came back, we ran up the beach and onto the hillside, staying low to the ground. We started the climb, our feet sliding on the dry soil and loose rocks.

It was a twenty-minute climb to an outer perimeter wall of the monastery.

"This is it," Sethi told us. He reached for the rope and grappling hook over his shoulder. "Once we're in, there might not be any coming out again."

He lowered his head to kiss Jennifer.

"You've got no skin in this game," she told him quietly. "You can leave now. You should. You got me here, and that's enough."

He held her in his gaze. "Your brother is my brother."

"Wait," Constance said urgently. "What if there's another way?"

Sethi shook his head. "As far as I can see, this wall goes all the way around."

"Ssh," Jennifer cautioned. "I see something. Lights."

I whipped around to see what she was seeing. Flashlights. Dotted around the hills. "Hell. Where'd they come from all of a sudden?"

Sethi tugged his rope, making the hook tumble down.

The four of us crouched on the ground.

The flashlights seemed to crowd together, the people coming together and moving in a single line now. Coming closer. I held my breath. If they chose to walk around the perimeter, they'd find us. We were exposed here—no trees or large rocks to hide behind. If we were going to head away to a better position, we had to go. *Now.*

I turned my head to Jennifer, Sethi and Constance. They were looking around, and I could guess they had the same idea.

"We can't let them find us." Jennifer lifted binoculars to her eyes. "*God.*"

"What is it?" Sethi took the binoculars from her and looked through them himself.

"There's a group of people with rifles," said Jennifer. "They're the ones with the flashlights. They've got prisoners."

"Who? Who have they got? Can you see?" I asked quickly.

"Kara?" whispered Constance.

Sethi shook his head. "They're too far away to see clearly. Wait. *Gamóto!* Where did they go?"

He returned the binoculars to Jennifer. "I lost sight of them."

"Do you think they saw us?" Constance breathed.

"No," answered Sethi. "I don't think so. They were walking in a straight line. Not looking over this way, as far as I could tell."

"But if they've got night-vision binoculars, too? They might have seen us. Maybe they're hiding and waiting." Jennifer looked again through her lenses.

"If they just *vanished*," said Constance, "maybe that means there's a passage that goes underground to the monastery. Ancient castles had that kind of thing, didn't they? Hidden passageways?"

"Too risky," said Jennifer. "We can't assume something like that." She gazed straight upward to the top of the fencing. "Risky to go over the wall, too. But we don't have much of a choice."

Constance exhaled, turning towards the dark hills. Her voice flattened when she spoke. "There's a hidden passageway in the chapel. Petrina told me."

"What?" Jennifer hissed, grabbing Constance's arm. "You told Petrina where we were going?"

I stared at Constance in shock.

Constance shook her head, twisting back to face Jennifer. "No, she knows nothing. All I did was ask her about the image of the chapel. She and Rico found out some things about it. And about the monastery."

"Do they know where the island is?" demanded Jennifer, still clutching Constance's arm.

"No. They have no idea." Constance shivered, the shiver running straight through her voice.

"Are you sure about the chapel?" Jennifer asked.

"I'm sure." Constance bent her head. "At least, Petrina was sure."

"I know her," muttered Jennifer. "And she knows her stuff."

Sethi rubbed the back of his neck. "Okay, look, the thing that Constance did has been done. We can't change it. And you know, it makes sense about the hidden passageway. Maybe we should go check it out."

Jennifer let her hold on Constance drop. "Okay. I'm outvoted. We'll wait another minute and then head out. Everyone stay low."

64. GRAY

WE CREPT ACROSS THE HILLS TO the chapel, Constance and I following close behind Jennifer and Sethi. The captives and their captors had vanished there.

I couldn't shake the feeling that the members of the Yeqon's Saviours cult had simply switched off their flashlights, and they were waiting here to ambush us. But this was the better of two bad options *if* there really was a secret entry in the floor of the chapel.

Sethi's face held a sheen of sweat. "Could be a trap walking into that."

Jennifer pulled a balaclava over her face. "I'll go check."

"Not you." Sethi touched her arm. "I'll go."

"I'm better at this," she told him. "I've been doing this for years." Without waiting for a reply, she left and headed away, lithe on the rocky slope of the hill.

Sethi turned to us with a tight expression. "I know this is what we signed up for when we came here. But the practice is different from the theory."

"I know," Constance whispered back. "We're soldiers in a war. That's what it feels like. A war." She gazed back at the high walls of the monastery. "We can't win this, can we?"

Sethi bowed his head in acknowledgement. "Stay with us, Constance Lundquist. If your daughter is here, may you get the chance to see her. If we don't win the war, maybe we can win the battle."

Constance nodded, closing her eyes and taking a deep breath.

I looked away, trying not to let a bitter sense overtake me. All this just to win a battle? Evie might already be dead. And all I'd get was the chance to know what happened to her. But Sethi was right. This was what we signed up for.

Jennifer reached the chapel, glancing back once at Sethi. I understood now that she would stop at nothing to find out what happened to her brother. She'd already given her life for that cause. But was she going to take us into danger without a second thought?

She circled the chapel to a point where we could no longer see her. Within a minute, she re-emerged, waving us forward.

We made our way up to the chapel.

The interior of the chapel was a simple affair: stone floor and walls, a small altar and a rope hanging down from a large bell.

It didn't take us long to find the trapdoor. It wasn't in the floor. A set of four wide stone steps led to the altar—the entire stairway lifting up as a door to reveal a hidden tunnel.

Inside, stairs led down.

Crouching, we stepped in and onto the stairs. Sethi closed the door behind us.

The passage walls were close enough to reach out and touch on either side. My shoes stuck to the damp floor. The same rain that had poured down the day that Constance and I had first tramped up the hill to Jennifer's house had trickled in here, the smell of wet mud rising from the ground. Our shoe prints wouldn't be noticed—lots of shoes had just tramped this ground.

A light shone on the wall around the next bend. If we walked on, we'd be exposed.

Jennifer stopped, turning back to Sethi.

Wordlessly, he stepped around her, drawing out a gun from his pocket. Pressing his back against the wall, he angled his face to try to see around the bend. He inched along the wall.

Suddenly, he charged ahead.

Had he been seen by the Saviours?

Pulling out our guns, we followed him around the bend.

Sethi bent over the crumpled figure of a woman. She was blonde, middle-aged and thin. There was no one else. A dim lamp was fixed to the wall overhead.

The woman turned to view us with dulled, dazed eyes. A bullet hole and blood darkened the side of her face, just above her ear.

Constance inhaled sharply.

Jennifer knelt down to the woman. “What’s your name?”

“Louelle May Gibson,” she answered in a laboured but automatic tone. “I’m a librarian from Grand Rapids, Michigan. I have a husband and three children. Two cats. I’m addicted to prescription drugs.”

Jennifer cast a confused glance at Sethi then brushed the woman’s bloodied hair away from her temple. “Where were those men taking you?”

“The cellar . . .” A thin line of foamy blood trailed from the corner of Louelle’s mouth. “I’m no good to them anymore. They left me here . . .” At that point, Louelle May Gibson went beyond the point of being able to talk to us.

My chest squeezed inward. The horror of the Saviours had just become real.

“We have to go.” Jennifer motioned to us.

We continued on down the passage.

The stench grew thicker. Foul.

Shots of electricity crisscrossed my body, surging into my brain, warning me to get the hell off this island. But getting off the island wasn’t an option. Not until I found Evie.

65. EVIE

BROTHER VITO TOOK ME DOWN TO the cellar.

Other members of Yeqon's Saviours took the rest of us.

Why didn't I go with Louelle and the others?

Vito fixed the chains to my arms and ankles in the same gentle way that he'd fixed the wristband to me, as though the two were no different in his eyes.

"I have children," I pleaded. "You can't—"

"I have two young ones myself. I adore them."

"Yet you can rip parents away from their own children?"

"It's the way the world operates. Some win. Some lose. We are what we are—Evie—all of us," he said, his voice in that same soothing register he always used, only it was chilling now. "Each person must remain true to themselves. I wouldn't have chosen for you to see the cellar at all. The final six contestants are always given the quickest death. The six have their final meal, and then we hold our ceremony. And then we prepare the challenge rooms again. Six new challenges, all held later tonight. Each of the new challenges is deadly, and when you die, death is fairly instant. But seeing as the remaining six are the best, you have a slight chance of lasting until the sixth challenge. If that happens, your death will occur by drowning in the cenote." He eyed me indulgently. "I hope that will be you, Evie. You can make it to the end. And when you die, your body will be whole and unmarked. A beautiful death."

A guttural moan rose from my throat. "Where are the others? Did they leave the island?"

"Don't you understand? None of them left the island. They either died here in the cellar or they died out on the hills. Each night of the six challenges—just before dawn—we release half of the losing contestants outside to the hills, where we hunt them. You see, some of our Saviours prefer to hunt than to get up close with their quarry. We cater for all tastes here."

Staring at him in revulsion, I recalled the raucous noise of the peacocks before dawn each morning and the distant screams I'd dismissed as being bird calls. Each morning when I'd woken in my bed, sleepy, excited and wondering about the next challenge, people were being hunted to their deaths out there on the island.

"Shhh," he crooned. "Sweet Evie, you'll only upset yourself. I apologise for this change to our schedule. It wasn't supposed to happen this way. But within a few hours, you won't be here anymore to feel the pain and sorrow that brought you to the monastery in the first place."

My arms sank with the weight of the chains. "Is that why we're here? Because we're addicts? You want to put us out of our pain? Or because we disgust you?"

He took a deep breath, his dark eyes on mine. "No. I know that you're smart enough to figure that one out. Perhaps your fear is blinding your senses."

"Tell me," I said, all colour drained from my voice. "I need to know why."

"Very well. You'll find the reasons why we choose addicts quite clever, I think. Your addictions do not interest us, but your addictions are helpful to use in a number of ways. They provide us with a compelling reason to get you to come to the island. And of course, your reasoning is blunted by your desperation. You'll agree to anything to relieve yourselves of the painful situations in which you've found yourselves. The money and the treatment program are impossible to refuse. And your addictions provide a very good cover for the fact you've gone missing. People with addictions are the ones who are most likely to vanish. The drug addicts and drug-addicted prostitutes. The gamblers with massive debts to their names."

My teeth set firmly together, my jaw trembling. "You prey on the desperate. Why even bother with the challenges? Why not just kill us as soon as we step foot on the island?"

"The challenges are not for you. They are for us," he said, fixing a chain to my left ankle. "It's a commemoration of our history. We chose all of you because you have talents." He smiled briefly. "You are addicts, yes, but each of you are talented in some way. Each year, the four mentors choose their teams. Six people each, cherry picked from the world. The mentor who ends up with the most people out of the final six who have the most points to their names wins."

"It's all just a *contest*?"

He shrugged. "Yes. As I said, each one of the people we choose is very adept at something. Good at figuring things out. Quick minds. Mathematical ability or intuition or the ability to stay calm under pressure." He caressed me beneath the chin. "You're my prize, Evie. You won the most points of all the participants. And you, of course, were chosen by me to be on my team. You were a whiz at the poker table. When you moved past that to an addiction, Brother Wilson took a keen interest. He told me about you."

Unable to brush his fingers away, I turned my face. "Everything was a lie."

He touched my hair fondly before he dropped his hand. "Rest now, Evie. Think of your children and kiss them goodnight one last time."

Brother Vito left.

A blinding terror coursed through every nerve in my body, searing me.

I could trust no one here.

Who else was pretending to be what they were not?

I hadn't even sensed the cold emptiness behind Brother Vito's words and charm. I hadn't figured out why Kara had turned so cold when I first spoke to her here. And God, *Poppy* . . . why hadn't I guessed what she really was? When Richard and I had witnessed Brother Vito pushing Poppy's advances away, he must have been worried they'd be seen.

A door slammed open somewhere behind me, on the other side of the half wall where I couldn't see. I guessed it was the door that we'd been unable to open.

My heart fell through my chest as I watched a group of Saviours bring in Hop, Yolanda and a few of the others who had escaped from the cellar.

Yolanda's dark eyes raged as she held up her arm to me. "The wristbands. They've got trackers in them. We should have cut them off."

A Saviour roughly chained Yolanda to the left of me, one space over. He looked over at me and grinned. Harrington. Harrington was one of *them*, too.

"Why?" she asked him weakly. "Why did you pretend to be one of us?"

"It's a privilege," Harrington told her. "Each year, four of us are chosen to be part of the challenges. We get to be up close and personal with our victims, right up to challenge five. What could be better?" He kissed her loudly on the forehead.

She spat at him.

"Knew it," slurred Richard. "There were four too many, right from the start. Twenty-eight made no sense. There were really only twenty-four of us. So, Harrington, Kara and sweet, treacherous little Poppy . . . Who else? I know there's another one of you."

Harrington stood, slinging his rifle over his back. "Eugene Bublik. Stupid jerk got himself killed out in the hills by that one over there—*Ruth*. Smashed his head in with a rock. She should be one of us."

"Good. One down. The rest of you to go." Richard moaned as he leaned his head back. The Saviours had retaliated brutally when he'd tried to stab Brother Sage, throwing him to the ground and kicking him in the head and chest.

Stepping away, Harrington smirked. "Your odds are a million to one, Mister Vegas High Roller."

Richard had guessed right. There had been four pretenders. I didn't know Eugene at all and hadn't been in a challenge with him, but I was glad he was dead.

Louelle hadn't been brought back. Louelle, with her distant expression, who'd known things were wrong here in the monastery. I clung to the hope that she'd escaped—that she'd gotten away on a boat and could bring help. Mei and Thomas hadn't returned either. *Please, please, if you've all escaped on boats, keep going and bring help.*

My rational mind knew that they had no chance. Anyone trying to escape in a rowboat was no match for a Saviour in a fast speed boat.

I turned to ask Yolanda about Louelle, but her eyes had glazed over. She began singing something in a faltering, trembling voice. A song a parent would sing to a small child.

Next to Yolanda, Ruth woke, groaning. She rattled out a flurry of garbled swear words at the Saviours, as if her jaw was numb and she could barely form words. *The side of her jaw held a dark purple bruise. They must have done that to her when she killed Eugene.*

On a nearby wall, machetes, chains, knives and other instruments of torture were hanging on hooks.

I screamed out every swear word I'd ever known at Harrington. To be Ruth's voice, because they'd taken away her ability to curse them herself.

Stomping back to us, Harrington leaned down to smack me hard across the head.

I felt my skull crack against the stone wall behind me.

Everything turned black.

66. GRAY

THE TUNNEL THROUGH THE HILL BROKE into two.

Straight ahead, a door with a keypad lock had been left propped open.

Sethi indicated towards the open door. Jennifer nodded. We stepped through and kept walking, not speaking, listening hard for any noise in the tunnels.

Another door stood in the distance. A small patch of light glowed from a pane of glass about three-quarters of the way up.

Instinctively, the four of us moved alongside the left wall, walking in single file. If someone burst through that door, we'd be seen, but at least if someone looked out through the pane, they might miss seeing us.

Keeping low and in the shadows, we ran up alongside the door.

Jennifer pointed at a small red light beneath a keypad. "Alarm," she whispered.

Pulling her hood low over her forehead, she inched towards the pane, just enough to see through it and back away again. She clapped a hand over her mouth, her eyes grown huge.

Whatever she'd seen was horrific.

With my breath caught fast in my chest, I waited for Sethi to look, and then I took a quick glance.

I'd been warned. But seeing it for myself sent my mind scattering.

Bloodied, dirty men and women—sitting or lying against a half wall of stone, facing me. Chained like animals.

Some of them seemed dead.

Bile shot up into my throat.

My heart stopped cold.

In desperation I scanned the rest of the room. I needed to see the other side of the cells, but I couldn't view that from here.

None of the people in my range of sight were Evie or Kara.

I could see the bottom end of a spiral staircase.

Beyond the half wall, people in dark robes were busy with some kind of preparations. *They were the ones who'd done all this.*

Bright lights snapped on in the dark recesses of the cavernous space. Wooden scaffolding surrounded an enormous natural pillar of stone—the pillar as wide as a house and shooting upwards farther than I could see.

Mother of all hell.

What *was* that thing?

67. EVIE

LIGHTS WERE FLASHING ON IN FRONT of me. My eyes remained shut—the only barrier I had between the Saviours and me.

But the bright glow disturbed me and wouldn't let me escape, not even inside my own mind. The Saviours wouldn't even grant us some quiet moments before our deaths. My head felt as if it had been kicked by an ox. I remembered then. One of the Saviours—Harrington—had thumped me hard.

The choking gasps of Richard and Yolanda on either side made me open my eyes to see what they were seeing.

My blurry vision pulled into focus.

At that moment, a silent scream ripped through me.

The scene before me was too shocking to grasp.

There was death—*bodies*—on a scale that made me want to tear my own eyes out, so that I could never again see it.

So many bodies.

Hundreds and hundreds.

In a vast tank of glass that had been cut into a soaring pillar of rock. Bodies floated in the water like ghostly spectres in a horror movie.

Yolanda began singing again, her words dissolving into a series of unintelligible gasps and stutters.

Ruth was mumbling, this time not swearing, but praying.

I needed escape, escape, escape . . .

My thoughts sped backwards. All the way back to when I was a child. A desperate, flashing show reel of images, sounds, memories.

I heard the words my father used to sing to me—when I'd had nightmares and couldn't sleep. Bob Marley's "Redemption Song." Dad would grab his guitar and sing that. I concentrated hard on Dad's voice.

But I couldn't keep hold.

The memories were already fading to black.

68. CONSTANCE

JENNIFER REFUSED TO LET ME LOOK through the glass panel, even though she, Gray and Sethi had. She'd already pulled Gray back—Gray suddenly disoriented and struggling to breathe.

What was in that room? Gray had rigidly shaken his head when I'd spoken Kara's name.

I could do nothing but follow the others as we retraced our steps and took the tunnel to the right.

My limbs felt cold even though the air wasn't. The passage ahead seemed desolate, like walking through a place not on the Earth. It was ancient, empty . . . dead.

I turned sharply then, certain someone was following me. I had Sethi shine his flashlight into the darkness. But there was no one we could see. He went back to check but still nothing.

I was hearing things that didn't exist. Shadows and ghosts.

The passages began bending and twisting in all directions. We were in a maze. I'd lost all sense of which way we were headed. Seconds ticked away like beats of a drum in my head.

Jennifer stopped, as if she'd tuned into my thoughts. "We're going around in circles. It's crazy, but I think the passages are going around each room."

"I think Jen's right," said Sethi. "You can trust her on things like this.

My expertise is out in the water. Jen's is in orienteering on land. She's been orienteering for years. Preparing herself for this day."

I nodded, the drumbeats in my head growing louder. "We need to find our way. We have to find Kara and Evie."

We had no time to waste. Gray was still walking stiffly, not looking at any of us. I guessed he still hadn't processed what he'd witnessed.

Voices boomed along the tunnel, drowning out the sound of my imaginary drumbeats and making my heart jump.

Get back to the infirmary, Poppy, came a male voice. *We didn't finish your transfusion.*

I'm fine, said a woman, her voice high and dismissive. *I need to find her before the others do. She stabbed me. That goes against the rules, and that means she dies.*

Brother Sage won't agree, said the man.

The woman laughed. *Why should she get special rules? He won't know who did it. I'll be back in the infirmary straight after.*

The voices stopped.

"This way," said Sethi under his breath.

Trying to stay as silent as possible, we moved along the passage in the opposite direction.

The passage ended in a wide-open space that led to a dormitory—the room enormous and hexagonal in shape. A dozen or more double beds were set up among closed-circuit screens—bottles of wine on the bedside tables. Flickering lamps dimly lit the room.

Placing our backpacks behind a cupboard so that we didn't knock over any of the bottles of wine, we began searching the room. At least, Jennifer and Sethi were searching. I didn't know what they were looking for.

The TV screens flicked from showing the various hallways to scenes of a room. I stared in horror. The screens showed black-and-white images of people hung up on a wall. *People being tortured. Just like the pictures in Rico's book.*

Gasping for air, a series of shivers ran vertically through my body. My limbs started shaking, every muscle caught tight.

Sethi glanced at me and then tilted his chin at Jennifer. "Gray and I will go see if there is another way out."

Jennifer nodded, gently grasping my shoulders and taking me over to sit on a bed. "Be strong for your daughter, Constance. You have to be."

I flinched beneath Jennifer's hands at the sound of voices coming this way. Five or more men. Saviours.

Sethi and Gray were across the other side of the room. Jennifer inhaled sharply, jumping up to tug me backwards into the dark hallway.

The men strode straight past us into the dormitory, with only a split second to spare. "Hey, what are you doing here?" one of them called.

I froze. They'd seen either Sethi or Gray—or both.

"There's too many of them for us to take on," Jennifer whispered.

Swallowing, I pressed my back against the wall. "What do we do?"

"Continue." Her answer was quick, sharp.

"Without them?"

"We have no choice." She prodded me, forcing me to move.

We made our way along in the complete darkness. We had nothing with us now. No night-vision goggles. And almost none of the ammunition and weapons, only what we carried in our pockets.

In a panic, my vision blurred.

Specks of fuzzy light pinpricked the darkness.

I let my eyes focus. Farther down the tunnel, tiny spots of light glinted through the wall. Without thinking, I ran to the nearest yellowish spot and pressed my eye to it. Old statues and paintings came into view. Jennifer was behind me as I turned to her. "I can see a corridor."

She took a turn to look through. "Let's follow it along."

The specks of light persisted as we walked on. At times, we had to climb up and down ladders to continue, sweat trickling down my back. This place was insane—I sensed the madness of it as if it were a living thing.

The passage swung sharply to the right.

We climbed another ladder and crawled into a passage that didn't allow us to stand upright. I twisted around, again sensing that someone was behind me.

"What's wrong?" Ahead of me, Jennifer stopped.

"I don't know. I think someone's in here with us."

"You heard someone?"

"No."

"Then?"

"It's nothing," I conceded. "I thought I saw movement, but it's so dark . . ."

"Let's go quicker, just in case."

We climbed down the ladder, now on the opposite side of the corridor.

"Whoever built these passageways wanted to spy on people." I frowned as I peered through another peephole. The area outside was much wider than a corridor, a large sculpture of a bird hanging from a chain. "I think it's the entry."

Jennifer touched my back, and I moved to let her see. "Just where we don't want to be. We need to get back to the centre of this place. Let's head towards it."

I followed Jennifer's swift footsteps. She didn't say it, but we were on borrowed time. The Saviours had Gray and Sethi, and they were sure to have found our backpacks, too. They'd know there were two more. This whole thing had already fallen apart. Had the Saviours killed them? That must be weighing on Jennifer's mind. The man she loved was in the hands of people that strung people up on walls and carried out unimaginable cruelty.

My top soaked through with sweat, and my face itched under the balaclava. It seemed that we'd been travelling through this black maze for days.

Ahead, noises echoed through the air. Then voices and footsteps. Men and women.

"Where the hell could she have gone?" one of them complained. "She has to be out there somewhere on the island."

"Brother Sage just sent a dozen of us to look outside the gates. If she's there, they'll find her."

Jennifer grabbed my arm and pulled me on. We headed straight up a set of stairs.

I drew a tight breath and held it fast as the people went running past below the stairs. I was at least grateful that we'd made it inside the monastery before the Saviours had gone to find that woman. Whoever she was, I hated to think what kind of desperate state she was in, running from these people. And whoever Brother Sage was, this was the second time I'd heard his name. He must have some measure of control here. Maybe he was even the one who led the entire order of Yeqon's Saviours.

We continued upward.

The stair landing led into a space much larger than the dormitory room had been. Lamps dimly illuminated settings of plush leather armchairs and viewing screens, the screens all dark and not showing the terrible images of the dormitory. Persian rugs partly covered the wooden floorboards. There were peepholes here too—but nothing like the tiny holes that had been drilled into the hidden passages. These were made of dark glass, about the size of a coffee table, with expensive-looking cameras pointed at them. I suspected they were two-way mirrors.

Whatever happened in the rooms below had to be of major interest. Why were these people so obsessed with watching others?

While Jennifer examined things in the room, I peered down through a mirror into a hexagonal room that had nothing in it except for a stand of the same shape in the centre of the room. What on earth did they watch in this room?

A blur of movement in my peripheral vision made me jerk my head up. Hooded figures separated themselves from the darkness on the other side of the room.

"Jennifer!" I called in desperate warning and raced back to the stairs.

In alarm, she dropped what she'd been looking at.

By the time we'd reached for our guns, more figures moved out behind us.

They'd been there the whole time. Waiting.

69. EVIE

BILE BURNED MY THROAT.

Beside me, Yolanda stopped her broken song and began screaming.

The thing before us was a nightmare vision.

A wide, carved pillar of rock ran from the floor and up through to the underside of the rock ceiling. Huge glass panels were set into the pillar, all the way around—some kind of massive, upright, cylindrical tank filled with water. A rusting metal cage that seemed to me as large and tall as a mansion filled the tank. What was inside the cage squeezed the air from my lungs. Layers and layers and layers of bodies. Skeletal and crumbling at the bottom and in all stages of decomposition to the top layer, where the bodies were fresh.

The macabre scene was medieval and like the mass-extermination graves of modern war all at once.

I could see some faces that were turned my way in the top layer.

Greta. She was never taken to the mainland.

Andre. He'd lost after the very first challenge and would have been among the first to discover the horror of our fate.

Saul. The police hadn't returned him to his family. Whoever had come to the monastery that day were part of this—they were Saviours.

My body shivered relentlessly. I was suddenly deathly cold.

Kara had mentioned the missing participants *floating*.

Now I knew.

I was in the final six. I was going to be sitting here watching the others get tortured by the Saviours and then see their discarded bodies float down through the water.

Knowing I will be joining them.

70. CONSTANCE

THE SAVIOURS MOVED IN AROUND JENNIFER and me. Terror washed through me, making me lose control of my bladder. Men on either side of me kept a grip on my arms so tight it dug into my bones. They searched our bodies, taking away our guns and knives.

Jennifer and I were forced down the stairs and then into a hidden passage. We were being taken to the level immediately below the floor with the cameras and two-way mirrors, into the dead centre of the monastery.

A door stood in front of us. A door with a keypad and a screen with the image of a handprint. Whatever was behind this door, I understood immediately that it was something terrible.

My heart pounded so hard it hurt.

One of the men tapped in a code and then pressed his hand to the screen.

The door opened.

Ahead, two hundred or more of the Saviours stood on the rock floor of a cavern in a wide semi-circle.

I trembled and stalled at the sight of so many of them at once. A collection of monsters. One of the men pressed the point of a knife into the back of my neck, forcing me to move again.

I saw now that the Saviours were gathered around an enormous, gaping hole in the rock floor.

High, man-made walls surrounded the cavern in a hexagonal shape—the walls of the strange rooms that I looked down into from the floor above. One of the walls was made of glass—an aquarium with fish swimming in it.

Faces turned to us in shock and confusion.

Pale blue light rippled on their faces. There had to be water in that hole in the ground. Their eyes quickly turned hard and glittering, devoid of human emotion.

My bottom lip quivered as I caught Jennifer's eye.

Her eyes seemed to say, *sorry, I told you what you were up against, but you didn't listen.* She looked so much calmer than I felt. I knew she'd been preparing for this for a long time.

My life was about to end. Here and now. As was Kara's, and I hadn't even gotten the chance to see her. Neither of us would leave this island. Nothing of us would be left in this world—a cold, tight thought.

Last-minute regrets churned inside me. All the things I'd done or hadn't done. Thoughts whipped through my mind.

I hadn't spoken to my parents and sisters in a long time. Years might go by before they'd even notice Kara and I had vanished. I should have made more of an effort when Kara was small. I shouldn't have isolated her and myself from them. Then I saw Otto's face. Why didn't I do more to help him get better? Instead, I'd been part and parcel of the maelstrom. I pictured James and the house I'd left behind. Would my husband finally show his feelings for me when he realised I was missing, too? I'd never know.

"Brother Sage!" one of our captors called. "We found these two in the viewing room."

Four people in dark robes stared at us from beneath their hoods. Two women and two men.

One of the four—a man—gestured for us to be brought over to him.

Roughly, we were taken across to stand before them, our balaclavas snatched away.

I watched the mouths of the four gape open at our revealed faces, but that was all I could see—their own faces largely shrouded by their hoods and the dark light.

One of the women spoke first. "Jennifer Bloom. You finally found us."

Jennifer didn't answer.

"I'm Sister Rose," the woman told her then fired sharp questions at her. "You've been searching for us a long time, haven't you? How did you find us? And how did you get inside the building? Who did you come here with?"

"We came alone," said Jennifer, her voice firm. "And we got inside because your security isn't as good as you think it is."

"And you expect us to believe you came here without any supplies?" Sister Rose threaded her fingers together tightly, like a schoolteacher admonishing a student. Her voice was so ordinary, American like my own.

"We had all we thought we needed," replied Jennifer. "We didn't realise there were so many of you. In any case, when the police arrive, they'll have better weapons than anything we could have brought."

Hope jumped inside me but was immediately quashed. There were no police coming. Jennifer was just buying time and trying a last-ditch attempt to save us.

The woman tilted her head but didn't show any alarm or anger at Jennifer's words. "Nonsense. You wouldn't arrive by yourselves ahead of the police. We have extremely high-level police and politicians who are members here. I know for a fact you couldn't get a search warrant for this island, but if such a thing did occur, then our contacts would have informed us well ahead of time. We'll be thoroughly searching the monastery and grounds to see who and what you did bring with you." She gestured towards the Saviours. Immediately, groups of them moved off towards the exit.

Jennifer gazed at her defiantly.

The woman's mouth drew into a hard line. "We already know who you both are. Jennifer and Constance. Of course, the question is, what brought the two of you together?"

They knew me?

Of course they did. I was Kara's mother, and I'd been searching for her.

My voice shook as I mustered the courage to speak. "All we want are the people we came for. And then we'll leave."

"No one may leave here," said Sister Rose in a harsh tone that belied her round, pleasant face.

"What is this place?" I pressed. "This room and the water—what does it all mean?"

Sister Rose pursed her small pink lips. "This is our remembrance hall. Where we remember the past and all who came before us. The pool is a cenote."

"Sen-oh-teh?" I queried. "I don't know what that is."

"It's a natural formation," she replied. "It's been here thousands of years, caused by rain seeping into the limestone. Cenotes go deep and narrow into the earth. This cenote is sacred to us."

She spoke as though this was all so normal, like a teacher explaining something to a student.

"Did you know my brother?" Jennifer's voice was finally thinning and showing cracks. "His name was Noah."

I let my eyes close for a moment, sad and terrified for her at what she might hear.

"I knew Noah," came the sharp voice of the other woman. "You can call me Sister Dawn. I remember Noah Bloom. Oh yes, an angry young man with a talent for mathematics. A very smart boy. He found out about us and staged an escape in the middle of the night. Fortunately, we found him and brought him back. Don't worry, Jennifer, we remember your brother. We remember every single one who enters the island. They aren't forgotten."

The muscles in Jennifer's face drew taut. "Did he suffer?"

Sister Dawn sighed. "We all suffer." She had a more angular face than Sister Rose, appearing to be of Indian heritage. Her voice was a mix of Indian and English and very authoritative.

"Who killed him?" Jennifer's eyes opened large and focused. "Which one of you murdered my brother?"

A slight smile indented Sister Dawn's face before she straightened and made her expression go blank. "That pleasure was mine. You see, you don't get closer to a person than the moment you take their life. I already feel close to you because you are of Noah's blood. And I'll be the one to take *your* life."

Jennifer stared at her unflinchingly. "You will pay. For my brother and my parents."

"The murder of your parents gave us no pleasure," said Sister Dawn, dropping her smile. "Unfortunately, when Noah set off on the boat, he'd managed to steal one of our phones, and he had it with him. While at sea, he texted your father. If he'd contacted the coast guard instead, it might have been all over for us. But he didn't. That was his mistake and our fortune. We located your parents by their phone signal and sent one of our own who lived the closest to that location to take care of it."

I heard a gasp under Jennifer's breath. It must be hard for her to hear that small detail and know that Noah had come so close not only to escaping but to destroying the Yeqon's Saviours.

Sister Dawn nodded to indicate the conversation was at an end, and she turned to the tall man beside her. "I'll leave the proceedings to you now, Brother Sage."

Brother Sage bowed his head and slipped the hood back from his face.

All breath left my lungs.

His features.

Features I knew so, so well.

Steel-blue eyes. A firmly set mouth and chin. An expression that was fixed and vague at the same time. As though he saw right through you, but his mind was operating on another plane.

My husband.

James.

Mentally, I tried to push the image of him away. This wasn't real. It wasn't—

It was.

It was real.

No hallucination. My life of the past ten years instantly rearranged itself and turned into something completely *other*. A horrific lie.

He waited with that veneer of patience I'd seen so many times before.

"Constance," he said. "You weren't meant to see . . . any of this. How is it that you made your way here?"

"I don't—" I gulped breaths of air that caused my lungs to burn.

"Of course you don't understand," he said. "You can't process any of this. But I'm afraid it doesn't matter. I think you realise what's going to happen here next. I see it in your eyes. In any case, it wouldn't have gone well for you had you done what I requested and come home. Your daughter would have remained missing. And then I would have divorced you. Without Kara, I'd have had no reason to stay with you."

Horror and confusion raged inside me, and my voice rose to a scream. "What do you want with my daughter? Why did you bring her here? *Why?*"

He stared at me coldly. "She's been coming here since she was seven."

My knees weakened. Gasping, I shook my head wildly. "That's not true. *It's not*—"

"It *is* true," he insisted coldly. "You were only too grateful for me to take her away on my overseas business trips. You got your time alone without her. She was too much for you to handle. Too strange. You never understood her. Well, *I* understood her. And I showed her the ways of the Saviours."

His words cut into my skin like razor blades.

All this time. He was bringing my little girl *here*.

I wanted to tear him limb from limb. "My God, why would you do that to a child? You're evil. A monster."

"Stop pretending, Constance. Kara was never the sweet little girl you pretend she was. And you were *far* from the perfect mother. The best thing that happened to both of you is when I married you and adopted Kara."

"No, I wasn't perfect. But I never—"

"You were living in the poor end of town—you and your useless boyfriend. What was his name—*Otto*? Yes, it was Otto. A scum-of-the-earth drug addict. You two spent all your time at your drug-fuelled parties, barely taking care of your own daughter. She was alone and frightened so many times that she kept knives hidden under her bed. She even invented an imaginary brother for herself—*Santiago*."

"That's not true," I breathed. "I didn't—"

But I couldn't finish my words. Because it was all true. I *had* found knives under her bed more than once. She *did* invent a naughty little brother that she named Santiago. Otto and I *had* partied too much.

But I hadn't used drugs since I'd found out I was pregnant Kara. I'd been devastated by the discovery of the pregnancy. But then, something changed everything. I'd started bleeding and felt a sudden, unexpected terror at losing the baby. Like a miracle, the bleeding stopped and the pregnancy continued.

And I'd never left Kara alone. Except for one night. Just one night. Otto was the one who couldn't manage to stay off the drugs. He'd been growing increasingly erratic, to the point where he was threatening to kill himself. He sped off in his car, leaving me terrified. I'd jumped in my car and followed him, leaving Kara asleep upstairs. Otto did die that night, but not through suicide. A man driving his elderly mother home from the hospital somehow misjudged a turn and plunged his car straight into Otto's.

"That's exactly how it was," James told me in a cruel voice. "It's what the newspapers all reported. Kara's terrible, neglectful parents. You and Otto left her all alone one Tuesday night, when she was just seven. A strange man entered the house—a thief who knew you kept drugs there. Kara ventured downstairs. You know what happened next. She killed him. Stabbed him twenty-eight times, the coroner's report said. The moment I read about her, I knew she was special. One of us."

"One of us . . .?" I stared at him in confusion, my mind numbing.

"She's psychopathic," he told me flatly. "Most children would hide in a cupboard should a stranger break into the house at night. But little Kara took two knives she'd been keeping under her bed—one for herself and one for Santiago—and she went downstairs and stabbed the intruder to death. Like a tiny assassin."

Tears wet my cheeks.

"You would have lost her back then if not for me," he continued, enjoying how his words were crushing me. "I arranged for one of the Saviours—Judge Reynolds—to go easy on you, and he ordered you into rehab instead. After two months, you got Kara returned to you."

I'd long tried to put that terrible episode behind me. I lost sight of Otto on the roads that night and returned home, not knowing that he was already dead. Police had been swarming everywhere out the front of our house, and I'd imagined it was a drug bust. But instead, my seven-year-old daughter had just killed an intruder. With blood on her hands, she'd calmly picked up the phone and called the police, telling them what she'd done. Because Kara had been a minor, the newspapers hadn't been allowed to report her name—or, by proxy, my name. No one found out about Kara except the police. I met the charming Englishman, James Lundquist, soon after. He'd given a sizable donation to the rehabilitation centre where I was receiving treatment, and then he'd visited it. We bumped into each other in the rehab garden. He'd seemed enamoured by me. He swept me off my feet, promising a beautiful new life for Kara and me. At the time, I'd been desperate. I had no money, nothing to offer my poor little daughter. Even though she didn't show her feelings, I knew she must be traumatised. Her father was dead. And she'd killed someone. But together with James, I'd been able to collect her from the foster family she'd been put with and give her a real home. He moved from his home in England to America to be with us, and then we married.

Everything ran through my head. All the charity dinners and walks in the park and family things with James. All of it was a charade. All the times he'd taken Kara away with him on business trips to other countries, telling me it was enriching her education. I'd allowed it all to happen, and I'd allowed myself to believe we were a real family.

I'd taken my daughter from the frying pan into a burning, raging pit of hell. I'd delivered her into the hands of Yeqon's Saviours.

71. I, INSIDE THE WALLS

I HAVE ALWAYS LIVED INSIDE THE WALLS.

I never felt like I truly belonged at the monastery, but I didn't belong in the outside world either. I was stuck somewhere inside the walls, neither in nor out.

Daddy James told me I belonged here when I was a little girl. He told me that I was special, that people like me can do extraordinary things because we're one of the elite, and we don't have to abide by the rules of ordinary people. He said we were angels who'd become gods on earth, symbolic descendants of Yeqon, with our own religion and our own history. We were saviours of Yeqon's legacy.

He shielded me from the terrible things that happened here until I was about ten. Little by little, he drew me in and made it all seem normal. I grew numb to the murders. The Saviours called them sacrifices for the greater good.

The concept of normal is a strange thing. If a person is persuasive enough, they can tip you on your head and make you believe that your new view of the world is normal. James was that kind of person.

Real Daddy died when I was seven, and my mother was taken away, after I killed a man. Daddy James came to visit me at my foster home, saying he was a good friend of my mother's. He became my lifeline, my only friend and my only way back to my mother.

Santiago, how did this happen? How did Mom find the monastery?

I see terror in your eyes. Please don't be scared. I'll always protect you. Remember when I first found you? I was five and it was my birthday. Mommy and Daddy were having a party, but it wasn't for my birthday. They'd forgotten all about it. They forgot stuff all the time. They didn't mean to, but they did. That was when you walked in and wished me happy birthday. You were the brother that I wished my Mom and Real Daddy had. Then Real Daddy died, and Daddy James came to live with Mom and me. Mom turned into a different person and wanted me to forget Real Daddy. But you stayed the same. You were always the same, Santiago. You came to the monastery with me and we played hopscotch in the halls. You helped me kill the Saviours that came after me with lust in their eyes when Daddy James wasn't watching.

Daddy James told me that the universe crunched the numbers and made me what I am. The universe knew what I was long before I did.

I was fifteen when I started to question everything Daddy James told me about myself and my mother. I didn't believe in his speeches about the right and might of the Saviours anymore. I tried to get away from him. The second that I could, I went to the other side of the world. But Daddy James wouldn't let go. He stopped the money that Mom was sending and had Brother Wilson watch over me. Brother Wilson forced drugs on me, forced me to sign up for escort websites. It was punishment from Daddy James for leaving home and trying to strike out on my own. And if I kept doing the wrong thing and the monastery had to kill me, then there would be a trail of things that would make the police and public less sympathetic about the task of finding me. People tended to shrug when drug-addicted sex workers went missing, even when they were just kids, like me. They had it all worked out.

If I didn't do as I was told, then something bad might happen to Mom. He never said what. But he didn't need to. I already knew too well about the bad things that the Saviours did.

And then I was forced to make contact with Evie Harlow. I knew from that second what their plans for her were. But I didn't know how to stop it. I didn't know how to make it end. But it was Evie who changed everything for me. When I saw her here on her first morning, I finally understood how wrong everything about the monastery was. She had two little kids. She'd shown me photos of them. It made it all too real.

Daddy James already knew I was in mental turmoil. He forced me to take part in the challenges just so that the Saviours could keep an eye on me. I had a knife with me in the bed the night that Evie was first brought to the dormitory. I wanted to cut everyone's throats while they slept so that they'd never know the truth about the monastery. They'd never be subjected to the tortures that awaited them. They'd die happy. But other Saviours were keeping watch behind the walls.

I ran now through the hidden passages, away from the remembrance hall. Would Daddy James be explaining to my mother all the secrets we'd been keeping from her? I never wanted her to know. He promised me that if I did all he asked, she would never, ever know.

My eyes burned with tears I couldn't cry.

I'd followed Mom all the way through the tunnels, scarcely believing that she'd come all the way here, straight into the nest of the Saviours, to find me.

Who would knowingly do such a thing? It's certain death.

72. GRAY

TWENTY MINUTES EARLIER

A GROUP OF SAVIOURS WAS HEADING our way.

The four of us were about to get caught in the dormitory. Jennifer swiftly pulled Constance back through the doorway. Sethi and I were on the other side of the room, like deer caught in headlights. No time and no room to hide.

I spun on my heel. I'd seen a rack of the gowns that the Saviours wore a few seconds ago. I grabbed two gowns, tossing one to Sethi and throwing the other one on. I pulled the hood down over my forehead and picked up an open bottle of wine from a table. Sethi followed my lead. I sweated bullets as we walked towards the exit of the room, drinking bottles of wine.

They'll slaughter us without hesitation if they find out we're not one of them.

"Hey, what are you doing here?" one of them called roughly.

Sethi merely raised a full bottle of wine by way of explanation.

"That's Brother Harrington's," said a thick, red-bearded man. "The '92 vintage. Special treat from Sage."

Sethi shrugged, making a dismissive sound.

The man laughed. "Can't wait to see his whiny face. He hasn't stopped whining since he got hurt in the challenges."

The Saviours brushed past, laughing to themselves but without any more interest in us.

"Lucky," I said under my breath as Sethi and I continued down the passage. The room had been dim, and we'd managed to conceal our faces.

"Here." Sethi indicated towards a set of stairs. "We'll wait here until they go. We need those backpacks."

At least five minutes passed before the Saviours left, and then we retrieved all four backpacks. Sethi stalled for a moment, and I could guess that he was hoping that Jennifer and Constance would meet us back here. We went back into the passages, searching for them.

Sethi's voice hoarsened and cracked as we rounded another corner. "I managed this badly, my friend. Wherever they are, we've gone the wrong way. I don't know if we're going to find them before someone else does."

I swallowed. "Maybe they couldn't come back. Or maybe they've gone to find the cellar."

"I think that's our only way forward now," he agreed, but a twinge of uncertainty remained in his words.

We ran now, keeping an eye on our location through the peepholes we'd found in the walls. We found hidden doors, too—the exits marked with tiles set into the floor. I missed them until Sethi pointed them out. My mind was raging, set only on getting to Evie.

My lungs almost exploded as we passed two more of the Saviours, attempting to steady my breath and pretend like I hadn't just been rushing somewhere.

But I'd slowed too late.

"What's the emergency?" a woman demanded, shining her flashlight over us.

Sethi held up his wine bottle, slurring the words, "Drink with us?" He shot me a warning glance and I immediately understood it. *Don't speak. Your accent will stand out.*

"Don't let Brother Sage catch you drunk. It's the night of remembrance," she cautioned.

Sethi nodded contritely.

We continued on, walking but keeping up a quick pace. If the pair suddenly realised there was something wrong about us, we needed to be as far away from them as possible.

Catching sight of another peephole, I stuck my face against the wall, squinting through. "Sethi. Look at the stairs."

At the end of the hall, a set of spiral stairs led down. The stairs looked the same as the set we'd seen in the cellar, only this would be the top of the stairs and not the bottom.

Sethi peered into the peephole. "Spiral stairs. Same handrail. I think we've found it. The stairs are in the right location to lead into the cellar."

My heart juddered against my chest wall. "We need to get in there."

"Let's go," he replied. "Are you sure you're ready? If Jenny and Constance have been captured, then the alarm has been raised, and there is no margin left. You might be living your last minutes on this earth."

"I have to."

"Okay. There was an exit a minute back. We take it and we go."

Every nerve in my body fired as we located the door and pulled it back.

The hall was empty. There was no one to stop us. Ditching the wine bottles behind a statue, we strode out and to the cellar then onto the spiral stairs, past cut chains hanging limply from a metal gate.

Dank, overpowering odours rushed up from below. Sweat, blood and mildew.

"Follow my lead," Sethi told me quietly, angling his face back to me. "Stay away from the prisoners. We need to get to the Saviours."

We stepped out into the cavern.

The chained prisoners along the half wall were shrouded in darkness beyond the immense structure I'd glimpsed before.

My blood turned cold.

Thousands of bodies were trapped within a watery cage—the cage suspended on long cables that reached upward past where I could see. A nightmare of insane human depravity. All lit up and on display with strong lights. Crumbling messes at the bottom of the cage that had once been human. Bodies resting at the top that had not been long in their grave.

Rage twisting through me, I searched among those bodies on the top layer, searching for Evie—for the familiar curves of her body and cheekbones, her exact shade of hair.

Three Saviours stood on the scaffolding surrounding the pillar, peering in through the glass. Fewer of them than before. I guessed what the scaffolding was for. So that the Saviours had a perfect view of all the layers of bodies, so they could gaze and gloat on their killings. Another Saviour stood inside a tiny room, looking through sets of knives and screwdrivers and other cutting instruments that were displayed on a bench and hung up on hooks on the wall. Half of the instruments were crusted with blood.

None of them had noticed us—yet.

Sethi knocked his shoulder against mine, sending my mind reeling back to what we'd agreed upon. I had to be like one of *them*.

Sethi walked into the room with the tools. Moving alongside the man, he lifted a knife down from a hook. Before I understood what was happening, Sethi had one hand over the man's mouth and the knife at his throat. The Saviour slumped in Sethi's arms.

Wake up, Gray. Forget who you are. Do what needs to be done.

Rushing over, I helped Sethi hide the man under the bench. Blood gushed from the cut in the man's throat as we shoved supplies and thick ropes over him.

One less Saviour.

"If we go out shooting guns, we'll get a horde of them down here," said Sethi. "And we can't fight them all. Maybe we have to stay here and ambush them."

I gestured subtly at a camera I'd just noticed high on a wall. What we'd just done had been broadcast somewhere else within the monastery. Maybe no one had seen it. But someone was going to see us here eventually.

Sethi cursed under his breath. "Stay with me."

The three men on the scaffolding wheeled around as we emerged from the room. Walking beside Sethi, I crossed the floor and stepped onto the scaffolding, ignoring the gazes that were set on us.

"We're on watch here." A blonde, slightly built guy lifted his chin. "You're supposed to be at the ceremony."

Sethi shrugged. "Sage sent us."

A tense moment passed before the man standing closest to us cocked his head—an anaemic-looking man in his seventies with hair thinning over his age-spotted scalp. "Checks out. Brother Harrington thought he saw something on the infra-red. Brother Sage might want more security."

A chill sped through me. This man was probably some kid's grandfather. A serial killer who looked like any harmless and slightly unwell old guy you'd see in the street.

"No way," the blond scoffed. "He's a looney. The knock to the head wouldn't be helping."

The third man viewed us coolly, his eyes dead, ice cold, a scar running the length of one side of his face. "I don't know who these two are. Did we get new Saviours? We never do that just before the challenges."

The blond guy studied us curiously. "Take off your hoods."

Sethi acted quickly, pulling the older guy towards him and hooking his arm around his body. With his free arm, Sethi held a knife to the man's throat. "Do what we say, or we'll kill him."

A moment of shock lapsed into a sneer on the face of the man with the scar. "Who the fuck are you, and how did you get onto the island?"

"You've got one second," said Sethi.

In response, the two Saviours took out guns from their pockets.

Sethi sliced his knife across the old man's throat and let him drop to the floor.

The Saviours barely reacted.

"Your deaths won't be that quick." The guy with the scar gestured at us with his gun, telling us to walk back down the ramp.

I turned and walked with Sethi.

They weren't going to shoot us in the back. Whatever was coming next was worse. They forced us off the scaffolding to a desk against a wall, where they picked up two sets of handcuffs.

A set of three monitoring screens on the desk displayed live scenes, constantly flipping from the island to the halls inside the monastery to the prisoners chained to the wall.

The blonde man picked up a fixed phone.

"What are you doing, Lewis?" the other man hissed.

"Calling Brother Sage," Lewis answered, nonplussed.

"We'll have some fun with them first." The scarred man stepped around us, snatching back our hoods. "I can tell you they're not undercover police."

"What if they are?" A nervous energy charged Lewis's voice. "And if they are, someone needs to deal with this and shut it down."

One of the monitors swapped to showing an area of the monastery in which a huge number of Saviours were gathered. *Hundreds of them.* My bowels went ice cold. We'd had no chance from the second we'd stepped foot here. Another monitor swapped to a view of the prisoners. Different prisoners to the ones I'd seen before, on the other side of the half wall.

Then I saw her.

My wife.

Her head down, dark hair in tangles.

I knew it was her before she raised her face, staring ahead in numb confusion.

I lost sight of her just as quickly as the display switched to a view of the hall outside the cellar.

"*Evie! Evie!*" I roared her name, charging away, ignoring the guns that were suddenly raised and pointed my way.

73. CONSTANCE

JENNIFER DIDN'T ATTEMPT TO HIDE HER shock as she stared from James to me. *My husband—the head of an insane cult.* I guessed that Jennifer was calculating the same things that I was. If I'd suspected James, I could have had him tracked, had his computers logged and eavesdropped on him.

But I hadn't done any of those things because I never had an inkling.

Why didn't I know?

Terror pierced my body with sharp, ice-cold pins.

Kara.

My daughter had been in the hands of a monster. And I'd put her there.

"I need to see her," I pleaded. "Just let me see her."

James merely made a tutting sound at my anguished face. "She's elsewhere in the monastery, and she's told me she has no interest in ever seeing you again."

His words socked me in the centre of my chest. "I want her to tell me that in person."

"I'm sorry, Constance," came the reply. "But it's out of the question."

He was no longer my husband. He was an unknowable stranger. A mass murderer. The hands that had touched me in intimate ways had done terrible things to other human beings. "Who are you people?"

His eyes hardened and grew distant. “Our order began a long time ago. You don’t possess the ability to understand it.”

“I need you to tell me. Give me that much, *Brother Sage*,” I replied bitterly.

His left eye twitched. “I don’t need to give you anything. I already gave you far more than you deserved over the last decade of your life.”

“You owe *me*. You people took everything from me,” Jennifer told him. “Everything.”

“Life is filled with sacrifices and consequences, Jennifer,” he said.

“I’m sorry . . . so sorry . . .” I whispered to her. I was empty, humiliated, raw. Turned inside out. How many families had James and the Saviours destroyed?

“You’re apologising for me?” James said to me, sounding annoyed. “I have nothing to apologise for.”

“You’re insane,” I breathed. “A psychopath.”

“A psychopath, yes,” he replied. “But not insane. Psychopathy is not regarded as a mental illness. We’re not evil, either. The depths of the human psyche may be terrifying to you, but it is what it is.”

“If I’d known what you were, I’d have killed you with my bare hands.” I meant it. I’d do it now, right now, if I had the chance.

“And so, you admit you would kill if you had a reason for it.” His tone was as dry and as vast as a desert, terrifying me.

I struggled to control my own voice. “I would not kill for my own pleasure.”

“Are you sure, Constance?” he said. “I see it in your eyes now that it would bring you satisfaction. But you don’t understand the merest thing about me or about those like me. Psychopaths exist because human evolution had a purpose for us. Unburdened by the same emotions and conscience as the rest of you, we do the things you only wish you could. Throughout history, we’ve led corporations and we’ve waged war. And we’ve been calm minded enough to succeed.”

“If not for the monastery,” said Sister Rose, “far more people would die. People like us would be responsible for the murders of hundreds of people each year. But here, we take a relatively small number of people each year, and we share in the kills. We also keep the worst of our kind here, far away from society. They never leave.”

Jennifer stared at her sharply, fire rising in her eyes. “Do you imagine that any of that excuses what you do?" she accused. "And serial killers are rare—how is it that there are so many of you here? And tell me, how do you all even find each other? I don't understand that. Decade after decade, century after century. *How?*"

Jennifer broke off, her voice gone. I guessed that all the questions that she'd had to keep inside her all these years had finally exploded out in a ball of fury.

Sister Rose's lips twisted into a smile. "We have a number of pathways, but the usual route is through our psychiatrists. I myself am a psychiatrist. When people confess to me that they have conducted a series of murders or they express a desire to do so, I begin a rigorous screening to see if they belong with us. We have many members who have never actually killed anyone, but who just like to watch. In medieval times, it was easier. Serial killers among the wealthy didn't need to hide themselves as much as they do today."

"We should begin the ceremony, Sister Rose." James cast his eyes over the crowd of Saviours, a growing impatience evident on their faces. "We've already had many delays. My wife and Jennifer can perhaps discover all that they wish to know in the speeches."

Sister Rose nodded. "Yes, of course. We should begin."

The four mentors made their way to the opposite side of the cenote.

The handsome, olive-skinned man standing beside James led the hundreds of assembled Saviours into a song that sounded like a Gregorian chant—the deep tones of hundreds of voices vibrating through my teeth and bones and echoing into the dark reaches of the hexagonal cavern. The sounds were ancient and surreal, with an edge of savagery in the way the voices relentlessly pressed into the air.

James strode to a podium. All faces looked to him.

The chant came to an end.

James leant his hands on the podium, reminding me of so many speeches he'd given at business and charity events. His stance and the expression on his face were exactly the same.

"My brothers. My sisters," he began. "We are, once more, in the final hours of the challenges that we hold to commemorate the history of Yeqon's Saviours. We begin the ceremony in our traditional remembrance of our origins. We do not pay homage to the order of monks who built this monastery, nor do we speak their names. These monks of the twelfth century held the belief that they could heal the mentally ill through a direct line to God. The monastery was to be the treatment centre. Built on a system of God's holy numbers, all rooms hexagonal. And in the exact centre, a cenote, to remind the unfortunates who would come there of the depths of God's soul." He paused. "The good monks then set about trying to cleanse the addled minds of the afflicted. On this day each year, we remember the torture of these unfortunates. The monks treated the unfortunates by locking them in cages and thrusting them in and out of the cenote. And they would wake them every midnight to force them through sets of cruel challenges. They kept metronomes running day and night in an attempt to push out supposed demonic possessions and insane thought and allow the minds of the unfortunates to be restored. The worst of the afflicted were kept in metal cages and chains down in the cellar, and the monks would drill holes through their skulls to release their madness. When all failed, the half-dead unfortunates were left out on the hill with the belief that God would save any that deserved saving. The birds would tear at the flesh of those who died on the hill. They all died, of course. These people were then buried out there on the hill, with gravestones that marked not their names but their supposed crimes and afflictions. After decades, the afflicted could take no more."

James lifted his arms to the ceiling. "Brothers and Sisters, the afflicted rose up and took vengeance on their tormentors, throwing them into the cenote to drown." I could barely hear his voice now over the erupting cheers. "The afflicted took control of the monastery. Forever more to be in control. They wore the garb of the monks and pretended to the outside world to be the same order of monks. And so we endured. And will continue to endure. The monks had no idea what they were fooling with when they built this monastery with all its mathematic precision. The order of Yeqon's Saviours is a creation of the monastery itself. It brought us together and brought us into existence. The monastery became a beautiful mind, free of all pretence."

I stared at James. All the pieces of my life, of James's life, of Kara's life, and the long history of this place and the Saviours were a jagged whirlwind inside my head.

74. I, INSIDE THE WALLS

I WATCHED MY MOTHER AND THE tall woman get taken to the remembrance hall.

It will be the last place they go.

Wait, Santiago, we can't follow her in there.

There are two things I must do now.

I stole along the passageways and into the control centre for the camera network of the monastery. It was the only place that wasn't watched by cameras, aside from the hidden passageways.

There were many computers here, too. Brother Harrington had one of the computers open, typing up replies to one of the prisoners' profiles on a sex workers' website. That was one of his jobs. To pretend to be the people who came to the island.

I love red wine and red stilettos and Latin dancing, Brother Harrington wrote on a woman's profile, all the while humming as if he were writing a letter to his grandma. He pretended as if the woman were freely living her life. In the future, when someone finally noticed that she was missing, the police would find her profile online and think she was alive but merely didn't want to be found.

Her name was Greta. She was dead now. I saw her, during Challenge Two, desperately trying to signal us with a lit candle from the remembrance room. I was drowning at the time, stuck in the tank. The Saviours thought they'd tortured her to death—they were about to dispose of her body in the cenote when she struggled and broke free.

But her freedom didn't last long.

I hate it—the desperation in their eyes when they know they're about to die.

But the numbers are clear.

The numbers led them all here, to the island.

There is no escape from death, here.

But I need to buy time. There are things I have to do.

While Brother Harrington wasn't watching the cameras, I set the cellar surveillance footage onto *loop*.

75. EVIE

A SAVIOUR CALLED MY NAME AND came rushing to me.

He knelt before me.

How does he know my name? Why does he sound so anxious? So . . . unlike a Saviour?

"You don't know me, do you?" His voice soft now as he stared at me strangely. "What did they do to you?"

I let my eyes focus on him.

"Gray . . ." The name dropped from my tongue, but I could not trust what I was seeing.

Gray, in *Saviour's* clothing.

Here, in the monastery.

My mind searched for explanations but found none.

I touched his gown with stiff fingers, not allowing myself to believe. This was yet more cruel trickery. He was a very different man than my husband, with dark hair and stubble.

"I'm not a Saviour," he told me. "I'm with you now, Evie . . . I'm with you." His arms came around my body, cradling me.

He kissed my forehead.

A gasp tore through me.

He was Gray. But how? Had the Saviours brought him here?

Two Saviours moved into position behind Gray—Lewis and Valdez.

They had a third man with them—a prisoner in handcuffs. I didn't know the prisoner.

Valdez rubbed his scarred temple, a glint in his black eyes. "This is too perfect. This man named *Grayyy* has come in search of his dear wife, only for her to watch him die before her eyes."

I clung to Gray, burying my face, the scent I knew so well warm on his neck. He'd come in search of me? Valdez had just said that. Gray shouldn't be here. He couldn't die. He was meant to be at home, safe with our daughters.

Tears wet my cheeks. "How did you get here? *How?*"

In response, he hugged me tighter.

"Sage would want these two delivered to him," said the one named Lewis.

"We'll take *one* of them to Sage." Valdez shrugged.

"Brother Sage shot Marko when he went after that Saul guy. Marko didn't get any second chances," said Lewis.

"Marko broke the rules," Valdez retorted. "He set the guy free so that he could hunt him through the monastery. We're not breaking rules. These two came to us."

Now I knew what had really happened to Saul.

The prisoner in handcuffs gazed down at Gray with soulful eyes. "This didn't go well, my friend. We tried and we lost. I'm glad you found your wife."

The prisoner had a Greek accent. Who was he, and how did he and Gray know each other?

Gray gave him a tense nod.

All breath left my chest as Valdez pulled out a large knife from inside his robes. "Lewis, undo Yolanda's chains, move her, and help me chain up this guy here next to his wife. After that, we hang the Greek guy up in the fun room. Then I return to play with *Grayyy*. Evie can hold him while he suffers."

Gray's eyes switched back to me. I saw a goodbye in his expression. I saw regret and love and fear. I saw Willow and Lilly's features.

"*No . . .*" The word tore from deep within me.

"You bastards will burn in hell," came Cormack's voice.

"I don't believe in hell," said Richard, staring at Valdez with glazed, savage eyes, "but may a thousand hells find you in this life."

"That sounds very Scottish," called Cormack.

"Told you I'd turn Scottish before this night was out," Richard quipped, his voice eroding in a tight rasp.

Valdez's face warped into a grisly, dismissive grin as Lewis helped him carry out his requests. They put Gray next to me, in chains.

The prisoner was taken into the room where the Saviours kept their victims hung on rope hoists. I heard the man cry out something in Greek. I turned my face, not wanting to see Duncan's body still hanging in there limp and dead on the hoist.

Valdez stepped in front of us, then crouched to the ground and drew the point of the knife along the stone floor, making a chilling sound. "Who goes first? Maybe her? Yes, I think so. Something to break the ice. You're both so . . . *tense*."

Instinctively, I put my arms up to protect myself.

I felt quick, sharp cuts to my flesh.

Beside me, Gray yelled and tried to grab at Valdez. But the chains held him back.

In the space between my arms, I watched a figure move from the dark recesses of the cavern. A figure dressed in Saviour garb. Slightly built. Face obscured by the hood. Slowly, silently stealing forward. How long had they been there in the shadows? Were they stealing out now to watch Valdez hurt us? Or join in?

Valdez didn't have time to completely turn around before the other Saviour plunged a knife into his back.

Valdez jack-knifed, roaring in pain. The attacking Saviour backed away, but Valdez was quicker and gave the attacker a violent shove.

The attacker landed hard on the ground and their hood slipped back. The attacker was Kara.

Valdez staggered forward to hit Kara again. "What the hell do you think you're doing?" He looked back towards the torture room. "*Lewis!* Get this knife out of me and get this crazy little bitch sorted."

But the man who emerged from the other room was not Lewis. It was the prisoner.

76. GRAY

"SETHI!" I BOOMED, YANKING AGAINST MY CHAINS. "He's going for his gun."

Sethi ran hard at Valdez, knocking him flat to the ground before he'd had a chance to retrieve the gun from a holster inside his robes. The knife, still in Valdez's back, penetrated deep from the force of his landing. Valdez's head lolled to one side, his eyes deadened. Bright blood seeped out on the floor.

Without missing a beat, the girl crouched beside Valdez's body and stole the gun. She pointed it at Sethi. "I saved your life, but I don't know who you are. So, who *are* you?"

She'd saved Sethi's life? This girl must have killed Lewis and then cut Sethi down from the wall. And then she'd come out here to kill Valdez. No mean feat. She looked like a mere teenager.

Sethi frowned for a moment, then recognition seemed to enter his eyes. "I'm a friend of your mother's."

Then I understood. This girl was Kara Lundquist, Constance's daughter. She'd looked familiar, but I'd been unable to place her. In the photos I'd seen, she'd been wearing heavy makeup. But how and where had this kid learned to become a killing machine?

"How do you know my mother?" Kara demanded of Sethi.

"She is one of a small group of people who have been searching for the location of the Saviours," he answered. "Gray over there is one of the group."

She glanced over at me.

A chorus rose up from the other prisoners, pleading for their chains to be unlocked.

"Quiet!" Kara scolded. "You'll have the Saviours running in here soon." She stared at Sethi with cold anger on her face. "Did you and Gray bring my mother here? You shouldn't have done that. She was never supposed to know about this place."

"I didn't say she was here," said Sethi, his voice pulled taut.

"You don't need to lie to me," Kara told him flatly. "I've followed the four of you since you arrived on the island."

"Do you know where they are now—your mother and the other woman?" Sethi questioned.

"They were captured by the Saviours. They're in the remembrance hall right now," Kara told him.

Sethi's chest sank inward like he'd been punched.

"She's one of *them*. A *Saviour*," cried the girl named Yolanda. "You can't trust her."

Sethi's expression changed to stunned disbelief as he stared at Kara. "You're a *Saviour?* Tell me that's not true."

Kara's expression turned stony. "Yes, it's true. I'm a part of the monastery."

Kara's words embedded themselves deep in my brain. She was a Saviour. All this time, the daughter Constance had been trying to save had been one of this murdering cult.

Sethi put the palms of his hands up. "But you helped us. Please, put the gun away and let me get the chains off these people."

"There is no point." Kara raised the gun higher. "I came down here to kill all the prisoners. So that their deaths would be quick and none of them would have to suffer. Then I'm going back to do the same for my mother."

I heard Evie's sharp intake of breath beside me. "Please, Kara. Let us go. I know you're trying to help us. What we want is for you to let us go."

Kara shook her head. "You know nothing. They'll only capture you again. And your deaths won't be as easy as they could be now. I tried to take you all down to the beach before. So that you could die with the sound of the ocean in your ears. Instead of dying in here, upon the cut of a

Saviour's knife—or worse. Not one of you is going to leave this island. You all signed your death warrants the moment you stepped foot here. The Saviours have everything. Every weapon you can imagine. And my stepfather has put new safeguards in place over the past few years. There is no escape."

"Your stepfather?" Sethi shook his head in confusion.

"The man who heads the Saviours is married to my mother. James Lundquist." Kara's voice thickened with loathing.

Constance's husband was the head of the Saviours? And her daughter was a Saviour? I tried to fit it all together, but it was not making sense.

"You won't get near him," Kara added. "There are hundreds of Saviours here right now in the monastery. Minus a few." She glanced briefly around the room at the dead men.

"Please," called a young guy with straggly black hair, his face angular and handsome. "Kara, let us choose. If I'm going to die, I choose to die on my feet."

"You don't understand what you're asking, Cormack," she replied, her hands curling into loose fists by her sides.

Desperate cries echoed around us.

Letting her head drop, Kara silently nodded. She shoved the gun into a holster inside her clothing. "If that's what you want. But I warn you, the deaths you all face might be brutal beyond your wildest nightmares."

Sethi found the keys on Valdez's body and raced around undoing the lock on every chain, even the chains of the unconscious prisoners. We weren't going to be able to take the unconscious ones with us, but at least they had a shot of escape if they woke up.

Evie stood, trembling, her eyes filled with fear and shame as she gazed at me. "I'm sorry, Gray. So sorry. You shouldn't have come."

Her body was tense and rigid as I brought my arms around her and held her close. She felt cold, and smaller than I remembered. She asked about Willow and Lilly, and I answered as best I could, telling her they were safe and loved. She didn't need to know about Lilly—it would only wound her.

"I love you," I said, knowing that was inadequate. There wasn't time now to tell her everything I wanted to say. There might never be a chance.

"Kara," said Sethi. "All that just happened would have been seen on the cameras, yes?"

"No," she answered. "I put the footage on *loop*. If anyone looks, all they'll see are the prisoners sitting there. Chained-up people don't move much. There's not much that changes from minute to minute."

I blinked my eyes tightly in relief. That bought us some time.

Everyone made quick introductions—just their names and nothing else.

"What's going on here?" demanded Richard, a small, blonde man with a goatee. "How in the hell did everyone's relatives suddenly rock up? If my father is about to walk in here, too, I want some warning." There was an ironic, harsh edge to his voice.

"That door!" said Yolanda, ignoring Richard and pointing to the other end of the cellar. "Kara would know how to disable the alarm and unlock it. It leads straight outside."

Kara ran her lip across her bottom teeth as she eyed Yolanda. Not in the timid way of a teenage girl but in a slow, controlled way. "Yes, I do. But the Saviours know that there are intruders on the island. And there are Saviours running all over this island right now. With AK-47s. If you want to be shot at like it's duck season, go for it. They don't shoot to kill, by the way. They aim to maim and then have their fun with you."

The room fell into silence.

The slight sway of the enormous cage in the tank with its macabre collection of dead bodies captured everyone's attention.

"What the hell *is* that thing? Why are they keeping bodies there?" I asked Kara.

Kara turned from Yolanda to me. "The Saviours keep the dead in the cage so they can see their victims at any time they wish, at all stages of decomposition. The entire thing is a natural pool. A cenote. Long ago, the Saviours drilled into the rock and made the windows of glass that you see, so that they had a view inside."

I cursed the Saviours under my breath.

Evie raised her head, her gaze travelling up the fearsome length of the cenote. "Where does it go?"

"To the ground floor," Kara told Evie. "In the centre room of the monastery. The Saviours call it the remembrance hall. It's where my mother and the other woman are right now."

"If that cenote is where we're all going to end up," said Richard, "why not fight? I'll take as many of the bastards with me as I can before I die."

"I'm with you." Cormack shook back his mane of black hair.

Yolanda and Hop went to stand beside Richard and Cormack. "I know how to shoot," said Yolanda darkly. "And I'll start with the mentors."

My mind roared. Maybe fighting to the death was all we had left. But I refused to give into that thought yet.

"Sethi," I said, my jaw rigid. "Can we talk for a minute?"

Sethi nodded.

I crossed the room with him, bringing Evie with me, keeping out of the glaring lights of the cenote. We stopped near the three-screen video display that showed different scenes of the monastery and the horror inside the cenote.

"I want to try to figure out a way off here," I told Sethi. "You've got guns and grenades. We've got to try."

"Please," added Evie, her voice paper thin. "Gray and I have children. If we try to fight them without some kind of plan, neither of us is going home."

Sethi expelled a stream of air. "I'm afraid to say Kara's right. Planning an escape is a fool's mission." He bent his head. "Even if it were possible, I couldn't leave Jenny and Constance in the hands of the Saviours. The best I can offer you is that I'll create a diversion—and let you and Evie run as far as you can get."

Evie shook her head, her eyes huge.

Heart beats pounded in my chest. "*No*."

The shadows and ripples of the cenote set ghostly lights in Sethi's eyes. "There isn't anything else. There are too many of them."

With anxious steps, Kara made her way over to us. "They'll be coming to get the prisoners soon. You'd better make a decision on what you want to do, or the Saviours will make that decision for you. I'm going to sneak into the remembrance room now. My mother won't see me, and she won't feel anything when I fire my gun. I'll make sure of that. She'll die instantly."

Evie shivered. "They'll hurt you, Kara."

"If they catch me, they'll be brutal," she admitted. "Sage won't protect me now. But if I'm quick enough, I'll have killed myself before they can reach me."

The young guy named Cormack was suddenly behind her. He encased her in his arms, his eyes wild. "I'll not let you do that, Kara," he said.

Near the half wall, the others had gathered in a tight bunch, making their own plans.

I glanced at Sethi. He was staring fixedly at the left-hand screen, a frown making a deep shadow between his eyes.

He turned sharply to Kara. "What is that object on the floor of the cenote?"

I peered at the screen. All I spotted were some old skeletons and a glimpse of a metallic curve before the view swept away to another section of the cenote floor.

Kara inclined her head, her brow furrowing. "I don't know. Probably the remains of a broken cage. They don't last forever."

"No," insisted Sethi. "I could only see a tiny piece of it, but it looked to me like the shape of a mine. Maybe a World War Two issue."

Kara grasped Cormack's arm as though to push him away, but then she didn't. "A mine? Yes, it could be that. There are three down there. No one knows they're there except for my stepfather and the last leader of the Saviours, Brother Angelo. He's dead now. I used to listen in on them talking all the time when I was very young. Not hard when there are holes in the walls."

"Why are the bombs there?" Sethi pressed.

Kara shrugged. "It's an insurance policy. In case the Saviours are ever exposed—so they can destroy everything. Sage told Brother Angelo the mines are too old. They're from the last world war. Sage is going to buy in new explosives."

Sethi turned to me, his expression dark. "If we could get Jennifer and Constance out of there and then detonate the mines . . . perhaps we have a chance."

Kara was already shaking her head. "No chance at all. The detonators are down in the cenote itself. You'd need full diving gear to even get to them. Then you'd need to get out of the cenote again. All while hundreds of Saviours watch on."

Sethi's eyes widened in frustration. "The detonators are in the cenote? Why in the name of—?"

"So that no one could get to them, if they discovered the mines were there," Kara explained quickly. "The monastery is full of mass murderers, after all. Some of them like explosions. No explosives or guns are even allowed in the remembrance hall. Apart from the mentors—they are the only ones allowed to be armed in there."

"Did you find out how the detonators work?" he asked her.

"Once switched on," she said, "they're wired to count down for twelve minutes and then emit a sound like a submarine."

"Okay," Sethi breathed. "So, they're what you call *influence mines*. Back when I was in the naval division, part of the job was to find old mines and explode them. Many of them last a very long time. There's a good chance they will explode."

"It's a suicide mission," said Kara. "But even if one of you is willing to undertake it, you can't even get into the remembrance hall. You need to scan your hand. My handprint won't work. I'm not trusted anymore. It was going to be difficult enough to sneak inside myself. I can't get more of us in there."

I pointed at the nearest of the dead Saviours in the room. "We have *hands*."

I heard Evie's breathing escalate beside me.

"Yes, you're right. We can use that." Kara nodded coldly, not even flinching at the suggestion of hacking a dead man's hand off. "But you can't get to the detonators without diving equipment. You'll drown before you reach them."

Sethi inhaled deeply. "Not necessarily. Do you know exactly where the detonators are located?"

She nodded, pointing at a set of large metal cabinets that were fixed to the wall. "There is a diagram in there. Brother Clarence would have the key. He was the senior. The old man that you killed."

Cormack sprinted over to the scaffolding and felt inside the dead man's pockets until he found a set of keys. Within the next second, we had the cabinets open. Inside were sets of pumps and switches, all well maintained.

"The switches hoist the cage when it needs repair," Kara told us. "They also work a pumping system for times when the cenote gets blocked. And here's the map of the cenote." She took out a laminated illustration of the entire cenote.

The cenote consisted of a vertical shaft that led straight down from the surface, almost seventy feet deep into the earth, continuing down underneath the cellar. The cage was situated maybe twenty feet down from the top of the cenote, suspended on steel cables. The cenote shaft had horizontal arms that reached through the mountain and out to the sea. The top arm was marked with tiny letters.

Sethi studied the drawing, finally placing a finger on the top arm of the cenote. "That's where the detonators are, right? It has the World War Two code for this type of influence mine."

"Yes," said Kara. "That's exactly where they are. But you won't get to them. And I will have lost my chance to kill my mother."

"What if you can save her instead?" said Sethi. "I am trained to hold my breath for a long time. I can do it. I don't need to resurface. I've got twelve minutes. I can swim out through the arm of the cenote that leads to the ocean."

I glanced from the cenote illustration to Sethi. "The sponge diving, right? You learned to dive on the island where you grew up—Constance told me."

He gave an abbreviated nod. "In Kalymnos."

"You sure you want to go down *there*?" I asked him. "Where the bodies are?"

"Yes." His eyes flashed with adrenalin.

My chest tightened. It was an impossible plan. But it was our only plan. Our only chance of escape. For it to have a snowflake's chance of working, things had to happen in the right sequence.

"We'll take them by surprise and buy ourselves some time," I said. "You and me, Sethi, we go in there as captured prisoners. Kara, in Saviours' robes, pretends to be that blonde-haired guy, Lewis. She and he are about the same height. Sethi, you will run and dive into the cenote and do your thing. Kara and I will cover you and get guns to Constance and Jennifer. We'll take the grenades you and Jennifer brought in your backpacks to cause as much mayhem as possible."

A cold sweat prickled the back of my neck. What I was proposing—going into a hall of hundreds of brutal killers—sent waves of raw terror coursing through my veins and breath pumping hard into my lungs.

Kara's eyes grew round and were still filled with doubt, but she gave me a nod.

"Let's do this," said Sethi.

Evie's hand caught fast in mine. "I'm coming, too." Her voice sounded so definite, nothing like the Evie I knew.

I shook my head, catching my breath. "They'll know straight away what's happening if any of you come with us. It can only be Sethi, me and Kara. Everyone else should get out to the chapel and wait there for us."

"Like fun I'm being shuffled out there," said Cormack.

"Cormack, you can't come with us," said Sethi. "The cameras will pick up everything the whole way. You stand out too much. You're taller than everyone. And that bushy beard . . . We have to hurry."

I grasped Evie's face in my hands. "If I don't come back, promise me you'll get off this island. Get back to Willow and Lilly."

"You promise me you'll come back." She kissed me. Her lips were cold.

77. I, INSIDE THE WALLS

CORMACK, RICHARD AND YOLANDA VOLUNTEERED to lead the others to the chapel. Richard and Yolanda were the only ones who knew how to shoot. I found myself disturbed by the thought of what could happen to Cormack should he have to take on a Saviour by himself.

I took the three of them out there to show them the right path and make sure they understood they had to hide in the chapel until the mines exploded; otherwise they'd ruin the whole plan. And I told them where to hide along the tunnel in order to ambush any stray Saviours.

Back in the cellar, Sethi was busy hacking off Brother Lewis's hand. Any second now, Gray, Sethi and I would have to go.

Santiago, stay with me.

But I watched Santiago drift away, almost swallowed up by the black tunnel, confused by what was happening. The terror of losing Santiago shot through me.

It was hard for me helping these people. Not because I didn't want to. But because I'd acted alone for so many years. Even before I met Daddy James, it was how I'd been. Locked inside myself, with a brother who only had life inside my mind.

Daddy James had my brain imaged when I was a child. I have the brain of a sociopath. Having a brain scan is essential before you're allowed to be a Saviour. You have to have the right brain.

Some people think you can change and get better. And some people think that a sociopath always murders. Neither is true. I can't change my brain, and neither do I wish to. I like my brain how it is. Maybe that's because of the egotistical side of sociopathy. But I don't want to kill anyone. *Except for the Saviours.* I'd kill every one of them if I could.

Catching my hand in his, Cormack pulled me out of the light that streamed from the plate glass in the cellar door.

I thought a Saviour must be coming our way, my hand reaching instinctively for the knife in my pocket.

But Cormack was strangely hesitant. "I don't like you heading into a whole nest of Saviours. It's too dangerous. Kara, I didn't understand before how you could be one of *them*. Now I know that you're not."

The way he said my name in his Scottish accent made it sound beautiful. I'd never thought of my name as beautiful. "You don't know anything about me."

"I know that you didn't want to do what they've been making you do."

"You don't understand. They could only make me do any of this because of who I am. Any normal person would have gone some kind of batshit crazy at the things that happen here."

"Have you considered that you might not even know who you are? Brother Sage has forced all this on you, the bastard. I want to kill him for what he's done to you."

"If everything goes to plan, you'll get your wish. At least, he'll die."

"No matter what happens next, I've got your back. Just wanted you to know that."

"You're kind of noisy for someone in a place filled with serial killers." Despite everything, I had a smile in my voice. He was so . . . *earnest.* No one around me was earnest. Everyone was a liar. That went with the territory of being sociopathic. Even Mom had been lying about her past for the last decade—and she was normal.

"In case all of this goes to shite and we don't make it off this island," he said, "just know that a guy named Cormack liked a girl named Kara. Very much."

He moved closer, his breath on my cheek. And kissed me.

Why was I so breathless when he broke away?

I'd never let a boy get this close.

Never.

Cormack had no idea what he was doing. He'd seen a face and projected all kinds of things onto the person behind that face. Just like the boys at school. Cormack was the first boy to see behind the face, but he still didn't understand. He couldn't. He was a neurotypical. A normal brain with normal thoughts.

I looked around in a sudden panic. I'd forgotten Santiago.

He'd gone. For the first time since he'd come into my life, I couldn't sense him near.

Santiago. Where are you?

78. CONSTANCE

JAMES PAUSED THE SPEECH HE WAS GIVING to his twisted, macabre congregation. I could tell he relished his role as leader of the Saviours, his lips curling up into a satisfied smile. "And we," he continued, "broke free of our shackles in Plato's cave. We saw beyond the shadows into what was real. Our eyes are open. We believe in the regime of aristocracy and the philosopher king here among our fold. We are rich and boundless and will continue our tradition of bringing those who belong with us to Saviours of Yeqon's legacy."

A cheer went up around the Saviours—a deep, resonating cheer that sent an ice-cold shudder down my back.

The terrible ceremony of the Saviours was done.

"We cannot delay longer," James told his congregation. "Many of us have lives and businesses to attend to and must return to home. We will soon watch over the final challenges. First, we will need to deal with Constance and Jennifer."

"I would be happy to have the honour of bringing Jennifer Bloom to her last breath," said Sister Dawn, flicking her gaze to Jennifer. "Naturally, first we must find out all you know, Jennifer. We have ways of breaking all the small bones of the body first, and then the large. At some point, your mind will crack along with your body, and you'll tell us everything. Everyone does."

"No." The word stuttered in my throat.

"Constance," said the vile stranger who was my husband, "if we don't get enough information from Jennifer, I'm afraid you will be next."

His words made my mind recoil into the tightest possible place, my heart slamming against my chest wall.

Faces turned sharply as people entered the hall.

Jennifer cried out.

The Saviour had Sethi and Gray captured, a gun pointed at their backs. Silently, the Saviour held up four backpacks—ours.

"Well done, Lewis," called James.

The man named Lewis nodded in acknowledgement, his hood drawn too far over his forehead for his face to be seen.

Wilson Carlisle stepped across to them with a mocking look set into his pudgy face. "Gray Harlow, you should have stayed at home. Jail would have been a safer proposition than this."

"I'm just glad my wife won't have to suffer this alone," said Gray.

Wilson's face stretched into a bland smile. "We all die alone." His attention turned to Sethi. "And who have you brought with you, Mr Harlow? We're going to have to discover everything you two know and who else you've told."

"That is Sethi Ambrosia," said Sister Rose. "I was the one tasked with keeping tabs on Jennifer and her liaisons. He's her on-again off-again lover."

"There was no *off*. I have always loved Jenny." Sethi stared at her coldly.

"Well, you certainly tricked me," she retorted.

"Because you don't know love." He wasn't looking at Sister Rose anymore but directly at Jennifer. His jaw drew tight. "Jenny didn't want me to get too involved with her because she was afraid I would get hurt by the Saviours. But she always had my heart. And because of that, I cannot bear to watch her die."

Amid the choked gasps of the Saviours, Sethi turned and sprinted the short distance to the lip of the cenote.

And dived straight in.

The Saviour named Lewis shot at Sethi twice and missed, the bullets striking Wilson and forcing the assembly back.

I whirled around to Jennifer, catching sight of her stricken face just before I heard the splash far below in the cenote.

I caught sight of an odd object on the floor.
A severed hand.

79. GRAY

SETHI'S LONG BODY HAD VANISHED INTO THE CENOTE.

The four mentors whipped out guns, shooting at the water. *Good, let them use as many of their bullets as possible.*

I sweated terror and adrenalin. Kara seemed to be right—no one in the remembrance hall other than the mentors had guns.

"The man is a deep-sea diver!" came the loud, shrill voice of Sister Rose. "I've looked into his early history before."

Sage's expression turned to an incredulous rage. "Can he get out to the ocean?"

"It's impossible, but—" Sister Rose stared down into the water.

Any second now, they'd realise this was a set-up. And they'd find out that Kara was pretending to be Lewis. Lewis's severed hand had gotten us through the door. Kara had told us that Lewis's ID would have flashed up on the special apps the mentors used on their smart watches.

But the trick had only bought us minutes at best.

And that time had gone.

My turn to act.

Whipping out my gun, I took point-blank aim at the Saviour who was holding onto Jennifer.

Kara shot the Saviour who held her mother.

The crowd of Saviours jerked their heads around, trying to find the source of the new blasts.

Breathing hard, I took out the grenades from my pockets.

The pins—don't forget the pins.

One chance. One chance to get this right.

Wait, wait, wait.

Now throw.

I tossed each of the grenades.

One at the mentors. One into the crowd.

Blood hammered in my head so hard I barely heard the explosions.

The Saviours scattered in chaotic patterns.

Kara walked up to Wilson Carlisle and shot him.

Constance's expression turned to open-eyed shock as she caught sight of her daughter's face.

Kara whipped out additional guns from her pockets and handed them to her mother and Jennifer.

Jennifer was the quickest to understand, not needing any explanation before raising the gun and firing off rounds.

"Run! *Run!*" My voice sounded far away to my ears.

Kara tugged her dazed mother along while turning back and shooting.

I pulled the pins on the next two grenades in my store and threw them.

It was enough. Just enough. The Saviours were running for cover. The mentors were sprawled on the ground—hopefully dead.

Any minute now, all our ammo would be gone, and hundreds of Saviours would be chasing us down through this monstrous place. And they had rooms full of guns.

Some of them were advancing again.

"Kara!" Constance screamed. Running back, she thrust her daughter behind her, shooting at the Saviours.

"Out!" Jennifer yelled. "Out now! All of us!"

We fled behind the door and slammed it shut.

Kara shot at the keypad lock. "They can't get through it now."

Constance grasped Kara's face between her hands. "Are you okay? Are you hurt?"

"I'm okay." Kara stared back with the same large blue eyes as her mother, suddenly seeming as young and fragile as the seventeen-year-old that she was.

Jennifer spoke in sharp, ragged breaths, her fist clenched on the gun. "What's happening? Why the hell did Sethi dive into—?"

I shook my head. "We need to run. This whole place is going to blow!"

Constance gasped, looking to her daughter for an explanation.

Jennifer stared at me as if gathering herself mentally.

"We've got ten minutes," I roared. "*Go!*"

Rain slashed down in the garden as we charged out—wet branches whipping our faces.

We entered what Kara had called the cloister and then rushed inside.

A voice rang out from the hazy darkness at the other end of the hall. Three Saviours charged towards us.

Before I had a chance to react, Jennifer and Kara shot them dead.

"They all know now. They've all been told." Kara gestured frantically in the direction of the cellar. "We have to get out of here. More of them will be coming."

The cellar was empty now as we raced down the spiral stairs.

Everyone gone, except for the unconscious prisoners.

Loose chains everywhere.

Dark blood on the walls.

The dead hanging in the torture room.

And the bodies caught in a rusting cage in the cenote.

I heard Constance and Jennifer's gasps and cries of shock.

Kara slipped across the room to the door that led to the outside. She entered a code into the keypad.

I inhaled a short breath of rancid air, turning quickly to face Constance and Jennifer. "Here's the plan. Sethi's attempting to swim through the cenote and out to sea. There's a lever down there that can detonate three mines lying at the bottom of the cenote. He's got a twelve-minute leeway. If it works, the cenote's going to blow. We need to get out. Sethi will meet us at the beach." Even as I spoke the plan, it sounded impossible.

Jennifer's eyes were huge as she nodded, but she didn't speak.

Her expression was plain. She knew as I did this plan had the smallest chance of working.

Were Evie and the others still alive out there? There were no guarantees.

Evie, I need you to survive this. If I don't come to you, get to the boats and leave this island.

Kara's code set off a click within the door. She pushed it open.

We slammed the door shut behind us as we sprinted through the tunnel.

Breaths like charging bulls.

Terror spiralling through me.

I forced my mind to shut down.

There was only the tunnel and the darkness and getting through to the end.

80. EVIE

WE HUDDLED INSIDE THE CHAPEL LIKE the damned seeking refuge. The light of the approaching dawn seeped into the sky in tones of the darkest grey. Each thrash of the ocean far below set my bones on edge as I waited for the explosion.

Louelle hadn't made it home. We'd found her in the tunnel on our way out. Her family would never know the Louelle she wanted them to know.

Ruth had vanished as soon as we travelled through the passage and climbed up into the chapel. We were to guard Gray, Constance and Kara when they emerged from the tunnel, but she hadn't bothered to stay and help us. Who knew what her game was?

A dozen or more Saviours had been combing the hills since we'd entered the chapel. We'd taken turns watching them. They couldn't see us behind the thick stone walls with their infra-red viewers, but they could see a human face peering through the glass-less chapel windows, so we had to be quick.

A swift change came when all of a sudden they were running and shouting. I knew then that they'd been radioed about Gray and Sethi. About the plan.

Sethi, Gray and Kara must have made it to the remembrance hall.

What happened? Did the plan work? Did they get out?

Some of the Saviours had run towards the chapel—no doubt rushing to get to the cellar to check that their precious collection of lambs was still chained and ready for slaughter.

Richard held up a hand to us, letting the Saviours come closer. *Closer. Closer.*

My heart jerked against my chest wall.

Richard, Cormack and Yolanda jumped up with their guns—the semi-automatics that we'd taken from the supply room.

A terrifying back and forth of gunfire rattled the air, louder than anything I'd ever heard before.

Like a war.

It *was* a war.

We'd reached a place of savagery and entered it. It was fight or die.

Bits of sandstone flew across the small space, shattered by the Saviours' guns. But so far we were all alive. We were partly protected by the chapel walls, and we'd had the element of surprise in our favour.

Then, quiet.

I stole a quick look past Yolanda. Men and women had dropped dead on the rocky ground, the rest fleeing.

I turned to Richard. He shot me a tense grin. "Got them on the run."

At that moment came a sound like the earth splitting apart. A roar from hell itself.

Sethi had done it. The mine was detonating.

Columns of water thundered through the centre of the monastery, seeming as high and wide as a skyscraper, stone blocks flying into the night air.

Pieces of the monastery smashed repeatedly into the chapel, tremors running beneath our feet.

"Get out of here!" Cormack's eyes were wild in the thin, dark light.

Arms over our heads, we headed to the doorway.

Gray, make it out of there.

Please.

I hung back, the last to leave.

Richard spun around, grabbing my arm. "Don't stop now."

We both turned around to the monastery then, stunned by the sight of the immense waterspout plunging back to earth and the buildings beginning to collapse and sink.

Gray, where are you?
Where are you?
You promised . . .

81. CONSTANCE

OUR URGENT SCREAMS AND SHOUTS ECHOED in the narrow tunnel.

My last thought before the explosion was of Kara.

Far behind us came the roar of the world breaking and the glass windows of the cenote shattering.

A mass of water and glass was headed our way. The door wouldn't hold it back.

The ground swayed and pitched dangerously.

Kara ran faster than I could, forcing me along, breath raw in my chest.

The maelstrom surged behind us. I could hear it filling the tunnel.

Oh God.

Light.

Sky.

The exit.

The chapel was gone. Just rubble.

I heard Gray's anguished cry.

Were Evie and the others trapped under all that?

If they were, they were dead. All dead.

We climbed out and over the stone blocks and remains of the chapel.

An ear-splitting sound boomed—the rubble tumbling beneath our feet and then dropping.

We were sent downward, on top of what used to be the roof of the chapel. In terror, I jerked my head around. The ground had formed a pit about ten feet deep, and it was still dropping.

"Get out of here!" Jennifer screamed.

The sides of the pit were tumbling, while the ground below us sank farther and farther.

As we tried to climb the steep sides, torrents of dark seawater burst from the tunnel, pushing us down, drowning us.

I fought my way to the surface. "Kara! Kara!"

Gray and Jennifer surfaced just after me, coughing and spluttering, bright red blood seeping from cuts and slashes in their skin.

Glass. Swirling around and around us.

I glanced down at my arms—they were covered in blood.

Stone continued to fall in from the sides of the pit. The ground could continue to cave in, with the rubble above falling onto us, sealing us in.

"*Kara!*" I swam frantically, needing to get to her.

I gasped and shivered at the sight of bones in the water. Body parts. All the dead from the cenote in the cellar. And others—Saviours, their bodies fresh. I searched among them, looking for my daughter.

Then, a girl, white and unconscious, floating.

Kara.

Jennifer, a deep gash across her nose and cheek, stroked towards me, Gray following. We hauled my daughter onto a stone block at the side of the pit. Jennifer took charge, checking her breathing and then immediately starting to pump her chest.

Kara's body jerked within ten pumps, her head turning as she vomited.

"*Thank God*," I breathed, putting my cheek next to hers.

Gray gestured towards a set of staggered stone blocks. "We have to find a way out. Now."

Jennifer nodded. "You first, Gray. Constance and I'll help Kara up from this end, and you grab her from up there."

I didn't know how we were going to do that. The sides were so steep. All I knew was that we *had* to.

Two figures in black hoods peered down at us from the top of the pit. The weak light of dawn showed surprised sneers on their faces.

Saviours. A woman and a man.

The woman, red wisps of hair lifting in the breeze, took out a gun as she stared from us to Kara. "Fish in a barrel."

Kara stared back at the woman, unflinching. "They're all gone, Poppy. It's over."

"No, it isn't over, Sister Kara," said the woman, stressing each word in a cold, terrifying voice. "You destroyed everything. The only real home I ever had. And you killed Vito. You and your mother and whoever these people are killed the man I loved. Sage made a big mistake when he brought you here to the monastery."

"Then take care of Sage's mistake. But leave the others," Kara told her.

"*No!*" I cried when I realised what Kara meant. "Leave my child alone. You people have done enough."

The redhead gazed in the direction of the ruined monastery, tilting her head. "The monastery has to be built again. Somehow. None of you can stay alive. You'll only get in the way. Isn't that right, Harrington?"

The tall, lanky man beside her bit into his lip as he grinned. Taking out his gun, he took aim and shot at the water, laughing at us.

The Saviours turned sharply as a woman approached, her face and body silhouetted in the warm light of the sun.

The redhead gaped at her in shock. "Evie . . . ?"

I didn't even see the gun that Evie fired. The redhead fell to her knees.

"Evie!" Gray screamed as Harrington raised his gun.

Harrington screamed as a bullet hit his arm, his gun tumbling into the pit. Wheeling about, he ran off into the piles of rubble.

Two men emerged from the rubble, the smaller of them with a rifle over his shoulder.

82. EVIE

A FLOCK OF STARTLED PEACOCKS RAN across the distant hills, lifting into the air.

Richard and Cormack stood together, Richard lowering the rifle he'd just fired. "You didn't think we'd let you go back there alone, did you?"

I gave them a nod, jamming my eyes shut for a moment, my throat too tight to reply.

Stalking up to Poppy, Richard bent to snatch up her gun. "You won't be needing this, sweetheart."

Poppy raised her eyes to him, her sneering face turned ugly in defeat.

I ran to the pit, terrified at what I would find below.

The rocks and rubble beneath my feet lurched as I made my way to the edge.

Gray. He was there. Covered in cuts and bruises.

Kara and the two women I'd seen on the cellar monitor were with him—all of them in the same condition as Gray. But alive.

Alive.

Blocks of sandstone shifted, and I crouched to the ground, balancing.

Any second now, this pit and everything surrounding it could collapse inward. Everything was hanging on a thin wire.

"Evie, you were supposed to get off this island," Gray yelled at me, his voice hoarse and broken.

Tears wet my cheeks. "Hold on . . ."

"Kara, we'll get you out. We'll get you all out," Cormack called down to her.

In desperation, I eyed the slopes of the pit. They were steep, dangerous and threatening to collapse.

The curve of something smooth and large caught my attention, its surface brass and partly covered in a greenish patina.

The church bell.

It must have come loose in the pummelling from the explosion, as it was now lodged tightly between the rocks near the top of the pit. I remembered a rope that had hung from that bell. My eyes followed the line downward. The rope was still there, attached but covered in a number of stone blocks.

I twisted around to Richard and Cormack, pointing at the bell. "*This!* We can use this!"

Together with Richard and Cormack, I climbed down and levered the rocks to allow the full length of the rope to descend to the pit.

We got Kara out first, then Constance, Gray and Jennifer.

I wrapped myself around Gray. He was shivering. Cold, wet. Had he lost too much blood?

I lightly touched his wounds. "We need to bandage these."

"I'm okay. I'll be okay," he answered.

He pressed his forehead down to mine. A flock of peacocks in flight made us both look up, their pink-tipped wings spread wide as they came in for smooth, elegant landings. I hadn't even known peacocks could fly before this morning.

Poppy remained doubled over on the ground. She pushed her face up to me, a thin line of blood streaking from the side of her mouth. "The boyfriends I told you about? They didn't die of accidental overdoses. I killed them. Because they looked at girls who weren't me." Her lips pulled to one side in a small, cold smile.

I stared back. I hadn't known the first thing about her.

Turning my back on her, I walked away with Gray.

I didn't know how far it was to the nearest island. Hours? Could any of us even find our way to another island through the ocean? We could be lost out there for days. We needed Sethi, but none of us knew whether he'd made it out or drowned.

I turned to face Jennifer, catching her eye. Her eyes were terrified above the bright smears of blood on her face, and I knew that terror was for Sethi. "Let's go find him."

The seven of us made our way off the cliff top, through the hills. We found Mei and Thomas on the way. Both dead. Both seemed to have fallen off the cliff edge. Whether they were pushed or had chosen to jump rather than allow themselves to be captured, I couldn't tell. But I guessed they'd made the decision to jump. The Saviours would surely not allow any of their quarry to die so easily.

We closed Mei and Thomas's eyes as a sign of respect and continued on down to the beach.

"Stay here," Jennifer told us. "I'll go find Sethi."

Gray and Cormack stepped across to Jennifer.

"I'll be back soon," Gray said. "Sethi saved our lives. We need to find him."

The three of them sprinted away.

Richard tried to hold my arm, but I shrugged him away. Gray had almost not returned to me once. I needed to be beside him.

As I rounded the bend, a figure emerged from behind an outcrop, her eyes large and filled with adrenaline. Ruth. Instinctively, I reached for my gun.

"What do you want?" I asked her, pointing my handgun at her.

"You don't honestly think I'm going to hurt you, do you?" Her face was covered in cuts and bruises.

"Why did you take off on your own?" I demanded, choosing not to answer her question directly.

She raised her eyebrows. "I've been picking off any Saviour that I can find. I didn't want to wait for them to come to us. I used to go hunting wild boar with my father. I'm a good shot."

"I'm supposed to believe that's what you've been doing?" I said, my voice catching. "So many good people died. But you're still here."

"I didn't push you in Challenge Four in order to gain some kind of glory, Evie."

"Why did you push me?"

"Hear me out. I didn't trust Harrington. Not from the first day. So I kept him close. You know that saying about keeping your enemies close? I made him think I was just like him, just so I could try to figure out who the hell he was. I even told him I just pretended to lose my shit in the mirror challenge—because I was damned sure *he* was pretending."

I exhaled tensely, waiting for her to finish.

"And in Challenge Four," she said, "the moment I knew we were working with dangerous elements, I was watching him like a hawk. When you were bringing your puzzle piece up to me, Harrington was racing up behind you. He had his puzzle piece out in front of him. I caught the insane look in his eyes, and I knew exactly what he intended to do. He wanted to catch you in between the two magnets. There wasn't any time. And there was a bird swinging your way. I did my best to save you. Sorry you got hurt."

My knees weakened, and I replayed those moments in my mind. Harrington *had* been behind me. And I knew now what kind of man he was. I lowered my gun. "Thank you . . ."

"You don't need to thank me."

It was too late now to follow Gray. And I couldn't go on my own. I barely even knew how to use this gun. I leaned against the outcrop. "What happened after you were told you'd been eliminated from the program?"

She shrugged. "I thought I was going home. Of course. But I was taken straight down to the cellar. For a celebration wine, they told me. When I caught sight of their little *celebration* down there, I fought like an alley cat. They beat me up and chained me. And that's all I knew."

"I'm sorry I left you behind the first time. We couldn't take you."

"I know."

"We're going to get away from this place. *We are*. You said you've got two girls?"

Her eyes clouded. "I haven't seen them for two years. They were taken away into foster custody seven years ago. They're teenagers now. They don't know me. I'm a stranger to them. I hoped I could clean myself up, rent a small apartment. Keep away from heroin. And then try to start again. I can't be a mother to them, but maybe I could be a friend."

I gave her a tight smile. "Hope it happens."

Gunshots blasted into the sand. I lifted my head. Four Saviours stood on the cliff edge.

"Hurry!" Ruth ordered me.

We ran together in the direction that Gray had gone. Keeping close to the bottom edge of the cliff face, we threaded our way through the rocks and around the sharp curve of the island—making it as hard as possible for the Saviours to keep up. They had hills and crevices to contend with.

I knew that the Saviours needed us to die. We were the last ones who could tell the tale of what happened to people on this island and all that we'd seen and who the Yeqon's Saviours were.

Six people walked towards us in the distance. Four about as tall as each other and two shorter.

Saviours?

They stepped closer. One of the middle people was hurt, his companions with their arms around him, supporting him.

Sethi. With Gray, Jennifer and Cormack. They'd also met up with Yolanda and Hop.

"Watch out!" I screamed. "There's Saviours up there!"

Bullets rained down.

They raced for the base of the cliff as Ruth and I continued on our path towards them. We all stopped beneath an area where the edge of the cliff overhung the cliff wall. The Saviours couldn't see us or shoot us here.

"Sethi. Thank God!" I cried.

He gave a half grin. "I made it out of the water just before it all went kaboom. Yolanda and Hop came looking for me."

"The explosion was like a plane crashing," said Yolanda. "So scary but so damned beautiful. Hundreds of Saviours gone forever."

I turned, startled as people ran towards us.

Richard, Constance and Kara.

"Safety in numbers." Richard exhaled loudly. "Any idea how many of those bastards are left out there?"

"Yolanda and I saw quite a few out on the island just after the blast," Hop replied.

"I think we're about to find out." Ruth gestured upwards.

The Saviours had begun to descend the hills. Coming straight for us.

"We can't let them get down here!" cried Jennifer. "Whoever knows how to shoot, help me keep them at bay. The rest of you, don't get in the way. Just stay covered."

Ruth took a place beside Jennifer.

Gunfire filled the air, bullets striking the rocks.

"*No!*" cried Yolanda, pointing out to the shore.

Saviours were rowing small boats around to where we were. Making sure we couldn't risk a sprint across to the beach. Once they'd moored, they'd be moving in, trapping us.

I buried my head in Gray's shoulder. *Was this where we died? Was this patch of earth the place where our numbers ran out?*

I squinted into the horizon. Far beyond the rowboats, the first rays of the sun sparked off something large and metallic. "What *is* that?"

Sethi stopped shooting and turned to look. He shook his head, puzzled. Jennifer unzipped her backpack and took out a pair of binoculars. "Take these, Seth."

Breathing hard, Sethi peered through the viewing lenses. "It's the Hellenic Coast Guard."

"Would they have come because of the explosion?" queried Jennifer. "What's their nearest base to here?"

Sethi's forehead rippled in concentration. "Karpathos, I think. It's not so far away. Maybe there were reports from boats at sea. Maybe even an aircraft. I saw the water spout hundreds of feet. Someone would have surely seen it."

On the hills above us, the Saviours had fled.

"Well, thank Methuselah," said Richard. "Are the coast guard part of the Greek police?"

"They operate independently," Sethi told him. "They're paramilitary. Sometimes, the coast guard and the police step into each other's territory, and that doesn't go so well. Mostly, the coast guard patrols the waters, carrying out rescue of refugees and conducting drug and border control."

We watched as the Saviours in the water about-faced and rowed their boats away.

"We can go down there now." Yolanda's voice trembled. "We're getting out of here."

"Wait," Kara cautioned. "Some of the Saviours are insane. Literally insane. The ones who lived here at the monastery. You've destroyed their home, and they're not about to let you go, even if they die, too."

And then I saw them. Crawling over the rocks like shadows to our left, staying out of sight of the fast-incoming coast guard boat.

"Get ready," Sethi hissed. "But don't go crazy. Maybe they want that we fire off all our ammo."

Those of us with guns raised them, facing left.

Sethi fired first. A barrage of gunshots followed from both sides.

"Get down!" Jennifer grabbed Hop and Yolanda, forcing them below the rock that they'd been firing over. "They've got semis. Their bullets will take your heads off."

Hop and Yolanda panted, wild-eyed, pressing back against the surface of the rock.

The coast guard boat pulled close to shore, deploying an inflatable raft.

The Saviours who'd been hunting us directed their fire at the approaching raft.

"We need to get out of here!" Sethi yelled. "That boat has machine guns. Point fifty calibre. Move it!"

Jennifer and Sethi covered us with gunfire as we rushed along the beach, staying close to the cliff base.

"We're out of range now," said Sethi. "We can stay here. And hope."

A loudspeaker blasted through the air, instructing everyone on the beach to stop. The Saviours fired in response.

Machine gun fire followed—so loud it stole my thoughts away.

"We have to be careful now," Sethi told us. "If the coast guard think you're shooting at them, they'll shoot back. Hold your fire unless we're under threat."

To the left of us, shadows stretched across the sand. A group of people running towards us from around the bend of the cliff base.

Whether they were Saviours or coast guards I couldn't tell.

I glanced back at Jennifer and Sethi. At a distance to the right of them, three figures stepped along the sand, coming towards us. Dressed in ordinary clothing. All apparently hurt and limping.

As they came closer, Constance clutched Kara close, moving herself in front of her. "It's James."

My lungs tight, I watched the figures approach us. Brother Sage, Sister Dawn and Harrington. Cuts and dirt smeared on their faces. Brother Sage and Harrington in ordinary pants and white shirts, Sister Dawn dressed similar. Both of them with their hands in the air. Harrington had a thick layer of ripped cloth tied around the arm that had been shot.

"How on earth did he survive?" said Constance darkly.

"I can guess how." Kara shot a grim look at her mother. "One wall of the tanks in challenge room two faces the remembrance hall. They must have shot a hole in the tank wall, let the water spill out and then gotten through that way. Before the blast hit."

The three Saviours stopped together, their expressions unreadable.

Was this a trap? A trick?

Richard and Yolanda raised their rifles and shot, the bullets pinging into the sand.

Reaching across, Jennifer put a hand on top of the barrel of Richard's gun. "No! Wait. Something's wrong here. They're making it too easy."

"Stay away from Kara," Constance warned Brother Sage. "You're evil. I'd hoped you'd died."

Brother Sage just stared at her, impassive.

"Put down your weapons," Sister Dawn suddenly called to us in an authoritative tone, completely unlike the voice she'd used in the monastery. "This is Police Lieutenant Colonel Dimitra Georgiades."

"She's with the police?" Sethi exhaled a tight breath.

The people casting the shadows to the left of us pulled into view. A group of men in uniform. The Hellenic Coast Guards.

"This is Commander Liourdis. Lower your weapons," demanded one of the guards—a stocky blonde man with deeply olive skin. "Place them on the ground. One wrong move and we'll shoot."

Sethi nodded at us but not without an anxious look in his eyes. "Do it."

Members of the coast guard moved in to take the weapons. Seemingly emboldened, Brother Sage, Sister Dawn and Harrington stepped up close. The three of them suddenly had guns—they must have been concealing them in their waistbands behind their backs.

"We've got this under control," Sister Dawn told the blonde commander, flashing a police badge.

"No," roared Sethi. "Don't believe these people."

The blonde man held up the palm of one hand. "What's going on here, Lieutenant Georgiades?"

"It's a joint effort between the Hellenic and British police forces," Sister Dawn told him. "We've been watching this group, under suspicion of transporting narcotics, for months now. They're keeping stores of weapons and narcotics on the island. A number of the monks were involved in their operation. Unfortunately, we lost two other members of our special unit this morning."

"I'm sorry to hear it. We had reports of an explosion—" started Commander Liourdis.

Sister Dawn gave a quick nod. "Upon our arrival just before daybreak, they detonated a naval mine—attempting to destroy an extensive array of evidence. A World War Two mine if you can believe it."

He nodded and then glanced at Brother Sage and Harrington with interest. "Who are these people?"

"Sergeant Harrington Green and an American businessman named James Lundquist," answered Sister Dawn.

"I came in search of my runaway stepdaughter," answered Brother Sage. "I've been cooperating with the police for weeks now. This is Kara, over here, with her mother, Constance. Constance was involved with the murder of a British investigator who was assisting in this investigation. I'm afraid my wife got mixed up with the wrong people."

"Tell them the truth, James," cried Constance. "Look at us. Do we look like drug smugglers?"

The commander didn't answer, instead keeping his eye on Sister Dawn. "Who were the people shooting at us?"

"A small number of the same group," answered Sister Dawn. "My task force has them rounded up now. Thanks for your intervention. It was well timed. We weren't expecting the explosion of a naval mine—who would? But we now have this operation back under control."

"I have files of information to show you, Commander," said Jennifer. "I'd welcome the chance to hand it all over to you."

"I'm afraid the commander isn't interested in your subterfuge," said Sister Dawn. "He's able to check into your backgrounds via Interpol. Drugs, prostitution, armed robbery, fraud. This woman here—Jennifer Bloom—uses an art business as a front while she engages in combat training and buys up stores of weapons. And this woman here"—she pointed directly at me—"is the infamous Evie Harlow. A prostitute who faked her own death and then travelled overseas on a fake passport. A week later, her pimp husband joined her. Both of them abandoning their two small children."

My lip trembled. "I didn't abandon them."

"That woman is the one telling you lies," Gray told the commander. "Take us with you. We'll explain how everything happened the way it did and why."

Sister Dawn stepped forward, shaking her head. "This sting is under the jurisdiction of the British and Hellenic Police forces, Mr Harlow. Commander Liourdis is well aware of that."

Sethi and Jennifer exchanged worried glances.

I knew exactly what they were thinking. The same revolutions were happening in my own mind. *We couldn't tell the truth. It was too bizarre and shocking to be believed.*

Raw fear turned to raw adrenaline inside me. Talking was only making this worse for us. The Saviours needed the coast guard gone. They needed time to clean up their island and remove the lingering evidence.

The coast guard could leave without us.

I tugged my hand away from Gray's and crossed halfway to the guards.

"Evie!" Gray urged me back.

"Stop, or I'll shoot!" called Sister Dawn.

Ignoring her, I faced the commander, my heart jumping into my throat. "We're unarmed citizens. We came here because we were duped by corrupt people. We need rescue. I know you rescue people all the time. Some of us are seriously hurt. We need medical attention. They have no medical supplies. *Please*. We're willing to cooperate with you."

Commander Liourdis's gaze switched from me to Sister Dawn. "You are outnumbered. We're happy to assist your efforts and escort these people to the Greek mainland."

Sister Dawn shook her head emphatically. "Commander, we have backup soon arriving at the island. With full medical supplies. We need to process our prisoners and find out additional information. We've put too much time and effort into this sting to have its integrity affected at this point."

"Which members of the Hellenic Police Force are involved in the sting? We've had no word," he said to Sister Dawn.

Sister Dawn brushed his words away with an almost dismissive gesture. "I'll forward you full documentation."

"Regardless," said Commander Liourdis, "we have medical supplies on board. We can attend to this group and take them with us, allowing you to finish your investigations here."

I turned and watched her stare at him, unblinking, as if calculating her next move.

"What you can do is help us secure the prisoners here on the island," she said. "Please, we'll show you the way up to the vineyards."

"No!" I whirled around to the commander, electricity firing across my skin and scalp, no longer measuring my words. "It's a trap. They'll kill you.

They'll be waiting in ambush. They'll kill you and kill us. The truth here will never come out."

The muscles in the commander's jaw pulled taut. "Enough!" he told Sister Dawn. "What we saw when we arrived was a situation out of control in every which way. We're taking control. We are escorting this group to the mainland under armed guard and delivering them to the police."

A silent message passed between Brother Sage and Sister Dawn.

"Very well," said Sister Dawn. "You go ahead and do that, and I'll coordinate things from this end."

"Okay, people," barked another member of the coast guard. "Hands on heads and walk to the shore. Anyone who takes their hands from their head or attempts to run in any direction will risk being shot."

"Commander," said Sethi. "There are people up on the cliff with semi-automatics. It's not safe to proceed. You should move your men. They're already at risk."

"Lieutenant Georgiades, can you assure me of the situation at hand here?" The commander studied her face.

"Of course," she replied, turning and raising an arm straight above her head.

Immediately, the air filled with the rattle and roar of gun blasts. Two of the coast guards fell on the sand.

Commander Liourdis turned on his heel and scanned the cliff above, shock registering on his face. He made a call to his boat.

Gray sprinted to grab my hand, zigzagging with me back to the cliff base.

Harrington stood his ground, shooting at the coast guards, while Brother Sage and Sister Dawn ran for cover.

"No, you don't get to get away! This is for Noah." Jennifer followed them.

"Jenny!" Sethi charged after her.

Jennifer made a grab for one of the guns that we'd been forced to leave behind.

Sister Dawn shot at Jennifer, one of the bullets hitting her in the chest. Flung back on the ground, Jennifer shot back before she collapsed unconscious. Her third shot made contact with Brother Sage, and he grabbed his shoulder, wincing in pain.

Roaring, Sethi leaped to the ground and rolled, snatching up a gun and firing at Brother Sage and Sister Dawn.

A bright red patch bloomed across Sister Dawn's white shirt. She doubled over then tumbled to the ground.

The boom of the machine gun from the coast patrol ended it.

The Saviours that lined the cliff edge vanished.

The beach fell silent but for the rush of the ocean.

Sethi turned his head, crying out at the sight of Jennifer lying on the driftwood. Rushing to her, he gathered up her limp body in his arms.

Brother Sage came staggering towards us, one hand up in surrender.

"Thank God." Brother Sage had his other hand clamped onto his bleeding shoulder. "I was that woman's captive. She told me she'd shoot my wife and daughter if I didn't do as she said. They kept us chained up and drugged here. We've been hallucinating for days."

Kara walked steadily towards him, stopping immediately before him. "I am not your daughter." In a swift, tight movement, she plunged a knife deep into his stomach.

He stared back at her, his eyes glazed with astonishment. As he grasped Kara's arms, his knees buckled.

She pushed him back roughly, his blood spilling red onto the white sand as he fell.

83. I, INSIDE THE WALLS

I CAUGHT SIGHT OF THE SHOCKED FACES. My mother and Cormack, mouths open, unable to conceive of the girl who just killed.

Girls don't kill. No one thinks they do.

Until they do.

I let the knife drop from my hand as I watched a boat row out from the shore.

It's Santiago.

He's finally leaving the island I brought him to so many years ago. He waved at me.

I wanted to be sad, but I couldn't. He was never like me, and I shouldn't have kept him here. He's the brother I should have had if Real Daddy had lived. My mother never talks about Otto, my biological father. Didn't let me have photos of him and just shook her head and walked away if I mentioned his name. But I kept my memories. I have almost perfect recall.

Strange brain I have.

Everyone was gathering around. Trying to make sense of everything they'd just seen.

Cormack reached me first. His arms went around me.

His arms felt like walls, but not like the walls of the monastery. Walls of flesh and blood and warmth.

I sensed his mind marked and stained by the sight of me pushing a knife into Daddy James.

Like a sharp, unexpected night wind blowing down on the dandelions.

"Kara," he said quietly. "It's time to go."

84. EVIE

THE ISLAND BECAME A DARK SMUDGE against the sky as the Coast Guard boat headed back out to sea. I kept watching, needing to witness the moment when the island vanished altogether.

Commander Liourdis had requested that we not tell him our stories yet. He said he couldn't determine what was truth or fiction. I didn't blame him. He'd called for Hellenic Coast Guard patrols and the Hellenic Police to head out to the island and investigate.

I didn't know whether the guards and police would find Poppy dead or alive when they got there. A dark part of me hoped that she'd live and be put away in jail the rest of her life. She'd be mourning the loss of the man she loved—Brother Vito—for a long time, just like she'd made so many others suffer the loss of loved ones. She deserved to know pain.

Constance stood on the deck with her daughter, holding her as though she was terrified that if she let go, Kara would be gone forever. Kara stared out to the island with a frozen expression. Her wrists were bound in handcuffs, one of the guards standing watch over her.

Richard and Cormack leaned on the boat's railing, Richard gazing up at the sky, Cormack casting quick glances in Kara's direction. I caught Kara stealing a return look.

The others were still having cuts tended to.

The lives of Jennifer Bloom and James Lundquist were on tenterhooks.

Both had lost a lot of blood. I prayed if only one of them were to survive, that person would be Jennifer. I'd last seen Sethi by Jennifer's side, with his forehead bent down to her chest and his shoulders hitching as he sobbed. She hadn't regained consciousness.

I was both terrified of someone as dangerous as James living and terrified of him dying. If he died, all his knowledge about the membership of Yeqon's Saviours would be gone. As their leader, he'd know more than anyone. Kara had told me there were yet more Saviours out there in the world. Not all of them had come here for this year's round of serial killings. And the few that had been left alive on the island might be sailing away right now. My stomach twisted at the thought of Saviours living freely, ready to rebuild that cult of evil.

A bandaged Gray emerged from the interior of the ship. Moving behind me, he locked his arms around my shoulders and kissed my temple.

A tremor passed through my body as I moved around to face him. "Are you okay?"

"Yeah. Better than new." The familiar creases appeared at the outer edges of his eyes as he smiled. The handsome face that had grown pale during the Sydney winter had suddenly become sun browned under the Mediterranean sun. He had a week's growth of light-brown stubble, which I'd never seen him with before. And he'd dyed his blonde hair dark. He was a different man than I'd known. I was still having trouble processing the fact that Gray had come all this way to do the things he'd done.

Had this whole insane thing changed him, or had this man always lurked inside Gray? I didn't know. What I did know was that I didn't deserve either version of Gray.

"You almost died," I said. "I have to live with myself knowing that."

"It was my choice to come here, Evie. Constance, Jennifer, Sethi and I . . . we knew what we were walking into. *You didn't*. You had no idea what this island was. Remember that."

"I half think I'm still there, trapped in that cellar, and I've gone crazy. Imagining you and everything that happened afterwards."

As I turned back to the ocean, his arms came tight around me.

Gray's heartbeat was a tattoo against my back—or at least, I imagined I could feel it.

The island became a speck, then it slipped from view, a thing existing only in nightmares.

The sun glinting on the ocean and the breeze whipping past me couldn't erase the images of the cellar or take away the incessant echo of the metronomes.

My head hurt. Pounding. A thick, disorienting cloud hazing my brain.

I let my eyes close.

In shock, I felt myself pulled straight back to the cellar. The heavy weight of the chains. The stone wall against my back. Whispers and whimpers and choked pleas in my ears. The foul, coppery odours of death.

Gasping, I struggled to find the breath in my lungs that wasn't there.

Open your eyes, Evie.

Open your eyes.

EPILOGUE

ONE MONTH LATER

TWO LITTLE GIRLS STOOD ON THE SHORE, hand in hand. Silhouetted before the deep pink and orange sunset, waving goodbye to the sun.

They'd call the sun back again in the morning, racing down to the sand with buckets and spades. Everything certain and forever in their world.

If I looked past them, I could almost see my brother bodysurfing in the curling waves, making the most of the fading light, never wanting to come in. And Dad walking along the shore with his fishing rod, coming back to make us dinner with what he'd caught. Only, it was winter now, and that picture was all wrong.

Gray sat beside me on the edge of the deck. "No wonder your parents kept coming back here. Perfect spot." He handed me a hot coffee.

"Thanks." I leaned against his shoulder, watching Willow and Lilly chase each other across the sand.

It really was a great spot. I'd been amazed that this holiday house was still here, the furniture and pictures on the walls the same as I remembered. My mother had rented it for us this time, insisting that Gray and I come and stay for a while. She was somehow different, but in another way exactly the same. If I wanted Willow and Lilly to have a relationship with her, I was going to have to bite the bullet and just accept that she was always going to have a prickly personality.

Gray and I had only been back in Sydney for two days before we'd come here. We'd stepped from the hot summer in Greece to the cold Sydney winter. I was glad to be away from my street and from the people who knew us. I didn't want to have to answer any more questions. We'd been kept overseas for almost a month while the authorities untangled the story of the monastery. Finally, they let us go home.

James Lundquist had come close to dying on the coast guard boat that had brought us all back to the mainland of Greece. But he'd hung on, probably using the same tenacity that he'd used to lead his flock of Saviours. He'd protested his innocence until too much evidence was stacked against him. Then he'd fallen into a cold, terrifying silence and he'd been locked away.

The Hellenic Coast Guard and special police units managed to gather up a few more of the Saviours from the island, but not many. Most had died. A few escaped in boats but were picked up later.

Poppy had vanished. She'd been in no state to escape, yet she couldn't be found anywhere on the island. I assumed that perhaps she'd fallen into the watery crater that had opened up after the explosion. During the enormous task of recovering the remains of all the victims, it was thought that Poppy's body would be found among them. But her body wasn't there. Dead or alive, Poppy was gone. I liked to imagine that her body was hidden deep in the waters beneath the island. But I couldn't be certain of that, and my chest felt cold inside whenever I thought of her.

Jennifer Bloom, after three weeks in a coma, had opened her eyes to find Sethi, Petrina and Rico at her bedside. Her long endeavour to find out what had happened to her brother and to expose the Saviours was over. I'd been to see her before Gray and I left Greece, and we'd talked about Noah and Ben and how we'd both lost a treasured brother. My throat went dry and my face became wet with tears when I tried to express my gratitude that she'd never given up and that she'd come to the island—even though she'd known in her heart that Noah was already long dead. She'd shaken her head emphatically, grabbing my hand and telling me that Gray and I were the last pieces of the puzzle that she'd needed so desperately. And she'd said that her paintings could be *true* now. She didn't have to hide behind the blue skies and fluffy clouds of her work anymore, because she could step back into that world and be at peace. She gave Gray and me one of her lovely paintings to take home with us.

Kara and her mother were in Scotland right now with Cormack. Constance had been glad to get her away from the media spotlight in America and escape. Of all of us, the media were most interested in Kara and her story. The story of a seven-year-old who'd killed an intruder and had then been sought out and adopted by James Lundquist—a man who intended raising her in a psychopathic cult—had created a media storm.

I'd spoken to Cormack on the phone this morning. He said that today he was on a mission to show Kara a place that had been special to him as a child—a place named Fingal's Cave, located on a tiny uninhabited island in Scotland. On the edge of the sea, the cave was about seventy feet high and two hundred and seventy feet deep, and composed of soaring, cathedral-like hexagonal columns. Cormack said he wanted to show Kara a place of hexagonals created by nature. As a boy, in the middle of the cave, he'd had the sense that nothing humans could create or understand could match the mystery of nature. He hoped that it would help Kara heal and come to understand that the teachings of the Saviours hadn't been real or true.

I'd heard from Richard, too. He and Ruth and Yolanda were hanging together for the moment. Richard had big dreams of the three of them starting a business together—that was so like Richard. I understood why the three of them were clinging together. None of them had much in the way of family to return to. Both Richard's and Yolanda's families had completely disowned them when they heard the news about the monastery. Ruth had finally met up with her daughters again, without the money she'd thought she needed to be able to do that. But there was still a long road ahead for Ruth—her daughters barely knew her.

Hop had abandoned his studies and he'd flown back to China to be with his mother and family.

Louelle and so many others didn't get to return to their families. The horror and the shock of those families was everywhere on the news. I couldn't bear it, especially knowing that I had come close to not returning to Gray and our girls, and I would have put them through that kind of agonising grief. I knew that Ruth had visited Louelle's family in America and had told them how much Louelle had loved them and wanted to come back to them as a new person.

Twenty-four people had travelled to the monastery in the hope of healing and a new life. Only six had survived to tell the tale. The media had dubbed us *The Six*.

I hated that. It made us sound somehow victorious—like we'd emerged as the winners. As if it had all really been just a game. We weren't winners. And it hadn't been a game. Worse, the name—*The Six*—gave no respect to the victims who'd died there on the island.

The real *Six* was the number that the monastery had been founded on. But that had somehow been lost in all of this.

A shiver ran over my skin beneath my thick jacket as the sunset darkened. Rising abruptly, I called out to Willow and Lilly, spilling a little of my coffee. I tried to keep any note of anxiousness from my voice but failed. I had trouble with dark places now. As if the entire world could suddenly plunge into pitch darkness and a set of insane challenges could begin. Challenges that you could never win.

The girls ran to us from the beach—Willow to me and Lilly to Gray. It was like that with Lilly now. Lilly had forged a deep connection to her daddy when she was sick and when I wasn't there. And she seemed a little wary of me. But then she came to me for the first time since I'd been home, and she cuddled in tight, while Willow swapped to sitting on Gray's lap.

The girls' cheeks were stung pink, their hair windblown. The four of us leaned in close, against each other and against the bracing cold. The sunset turned bronze and somehow even more beautiful, because it was on the edge of vanishing.

Challenges lay ahead for us, as they did before. But what we had right now—this, being together—was everything. We had a new challenge in Lilly's illness. I was terrified and scared for her, but we just had to find the best way forward from this point. Gray and I were going to find somewhere new to live, somewhere near the ocean where the weather was warmer. For Lilly's sake.

We stepped inside the house, the girls racing ahead to jostle for position on the scruffy rug in front of the fireplace—the same rug that Ben and I used to sit on and play board games during the long summer evenings here.

ABOUT 'THE SIX'

Thank you for reading **THE SIX**!

I hope you enjoyed the high adventure, dark games and chilling aspects of the story.

If you enjoy audiobooks, you can now listen to **THE SIX**—narrated by the highly talented **Barrie Kreinik** (actor, singer and acting coach). Her voices are nothing short of amazing!

Anni Taylor
http://annitaylor.me

ANNI TAYLOR BOOKS

SERIES

TALLMAN'S VALLEY DETECTIVES

The books of the Tallman's Valley series can be read as standalones. They are best read in order.

BOOK 1: ONE LAST CHILD

Five nursery-school children vanish from a picnic. The kidnapper returns them years later. All except for one last child - the granddaughter of homicide detective Kate Wakeland. Speculation grows that the kidnappings were a revenge plot. Is the kidnapper someone Kate put behind bars years before?

BOOK 2: THE LULLABY MAN

A decade ago, The Lullaby Man preyed upon young girls in Tallman's Valley. Detective Kate Wakeland will find dark, twisting tunnels of secrets that will blow this small town of Tallman's Valley apart.

Book 3: THE SILENT TOWN

Coming soon

STANDALONE THRILLERS

THE GAME YOU PLAYED

Cruel notes in rhyme taunt Phoebe about her missing two-year-old son, Tommy. The game has just begun.

THE SIX

Young mother, Evie, is desperate to find a way to repay her secret gambling debt. But travelling to an island that runs a mysterious program for addicts is the worst mistake of her life.

POISON ORCHIDS

Two backpackers arrive at a remote fruit farm, desperate for work. They find a strange cult and a charismatic owner who seems to be hiding his true intentions.

ACKNOWLEDGEMENTS

Enormous thanks to my partner, Tim, for the fantastic map he created of the monastery. And for listening to my waffle about story plots and twists and other angsty writer's stuff.

Thank you to my writers' groups and others who assisted me with my research.

This book was a long time in the writing—a year. There was a crazy amount of research involved. I spoke with engineers and naval bomb experts to get parts of it right. I also gained knowledge from people with extensive knowledge of travel/travel times within Europe.

Gratitude to my beautiful sons always for supporting my writing and giving me a reason to work so hard at this author gig!

Endless thanks to my first readers, who gave me their wonderful thoughts and suggestions: Brenda Telford and Carolyn Scott.

Made in the USA
Thornton, CO
11/11/22 11:55:26

5187c708-671e-401b-a911-b8b95e3b609cR01